Paradise Interrupted

Kayla Danoli

Copyright

Cataloguing-in-publication data
Creator: Danoli, Kayla, author

Cataloguing-in-Publication details are available from the National Library of Australia
www.trove.nla.gov.au

ISBN: 978-0-6483950-3-4 (paperback)
ISBN: 978-0-6483950-4-1 (digital)

Cover by T A Marshall, Mackay, QLD Australia

Contents

Acknowledgement

This book, *Paradise Interrupted,* became a reality in part due to the work of author, Robert Thorogood. It was thanks to his series of novels set in the Caribbean, and the subsequent *Death in Paradise* television series based on those works, especially the creation of the island of Saint-Marie and its police force, which allowed it happen.

With the story line well mapped out for *Paradise Interrupted,* writing was delayed for want of the perfect setting for the story. Several tropical areas were considered but none seemed to fit. Viewing a repeat episode of *Death in Paradise* solved the problem. Thorogood's fictitious island of Saint-Marie and its Honoré township were the inspiration for the equally fictitious privately-owned tiny dot of a Caribbean island of Île Verte. Located just across the bay from Thorogood's island, it comes as no surprise there is interaction between those on the adjacent islands of Île Verte and Saint-Marie.

My thanks to Robert Thorogood for his entertaining stories and his creation of the island of Saint-Marie and its police force.

Chapter 1

The call came as I was about to climb into bed. Late-night calls always create a touch of apprehension and rarely deliver good news. This one was an exception. It didn't deliver bad news. Both surprising and intriguing, the caller was someone I hadn't heard from in over a decade.

"Frankie...! It is so good to hear your voice again." The accent was still there, but more subtle now than I remembered. "Your birthday... Of course I'll come ... When? Oh Lord, that's only about three weeks away. Just give me the details. I wouldn't miss it for the world." She paused a tad too long before asking if I were sure it wouldn't be too difficult for me to attend. "No, I won't have any trouble getting away, and I can take as much time as I want. That's one of the few benefits of being self-employed. But, how many days do you envisage this birthday bash of yours will last? ... Two weeks! ... No, no. That's not a problem. I'll be there. Send me the details."

Francesca (Frankie) Dubois, Dervla O'Reilly and I met at university on our first day as undergraduates. In spite of us all taking different courses, we became firm friends. Through those heady student days, we lived together in a house Frankie's father bought for her, and studied and got into scrapes together. The friendship lasted beyond our student days but, as with so many friendships, in our case, life and the tyranny of separation intervened. After Frankie returned home to France and Dervla transferred overseas with her work, we lost contact. Nevertheless, this was the strongest and most long-lasting friendship I've ever had. With Dervla invited to the party as well, I was excited about our reunion. Two weeks in France wouldn't be half bad either.

While we waited for Frankie to make the arrangements and send the details, Dervla tried researching Frankie's life over the intervening years. By pure chance, Dervla and I rekindled our friendship about 18 months ago. We had caught up on all our stories. It seemed beneficial to know something of Frankie's life before we met up again. Dervla's research and the details of our trip Frankie provided brought more surprises.

Dervla's research discovered the only one of our trio to marry during the past decade was Frankie. She had married the writer, C B Allerton. She found little else to tell us anything more of Frankie's life since we all lost contact. I confess to wondering for a brief moment whether Frankie's marital status might impact in some way on we three old friends spending time reliving past memories. The thought only last a moment before being dismissed as nonsense.

Surprising and interesting as Frankie's marriage was, the biggest surprise awaited when we checked our airline tickets. We would not be spending our time with Frankie in France.

With only two weeks until our departure, life became a blur of shopping, packing, unpacking and repacking, and arranging all those things needing to be in place when you leave the country and your home unattended for a couple of weeks. Then the day arrived. After a nervous check of everything again, it was time to spend the night in a motel before the flight next morning. In spite of having arranged an early morning call, and booked a cab for the short ride to the airport, I spent the night with one eye on the clock watching the hours creep by.

There followed a long day of flights, broken only by having to change planes several times. But, at last, the waiting was over. We had arrived in *the Caribbean.*

Ever since details of our trip arrived, I was consumed by curiosity and intrigue. Our unexpected destination alone was enough to cause that, but what awaited us on our arrival only served to strengthen those feelings. Our venue and accommodation were beyond my wildest dreams. Frankie's family came from 'old money' in France but, even so, it all seemed beyond belief – almost unreal somehow – and then there was Frankie.

She too seemed not quite real. Over time, life and age change us all. I could accept such inevitability, but Frankie wasn't Frankie. The person who met us looked like Frankie, but she wasn't Frankie … not the Frankie we knew.

Our arrival brought with it a whole lot of learning experiences. We met C B (Charles) Allerton. He seemed strange, but, for now, I was prepared to make allowances for the fact he had never met us before. Our 'home' for the next two weeks was the greatest shock.

It was huge. My first impression of it was of a fantasy castle snatched from some dystopian world and transplanted on the minuscule privately-owned island of *Île Verte*. Built from blocks of stone, in my mind, it resembled something a child might build with Lego blocks, adding to it as they came to mind all the frills and trimmings associated with castles. While still reeling from the sight of the building, there were the staff and other guests to encounter.

Three staff members appeared to run the place. Delphine was the stern-faced housekeeper, while Sampson and Dwayne took care of everything else. Of the latter pair, Sampson seemed to be in charge. The kitchen was Delphine's domain, but she also managed the household with an iron fist. Other guests had arrived earlier: both couples also were accommodated in the main building.

We received no warm, enthusiastic welcome from anyone; not from the other guests, the housekeeper … or from Frankie herself. Oh, she was polite enough and the perfect hostess on our arrival. After that, the whole atmosphere about the place was strange and a bit mysterious. There was a distinct lack of contact with Frankie once we settled in.

Nothing changed over the next couple of days. In my own mind, I began questioning why we were invited, and whether I wanted to spend two weeks enduring the prevailing atmosphere. Still, good manners dictated we should stay at least until after Frankie's birthday party. I found myself filling in the time until then as best I could. ...And the birthday party itself was another of life's mysteries which remained unsolved.

At last, the night of the birthday bash arrived. More guests flew in during the day to swell our numbers for the party in the evening. Maybe Dervla and I had forgotten how to party. While other guests slipped straight into party mode, we seemed sidelined, almost relegated to the role of onlookers. The word 'wallflowers' came to mind. After what we judged to be an acceptable period of attendance, we took the first opportunity to slip away to our rooms. Our escape from the great hall and out into the lobby went unnoticed by everyone. As we crossed the lobby, the night changed.

That's when the storm hit.

Chapter 2

The morning dawned clear and bright after the tumultuous night of the party. As I lay in bed half awake, I ran my mind over the events of the previous night. It was one to remember for all the wrong reasons. For a brief moment, I wondered how Frankie felt about how her party turned out. Then, a thought from left field fluttered in. I'm not sure she knows much about it. I'm almost sure she disappeared even before Dervla and I made our escape. If I'm right, it adds another inexplicable dimension to the night.

After last night's events, all I wanted to do this morning was dawdle over breakfast. Instead, Dervla's constant babbling had me rushing breakfast so I could escape the dining room. "I've a few things to do in my room. You won't miss me too much will you, if I leave you to finish breakfast alone?"

Surprised, she gave a half-hearted shake of her head. While it might be rude to abandon her, for me, it's about preserving my sanity … and I have a sneaking suspicion I might need rational thinking today. Having initiated my escape, I got on with it. After crumpling my napkin and throwing it onto my plate, I pushed back my chair and stood up.

That's when Frankie arrived in the dining room. Today promised to be 'different'.

Dishevelled, wild-eyed and pale, Frankie looked like an escapee from *Wuthering Heights*. She bordered on hysterical. "Have you seen Charles? Has he come in for breakfast? Do you know where he is?"

This was not the Frankie I knew; the Frankie who was a tight bundle of self-control, and never lost her composure. Taken aback by this morning's performance, I was struck dumb for a few moments. In those few moments, she rushed back out of the dining room. The housekeeper, Delphine, caught up with her in the lobby. She wrapped an arm around Frankie and, speaking in low soothing tones, spirited her away, presumably to Frankie's quarters.

"What was that all about?" Dervla whispered.

"No idea … other than she seems to have misplaced Charles." My flippant response resulted from my still somewhat shocked state. But, Frankie's performance made me wonder if it was linked to the something else which had tried to grab my attention since we arrived … if only I knew what it was. It was something I sensed in her, rather than something openly manifest, but I couldn't identify what it was or why it nagged at me.

Time to resume my escape plan, and before Dervla decides to come with me. Thwarted again! As I stepped out into the lobby, Sampson strode in through the front door. A gaggle of guests from the bungalows in the grounds rushed along behind him. The Nettletons on their way down from their room almost collided with the incoming cavalcade.

"Good Lord, man, watch what you are doing. You shouldn't go rushing about indoors like that. …Almost knocked my Old Girl here off her feet, you did." Terrence Nettleton's 'upper crust' tone brought the procession to a halt.

Sampson rose to the occasion. "Apologies, Madam. Sir, if you would be so kind as to take your wife through to the great hall… You too, Miss." He motioned me towards the hall. "…and your friend; please move into the hall."

There was something authoritarian about his demeanour this morning. None of us felt inclined to argue. We all traipsed into the hall. While it is fair to say none of us was happy to be ordered about so early in the morning, the Nettletons looked particularly put out about it. Marian began a high-pitched whine about not having finished breakfast in her room before being herded downstairs. It was a relief when her husband interrupted her performance. His comments, several decibels lower than his wife's, were much easier on the ears. Once again, he adopted his best English upper crust accent.

"My Good Man, this is a totally unacceptable way to treat guests. I assure you I am left with no recourse other than to bring it to Mr Allerton's attention at the earliest opportunity. Perhaps, if you might explain what in God's name this is all about, we might feel inclined to be more accommodating."

"All I can say is, the police will be here soon, and they have asked for everyone to remain inside here until they arrive."

Sampson's reply didn't suit Nettleton. "The police ... Mr Sampson, I asked why this is happening, and all you tell me is the police are coming. I think we are entitled to at least a little more explanation. Why the police are coming might be a good place to start. By the way, what was all the smoke I saw coming from further around the island early this morning? Are we safe here – or anywhere on the island – if the place is ablaze? Come on, Man, give us the details."

"Sir, I don't know any more than I have said but, for your safety, you must remain inside until the police arrive."

"Safe inside here...! This is ridiculous. Where is Charles? Why isn't Mr Allerton here to explain what's going on? I would think it the least he could do under the circumstances."

"I'm not sure where he is, Sir." Sampson looked desperate to escape. Nettleton had awoken my dark side. It was better listening to Marian's whining than to this toffee-nosed prick.

"Oh, for Christ's sake, the man simply works here. He is only carrying out his orders. He can't tell you anything because he doesn't know anything. You, like the rest of us, will have to wait for the police, or whoever, to enlighten us. So, cut the crap, and give the man a chance to get on with the rest of his duties this morning."

While I gave my best shrew impersonation, Sampson escaped; last seen disappearing out the front door. A stunned silence settled over the previously babbling gaggle of guests. Terrence Nettleton spluttered a couple of *well really* responses to my outburst, but a steely look from me silenced him as well. As a result of my speech, I found myself standing a little removed from the rest of the guests who had moved a safe distance away from me. The silence didn't last long. Soon, the others were in a huddle and sharing their mutual displeasure at the morning's turn of events.

Dervla broke away from the group and cautiously came to stand beside me. "Is it safe to stand so close?" I gave her a wry grin. "Any idea what's going on? ...And, where's Frankie? She didn't look too bright at breakfast. I expected she would be here with everyone. Do you think she is all right?"

"I've no idea about Frankie or about what's going on. I suspect Delphine is the only one who knows about Frankie."

As I finished speaking, a stern-faced Delphine wheeled in a trolley loaded with coffee, tea and a selection of both sweet and savoury morsels to help keep guests quiet for a while. Her look killed any inclination to cross examine her on the morning's activities. It was so soon after breakfast, yet guests pounced on the trolley as if they hadn't seen food for a month ... Dervla as well. I made the best of the moment to slip out of the hall and run upstairs.

Cloistered in my room, the journalist in me surfaced. Notes on everything from this morning went onto my laptop and into the notebook I tend to carry all the time ... even on holidays it seems. My next challenge was how to escape the building. I needed to investigate the light I saw moving about in the rain-forest early this morning. I saw it on one of the several occasions I woke during the wee small hours of the morning. ...And what about the smoke Nettleton was on about? I need to know more about it too. But first, I need to be outside.

Hunched over and hugging the wall, I sneaked down the stairs. No one moving about in the lobby... I ran on tiptoes across to and out the front door. My escape didn't take me far. When halfway across the lawn on my way to the rainforest, Sampson appeared from nowhere.

"Miss, you are supposed to stay inside. Please go back to the others."

"Thanks, Sampson, but I don't think I will ... not unless you give me a really good reason to do so." He shook his head and became agitated. "What is it, Sampson, what's going on? Something has upset you badly. Frankie was in a bad way, and now the police are coming. I'm a freelance investigative journalist. I'm used to dealing with all sorts of unpleasant situations."

It took some coaxing, but at last I won him over and he made a hesitant start. "Something terrible happened here on Île Verte last night. …And Miss Dubois saw it this morning. It was such a terrible shock, she almost collapsed. And now we don't know where Mr Charles is. The phones were not working after last night's storm. It took a while to get through to the Honoré police on Saint-Marie. They gave me instructions about what to do until they arrive."

"Okay, it's good they told you what to do, but why are they coming here? What was the terrible thing that happened? … And, at the risk of sounding like Mr Nettleton, why is there so much smoke around?"

"Oh, Miss, there was a terrible accident at Mr Anton's studio. The smoke is from the fire there."

He had time for only a few more words before Dwayne drove up on one of the golf buggies. After a quick word to Sampson, he drove off again. "I'm sorry, Miss, but I have to go to wait at the airstrip for the police. Please go back inside. Please try to stop any of the others coming outside. And, please don't mention what I told you to any of the others. The police said not to tell anyone." There was little fear of that. He hadn't told me anything – not really.

Then he was off jogging across the lawn. As I reached the front steps, the second buggy raced away down the driveway. I couldn't stand the thought of joining the others in the hall. Besides, I wanted some time alone to think. While I still didn't have details of what happened last night, I knew it was serious, more serious than just Anton's studio burning down. When I reached the top step, I decided it was far enough, and eased myself down to sit on the cool stone.

As I sat there, I reminded myself of how it all began, this Caribbean drama I now find myself mired in. A drama in which much seems unreal, and people are not as I remember them. On reflection, maybe I was wrong about the call which started it all not being bad news. In hindsight, perhaps that's exactly what it was.

While it is hot and humid outside the building, the stone steps are hard and cool against my bare calves. Their coolness seeps through the light fabric of my shorts. A panorama such as I've never seen before spreads out before me. Lush green lawns stretch down the incline for a couple hundred metres to meet a narrow belt of rainforest. This vast green carpet is interrupted at random intervals by dozens of clumps of shrubs intermingled with splashes of vibrant colour from flowering Bougainvillea and Heliconia. From my perch here on the front steps, my view stretches across the rainforest canopy to the startling azure sea beyond this island's shore. Mesmerised by the scene before me, I indulge in my own form of 'escapism' in a bid to ease my mind into neutral.

Now familiar footsteps clatter across the tiled floor towards me to interrupt my few stolen moments of solitude.

"Excuse me, Miss McNally ... I'm sorry. I mean, excuse me, Miss Tessa. Morning tea is being served under the big tree in the back garden, if you would care to join us please."

"Thank you, Delphine, but I think I will pass on morning tea today."

"That may be so, Miss, but Inspector Bennett insists everyone is to remain together until all of us are interviewed. He wants us in the great hall, but has allowed morning tea to be outside. So, please, if you would be so kind as to join us..."

My inclination was to ignore the request. If Bennett wants me in the hall, he can come and tell me himself. I knew such belligerent thoughts were a waste of time and emotion – and probably not in my best interest on two fronts. Delphine is housekeeper here, and more than that I suspect. Having fallen afoul of her once already, doing so again would not be good form. Finding myself on the wrong side of her is unlikely to do me much good at all. As for Inspector Bennett, he simply is doing his job. The sooner he does it and leaves, the sooner life returns to normal, or at least whatever passes for normal around here.

Determined to comply with Inspector Bennett's request for all guests to remain together, Delphine stood her ground a short distance behind me until I showed signs of complying. I raised my arms above my head and stretched, then thrust my legs straight out in front of me and rotated my ankles. She remained there, right behind me. I heaved myself off the step and eased myself upright on stiff legs. "I didn't realise how hard these steps are. My backside is quite numb now. I'll follow you out, Delphine, as soon as my legs work properly."

With nothing more than a contemptuous look in response, she turned on her heel and marched off ahead of me through the great hall and out into the backyard. I can't help wondering whether she reserves such 'special' treatment for me alone, or if all guests are treated this way. Still rubbing my rear end to encourage circulation, I dawdled my way out into the back garden.

Yes, we are all here now; all ten of us. On my joining the group, Delphine did a not too subtle headcount. Then, satisfied there were no absentees, she disappeared back inside, leaving Sampson to contend with the guests. Additional chairs added to the deck chairs permanently resident under the enormous Poinciana tree ensured everyone had somewhere to sit. I accepted a mug of coffee from Sampson, declined the cake, and took myself off a short distance from the others to sit on a low stone wall near the perimeter of the Poinciana's canopy.

Dervla's eyes followed me as I moved away. It was obvious she wanted to come with me but Marian Nettleton was not about to let her escape. Marian's shrill whining voice rose above all other murmured conversation as she complained to Dervla O'Reilly of the inconvenience of our current situation. I didn't much feel like company and wasn't in the mood for polite conversation.

A young constable came out and asked everyone to return to the hall. Marian and Dervla, empty-handed and standing closest to him, had no option other than to comply. Others returned their empty plates and mugs to Sampson's tea trolley before falling in behind Marian and Dervla to straggle back inside, like the proverbial Brown's cows. With everyone appearing to comply, the constable joined the procession into the hall. Sampson collected my mug, added it to his trolley and wheeled it around the side of the building to the kitchen.

I was left alone still perched on the stone wall. A sudden heavy silence descended over the backyard. It was as though someone turned the volume off in the middle of a program. Far more appealing than the clamour drifting out of the hall, I chose to stay in the silence and nurture my maudlin thoughts.

Serving morning tea out here under this tree was in poor taste given the events of the past eighteen hours or so. My memory of yesterday's afternoon tea out here, and of being introduced to a handsome young artist, remained raw and clear. It was when I met Anton … the now deceased, Anton Benoir.

My replay of yesterday afternoon's events progressed no further. The young constable was on my case. He strode towards me, his face grim. I half expected him to click his heels as he snapped to attention in front of me. "Miss, you are supposed to be in the hall with the others. Please take yourself inside now to join them."

A ball of spit and polish with knife edge sharp creases down the front of his trousers, the young constable was of medium height, looked like he worked out, spoke both English and French well, and was blatantly fluent in ambition. While his request was polite enough, my mood demanded I challenge it. So, I tried … and managed only a handful of words before being cut off.

"We are not trying to be difficult, Miss, or to inconvenience you. I understand you know about Mr Benoir." I nodded. "So far, we do not know how, why or by whom Mr Benoir ended up dead. Whoever is responsible still might be roaming around out here. For now, to keep everyone safe, we need you to remain indoors and to stay together as much as possible. Please, Miss, go inside now and wait in the hall until you are interviewed."

It was obvious his patience was at its limit. He assured me I would be returning to the hall with him now … in handcuffs if necessary.

"That won't be necessary," I snarled over my shoulder as I strode off ahead of him, leaving him stunned and wondering what went wrong with his game plan. After catching with me as I entered the hall, he made a show of escorting me inside and taking down my details.

Interviews were progressing well, with three people already interviewed and another guest being processed by the time the young constable was finished with me. Dervla, already spoken to, came over as soon as the constable left me alone.

After a conspiratorial glance around the room, she whispered, "There's still no sign of Frankie. Wouldn't you expect the police to interview her as well? I'm surprised she isn't here with us, and showing at least some interest in what is happening with her guests." The best I could offer was a shrug. "Something is not right, Tess. I'm sure of it."

The appearance of Delphine saved me from having to speculate on the matter. She marched into the hall and exchanged a few words with the young constable. He consulted his clipboard before responding. Then Delphine moved to the centre of the hall to deliver an update. "If I could have your attention everyone; lunch today will be delayed until one o'clock or as soon as possible after that, depending on the completion of the police interviews." Having delivered her news, she turned on her heel and left the hall.

During Delphine's announcement, the young constable drifted over towards me. I braced myself for whatever was to come, but he ignored me and spoke to Dervla. "Miss O'Reilly, as you were told, once you have been interviewed, you are free to leave the hall. You must remain in the building for a while longer, but are free to return to your room or go to some other part of the house. What you are not to do, is speak to the others still waiting to be interviewed."

Poor Dervla was quite flustered by being openly chastised. She shot me an apologetic look before retreating to the far corner of the room where Marian Nettleton and another woman were engaged in earnest conversation. The incident left me feeling like a leper. Guests formed into small groups: those already interviewed, those yet to be interviewed …

and me, alone some distance from the others. It's okay, I told myself. I don't much feel like conversation anyway.

It appeared guests' particulars were recorded in the order in which they returned to the hall after morning tea. Hence, Marian and Dervla were the first interviewees, while I, the reluctant last arrival, was at the bottom of the list. By one o'clock, I was the only one still to be interviewed. Delphine came to check on progress. I suggested the others go to lunch as soon as it was ready. I would join them after my interview. She seemed relieved by my suggestion, and promptly asked everyone to adjourn to the dining room.

There was a delay of a couple of minutes before I was summoned into the library where the interviews were held. Inspector Bennett rose from behind an impressive wooden desk and strode towards me. "Miss McNally … Miss Teresa McNally, I'm pleased to meet you. Welcome to the Caribbean. I'm something of a fan, having read many of your articles in the past."

Lost for words, I smiled politely in response as the Yorkshire export paused to draw breath before continuing. I didn't think 'Bennett' a traditional Yorkshire surname, but there was no mistaking his accent. How should I react to his admission of being a fan? I didn't have long to wait to find out.

Bennett addressed the young constable standing to attention beside the desk. "Williams, you may stand down. Join the others for lunch perhaps, and keep an ear on what is discussed around the place." The constable began to object. "No, Constable. You will not be required to record this interview. It will not be conducted along the same lines as the others. Go and enjoy your lunch. If any of the staff are around, tell them Miss McNally and I will require lunch a little later."

Okay, how do I feel about all that? I doubt being interviewed without at least a third person present is kosher police procedure. I didn't have to wait long to find out how this interview would play out. Bennett directed me to the two leather armchairs in a corner of the room. We sat facing each other across a low table.

While all the pre-interview faffing about happened, I took the opportunity to assess this Inspector Bennett. Lean, but not gaunt, he stood about six inches taller than me, sported a thick thatch of wavy reddish brown hair. The Caribbean had given his pale skin a soft golden patina, which provided a perfect backdrop for his incredible green eyes. For a moment, I idly wondered if there was a Mrs Bennett. Further scrutiny of the man suggested there wasn't. While appropriately attired in lightweight slacks, open necked shirt and light jacket, there was a slight 'unkemptness' about his appearance. No, I decided, definitely no wife looking after him. Why should his marital status interest me, I wondered? Then, there was no time to ponder the question – or to further scrutinise the inspector.

My 'interview' began. "Miss McNally…"

Chapter 3

"Tessa please, Inspector. Please call me Tessa"

"Thank you. Tessa, this is so exciting for me. Not only do I get to speak face to face with Teresa McNally, but one of the people involved in my current case is a seasoned investigative journalist. Oh, before we begin, I must stress nothing to do with this case must appear in the media. There is a complete media embargo in place for now." I confirmed my understanding of the situation and assured him I was here on holidays and not looking for a story.

"Good, good; now tell me how do you come to be here anyway? I don't recall seeing anything to suggest you are a regular visitor to Île Verte, or to the Caribbean in general."

"No, this is my first time to this area. I admit to being surprised to learn this was my intended destination."

"So then, how do you come to be the Allertons' guest?"

"I suppose the best place to start is at the beginning. It all started with a late night phone call inviting me to Frankie's – Miss Dubois' – fortieth birthday celebration."

"Fortieth birthday…?"

"Yes, I know. That was a few years ago now but, if that's how old she thinks she is, why would I argue?"

"I'm sorry for interrupting. Please walk me through what happened step-by-step, and include every detail." My mind fought the request to reflect on how I came to be here. It already had taken me down that path several times since my arrival on Île Verte. I don't want to revisit it all again; not today – but it seems I must. Did it all start only a few weeks ago? The memory of the night it all began flooded back.

"The late night call came as I was about to climb into bed. The call was both surprising and intriguing. My caller was someone I hadn't heard from in over a decade." Once in the 'zone', the story of my visit to Île Verte spilled out almost verbatim as the memories returned clear and sharp.

"Frankie...! It is so good to hear your voice again." The accent was still there, but more subtle now than I remembered.

"Your birthday... Of course I'll come ... When? Oh Lord, that's only about three weeks away. Just give me the details. I wouldn't miss it for the world." She paused a touch too long before seeking reassurance I would be able to visit. *"No, I won't have any trouble getting away, and I can take as much time as I want. That's one of the few benefits of being self-employed. But, how many days do you envisage this birthday do of yours will last? ... Two weeks! ... No, no. It's not a problem. I'll be there. Send me the details."*

"Francesca (Frankie) Dubois was someone from my university days. Way back then, the three of us, Frankie, me and Dervla O'Reilly, were best mates, and shared the house Frankie's father bought to accommodate her during her student days in England. During those university years, we called ourselves the Three Musketeers: one pencil-thin blonde, one well-rounded redhead, and one brunette built like a tall pillar box. At 168 centimetres tall, with olive complexion, black eyes and thick almost black hair, I looked different from the other two. Regular gym work-outs kept me trim and well defined. It wasn't about body shape. I believe physical activity stimulates creativity. Nevertheless, although not fat (it's more a basic structural thing), I look sturdy; more like a pillar box than a pencil."

"While Frankie and Dervla knew from the outset what they wanted to be, and chose the appropriate courses to achieve their ambitions, I was not so focused. For me, Teresa McNally, adulthood and the future seemed light years away, and I had no clue how I wanted to spend that time when it arrived. As a result, I changed courses several times and, after the other two left, ended up spending further years at university before I too graduated."

Bennett nodded sagely but made no attempt to record anything, so I continued.

"We kept in touch and met regularly for some years after university. Although Frankie's family and her home were in France, after graduating, she stayed on in England for a while to further her experience before returning to her homeland. About five years after Frankie and Dervla graduated, Frankie returned home and Dervla moved to Canada on a transfer within the company she worked for. At first, we emailed and skyped on a regular basis. As is so often the case, within a short time, contact was sporadic and gradually became relegated to Christmas and birthdays before ceasing all together." More nodding from Bennett; keep going, I told myself. Get it over and done with.

"About eighteen months ago Dervla returned to England and, as fate would have it, moved into a unit only a couple of blocks from where I live. We bumped into one another at a bar one Friday night and the friendship resumed as if never interrupted. On the other hand, Frankie remained lost to us in whatever her new world was back in France. That is, until her late-night phone call rekindled the bond between the three of us. After the call, and over a single malt, the memories flooding back kept me out of bed a long time that night. Somehow, the excitement created by Frankie's call softened the regrets I felt about having neglected such precious friends from those happy times together."

"It so often is the case with friendships forged at university," Bennett commented. It didn't require a response, so I continued my story.

"While my contact details remained the same as when we communicated regularly, Dervla had moved about a bit. Frankie had no current contact details for Dervla and asked if I knew them. I explained our renewed friendship and gave her Dervla's details. By the time the call ended, it was quite late ... or quite early the next morning! I didn't think Frankie would try contacting Dervla at that time."

"My first thought when I woke was to call Dervla. The excitement caused by Frankie's call the previous night persisted.

While it was possible Frankie did call Dervla after she spoke to me, a part of me hoped she hadn't. I wanted to break the news to Dervla. I remembered Dervla was not a morning person. Unless she changed over the years, she was unlikely to get up for another hour or two later than me. I accepted there was nothing for it but to have breakfast and bide my time before calling her. It didn't work out that way."

"It must have been hard to take it all in. How did Miss O'Reilly react to the news?"

"As I sat down to breakfast, Dervla called me, the excitement in her voice a dead giveaway. *"What do you think about Frankie's invitation,"* she blurted out as soon as I answered.

So you had a late-night phone call as well? ... Do you think you'll be able to organise time away from work? It won't be a problem for me, but it would be a shame if the three of us couldn't be there together.

"Dervla assured me she would have no problems organising a couple of weeks off work."

You know what's funny, Tessa? I always thought Frankie was older than us; at least a couple of years older. But, here we are invited to her fortieth birthday bash, when both of us can recall our forty-first birthdays.

"Dervla was right. Thinking about it, dredged up a vague recollection from a time at university, when I saw a document which showed Frankie was born about three years before us. I wondered how she could be turning forty in three weeks' time, when she should be talking about her forty-fourth birthday. Perhaps it's a French thing, I told myself. After all, French women seem to have the ability to look younger for much longer than the rest of us. Maybe they 'adjust' their age to complement their looks."

"I think I'll refrain from comment," Bennett chuckled. Mildly irritated, I pressed on.

"Our excitement at the prospect of spending a few days in France grew as we discussed what the birthday girl's party might be like. Frankie was never one to do things by half, and her family were not short of cash. They were old money and somehow part of the nobility. Through all our speculation about the party, I felt a couple of thoughts trying for home runs. They buzzed around just out of reach of conscious thought until Dervla helped one of them break through."

What do we know about Frankie after she returned to France? Did she marry? Her father always was a bit pushy. I'll bet he lined up an appropriate well-heeled husband for her.

I don't know. We lost contact so soon after the two of you left England. The last time I spoke to Frankie was about ten years ago. She was still single then.

Well, you and I are still single. I suppose it's possible she still is too. You don't think her birthday party will run for two weeks, do you?

No, I'm confident that's not the plan. I'm sure her intention is for the three of us to have time together to catch up on all we've done over the past decade, and to re-establish our friendship.

"It wasn't a lie when I said it; just rational thinking. Trouble is, even at the time, while it sounded reasonable, I'm not sure I believed it."

"As soon as Dervla's call ended, I headed for my computer, confident Google would be well acquainted with a forty-something year old Francesca Dubois. In the few moments it took my computer to boot up, my mind harked back to those utopian days at university."

"Google had a bit to say, but it was early information. The lack of anything recent about Frankie surprised me. Her career was going ahead in leaps and bounds and indications were she would become an important player in her chosen field. Then information about her came to an abrupt end. It didn't make any sense ... unless she joined a convent or something similar. The Frankie I knew was unlikely to take on a cloistered existence. As I closed Google, I giggled at the thought of her father having her locked away for some reason. Not only was it a ludicrous idea, but impossible. The Frankie I knew would not stand for it. Besides, she was having a birthday bash. I don't think such events are a feature of cloistered life."

"Probably not; so, I take it you knew nothing about this island at the time."

"No. I thought we were going to France. Curiosity was killing me. I visited my inbox several times during the day, hoping for something from Frankie. When Dervla rang after dinner to ask if anything had arrived, I tried to be upbeat about the situation and was thankful that, over the phone, she couldn't see I didn't believe a word I said. I stayed up late, and went to bed still harbouring the hope Frankie would contact me again. Disappointment does not make a good bedfellow."

I was beginning to feel self-conscious about revealing so much of me. An escape was called for. "Look at the time," I exclaimed as I checked my watch. "Delphine will not be happy if we delay lunch for much longer. Perhaps we should join the others now, and continue the interview afterwards if needs be."

Bennett seemed genuinely surprised time had slipped by so fast, and was most apologetic to Delphine when we arrived in the dining room. Most of the others were gone, so we ate lunch in relative silence. A call came for Bennett as we finished lunch. On his way out, he told me he would contact me later to continue the interview. Going back to my room held no appeal, so I wandered out onto the front steps instead.

After this morning's 'interview', the heady mix of tropical heat and the perfume of Plumerias wafted over me by the light sea breeze created the right environment for slipping into a deep and disturbing reverie. On my favourite perch on the top step, I found the setting ideal for recalling memories of yesterday's afternoon tea and my meeting with Anton Benoir. It started in much the same way as today. I had retreated to sit here on the front steps when tentative steps in my direction brought Delphine to interrupt my solitude.

It was happening for the second time today, but this time it was Inspector Bennett's steps approaching. "You seem lost in thought, Miss McNally; my apologies for interrupting. I wondered if you might be free to continue our interview. Perhaps we could talk out here." Bennett eased himself down onto the step beside me. It was obvious he wasn't interrupting anything important, so he continued.

"When we left off before lunch, you were waiting for information from Miss Dubois about your trip. Nothing had arrived by the end of the day. May we continue the story from there, please?"

"Next morning, I was finishing breakfast when the first mail arrived. The solid 'thunk' of something heavy falling through the mail slot caught my attention. I thought it probably a magazine and ignored it. Later, on my way through to my office, I noticed the mail on the carpet. There were the usual bits of junk mail, but the bulky envelope at the bottom of the pile caught my attention. Not only was it bulky, it arrived in one of those international express postage satchels. The sender's name in large black letters said it all: Francesca Dubois."

"I slit it open and upended it above my desk. A large white envelope slid out. Ripped open, its contents tumbled out. An impressive looking folder with a well-known travel company's logo on the front lay in the centre of my desk. As I admired the folder, Dervla rang to see if I received morning mail. She encountered the postman on the doorstep as she left for work. He handed her an international satchel as she rushed past, but her morning was hectic and provided no chance to open it. After confirming I had received my package but also hadn't examined it yet, I suggested she drop by after work for a drink and to discuss our envelopes' contents."

"It must have required great restraint. I'm not sure I would be able to contain myself for so long, regardless of what was happening."

"Not so much restraint, I'm afraid; while on the call, I used my free hand to flip open the folder. Its plastic sleeves held airline tickets. I remember asking my empty office how many tickets you needed to get to France and back. There were far too many tickets in the folder. For a moment, I thought Frankie might have included Dervla's tickets too but, if that were the case, why would she send Dervla a folder?"

"After reading the details on all the tickets, I sat confused and staring at the array of airline tickets spread out on the desk in front of me. Where the hell was *Île Verte?* It sounded as though it should be in France, but the tickets suggested I was off to the Caribbean. I'd never heard of the place, but that's not surprising. I didn't know much about the Caribbean area, so I woke up Google and sent it off to dig up whatever information it could find. The number of hits surprised me. I focused on the map of the area and, after enlarging it a couple of times, I found the tiny dot I was looking for."

"Ah, yes; not exactly a well-known place is it?"

"No. From my research, Île Verte appeared to be a minuscule dot of an island off the coast of the larger island of Saint-Marie. A search for more about the place brought up quite a bit of information, including several aerial photographs of it. In the photographs, it looked lush, green, tropical but scarcely inhabited. There was a small cluster of buildings at the margin of one of the aerial shots but, because of the angle it was taken, it didn't tell me much. One of the hits purporting to be a brief history of the place seemed like a good place to gain enlightenment about where I'd be spending a couple of weeks."

"I don't imagine there was much information to be found online. It isn't exactly a major tourist destination."

"You're right, but at last I found the Dubois name. After reading the article, I tried to construct the Dubois family tree from the information it contained. I learned the family appeared to own the island for quite some time. Then, several decades ago, for want of a male heir in the line, the Island passed to Frankie's great aunt, Lucille Dubois. The story contained a veiled reference to some sort of family upheaval when Lucille was still a young woman. Whatever it was appeared to result in Lucille's being ostracised by the family. While the article didn't say so, I worked out Lucille took herself off to live here. Not having any children of her own, Lucille opted to bequeath the island to the only child of her nephew, Frankie's father."

"What you discovered is fairly consistent with my knowledge of the place, but I suspect it is not all accurate, and there might be more to the story."

"I'm sure there is, and I intend digging further. While I hadn't envisaged such a web of family history, the story was intriguing. I wanted to know it all, and I told myself it was better to know the story before I arrived on the island, than to be shocked by what I learned after my arrival."

"Did you share your new-found knowledge with Miss O'Reilly? I'm sure she would be as curious about the place as you were."

"Of course; she came for drinks that night as arranged. Having walked the couple of blocks, she arrived with cheeks glowing from the chill night air. After a couple of sips of wine, we focused our attention on our forthcoming trip. I fetched the envelope containing the folder with the airline tickets and tried to tip it out onto the coffee table. It wouldn't come out. As I tried to free it, I realised something else was jammed in there. There were a couple of sheets of paper stapled together. Once flattened out on the table, I could see the top sheet was a note from Frankie. The second sheet was a brief itinerary of sorts. While I fiddled with the contents of my envelope, at the other end of the table, Dervla did the same with hers, and we soon had duplicate arrays of materials in front of us."

"No surprises in the focus of our discussion: our destination. It took me about two sentences to pass on what I'd learned about Île Verte from the potted history I'd found on Google. Despite her busy day, Dervla managed some research. She checked a type of 'Who's Who' used by senior staff at the PR firm she works for. They organise a many major events, so rely on such information. Research over her lunch break met with some success."

I found her name only once. Frankie didn't merit an entry in her own right, but her husband's entry included a brief mention of her. I suppose that could be because she is French, and the reference work we use focuses on UK individuals.

"At least then we knew she was married. Dervla recited the details."

Charles Allerton... His entry only appeared after he received a gong in the Queen's Birthday honours list not so long ago.

Chapter 4

"The name, Charles Allerton, sounded familiar, but I didn't know why. Dervla shared more of what she discovered."

His entry says he is a writer. I didn't have time to look him up, so I don't know about his work. I suppose whatever it is must be reasonably good for him to receive a gong for it.

"I fetched my laptop, keyed in Allerton's name and discovered he writes as C B Allerton. Information about him looked a bit strange; not many books. How could so few books earn him a gong, especially when they were all fiction? There were no major non-fiction works on subjects of world significance; no major treatise on anything. We knew big name authors need a mountain of bestsellers before the powers-that-be even notice them. There was little else of consequence about Allerton, other than research for his writing took him to many locations around the world."

"I've never read any of his works. It's hard to find time to read anything other than work stuff these days." Bennett's comment seemed more akin to thinking aloud.

"I know what you mean. I haven't read anything of his either. Anyway, with nothing more to be discovered about Charles Allerton, we returned to discussing our itinerary. We agreed, given the early hour we needed to be at Heathrow for our flight, we would spend the night before at a motel close to the airport. How we might fill in our two weeks at Île Verte and what the weather might be like also occupied our thinking. Not knowing whether Frankie's birthday bash would be formal, semiformal, or casual, made knowing what to pack difficult. I dashed off a quick email to Frankie requesting relevant advice and then waited more than twenty-four anxious hours for her reply."

"…And then you embarked on the long and tedious flight, broken only by a few plane changes between Heathrow to the Caribbean." Bennett looked almost apologetic as he spoke.

"Look, I don't mean to be rude, Inspector, but is any of this rubbish relevant to your investigation? All of this happened on the other side of the world, and some time prior to last night's events here on the island."

"I asked how you came to be here – you and Miss O'Reilly – and this is exactly what I wanted to know. I take it the next part of the story starts with your arrival here on Île Verte. I look forward to hearing about it."

"Judging by your accent, I'm sure you are familiar with the flight. The last leg of the trip, the light plane flight from Saint-Marie to Île Verte, almost did for Dervla. For her, it was a white-knuckle ride. She had just finished telling me she seemed allergic to small planes when we banked and dropped down suddenly to come into land. Again, as you are no doubt aware, the pilot has to apply all available means to bring the plane to a halt on the short private airstrip to avoid ending up in the rain-forest or the sea."

"Seconds after we came to a standstill, the pilot, Jackson, came through to open the cabin door and lower the stairs, and then he looked around in surprise. He expected us to be lined up behind him to follow him down the stairs. It took Dervla a few moments to prise her fingers from the armrests and make them responsive enough to unclip her seatbelt before we could vacate our seats. By then, Jackson had disappeared."

"What was your reception like when you emerged from the plane?"

"Frankie waited at the bottom of the stairs. As I came down, I watched a look of profound relief spread across her face. She thought something had gone wrong when we didn't emerge the moment the cabin door opened. After reassuring her everything was okay, we shared a threesome hug. Nevertheless, something did feel a bit off. She confirmed my suspicion she was tense about something."

I'm so glad you are here. I felt sure something would go wrong and you wouldn't come.

"Two golf carts were parked at the edge of the airstrip. As the pilot began unloading cargo and our luggage, one of the carts parked beside the plane. The pilot and the driver loaded everything onto the cart and it drove off. When the three of us released our hug, I noticed the second golf cart coming towards us. It stopped a short distance away and a grey-haired man climbed off. Tall and lean, and with a military bearing, he strode over and stopped about a metre behind Frankie, who did the introductions."

Oh, there you are, Charles. Ladies, this is Charles and, Charles, this is Tessa – Teresa if you must be prim – and this is Dervla.

"He came forward and shook Dervla's hand before shaking mine. As he did so, I told him, *whether you prefer to be prim or not, it's Tessa. 'Teresa' is likely to cause a hostile, even volatile, reaction.*"

"He clicked his heels and bobbed his head in mock salute."

Wouldn't dream of precipitating such a reaction, my dear Tessa. Right ladies, we should vacate the strip so Jackson can take off.

"As we made our way to the cart, Frankie shouted an apology to the pilot for holding him up. Charles drove off as soon as the four of us were on board the cart."

"Tell me your first impression of the place. Describe the trip from when you piled onto the cart."

"Are you sure you want to know this? I can't see its relevance to the subsequent events which brought you here today."

"Oh, I assure you, I do want to know every last detail; what you saw, smelled, felt … everything. Summon the journalist in you to tell me about it."

"O-kay… My first thought was about the airstrip. Sandwiched between the rainforest on one side and a narrow sandy beach on the other, to me it seemed short and capable of accommodating nothing larger than the light aircraft we arrived on. We travelled along a dirt track. A short distance along from the airstrip, the track took a slight bend before entering the rainforest. Rounding the bend provided a brief glimpse of Saint-Marie across the bay. Soon after that, we entered the rainforest and left the blistering heat behind."

"It was a different environment under the trees' dense canopy. While hot and humid, somehow it seemed cooler in there than in the world outside. Magnificent tree ferns and majestic old trees, many adorned with orchid plants, flashed by as we hurtled along a surprisingly smooth track. ...And there was a smell, not unpleasant. Somehow it shrieked 'damp leaf litter'. We broke out of the darkness of the rainforest and into a shady clearing. The elevated flat area ahead of us was reminiscent of a stage set in an elaborate backdrop of greenery. Our greatest surprise occupied centre stage."

"Aah, yes, this building … what was your first impression of it?"

"We were stunned and couldn't take our eyes off it. Dervla found her voice first."

Moorish, do you think?

"I thought it might be. I thought the definite Spanish influence strange. I told Dervla that, from my research, I knew Britain and France fought over this part of the Caribbean for years, with ownership changing hands several times. But, I didn't remember seeing anything about the Spanish ever being involved."

"Quite right … well, not here anyway ... but do go on."

"Dervla and I shared a few moments alone on board the golf cart. When we came out of the rainforest and into the clearing, the other cart sat idling off to one side. Frankie and Charles went across to speak to the driver, leaving Dervla and I alone to marvel at the panorama in front of us. On their way back to our cart, Frankie called back to the other driver to take everything to the kitchen, where Delphine would tell him what to do with the luggage. As though he was giving us a little more time to drink in the splendour of the place, after climbing back on board the cart, Charles waited a few moments before starting it. Frankie's comment seemed to confirm it."

Magnificent isn't it? Come on, Charles. Let's get them up to the house and settled in.

"He drove up and parked out front of this imposing entrance. Frankie took charge."

Come on, ladies, I'll show you to your rooms so you can settle in and freshen up. This way, ladies. I'm sorry; we don't run to a lift. You have to climb the stairs.

"She strode across the tiled floor and led the way up the stairs. We came to two doors standing wide open."

These are your rooms. This one is yours, Tessa, and the next one is yours, Dervla. Please check Sampson has put the right luggage in the correct room. I'll leave you to unpack and settle in. Take as long as you like. This will be your home for the next two weeks. Come down and join us when you're ready. We gather in the Great Hall at the same time every afternoon before dinner. That will be in about an hour's time, but feel free to come down whenever you're ready.

"With her hostess duties taken care of for the moment, Frankie headed back downstairs. As she strode across the entrance foyer, she stopped and looked up at Dervla and me leaning on the railing watching her."

When you come down, the Great Hall is through that door there.

"She indicated the centre doorway off the entrance foyer. Having delivered her message, Frankie continued across the foyer to disappear into one of the side rooms. Perhaps Dervla and I were awestruck, but we remained leaning on the railing without speaking for some time before Dervla broke the silence."

Who is that woman? What have they done with our mate? She is nothing like Frankie, not the one we knew anyway.

"A few heartbeats passed before I offered a weak explanation about it having 'been a while, that's all'. Dervla didn't buy it and persisted."

A bit stilted, don't you think? ...Never known Frankie to be like that in the past.

"I tried again, but I'm not sure whom I was trying to convince."

Like I said, it's been a while. If you think back to when we first met again in that bar after your return to England, it took us a while to resume from where we left off all those years ago; to become comfortable with one another again. I think maybe

Frankie is feeling a bit awkward about how to be with us, and whether we still accept her as she is. I agree, she seems to have changed somewhat, but so have we. Let's not be too quick to judge. After all, it appears we have two weeks in which to form our opinions.

"So, what was your reaction to your room? I assume it met with your approval?"

"In spite of Frankie's concerns, Sampson had the luggage in the correct rooms. I remember standing in the doorway surveying the room before entering. It is a large room, about the size of two of any bedrooms I'm familiar with, and its ceiling I estimate to be about twenty feet high. The good thing about ceilings like this, I told myself, is you never notice the cobwebs up there. God knows how you'd remove them anyway. All the furniture is wooden, heavy, dark, and features ornate carved decoration. A cupboard, incorporating wardrobe hanging space, occupies almost all of one wall. The centrepiece of the room is a huge four-poster bed with a substantial bedside cabinet on each side"

"…Not cramped quarters then? Anything else in the room?"

"Other furniture includes a dressing table, a large chest – like a footlocker – at the end of the bed, and something that is more a secretaire than a desk. An office chair on castors lives at the desk, and an inviting looking lounge chair and matching ottoman complete the furniture inventory. So no, not cramped quarters by any stretch of the imagination. I don't know why, but I remember the lounge chair looking inviting. After having spent so many hours sitting on planes, I didn't need a lounge chair."

"Was there any particular style discernible in the furnishings? They sound like they might be in keeping with the architecture of the place. What about the rest of the room, anything else noteworthy about it?"

"Yeah. The Spanish influence is reinforced by the rugs on the floor. They look straight out of the Alhambra, as do a painting and other wall decorations. To make a start on unpacking, I hoisted my suitcase up onto the chest and started hanging garments in the wardrobe. This huge cupboard stops a few feet short of the end wall. A door occupies most of the space between the wall and the end of the cupboard. It looks similar to the connecting doors you see in some motel rooms. It intrigued me."

"Mystery and intrigue, eh…?"

"No. I discovered the door was unlocked. After a moment's hesitation, I opened it, expecting to find myself peering into Dervla's room. I was wrong. It was my own ensuite. While not huge, it is more than adequate. Hot and cold water on tap to a bath tub, shower and granite topped vanity unit, and it includes my own toilet. Fresh towels were on the racks and a fluffy towelling bathrobe hung behind the door. A shower seemed like a wise move before I finished unpacking."

"I know how you felt after the flight from the UK. It takes me more than a shower to recover … and I don't have to face being sociable to people afterwards. You did go down for dinner…?"

"After a long refreshing shower and wrapped in my towelling bathrobe, I finished unpacking, donned a pair of patio pants and a sleeveless top in light cotton material, and added a pair of strappy sandals. I was ready to go, but kept putting off going downstairs until Dervla knocked on my door."

Shall we go down stairs and get this over with?

"It seems she felt the same way I did about the evening."

"Perhaps we might take a break … See if we can rustle up a pot of tea or some coffee or something. How does that sit with you?"

I checked my watch. "It is afternoon tea time. Perhaps, if we wander inside, we might find somebody already thought of that."

It was then Delphine came out to announce afternoon tea was being served in the hall. Shades of *déjà vu…!* It brought memories of yesterday's afternoon tea flooding back.

If I thought going in search of refreshment would give me some time away from Bennett, I was mistaken. He insisted on walking me into the hall. Delphine and Sampson were in the process of setting out afternoon tea for everyone. I made a point of wandering off to mingle with the other guests for a break away from the good inspector.

Chapter 5

Iced tea was on the menu again this afternoon; another dose of bad taste in my opinion. I noticed today's replay of yesterday didn't seem to bother anyone except me. And why should it? Iced tea was the offering every afternoon since we arrived. And the venue was different. I took my frosty tall glass, resplendent with the usual greenery, out onto the back deck. My intention was to sit under the big old tree in the back garden. Such a move most likely would bring someone out to round me up and herd me back inside. I settled for a boldly striped canvas deckchair on the deck instead. Dervla arrived a few minutes later and plonked down in the other chair.

"There you are. I looked for you inside. Have you seen anything of Frankie today? Apart from her distracted entrance at breakfast, I mean."

"No. Inspector Bennett hijacked much of my day, so I haven't seen anyone."

"Are you finished with him now?"

"I doubt it. I suspect he intends resuming after he has his 'pot of tea'."

"Are you okay? You don't seem your usual self." I reassured her. "Would you rather be left alone for a while?"

"Oh, yes please. After my hours of 'interview', I just want solitude. Please don't take offence. I just need a few minutes of peace and quiet."

A procession of expressions slid across Dervla's face. I half expected her to nag me. Instead she nodded, picked up her glass, heaved herself out of the deckchair and went back inside. I made a mental note to mend that bridge later. At last I was alone. My mind insisted on reviewing my conversation with Bennett.

From my viewpoint as a journalist, nothing about his 'interview' made sense. He was here to investigate Anton's death. At least, I thought it was why he was here. So, why is all the back story stuff about how I came to be here relevant to his investigation? And, how come my 'interview' is taking hours, when everyone else's took minutes? I replayed our conversation and paused at the point where I described seeing this place for the first time. The pause allowed me to relive the moment for myself, and without having to choose my words to describe it to a police officer.

Frankie described the place as 'magnificent' as Dervla and I, probably with our mouths hanging slightly open, sat there in the golf cart stunned by our first view of the castle. She was right. The building is magnificent and, up close, the place is no less imposing. It might have been copied from an image in an ancient Spanish reference book. Built from huge blocks of stone now greyed with age, it has at least two storeys, two turrets, a cupola-like structure on top … and it covers a huge area. A short flight of stone steps lead up to an entrance comprised of stone pillars positioned on either side of the doorway to support the huge stone lintels overhead. Thick wooden double doors (hardly ever closed I noticed) covered in ornate carvings open into a tiled spacious entrance foyer or lobby-type area. A number of doorways lead from this space. Off to one side, a grand stone and wrought iron staircase climbs to the upper floor.

There is something enigmatic about the place. I felt it from the moment I first saw it, and my time here has strengthened my opinion. As soon as things settle down, I plan to have a long conversation with Frankie about the history of the place … and a few other things as well while I'm about it.

Those 'other things' might even include such impertinence as to enquire into her marriage to Charles Allerton. He seems an odd bird, and not the sort of person I expected Frankie to settle down with. Apart from that, something seems decidedly off about the situation here. Come to think of it, where the hell is Charles today? After Frankie's performance at breakfast, I could under-stand it if she were heavily sedated and confined to her room.

But, that doesn't explain why Charles is so conspicuous by his absence, particularly as he is our host and might be expected to be paying attention to his guests.

My mind drifted on to other topics not discussed with Bennett – at least, not yet. I suspect our next session will move on to events of yesterday afternoon and last night. A stray thought slid in. If I continue the sweet and obliging routine with Bennett, I might be able to winkle some favours out of the inspector in return, like having a look at the crime scene for example.

Through the mist of relived memories came the realisation afternoon tea was drawing to a close. The babble of voices previously emanating from the hall had diminished to the point of almost having disappeared. I had two choices: continue to sit there feeling maudlin until someone came looking for me, or to go inside to discover what awaits the rest of my day. The latter option, while not the most appealing, made more sense. I wandered through the now all but empty hall, somewhere along the way deciding to go to my room.

It wasn't to be. Bennett virtually pounced from nowhere as I exited the hall to enter the lobby. "Ah ha, found you at last," he chirped. "Given the current situation here, when I couldn't find you, I became a little concerned about your situation."

"My situation…? I'm not sure what you mean."

"Well, we are trying to keep everyone safe by having them stay inside the building but, when you weren't around, I had some dark thoughts about what might have happened to you."

"Ah well, as you can see, I am safe and well, but thank you for your concern."

"Perhaps you might feel sufficiently refreshed to continue the interview…" I gave him a nod and my sweetest smile and he continued. "Then, unless you have a better idea, let's retake our seats on the top step."

I followed him out, and we went through the motions of settling ourselves comfortably on the hard stone step. I noticed some of the earlier heat of the day disappeared while we were inside. Bennett wasted no time in resuming the 'interview'.

"Let's move on to yesterday afternoon. What can you tell me about what happened then?"

"Nothing much to tell really until afternoon tea time. After lunch, I went to my room for an hour or so. Then, after I came downstairs, it was much like today. Other guests were starting to roam about inside in the lead up to afternoon tea. When you have nothing much else to do, food times seem to become keenly awaited events. I didn't feel like company, and wasn't particularly interested in afternoon tea. I came out here and sat on the top step as we are now, except then I was alone and was indulging in my version of 'escapism'. My solitude didn't last long."

"Tentative steps came in my direction. I recognised them as Delphine's as she clattered across the tiles.

Excuse me Miss McNally ...

No, Delphine. Remember; it's Tessa, please, not Miss McNally.

I forgot. I'm sorry. Miss Tessa ... afternoon tea is being served under the big tree in the back garden, if you would care to join us.

Thank you, Delphine. I'll be along in a moment.

"I admonished myself. Best I show a little more enthusiasm before she reports me to her mistress. Easing myself up off the steps, I made my way towards the young woman whose face reflected her displeasure at my unsociable behaviour. I smiled sweetly as I passed her on my way out to the back garden. She did not respond in kind. I remember thinking, upsetting Delphine is not a wise move. She runs this household and is devoted to her mistress ... not so much the master of the house, I'm thinking. Apart from her not taking kindly to my upsetting Frankie in any way, Delphine would be a useful ally to have, should one ever be needed in this exotic environment."

"I asked her if all the guests now had arrived.

No, Miss. Four will not be arriving until six o'clock this evening.

"With that, the tall, lithe young woman turned and headed back to where guests helped themselves to tall glasses of iced tea and whatever tasty morsels comprised afternoon tea."

"We – the guests – numbered eight yesterday afternoon, two extras having arrived around midday. Eight were sipping iced tea under the Poinciana tree when I joined them. They congregated there some time before the iced tea arrived. In part, it was their migration to the back garden which provided me with a chance to retreat to the front steps for a few stolen moments of blissful aloneness before Delphine's interruption.

Ah, Tessa, there you are. There's someone I want you to meet.

"It was as I arrived, Frankie grabbed me by the arm and dragged me towards a lanky, dark-headed young man whose sullen look suggested he was about as happy to be there as I was."

Anton, this is Tessa McNally. She is a houseguest who will be staying with me for a couple of weeks. Tessa, meet Anton Benoir.

"We settled for exchanging smiles and nods instead of a handshake before Frankie continued."

Tessa, Anton is … oh dear, excuse me please. Dervla is in need of rescuing from Marian. "With that, Frankie rushed off. Anton had his chance to say a few words."

She was about to say, 'Anton is our resident artist'. That's how she introduces me to everyone. I have a studio in a small bay further along the coast.

"His tone was flat, providing no insight into what he thought about his introduction, or anything else for that matter, so I studied his face. I found nothing there either to indicate how he felt. We exchanged pleasantries for a few minutes. He asked how much of the island I had seen so far and how I like it. It seemed we chatted for only a few minutes, but our iced teas disappeared along the way. Anton nodded at my empty glass."

Interested in a refill?

Ye-es, I think a refill might be good, thanks.

"With or without all the vegetation…? He asked as he flung the stalk of lemongrass and spring of mint from his glass into nearby bushes."

I can do without fresh greenery, thanks. The stuff already in the glass can stay there though.

"Moments later, he returned with a frosty refill from the fresh jug Delphine brought out. We sipped our drinks in silence for a few moments before I became bored with it, and the urge to seek refuge in my room prevailed.

There's only so much of this stuff you can drink before it loses its appeal. I'm thinking I should take myself off to rest and relax in readiness for tonight. Any idea how big this evening is likely to be?

Not really; I believe another three or four will arrive on a late plane to complete the guest list.

What about locals? Are many of them invited?

Île Verte is a private island. The only 'locals' are the owners, their employed staff, and me. On a couple of occasions, the pilot of the light plane stayed overnight to take people off the island at first light next morning.

Do they entertain like this often?

No-o, not really; maybe two or three times a year. If guests stay over for a couple of days or so, there's likely to be a dinner party, but that's about it.

Okay, thanks, I get the picture. This is a big night for Frankie, so I had better be on my best behaviour. I'll see you later…?"

"He nodded and grimaced when I told him I was off to prepare myself."

"Like so many of my best intentions and good ideas, I didn't manage to pull this one off either. Before going back into the house, I paused at the table to deposit my empty glass amongst the others of its kind. As I turned away from the table, I ran headlong into Marian. With Dervla now extricated from her clutches, Marian was forced to seek out another quarry. It seems she chose me as Dervla's replacement."

Tessa, isn't it? We haven't had a chance to catch up since you arrived. How are you finding the place? Not too overwhelming, I hope.

"If there is an upside to the conversation, it was that I didn't have to say much. Marian hardly drew breath during her opening salvo. I'm not sure if she expected me to answer her questions, but she didn't provide opportunity to do so. It didn't matter. She continued anyway."

So, tell me, how do you come to be here? How do you know Francesca ... or, is your invitation via Charles?

"This time, she did require an answer. There was a short delay while I weighed up the implications of her final question. As I did a quick scan of the gathering in search of Frankie, I wondered what inference I should draw from her mention of Charles. Frankie was on the other side of the group with her back to me. Short of yelling 'help, save me', there was little chance of her coming to rescue me from Marian as she had Dervla. There was nothing for it but to enter into polite conversation with the woman."

"As I didn't feel inclined to be expansive, I told her I met Charles for the first time when I arrived here. She drew a deep breath in preparation of what I knew would be a barrage of questions, so I jumped in to cut her off before she got started."

What about yourself, how do you come to be here for Frankie's birthday bash? Have you known her long?

Long...? Well, no, not really; I met her for the first time early last year – probably about eighteen months ago now.

"She seemed a bit wrong-footed by my question, so I made the best of it and pressed on."

Oh, so recently... You must've hit it off straight away to be invited to spend time here and be a part of her birthday celebrations.

We haven't been here all that long. We only arrived the day before you did, and we're due to fly out again tomorrow. If I'm honest, I'm not sure I would call my friendship with Frankie 'close'. The reality is, I don't know her well at all. My husband and Charles are close friends. That's how I met Frankie in the first place and, well you know how it is, you have to be friends with your husband's friends.

"I found myself liking the cow less by the minute, but her comments intrigued me. I decided to push a little harder; dig a little deeper – and maybe watch her squirm."

Sounds interesting ... Tell me about how you came to meet Frankie, and when it was.

"Ah, you journalists... always ready with the questions in the hunt for a good story. Did you get one?" Bennett was chuckling again.

"At the time, I wasn't sure whether her story was worthwhile or not, but she continued to intrigue me. In hindsight, my gut is telling me to think about it a bit more."

Our meeting was coincidental. My husband and a couple of his former work colleagues arranged a get-together to reminisce about old times. As usual, the wives were abandoned to their own devices while the men sat together boozing and reliving old stories. Charles had Francesca with him. I forget the name of the other bloke who was there, but he didn't have a wife, or maybe he hadn't brought her with him. That forced Francesca and I together to make the best we could of the long, boring evening.

I hope the evening was at somewhere nice, so there was at least one pleasant aspect to the night. Where was it?

It was at one of the best restaurants in Paris. The food was divine. It was the only memorable thing about the night. But, you didn't say ... If you're not here as a friend of Charles', I take it you met Francesca at some time in the past.

Yes. It was quite a while back. Frankie and I go back to our university days together.

I see. That dreadful Dervla woman also knew Francesca at university. Perhaps you two will have plenty to talk about; spend the evening swapping stories and the like.

Yes, I do know Dervla. She and I are here because of our long established friendship with Frankie which began when we were undergraduates together. We're really looking forward to helping her launch into her next decade in fine style tonight. Come to think of it; I really should get on. I've things to do before then.

"Having, I hoped, given the woman something to think about, I turned on my heel and strode up to my room. My focus for the next couple of hours was on what to wear last night. Frankie was sufficiently ambiguous as to leave me in a complete quandary about how formal or otherwise the evening would be.

I had an outfit in mind … until I met Marian. Somehow, I knew she would arrive wearing some Paris designer's latest creation – and possibly wearing a diamond tiara to boot. My original choice of outfit wouldn't measure up against such competition."

"I calculated, if four more arrived later, it would make us twelve for dinner, plus our host and hostess, and Anton. Some of us had arrived well in advance of the event. For me and Dervla, it was our third day on Île Verte. The middle-aged couple, Marian and Terrence Nettleton, and the Seymours were already installed as houseguests when we arrived. I knew the birthday party would be a lavish affair. 'Understatement' is not a word in Francesca (Frankie) Dubois' vocabulary."

"By five o'clock, I had made my decision, and it was not too far removed from my original choice. There would be no diamonds or ermine trimmings, but I would be elegant, cool and comfortable. As our instructions were to meet in the lobby for pre-dinner drinks at six o'clock, I felt I had enough time for a quick nap and a shower before joining the others downstairs. That was another of my good intentions gone west."

"My nap stretched on past the intended half hour. I have a form of inbuilt alarm clock. It wakes me on the dot of when I want to wake. Yesterday afternoon, it malfunctioned. Maybe it has something to do with being on the other side of the world; time differentials maybe. Whatever the reason, I slept for twenty minutes longer than planned. Up off the bed in a flash, I seemed to develop six arms and legs all going in different directions as I rushed about trying to meet the six o'clock deadline."

"I had barely dried myself off and climbed into my underwear when Dervla knocked on my door. I yelled at her to go down without me as I was running behind schedule. There's nothing like a degree of emergency to hurry things along. The outfit went on in a flash. A couple of quick swipes with the hairdryer had the hair almost dry and fluffed up a bit. No time to apply make-up; it would only melt off in the heat anyway. On my way to the door, I slipped my feet into a pair of wedge-heeled sandals, and I was ready to go."

"At the door, I took a couple of deep breaths to regain my composure before opening it ... actually, I'm not sure about 'composure'. It was more like checking everything I was supposed to have on was in place. Then, I was heading for the stairs. I paused for a second at the top of the stairs. This time it was about composure ... before slowly descending to the lobby. I was only five minutes late, but even the latest arrivals already mingled with the rest of the mob. Dervla sidled up to whisper to me.

Glad you could make it. Please don't leave me alone tonight. I think we need to stick together; safety in numbers and all that ... "

What are you on about? What's with the 'safety in numbers' stuff? Nothing is likely to happen here tonight. Our greatest risk is becoming bored witless before we finish dinner.

All the more reason to stick together! Maybe we can slip into a quiet corner for intelligent conversation. Whatever happens, if you see that Marian woman heading for me, run interference. Spilling something down the elegant brocade number she's wearing might work.

Chapter 6

"In spite of Dervla's misgivings, nothing untoward occurred before seven o'clock when Delphine announced dinner. Everyone traipsed into the dining room and went through the usual faffing about to find our places at the table. We were fifteen for dinner, all spaced neatly around a table capable of seating twenty. Charles and Frankie sat at either end of the table. I had Dervla on one side of me and Anton on the other. The delay while the first course was served gave me a chance to check out the others. What a motley lot we were. There wasn't time to form any preconceived ideas about those I hadn't interacted with yet. It felt as though a second sitting had been booked and was due to arrive at any minute, and the staff were anxious to have us fed and out of there as soon as possible."

"You were expecting a lavish night. What was on the menu last night, and did it live up to expectations?"

"Uhmm … yes, I suppose so. The first course was alternate drops of smoked salmon or pate, each with the usual accompaniments. Everyone received the same for the next course: a seafood plater of fish, prawns and oysters. Just as I was beginning to wonder for how many courses we might be parked at the table, we were told to pick up our glasses and take them with us into the great hall. Surprised murmuring accompanied the scraping of chairs as we complied with the request. Charles took Frankie's arm and led the way to the entrance to the hall. Like sheep, the rest of us straggled along behind them. The doors to the hall were closed. Our cavalcade stopped for a brief moment at the heavy wooden doors. Then, with a grand flourish Sampson and another young man, whom I now know as Dwayne, threw open the doors and ushered us in. Dervla, walking beside me, gasped and leaned in close to whisper to me."

This looks more like it. Someone has been busy since we were here earlier this afternoon.

"Streamers and balloons decorated the imposing but previously austere space. Lamps and small tables had been added. A small round table set off to one side reminded me of those set up at weddings to display the wedding cake. Dervla's question, when she saw me eying off that table, showed she shared my thinking.

Do you think that is for the birthday cake? If that's what it's for, why didn't they set up the cake before we came in?

Probably for fear it would melt in this heat before there was even a chance to light the candles.

"Sampson switched on fairy lights strung around the back deck and out to the big Poinciana tree in the backyard. Soft music fed into the space from some unknown source. People started swaying to the music. One couple took to the floor to dance. Others soon joined them. I hadn't noticed Anton in the hall until he spoke to us.

Would either of you ladies care to dance?

"I turned to face him and almost laughed. The question was nothing more than a polite gesture on his part. His face told the real story. Not a hint of enthusiasm to support his invitation evident there. We both politely turned him down, and all three of us strolled out onto the rear deck. On ground level and off to one side, Dwayne busied himself with a barbeque fashioned from half a large drum. Anton explained what was happening as we stood breathing in the aromas wafting our way."

Dwayne is cooking our next course. The smell of it suggests they are using traditional recipes for chicken and beef on skewers. The locals have proper names for it, but I can't remember what they are.

"A collective cheer from inside the hall lured us back inside to investigate. Delphine was putting the finishing touches to setting up the birthday cake on the small table. Charles tapped his glass to gain the guests' attention and to silence them. He then delivered a short speech extolling his wife's virtues. The platitudes seemed to make Frankie uncomfortable. The guests didn't see it that way. Sufficiently well lubricated by then, they cheered Charles' speech and broke into a lively rendition of *for she's a jolly good fellow."*

"So, everything was rollicking along smoothly and according to plan up until then."

"Yes, I think so. There were no apparent hitches. Anyway, the candles on the cake were blown out – I doubt there were forty of them – and the cake was cut before being whisked away again. Attention then swung to the large platters of barbequed skewers Sampson and Dwayne placed on tables in the centre of the hall. They smelled amazing and tasted every bit as good. While the rest of us were either still eating or trying to deal with our sticky fingers, Marian's husband, Terrence, called us to attention for another toast to the birthday girl. It caused a flurry of activity as people rushed to refill their glasses during his speech. While I politely waited my chance to top up my glass, I pondered the filthy look I saw Marian give her husband when he stood to propose his toast."

"All is not well in the Nettleton household perhaps…?"

"I don't know, but there is something odd there. Me thinks there is more to the couple than meets the eye!"

"We might discuss them at length later."

"After about another fifteen minutes or so, the platters held nothing more than piles of bare skewers. Most guests were on their feet and moving to the lively music. Dervla and I continued as wallflowers. Anton staged a disappearing act, seemingly without anyone, including me, noticing. I found myself wishing I knew how he did it. It seems Dervla felt the same way. She leaned in and asked if I thought anyone would notice if she escaped.

I, for one, wouldn't notice because I would be with you. I have been devoting some thought to how to achieve it with minimal fuss and attention.

"Further discussion of the matter was curtailed by the flurry of activity surrounding the arrival of an enormous cake stand loaded with slices of the birthday cake. As we stood closest to where the cake stand went on the table, it would look odd for us to move away without taking a piece with us. So, we each dutifully loaded a slice of cake onto plates provided, and grabbed a cake fork, before moving out of the way so others could help themselves to it. Dervla stopped to exchange a few words with a woman. I kept going and made it safely out onto the rear deck. After a couple of minutes on the deck, I went down and strolled out to the big Poinciana tree."

"Out there, far enough away from the music inside, the night sounds of the rainforest drifted in loud and clear. A choir of insects serenaded me, with a frog adding emphasis every so often with a deep throated croak. In the background, an unseen night bird played his monotonous single-note tune. The night air was cool and fresh. A jasmine somewhere close by allowed me to share its perfume. I found myself revisiting the question plaguing me almost since my arrival on Île Verte: why had I come here? Of course people change. I had changed since those heady student days. Life does that to you. Every time I asked myself that question, another question immediately followed it: why wasn't it true of Dervla? She was still the same Dervla. Maybe it was me and not Frankie who was the problem."

"If I'm hearing you correctly, you are saying you detected a major change in your friend, Miss Dubois. As you suggest, such a change might not be unusual after so many years. Again, if I am reading you right, you are suggesting the change in her was more significant than might be expected." I shrugged in response and Bennett continued. "We should revisit this matter, and at some length, later. But I am interrupting you. Please continue your account of last night."

"Let's see, where was I? Oh yes, out at the Poinciana tree… Thoughts of Dervla made me feel guilty about abandoning her. It was time to be sociable again. I started across the grass towards the back deck. The imposing structure looming up before me made me pause. Even in the low light from the combination of fairy lights and pale moon, it was breathtaking. It was the first time I really looked at the rear of the building. Over the short time I've been on Île Verte, the castle has lost none of its awe-inspiring magnificence for me. While lacking the imposing front entrance features, the rear of the building is just as impressive."

"As I stood there admiring the magnificence of the castle, I noticed a change in the air. The night sounds died away. I felt a brooding silence settle over the grounds. Then, a shriek of tipsy female laughter rent the still night air, reminding me of my intended mission. I trudged across the rest of the lawn, up the steps and into the hall."

"Nothing much had changed in there. The only change I noticed was Dervla. Pinned against one of the tables by a leering male guest, she frantically searched the crowd for a means of escape. I strode over to her and planted an elbow in the bloke's ribs."

Ah, there you are, Dervla. I've been looking for you. Come; I want to show you something.

"As I spoke, I inserted myself between her and the man. Then, grabbing her by the arm, I dragged her away with me.

Thank you, but what took you so long? I was almost at the point of kneeing him in his dangly bits. Where are you taking me anyway, and what do you want to show me?

Nowhere and nothing ... It was all I could think of at the time. But now, I do think I have something to show you.

What?

...Our rooms at the top of the staircase out there in the lobby.

Oh, yes please.

Don't rush; I'd prefer our departure went unnoticed.

"After skirting a cluster of people congregating around the coffee recently wheeled out on a trolley, we headed for the lobby. We were almost at the door to the lobby when the place plunged into darkness. I felt Dervla jump and move a tad closer to me. A hush descended over the hall. I stood still and kept hold of Dervla's arm. It didn't take long for my eyes to adjust to the darkness. The hall was nothing more than a black space dotted with even darker patches. I assumed those to be the guests. One or two of those dark patches moved a little, but remained in the same place. Others were unmoving, frozen like dark statues in the silent blackness."

"Not exactly what you want happening at your birthday party and, being in unfamiliar surroundings, the guests would find it disquieting."

"I agree, but we had been here three days and were reasonably familiar with the layout, familiar enough to continue with our escape. Pale moonlight streaming in through the front door cast an eerie light over a small section of the lobby floor. I wanted to get to the stairs, and it was light enough for us to find our way there. I needed to reach those stairs. Perhaps my life as an investigative journalist has left its mark. A sceptic from way back, I don't believe in coincidences. My past experiences taught me suddenly finding oneself in complete darkness is not a good place to be. A little voice in my head told me to keep moving; to find the stairs."

"If my guess was right, the stairs were not far in front of us, and we should keep moving in a straight line towards them. The moonlight did not encroach far enough into the lobby to reach the foot of the stairs. I told Dervla to stay close and tugged her arm to get her moving again. We shuffled forward only a couple of steps before a chance glance over my shoulder made me freeze and whisper to Dervla."

Stop! Stand still. Something is happening. Sshhh...

"Lights moving about far back in a room off the side of the lobby made the hairs on the back of my neck stand to attention. I urged Dervla forward. In short silent steps, we continued in what I hoped was the direction of the stairs. My free arm held out in front of me smacked into solid stone. It was either our targeted stone staircase, or the side wall of the lobby. Confirmation of where we were was critical to me as we came to a stop up against a cool vertical wall of stone."

"If my reckoning was correct, we were beside the lower section of the staircase. I knew a quick check of the stonework would tell me where we were. To avoid drawing attention to ourselves, I needed to explore our surroundings by myself. But, *in* order to, first, I had to prise Dervla off of me. As soon as we reached the stonework, she wrapped her arms around me, and was in danger of squeezing the life out of me. About to tell her to let go of me so I could do what I needed to do, I suddenly thought better of it. Those two lights I saw moving about in the side room had just entered the lobby area."

"Hmm, that would be inconvenient under the circumstances."

"I don't know if 'inconvenient' was the word I had in mind. I reacted on instinct. Throwing out my arm, I slammed Dervla hard back against the stonework. I heard the breath knocked out of her as I too pushed myself hard up against the wall. My pulse raced and my breathing was short and shallow as I watched those lights moving towards the hall. The silence was shattered by a female's hysterical scream. Both Dervla and I jumped … before resuming trying to ooze ourselves into the very fabric of the stonework. Noise, probably voices, drifted out from the hall. Then, the lights were coming out into the lobby again, but there now were three lights."

The bloody generator would pick tonight of all nights to pack it in. Let's get it sorted as quickly as possible. We should hope the problem is no more than the damn thing's run out of fuel.

"It was Charles' voice. The three lights moved through the lobby at speed and, soon after, three figures crossed the patch of moonlit tiles and disappeared out the front door. As I returned my heartrate and breathing to more normal levels, I noticed Dervla was shaking. I needed to get us upstairs. With the three figures – and their lights – disappeared out the front door, it seemed a good time to head for our rooms. A last check of the area before making a move made me change my mind. A soft glow escaped from the hall and travelled out to meet the patch of moonlight on the lobby floor.

Stay here, Dervla. I'm going to take a quick peek at what's happening in the hall before we do anything else.

"She wasn't happy about it, but I managed to disengage myself from her firm grip and tiptoed to the hall doorway. A number of lanterns were set up on the tables running down the centre of the room. One or two were battery powered LED type lights, while the others relied on lit wicks to do their job. The breeze coming in through the backdoor impacted the wicks in spite of their protective glass chimneys. It caused their flames to splutter and dance. Their flickering light added to the nervous tension in the room. Some of the guests were restless. Three men congregated at the end of the line of tables. An intense discussion was in progress when I turned and made my way back to Dervla."

"From my experience, I would say that's not a good sign. When a group of blokes decide to take matters into their own hands, they usually make the situation worse. But, do go on. Let's hear how this progressed."

"During my time outside earlier in the night, the gentle breeze increased in strength. While it remained pleasant enough, it did nothing to reduce the energy-sapping humidity. As I crossed the lobby to return to Dervla, I noticed there was no breeze. It had disappeared completely. I stopped to wipe the sweat from my eyes with the back of my hand, before retrieving a tissue from my pocket and mopping my face. The 'mopping up' operation completed, I was about to resume my trek back to Dervla when something took me by surprise. Somehow, during that brief pause in my journey across the lobby, the moonlight also disappeared."

"Oh dear; the gods were working against you last night. What had you done to upset them?" Bennett's chuckle was not appreciated. I chose to ignore it.

"When I started to cross the lobby, the moonlight was still there. Combined with the glow from the hall, it provided enough light for me to see Dervla still pressed hard up against the stonework supporting the stairs to the upper floor. Then, with the moonlight gone, she was cloaked in shadow. Nevertheless, I still could make out the outline of the stairs. I set my compass for those stairs and started forward again. Both Dervla and the stairs became clearer as I came closer. Taking her by the arm, I led her around to the bottom of the stairs and we started up them."

"I thought the figures we saw crossing the lobby were planning to investigate the problem with the generator, but I didn't mention that to Dervla. In itself, it wasn't likely to be a problem, but I wanted to watch goings-on from somewhere removed from the action … like from the gallery at the top of the stairs. Dervla needed no convincing to climb the stairs."

"As we stepped up onto the first step, a streak of lightning lit up the entire lobby area. Dervla tried to stifle her scream, but only managed to reduce it by a few decibels. It didn't matter. The deafening clap of thunder immediately following the lightning drowned out all other sound. We were experiencing our first tropical storm. As you suggested, I imagined a more gullible person reading something into all the gods chose to throw at us last night: the loss of power and then the storm. Was there something about Frankie's birthday bash to displease them? There was no time for such rubbish thoughts. My instinct insisted we keep going to reach the safety of our rooms."

"We raced up the stairs side by side. I went with Dervla to check her room. With no one hiding under the bed or in the cupboards, I left her to recover from the night's excitement behind her locked door. Once I heard her lock the door, I moved back along the gallery towards my room. My intention was to do a quick check of my room before finding a place on the gallery from which to watch for anything happening below. That plan changed."

"Thunder and lightning became intense, with barely a second between the flashes. The whole place shook as a lightning bolt came to earth somewhere close by. Then the rain came down in torrents. The wisest move was for me to go to my room but, instead of just checking it, to go to bed instead."

"As I reached my door, movement in the lobby below stopped me in my tracks. Two men carrying one of the lanterns came out of the hall. They seemed undecided. When about halfway across the lobby, they stopped and started back towards the hall. Almost at the door to the hall again, they stopped to confer for a few moments. The rain probably had something to do with their indecision. Then, their situation resolved, they strode back across the lobby and out the front door."

"Through the wrought iron railing, my perch on the top step of the staircase provided an excellent view of the area below. The performance I witnessed was perplexing. I shared my thoughts on the matter with the stonework."

Okay, now there are five men out there looking into whatever the problem is with the power. All of them probably are drenched, or will be by the time they return. If the first three can't fix it, what do those last two hope to achieve?

"With no answer forthcoming, I made myself as comfortable as possible and settled down to wait for the next instalment of the night's drama."

Chapter 7

"You might have been in for a long wait before anything happened. And then there was the chance nothing would happen. The rest of the night might settle back to being a perfectly normal event." Bennett had a point, but such notions did not occur to me at the time.

"I suppose intuition told me there was more to come, so I went with it. Regardless, my top-of-the-stairs vigil stretched on. Outside, the storm continued to rage with tropical ferocity. Experience told me, while it felt like a long time, it was more like five minutes since the last two men left the hall. To ease the boredom as much as for any other reason, I fished my phone out of my pocket and risked a check on the time. I was surprised to find it was a few minutes before midnight. Where did the night go? I didn't expect it to be so late."

"As you suggested, nothing happened below for some time. My eyelids grew heavy and drooped. I knew I should give up and go to bed, but something made me stay. The sound of voices woke me from a light doze. They sounded as though they came towards the front door. Moments later, the two men I watched leave earlier entered the lobby. In spite of looking half-drowned, without hesitating, they marched straight on into the hall."

"Almost as soon as the men entered the hall, a loud babble broke out as everyone spoke at once. I shielded my phone and checked the time again: a few minutes after one o'clock. The babble from the hall subsided. A lone male voice replaced it. He spoke too softly for me to hear. I kept watch for Charles and his two offsiders to return. They didn't."

"Okay, two had returned, but three men were still out and about. What happened after the two returned?"

"After a few minutes, voices from the hall no longer drifted up to me. The only sounds then were the scrape of chairs and clatter of shoes on the tiled floor. A group of bodies erupted out of the hall and stood in a tight group in the lobby. There no longer was any glow from lanterns coming from the hall as some members of the huddle below me now carried the lanterns. It appeared the night had ended. Frankie's birthday bash was over and her guests were taking to their beds. Five people, three carrying lanterns, broke away from the group and headed for the front door. With a final wave to those still in the lobby, they disappeared into the miserable night awaiting them outside."

"If they were going to bed, why did they go outside?"

"I assumed they were the guests staying in the cabins nestled in the gardens. Two of the cabins would be occupied by the last two couples who arrived that evening. Jackson, the light plane pilot who flew Dervla and me from Saint-Marie to Île Verte a few days ago, had the third cabin to himself. The remaining four guests, who followed the departing five to the front door to see them off, stood there for a few moments watching Nature at work."

"You said Jackson had a cabin. Was he at the party? His plane wasn't here when we arrived this morning."

"Yes, he was one of the invited guests. I think one of the other pilots flew him over sometime yesterday, and he was to fly back with the other guests when the plane came for them today."

"Okay; return to your account of last night please – or should I say, your account of the early hours of this morning."

"If I didn't want to encounter the remaining four guests when they came up to bed, I had to move fast. I eased myself onto my feet, willing my legs to regain full function as I did so. Then, with my back pressed hard against the stones, I slid along the couple of metres of wall to my door. Thank goodness I left it unlocked. In the space of a heartbeat, I opened the door a fraction and slipped inside … just as those guests, armed with two lanterns, made their way to the stairs. With no consideration for anyone else, they continued their conversation as they made their way to their rooms; Marian's distinctive voice shrill heard above the others as they passed my door. After that, there was only the sound of the storm outside. Inside, an eerie heavy silence settled over the castle's occupants."

"You said Marian passed your door. I take it you were referring to Marian Nettleton." I nodded my agreement. "So, the Nettletons had a room in the castle, and were not in one of the cabins. Interesting..." Bennett seemed to be thinking aloud rather than speaking to me, so I didn't feel the need to respond. "Apologies; I'm interrupting again. Please resume."

"She had been so nervous, I half expected Dervla to come banging on my door the moment the others were safely in their rooms. When she didn't, I thought maybe she was able to get to sleep in spite of everything. I longed to join her in slumber land, but it was a while before I fell asleep. Alone in my darkened room, I reviewed everything I witnessed after the power went off. I ticked everyone off on my fingers as I recalled what they did and where each of them went. My audit accounted for everyone except two people: Delphine and Frankie."

"Delphine didn't come back into the hall after bringing the cake and coffee. With Sampson and Dwayne rostered to look after guests and everything in the hall, I didn't expect to see her again. She would be busy in the kitchen both during the 'eating' part of the party and then the cleaning up afterwards. It's possible she went to bed before we lost power or, if she was still up when the power went off, went to bed then."

"Frankie was a different matter. She was not only the guest of honour – the birthday girl – but also our hostess. Under those circumstances, etiquette required her to stay until the last of the guests left the party. Perhaps that's what she did. Certainly, her sense of decorum would insist she did."

"The suite of rooms occupied by Frankie and Charles is in a different part of the castle from the guests' rooms. They are accessed rooms via a corridor off the lobby. After the power went off, at no time did Frankie come through the lobby while Dervla and I were there, and she did not come out of the hall with the other guests when they left. Perhaps the Allertons' rooms have an alternate access not via the lobby which Frankie used. Regardless, I would expect her to see off the last of her guests before she turned in for the night. She didn't."

While I didn't want to share my thoughts with Bennett, the more I thought about Frankie, the more disturbed I became. A heavy lead ball was forming in the pit of my stomach. Something was not right about the party, and I had a growing unease about Frankie. Last night was planned to perfection and went off without a hitch … until we lost power. Frankie laughed and mingled throughout the evening. Perhaps, to those who did not know her well, she appeared to be enjoying herself. But she was not the Frankie I knew. There was an underlying brittleness to her performance. To me, she seemed tense all night. The woman whom I knew for many years loved entertaining and did it with style and panache."

"My review of the night's events kept me awake for some time without producing any answers to the many questions I created for myself. I have no idea what time I fell asleep."

"That's good. What happened this morning?"

"What…? You know what happened this morning. You were here, and have been all day."

"No, that's not correct. We didn't arrive on the island until quite late this morning. I want to know what happened before we arrived."

"Well, let me think… The highlight of the morning might be my suffering lack of sleep and feeling decidedly unsociable. The other notable thing might be Dervla's being up and about much earlier than is usual for her, and arriving at my door looking even worse than I felt. Breakfast was a non-event until Frankie arrived looking like an escapee from Bedlam and carrying on about Charles being missing. Then, to compound my dismal start to the day, as I was about to bolt back to my room, Sampson marched in like the Pied Piper with the guests from the cottages trailing along behind him. He insisted everyone – including me and Dervla – was to congregate in the hall and stay there until the police arrived."

"… And this was the first time you heard anything about the police coming to the island? How was that received, and did he explain why the police were coming?"

"The police's imminent arrival was news to everyone. He offered no explanation, which probably didn't help matters. As for how the news was accepted … that was interesting. Sampson also rounded up all of the other guests who were staying in the castle. Before visiting the cottages, he banged on the doors of the rooms upstairs and told the occupants to get dressed and assemble in the lobby. I think Dervla and I were already in the dining room, so banging on our doors was a waste of time."

"You were going to tell me how guests reacted to that."

"Nettleton did an indignant rant and generally carried on like a toffee-nosed prick. Marion whined about the inconvenience of having her breakfast interrupted. I gave one of my better renditions of a shrew, during which Sampson escaped the building. My performance made me something of a leper and caused everyone to move a safe distance away from me. Dervla did eventually come to stand beside me … after asking if it were safe to do so."

"Then Delphine arrived on the scene with a trolley loaded with tea and coffee and food, and resumed herding people into the hall. At least it defused the situation in the lobby. It was only two blinks after breakfast, but the others pounced on the trolley as if they were starving. While everyone was so fixated on the food, I made the best of the moment and escaped to my room. A while later, while everyone remained ensconced in the hall, I sneaked down the stairs and out the front door. I was halfway across the lawn when Sampson caught me. He remained insistent I should be with the others in the hall and must remain inside until your mob arrived. I didn't feel so inclined and needed a damned good reason before I would comply. He might've felt a bit kindly disposed towards me after fighting in his corner earlier on. That's when I found out about Anton and 'the terrible thing that happened last night'. That was it. He and Dwayne took off on the golf carts to collect you lot from the airstrip. The rest of the story you already know."

"How much information did Sampson give you about last night's terrible event?"

"Nothing more than I've already told you. When Nettleton was giving him a hard time in the lobby this morning, Nettleton wanted to know why there was so much smoke around. I think he believed the forest was on fire, and the fire was a danger to us … and hence we had to stay inside. There was still a fair amount of smoke about when I came outside. Sampson indicated he already said more than he should, so I didn't press him further for details, but, my gut told me it was part of that 'terrible event'."

Bennett nodded, and proceeded to add to my frustration by saying nothing. I deliberately left the door open for him to enlighten me, but it was obvious he needed more enticement. Something more akin to a shove might work. A silent 'wait and see' game stretched on for a few moments. In spite of my determination not to be the one, I broke the silence.

"Inspector Bennett, what did happen last night, and what is going on?"

"How do you mean? Anton is dead. The police are here. What is so puzzling about that?"

"Okay, so that's how you want to play it. I have spent most of today supposedly being 'interviewed' by you, when every other interview took about ten minutes. Apart from first thing after your arrival, when the young constable spent some time organising everyone for their interview, he and your other officers have been conspicuous by their absence. And they are only some of those who seem to have evaporated into thin air. I want to know what happened – in detail – and what is happening with you and your blokes. I want to know, and I intend to find out. You can either tell me about it, or be prepared to have me getting in your way while you are here. What's it to be?"

"Is that some sort of ultimatum? I should tell you, I don't respond to threats."

Ah, at last I'm seeing his real colour now. Another prod might help. "I wouldn't dream of threatening a police officer.

There was no threat. I'm nicer than that. I made you a promise. Do what you will with it, but I will find out."

"I don't think that would be wise."

"I'm not interested in what's wise. Someone I only just met, but liked a lot, is dead. My friend and her husband are missing. I'm not about to play wise or nice. What I can tell you is, if you make my quest for answers difficult, the media will know about it ... and I can't guarantee it will benefit your career."

"Argh... Okay; please, can we call a truce and start again?"

"What ... start your so-called interview all over again? I don't think I want to waste another day in a gab-fest. If you want to interview everyone again and we each take no more than ten minutes – including me – I might be prepared to play along. By the way, where are all your officers? They have been invisible for most of the day."

"My officers are busy. We have a crime scene to investigate. Now about..."

"So, Anton's death was murder?"

"Yes, I'm afraid so. There is no doubt. But, if we could come back to your issue with the interviews..." I shrugged and gestured for him to get on with whatever he had to say. "Good. The other guests' interviews took no time because they knew nothing, saw nothing and, in a couple of cases, verged on becoming hysterical at the mention of Anton's death. And that was without any mention of murder."

"So, what made you think I saw, or knew anything more than the others?"

"I am familiar with your work as a journalist. I didn't think you saw or knew any more than the others. It was your view as a journalist of things here I wanted. This doesn't suggest I thought you had information about the crime. A journo notices what's going on about the place, and is articulate enough to put it into words. The journo's perspective is what I wanted from you, and it's what I got. Thank you. Now, I would like to explore further some of your observations. Do you feel up to it?"

"Oh, I suppose so, but I can't think what more I can tell you."

"I think there is plenty more. I'll ask questions and see where they lead. Do you want to continue now, or should we leave it until after dinner when you might feel fresher?"

"This might not take long, so let's make a start now and see how we go."

While Bennett went in search of a jug of cold water and a couple of glasses, I used the time to stretch my legs by strolling on the grass at the base of the front steps. While I needed the exercise, it gave me time to think. What more could I tell him? It came as a surprise when a couple of things did crystallise during those few minutes.

We returned to our perch on the front steps. This time, a tray holding the iced water and glasses occupied the top step, while Bennet and I moved down one step. A deliberate silence reigned for a couple of minutes, during which tumblers of water were poured and sipped and, more importantly, the time was devoted to clarifying and arranging our thoughts. Then, the stalling ended, and we resumed 'interview mode'.

"On more than one instance today, you commented Miss Dubois was not the woman you knew. I believe you noticed something was different the moment you stepped off the plane here on Île Verte. Tell me about what you noticed then."

"It's hard to explain, Inspector…"

"I think we've known one another long enough now to be on the first names basis. Please call me Tom. After all, you asked me to call you Tessa."

"Okay, *Tom,* I'll try to explain without sounding completely naff. I suppose I thought there would be a few awkward moments when we first met again. After all, it had been a while since we even spoke. And I expected there would be some changes. I'm sure I've changed over the years since I left university. The same is probably true of Dervla, but I hadn't noticed it in her. I'm thinking back to those first few moments when we stepped off the plane, the awkwardness was there, but it was more so than I expected. It didn't go away. If I'm honest, my expectation was, after we settled into our rooms, it would be full-on old friends catching up. You know the sort of thing I mean. You sit around sharing what each of you has done over the intervening years; reliving anything of note. Some time would be spent sharing gossip about other people we knew and what they had been up to. That didn't happen either."

"What did happen, Tessa? How was it different from your expectations? Try to explain; give me examples if it helps."

"To be honest, nothing much happened. During those first days, we had little contact with Frankie. There were no more than a few words here and there; at morning and afternoon tea, at dinner. We did not sit down together and chat. I'm still not sure why I'm here."

"So, things haven't panned out the way you expected. You still haven't explained what was so different about Frankie, as you call Miss Dubois."

"Yeah, I know, and that's the hard part. Frankie was outgoing and lively; fun to be around. She had loads of personality. Now, it's as though … as though … almost as though she has no personality. There is a brittleness about her. She is so brittle, you half expect her to shatter into a thousand pieces at any moment."

"Has your friend Dervla commented on any change in Frankie?"

"She hasn't said so as such, but subtle hints in our conversations suggest she also notices a difference."

"A few moments ago, you said you're still not sure why you're here. Earlier today, you made similar comment, and suggested coming here for Frankie's birthday party was a mistake. Tell me why that is."

"Argh, I'm a journalist. I'm supposed to be able to read nuances. If I think back to the late-night phone call when all this started, the clues were there. I just didn't pick up on them. Our phone conversation was a bit stilted, but again I put it down to her feeling a bit awkward about inviting me to a birthday party when we hadn't even spoken for over a decade. Before you ask what those clues were, I'm not sure I'm reading too much into something that was nothing. There was a hesitancy in the way she spoke. As I reflect on it now, it was as though she wanted to say something else, but for me to read between the lines and understand what she was trying to tell me. It sounded as if she was trying to say something but, for whatever reason, she couldn't. I've gone over that phone call in my mind so many times. Nothing needed interpretation. Everything in that brief call was quite straightforward; no hidden meanings, no lines to read between."

"She contacted you first; not Dervla. Is it possible Dervla's invitation was an afterthought, and it was really you she wanted here for her birthday?"

"No, that never occurred to me. The fact she called me first is easy to explain. My contact details are relatively easy to find, even if you have to contact one of the media outlets my work has appeared in. Dervla was a different situation. She spent a lot of time overseas and moved about a bit, only moving back to England about eighteen months ago. Along the way, she changed firms as well, making it even harder to find her. I only had her information because I met her by accident a while before Frankie's call … and she turned out to be living only a couple of blocks from me."

Our session came to an end when we noticed the sun had gone down, and dinner was not far away. I needed to change and freshen up before going to dinner. And I was beginning to feel in need of a break from the questioning. "Tom, what are the plans for tonight for you and your officers? Isn't it getting a bit late to fly back to Saint-Marie?"

"No problems; the former staff quarters are available to us for as long as we need to stay. My officers will have rooms there and will eat with the staff. I have a room in the castle and will eat in the dining room with the rest of you. So, if you feel up to it, we might continue our discussions after dinner."

I groaned silently and tried not to grimace. I've had enough 'discussion' for one day. My opportunity to escape to my room arrived in the form of the officious constable I encountered earlier this morning. After marching up and halting a short distance from the steps, he stood looking anxiously at Tom. It was obvious he wanted to speak to his superior, but wasn't quite sure about interrupting us. I helped him out.

"Tom, I think your constable is desperate for your attention. Perhaps I should leave you to deal with whatever issue he has. I'll see you later at dinner."

Before he could argue, I bounced up off the step and fled to my room. Closing my door, I leaned against it and whispered a prayer. "Please God, have him sit on the opposite side of the table tonight, or at least somewhere not next to me."

Chapter 8

Whatever the young constable wished to discuss with Tom must have been of some consequence. Tom arrived in the dining room a few minutes after everyone else was seated. Sandwiched between Dervla and Jackson, I sent God a mental thank-you for saving my ears and my sanity tonight.

Dinner was a sombre affair, broken only on occasion by the huffing and puffing of the Nettletons and the Seymours about the inconvenience of having to remain on the island ... and of having to change all their flight bookings to return home. Bennett, seated on the other side of the table and along a couple places from me, appeared to go deaf since I last spoke to him. He seemed not to hear any mentions of 'inconvenience'. I found myself unintentionally warming to his style.

I suppose it had to happen sometime during dinner. You can't have vacant chairs at either end of the table without someone noticing – and becoming curious about the absence of our hosts. Marian, having met Frankie in Paris some months ago, now considered herself a close friend of the birthday girl. She raised the issue of her *friend's* absence and made the most noise about it over the rest of dinner. Again, Tom let it all go past without showing any interest. It wasn't until he was asked the direct question about why the Allertons weren't at dinner, he was compelled to join the discussion.

"Perhaps one of them is feeling poorly, and the other is keeping them company. I'm afraid who chooses to eat with us and who doesn't is outside my jurisdiction – and my knowledge."

While the speculation about why the Allertons weren't with us continued, Dervla leaned in close and whispered, "How soon will it be polite to leave after everyone's finished eating?"

"I think how soon depends on when the first opportunity presents for our escape; in fact, the sooner the better for me. I would like to escape before our friend Inspector Bennett latches onto me again."

"Surely he hasn't got any more to talk to you about. You've spent all day with him. Now I think about it, the pair of you did seem to be getting on well."

She received a bleak look in response as Sampson and Dwayne arrived to clear the now empty dessert plates. When the deserts arrived as alternate drops, I waved them away in favour of a couple of chunks of tropical fruits from a large platter in the middle of the table. Dervla received something like a mini bombe Alaska, and complained about it being so sweet and loaded with coconut. Nevertheless, they removed an empty plate from in front of her.

Following Sampson and Dwayne's arrival, Delphine came in with coffee, port, cheese platters, and bowls of foil wrapped Swiss chocolates. She laid everything out on a side table and placed a stack of side plates alongside before inviting everyone to help themselves. I nudged Dervla in the ribs. "This might present the opportunity we were waiting for. Be ready to bolt at the first opportunity."

My concern about Bennett bailing me up again after dinner was ill founded. As Sampson removed the empty dessert plate from in front of Bennett, he leaned down and whispered in Bennett's ear. Whatever Sampson said didn't impress Bennett. As soon as Sampson moved on from him, Bennett was on his feet and excusing himself from the table. He wasted no time exiting the dining room, and a few moments later I heard him clattering down the front steps.

People already were milling around the side table. "Let's go," I hissed at Dervla.

As we made our unhurried – and we hoped unnoticed – exit from the dining room, Dervla asked, "Looks like Bennett found somebody better to talk to tonight. What do you suppose it was all about?"

"No idea ... Probably some message from his officers requiring his attention."

The rest of the evening was uneventful. After escaping upstairs, Dervla sat in my room and we chatted for a few minutes before she went to hers to read. It was my first real dose of time alone for the day. Like all good journos, I typed up my notes on today's happenings. Tonight differed from last night. No storm threatened. As I leaned on the windowsill listening to the sounds of the night and soaking up the perfume of the Murraya and Star Jasmine drifting by on the night air, the sky above was a dark ocean of twinkling stars. Lulled into a reflective mood by my surroundings, I hoisted my backside up onto the wide stone windowsill and settled down to think for a while.

As I reviewed the day, a persistent thought hammered on my subconscious. In spite of its best efforts, I couldn't bring it to the forefront, but something told me it was important. It was something I had missed. What had I missed? Bennett made sure I went over everything with him. Even that brought to light a couple of things I didn't know I'd noticed at the time. What else was there? Nothing else happened. Nothing… Short of divine intervention, there would be no answers to those questions, and certainly not from my empty room.

"Bloody hell, there they are again tonight! What's going on?" Now why didn't I mention them to Bennett today? It's another interesting question for which I don't have an answer.

Last night, during the storm, lights moved about out there in the rainforest. I assumed they were torches, but they were not in the area where the guests' cabins are located. I was heading for a nose-around in that part of the rainforest this morning when Sampson caught me and sent me back inside. And now those lights are back there again tonight. Do I tell Bennett about them and risk looking like a Nervous Nelly, or do I investigate first to see what I turn up? I don't know why I troubled myself with the question. Of course I would investigate before mentioning them to Bennett. So why am I wasting time wondering about the matter when I should be out there investigating it? You're an investigative journalist. Go and investigate!

The clear moonlight night might prove a hindrance rather than a help when crossing the wide expanse of lawn between the building and the start of the rainforest. Once in amongst the trees, it would be dark, their thick canopy excluding the moonlight. From past experience of being amongst dense trees at night, this rainforest is likely to be thick with mosquitoes and other biting things. To afford myself some protection, I slipped on a pair of slacks, and checked on the lights again as I struggled into a long-sleeved shirt.

"Bugger! … They've gone. Oh no, there they are. They're back again." I sat on the edge of my bed. "Come on; hurry up and get out there," I told myself as I laced on a new, so far blemish-free, pair of Nikes. Then, after retrieving a small torch from my bag, I was on my way down the stairs and out the front door. The babble of voices from the dining room suggested the guests continued to entertain themselves in there. If that's the case, those lights moving about in the trees are not likely to be guests.

A substantial garden bed about three quarters of the way across to the edge of the rainforest was my first target. Throwing caution to the wind, I raced flat out across the open expanse of lawn. The garden bed was a jumble of rocks inhabited by a mass of bromeliads, and home to a line of shrubs taller than me. My gallop across the lawn ended about midway along the garden bed. I picked my way to one end and peered cautiously towards the trees. There was nothing too frightening between me and the trees, and those lights were still moving about in there. A couple of tentative steps around the end of the garden bed and I was ready to dash for the trees.

"What the…?" I squeaked as something grabbed hold of me and pulled me into the shadow of the shrubs.

"Shssh," someone hissed in my ear. "What the hell are you doing out here, and where do you think you're going?" That 'someone' was none other than Inspector Bennett.

Before I had a chance to answer, I was dragged back around to the other side of the garden bed. Then, holding firmly onto my arm to keep me close, he leaned in and hissed in my ear. "Why are you out here? All guests are supposed to stay inside. Go back to your room and stay there."

He leant in so close I couldn't turn my head to speak directly to him, so I whispered into the dark night instead of his ear. "Not bloody likely! That's not going to happen. I'm going in there to investigate those lights."

"You are not required out here. Go back inside. This has nothing to do with you. I do not need you thrashing about in there."

"Here's a news flash for you: I am going in there to investigate those lights whether you like it or not. So, we can either go in together, or go in alone… But I will be going into those trees to find out what's going on."

There are times when you just know it's a waste of time arguing and, for Inspector Bennett, this was one of them. "All right…! But you must do exactly as I say. If you do not, or if I feel you are a threat to my investigating the situation, I shall drag you out in handcuffs and lock you in your room. Is that clear?"

"Yes," I hissed back at him.

"Okay, I'll lead the way. Wait here until you see me reach the trees, and then follow me in."

"If you actually go into the trees before I get there, it's so dark in there, I'll never be able to find you."

"I'll wait for you. If you can't find me when you reach the trees, don't venture in on your own. Come back and wait here by the garden bed until I return to find you."

I agreed, and it sounded pleasant enough when I said it. But a little voice in my head was telling me, if I did as I was told, I would spend the night out here beside the garden bed. That wasn't going to happen.

Bennett jogged towards the trees. That's not how I would do it. My approach would be to gallop flat out across to the shadows at the edge of the trees. When he was almost across the lawn, the little voice was in my head again. "He's not going to stop when he gets to the trees. He'll keep going and you'll lose him."

"Yes, I know that's his plan," I whispered to the night.

Then I took off flat out. I didn't expect to catch up with him. At that point in time, I really didn't care whether I did or not. I didn't want to be tied to Bennett. I needed the freedom to do my own thing. As I expected, Bennett didn't stop and wait for me at the edge of the trees. Like a wisp of smoke in the darkness, he disappeared into the rainforest. I was pleased he did. Now I could do my own thing free from Bennett's restrictions and constraints.

In the dark shadows at the very edge of the rainforest, I paused for a brief moment to listen. Was that the faint murmur of voices I could hear coming from somewhere deep in the trees? I stood still and let my eyes adjust to the darkness ahead of me as I scanned the forest for the lights. They were immediately in front of me, but I knew I wouldn't have a straight line trek to reach them.

As I stood there for those few moments, one of the lights disappeared. It caused pause for thought. Where did it go? Had it somehow been alerted to our presence? Snuggled hard up against the first big tree I came to, I lingered a bit longer. How long I remained there pressed hard up against the rough tree trunk I don't know, but it probably felt longer than it was, until that second light reappeared. I breathed a sigh of relief. Now I was right to go. A couple of deep breaths and I was ready to plunge into the dark abys beyond.

There was no sign of Bennett. I had to give him top marks for his stealth. Not only couldn't I see him or any sign of movement to suggest where he was, but I couldn't hear any strange sounds either; not even as much as a twig snapping underfoot. Here's hoping I can mimic his efforts, I thought as I stepped out from behind my tree trunk and took my first tentative steps into the rainforest.

A couple of birds startled by my presence took flight; not a good start. Having to watch where I placed my feet at every step made for slow-going. My new Nikes made a squelching sound as they sank into the deep, moist leaf litter. I was pleased I wasn't barefooted. Soon, the wet slush invaded my shoes.

My feet became mired in a slurry-like mess. Things grabbed at the sleeves of my shirt. I doubted it would be fit to wear in polite company again. Mosquitoes attacked my face and neck, and all around was the musty smell of composting leaf litter.

Despite my slow pace, the lights became closer and the voices more distinct. Those lights hadn't moved since I started in through the trees. Logic said the stationary lights meant whoever had them also was stationary.

Were they sitting down for a chat … or had they left the lights in some fixed position while they moved off some distance? The latter possibility was not encouraging. What if they heard something, and left the lights behind so as not to be seen while they investigated it? Such thoughts were not helpful, but worth considering nevertheless. I inched my way over to a nearby tree trunk of enormous girth and pressed myself hard against it.

Once I was standing still and my pulse slowed a little, I could hear two men talking. I listened for the length of a few heartbeats before being confident they were not moving about and their voices came from where the lights were located. Having ascertained – as much as I could – it was safe to continue, I moved away from my tree trunk and struck out again towards those lights.

After only a short distance, the trees ahead seemed to thin out a bit. It sent my warning bells wild. I would stand out like the proverbial if I continued into that area. But, it's where the lights seem to be situated. Perhaps just a few more metres will be safe enough, I told myself as I inched forward. How wrong could I be? A sudden development up ahead anchored me to the spot.

The lights began moving. I thought I could make out two figures. Don't just stand here, Tessa. Move! The little voice in my head screamed at me, but my feet were not inclined to comply. At last all internal systems were in sync. Not only did my feet want to move, but common sense now dictated I should find cover somewhere. A frantic look around failed to find a suitable tree to hug up to; a tree large enough to hide behind. The best candidate I could see was at least two metres away.

Don't rush … Don't rush … Don't draw attention to yourself … The little voice in my head was on a continuous loop chanting those instructions. It took everything I had not to abandon caution and race over to my target tree. With shallow breathing and clenched teeth, I picked my way cautiously across the intervening space to arrive at the tree with my heart playing jungle drums on my ribs and my blood pressure off the scale. It was only then I realised those lights and the men holding them were moving in the other direction. They moved away from me, not towards me.

Reassured by the realisation, I looked around in the darkness for a new safe track to take me a little closer to what I could now see was a small clearing in the rainforest. The agonisingly slow and careful trek forward began again. It occurred to me I didn't have a plan. What was my goal? What did I plan to do? If I should manage to get close enough to make out anything about the lights and the men with them, what then? Do I just turn on my heel and inch my way back out of the forest and return to my room? There is no point in telling Bennett what I discovered. He's probably already found out more than I know.

Another couple of steps brought me to a large tree. I peered around it to scope out the small clearing now only a few metres ahead of me. Christ, there is a building in the clearing. It looked like a small cottage; a small *neglected* cottage. What was it doing here, so far from the other guests' cottages? Maybe in days gone by it was accommodation for a staff member. Whatever its story, it doesn't appear to have been used for a while.

As I stood speculating about the cottage, the men's meeting appeared to end. One man turned and went into the cottage. The other one strode out of the clearing and into the forest. He adopted a track which took him on a wide angle away from me. But there was no mistaking where he was going. His destination was the castle. The thought which had hammered for attention all evening now broke free and came to the fore. Seeing the man heading back to the castle did it.

Whoever murdered Anton Benoir had to be one of us; one of the guests or staff on Île Verte.

That realisation created something of a pause in proceedings. How safe were any of us, regardless of whether we were in the castle or outside in the grounds? After a few moments, rational thinking returned. A new question occurred to me: why did it have to be someone already on the island? Why couldn't it be someone who came ashore unseen near where Anton's cottage is located?

The only two ways anyone can get here is by plane or boat. It's virtually impossible to arrive on the island by plane without it being common knowledge. Therefore, an outsider would have to arrive by boat. I made a mental note to find out about how difficult or otherwise that might be. Regardless of all the questions about WHO was involved in this murder, the big question for me remained WHY. Why would anyone want to murder Anton Benoir, supposedly an artist living in a grace and favour arrangement on the island?

While deep in such thoughts, I struggled to strangle a scream when something grabbed me by the arm. "What the hell are you doing here?" Bennett growled at me. "I told you to wait for me at the garden bed."

"…And that was never going to happen. And more fool you if you thought it was."

"We'll talk about this later. For now, let's concentrate on getting out here."

"You go if you like. I want to know more about the cottage, and the bloke who went in there."

"Eh…? What do you mean? Are you telling me you saw someone go into it? Did they come out again?"

"No, not that I saw…"

"Okay, now you do have to get out of here. Go back to your room and stay there. This is a police matter and not something for you to be involved in. Besides, it could become dangerous, and I don't need the paperwork associated with a civilian being injured, or worse, on my watch."

As he spoke, Bennett pulled out his phone and, shielding it with the lightweight jacket he was wearing, flicked through his contacts. While the number was dialling, he stuck a Bluetooth gadget in his ear. Then, in a whispered conversation, he called his troops from their beds and into action. For a moment, I wondered how his officers were going to find Bennett and this clearing. I didn't have to wonder long.

"Tessa, my officers should be out there on the lawns in a few minutes. Please make your way back out to that garden bed to wait for them. When they arrive, wave them over to you and point them in the direction of the clearing and the cottage."

My first inclination was to argue. Then I asked myself, how else were the officers going to know where to go? I agreed, and took a moment to orientate myself with the direction I needed to take. It was as I did that, I saw Bennett remove a small object from an internal pocket of his jacket. While it was too dark to see what it was, I saw enough to know it didn't look like a weapon of any sort. With no other reason to delay, I started back towards the lawns and the garden bed where I was to meet the officers when they arrived on the scene.

Mindful of the fact stealth was still required, I forced myself to pick my way carefully towards the moonlight in the distance. I was about three quarters of the way back through the trees when I stood on a fallen branch. It cracked underfoot. I lifted the offending foot off the branch and held it in the air while I stood stock still on one leg for a few moments. Nothing happened. No one rushed through the trees to attack me. I lowered my foot, making sure it didn't go back on the branch. Back on two feet again, I risked a look back at the clearing and the cottage to see if I had attracted any attention.

All was quiet; no change detected in that area. But something else did catch my attention. A very bright almost pinpoint of light shone out through the trees from where I last saw Bennett. The beam of light was directed out towards the castle. Me thinks I have discovered another of Bennett's ploys to get me out of the way. Those officers don't need me to find Bennett. Their instructions are to follow the beam of light he's providing as a location beacon to lead them to him.

Chapter 9

That's enough. I'm not playing this game any longer. My investigation has come this far. I want to see what happens next. I want to know who went into that cottage. If Bennett and his merry men round up the bloke and take him away, I might never know. My assessment of Bennett suggests he is unlikely to share any information with me. It leaves only one real course of action open to me: go back to the clearing to watch what happens.

With my next move clear in my mind, I started on my way back to the clearing. First, I went some distance at right angles to the track I was on. Then I turned towards the clearing and headed in a direction I hoped would take me further around the clearing from where I encountered Bennett. The temptation to rush so as not to miss anything happening at the cottage was almost overwhelming, but Bennet must not know I was still in the rainforest ... and I must not spook whoever was in the cottage.

After what seemed an agonisingly long time, Bennett's light beam became visible in the distance through the trees. I kept going and soon saw the clearing up ahead. There was little cover between me and the clearing. It was as though, at some time in the past, the area between me and the cottage was cleared. The rainforest slowly worked on reclaiming it but, so far, only managed spindly trees and some undergrowth. A slight detour once again adjusted my angle of approach.

My final vantage point had me opposite the front door and only a couple of metres back from the edge of the clearing. What better view of the site and any action taking place there could I ask for? I didn't have long to wait to find out. From where I stood, I could just see Bennett's light. I jumped in surprise when the light suddenly disappeared. His officers found him was the likely explanation. If it were the case, it was safe to assume, after a short briefing session, the group would move towards the cottage.

They were good. From where I stood, I couldn't detect any sound or movement by the police ... not until the whole operation turned sour. It appears Bennett and his officers went around behind the cottage in order to approach the place from the other side. I still couldn't see anything, but a loud crack gave away their position. I focused my eyes and ears on where the sound came from.

The occupant of the cottage also heard the noise. He opened the door and stood framed in the doorway for a few moments. His indecision was evident even from my distance. When nothing further occurred, he appeared to decide it was safe to go back inside. I didn't realise until he went back inside, but the tension of the moment had rendered my breathing shallow and slow. It's as well he went back inside when he did or I might have passed out due to a lack of oxygen.

It was while I was bringing my breathing back to normal I noticed the bloke had left the door slightly ajar. Was leaving it partially open deliberate? A safety measure in the event he needed to bolt in a hurry. Whatever the reason, it proved a wise move. All hell was about to break loose. Things were about to become lively around the cottage.

With their quarry now on high alert, Bennett chose to mount his take-down without wasting any more time. The police rushed out of the trees and towards the cottage. Their noise was enough to alert even a deaf man. Fearing a disaster might be in the making, as the police rushed across the open space between trees and cottage, I used their noise to cover beating a hasty retreat. My new position, while several metres further back in the forest, continued to provide a good view of the cottage and its immediate surroundings.

As I settled into my new watching position, the cottage door slammed wide open. The occupant, carrying his torch, raced out and headed for the trees. He barrelled headlong into the forest, stumbling and crashing about without concern for concealing his location. His direction was towards the castle, and his line of escape past me would take him only a couple of metres away from my current vantage point.

I had to do something, but what? At the same time as I pondered the question, the escapee realised the error in using his torch. With a flick of a switch, the place was plunged into darkness. The police with their less powerful lights were just entering the trees in pursuit. Between them all, they made enough noise to drown out any sounds I might make. I scrambled around in the darkness for something – anything – which might be useful in hampering the bloke's escape. Close to where I stood, a fallen branch about 80 millimetres in diameter lay half buried in the leaf litter.

When I lifted it free, I realised it was quite long and solid. This might have to do, I told myself as I held it at what I hoped was about ankle height above the ground. If my calculations were correct, the branch stretched across the escapee's line through the trees. I didn't have long to wait. About a second after I positioned the branch, the bloke reached the relevant spot.

His impact with the branch wrenched it from my grasp, but it did its job. The man caught his foot under the branch and went sprawling face-first into the leaf litter. If this were a movie, the police would be right on his heels, positioned to pounce on him the moment he went down. But this was real life. The police were several metres behind and unaware their quarry had gone down. It was up to me to make good the intervention I initiated.

Winded by his fall, it took the bloke a few moments to collect himself. That was my opportunity. I dived through between the trees and pounced, landing on my knees in the middle of his back. I heard the wind knocked out of him again. Where the hell were the police? I heard them crashing through the trees, but they were too far over. Where is this bloke's torch? If he dropped it when he fell, it could have landed anywhere … and would be difficult to find in the dark. Nevertheless, I frantically scanned the area around me in the hope of seeing it. Sometimes you can be lucky. That's when I remembered my small torch still in my pocket. It wasn't powerful, but it might help find this bloke's torch.

"Ye-e-s…," I whooped. There it was. The missing torch had landed beside its owner. It lay in the leaf litter beside the man's hip. So close and yet so far…! It lay a short distance to one side and behind me. Not being a contortionist, I couldn't reach the torch. Altering my position enough to reach it might give my captive the freedom he needed to toss me off him.

The next few moments were precarious as I wriggled backwards a few centimetres along the man's back. Then, by leaning back as far as possible and stretching my arm right out, I managed to reach the torch with my fingertips. I didn't have enough purchase to pick it up. By flicking it with my fingertips, I moved it several centimetres closer. While the manoeuvre buried it a little deeper in the litter, I could get my fingers around it. Triumphant, I held the torch tight to my chest for a moment before searching for its switch. I don't think I breathed at all throughout the retrieval exercise.

A couple of deep breaths as I located the switch, and then the scene was ablaze with torch light. By waving the torch in the direction of the police, and yelling as loud as I could, I hoped to speed the cavalry to my rescue. It worked, but it seemed to take ages before they arrived. Then, everything happened in a blur. The first two officers to arrive grabbed my prisoner's arms, and shoved me off as they brought his arms up behind his back.

It was all over in a flash. The man, handcuffed and hoisted to his feet, was being dragged along through the trees towards the wide expanse of lawn adjacent to the castle. Bennett remained at the scene when the officers moved off with their prisoner. His words to me before he stormed off after his men do not bear recording here. Suffice to say, *thank you* was not amongst them. Somewhat miffed by the final outcome of my night's work, I dusted myself off and, using the prisoner's torch to light my way, trudged back to the castle.

Once I reached the lawn, I turned off the torch. The moon-light was bright but gentle, and had something of a calming effect. There was no sign of the police. I was a short distance behind the police as I made my way out of the rainforest, but not so far behind as to allow them to disappear by the time I emerged. In spite of my thorough scan of the surroundings, there was no sign of them. Tired, filthy, and more than a little cranky, I marched back to my room for a shower and sleep.

*****

Morning seemed to arrive incredibly fast today. A few aches and pains as I eased myself out of bed reminded me of last night's adventure. Several scratches on my arms were a surprise. I don't recall them happening. My mirror doesn't flatter me this morning either. Another shower and shampooing my hair might help, but I'm doubtful.

As I made my way down to the dining room for breakfast, I realised Dervla hadn't knocked on my door this morning. Perhaps she did, but I was in the shower and didn't hear her. As I was feeling decidedly unsociable, that wasn't a bad thing, I decided. The dining room was empty when I arrived. That's another plus. So far, today is going well. I wonder how long it will be before something stuffs it up. Dervla's absence surprised me. After the last couple of earlier than usual starts, maybe she reverted to type and would come down to breakfast later.

I went straight to a side table where the breakfast fare was laid out, and loaded a small bowl with chunks of fruit. Was I early, or late? The issue of the deserted dining room nagged me as I munched my way through my fruit. I checked the time.

"Even if she were having a lie in, I would expect Dervla to be here by now," I murmured to the empty dining room. Dervla remained uppermost in my thoughts and I felt my stomach starting to tighten. When I arrived here this morning, I felt inclined to something approximating a full English breakfast. Somewhere during the few minutes I'd been in the dining room the idea lost its appeal.

With my coffee abandoned half drunk, I couldn't restrain myself any longer. My gut kept telling me to check on Dervla. After bounding up the stairs two at a time, I raced past my own room to pound on Dervla's door. The door swung open the moment I touched it. It wasn't even closed properly, let alone locked. My stomach was now a writhing mass. Every fibre of my being knew something was wrong. Applying restraint and caution, I eased the door open a fraction to scan the room.

Dervla lay on the floor just inside and to one side of the door. Her face was bruised and bloody. The room looked undisturbed. I left the door partly ajar and went to her side to check for a pulse. She was alive, but her pulse was weak. After tiptoeing across to the ensuite door, I checked there were no nasty surprises hiding in there. How do I deal with this in this godforsaken place, I asked the universe as I checked on Dervla again. Her room key remained in the lock on the inside of the door. I removed the key from the lock, let myself out and locked the door behind me. Now, where the hell am I likely to find Bennett this morning?

There was a vague recollection of his mentioning being given a room near ours. Was it the next one, or two down from Dervla's? I couldn't remember and I wasn't going to waste time trying to think about it. The door to the room next to Dervla's was locked and no amount of banging on it raised any response from inside. I moved to the next room along and repeated the process with the same result. This was wasting time, time I wasn't sure Dervla had for me to waste. Somebody must know where I can find Bennett this morning.

Down the stairs and across the tiles, I took the first door off of the lobby in my search for the kitchen. My expectation was Delphine, and maybe the other staff members, were likely to be in the kitchen at this hour of the morning. Surely one of them will know where I can find Bennett. My day had turned sour, and it was about to get worse. The kitchen, like the dining room this morning, was deserted.

At the far end of the long kitchen, an external door stood open. I raced towards it and almost barrelled into Delphine and Sampson as they came in from the garden. "Where is Inspector Bennett? I need him urgently. Something terrible has happened."

The two staff members exchanged a look I couldn't interpret. Delphine started to shake her head. I knew she was about to tell me she didn't know where Bennett was. I hoped that wasn't the case because I wouldn't believe her if she did. Perhaps the hard look I gave her changed her mind.

"I... uhmm I'm not sure. A little earlier he was in the staff quarters with his officers. He might be still there." Sampson nodded enthusiastically in support of Delphine's suggestion.

"Okay; where are the staff quarters?" They hesitated and exchanged another look. "Come on, don't waste my time. I said it was urgent I find Bennett. Now, where are these bloody staff quarters?"

"Come with me; I will show you the way."

"Thank you, Sampson, but can we hurry please?"

He responded by turning on his heel and taking off at a canter across the yard. Glued to his heels all the way, I remember crossing the lawn, skirting around a garden bed, and racing through a vegetable garden before coming to a long, low building reminiscent of a barracks or dormitory. Sampson didn't stop. He continued to the door, pushed it open and raced inside. I heard voices as I followed him in through the door.

"Inspector Bennett, Inspector Bennett, there is a problem," Sampson chanted once he was inside.

"You should know better than to rush in here yelling like that. This is police headquarters now, and we were engaged in discussing serious police business. What do you mean by carrying on like this?"

Bennett's tone brought out my dark side. "Get off your high horse you pompous Pom. Sampson brought me here because of a serious situation in the castle. You and your men might like to follow me back. If you don't hurry, you may well have a second murder to investigate. So, stop wasting time. Lift your arses and let's get moving."

I thought I was in for an argument. Bennett eased himself to his feet, pulled himself up to his full height and glared at me. My demeanour changed his mind. "Oh, perhaps we should humour her. Let's take a look at whatever this 'serious situation' is so we can get on with the business we are here for." His officers shrugged at one another before gradually finding their feet.

Sampson slowly inched away during my exchanges with Bennett. As the officers scraped their chairs and gradually rose to their feet, I told Sampson to leave. He hadn't deserved the spray he got from Bennett, and I wasn't sure there wouldn't be more heated exchanges between myself and the inspector. Sampson didn't need to endure any more of such stuff this morning. Once everyone was on their feet, I led the way at a brisk pace back to the castle.

Bennett and I were a little ahead of the others as we climbed the stairs to Dervla's room. After checking over his shoulder, Bennett leaned in close a hissed, "I don't much appreciate the way you addressed me in front of my officers. You will hear more about that from me in the near future."

"You deserved every word of it, but you're right, I shouldn't have said it in front of your officers. Sampson was only doing his job; a job he does well and as expected of him. And, you are the second toffee-nosed Englishman to abuse him for it in the last two days."

"The second one...? Who else made such an error of judgement?"

"Nettleton... And he got much the same treatment as you did."

"That's interesting."

I have no idea why he thought it interesting, but I wasn't going to pursue it. By then we had reached Dervla's door and I was busy unlocking it. Bennett watched me before asking, "Why is it locked, and how come you have the key?"

"I checked her room. There was no one else in there, so I locked the door when I left to make sure no one got in while I was gone."

"Why would you be so concerned about someone entering her room?"

I swung the door wide open. "See for yourself."

Dervla's room became a hive of activity. Bennett strode over to Dervla still prone on the floor. After signalling for the other officers to wait at the door, I watched as Bennett went into commanding officer mode. "Winston, in here, please," he yelled. Then in a quiet aside to me, "Winston was a registered nurse before joining the police."

Winston dropped to his haunches beside Dervla, inspected her injuries and took her pulse before speaking. "She's had a good going over, Sir; not in real good condition at the moment."

"Do what you can for her, there's a good chap."

"Does this place have a first aid kit of any sort?"

As Winston checked Dervla, Sampson came to the door. He looked beseechingly at me, and showed me the first aid box he carried. I didn't blame him for not wanting to again have to engage in any way with this lot, so I interceded on his behalf. I took the first aid box from him and set it down on the floor next to Winston. "Sampson anticipated your request." I gave Bennett a meaningful look as I said it.

"Good man, Sampson, thank you." Bennett accompanied the complement with a beaming smile at Sampson. It won't fix things, but it might go some way to mending bridges, I thought as I watched Sampson retreat from the scene.

"I need to clean her injuries. Is there somewhere I can get some warm water?" Winston was looking at me when he asked the question, so I answered.

"There's warm water in the ensuite through there," I said as I flicked my head towards the bathroom door.

"Williams…," Bennett bellowed. The officious constable, whom I now knew as Williams, rushed in and snapped to attention. "Warm water…," Bennett demanded.

Winston thrust a small enamel bowl at Williams and pointed him in the direction of the ensuite. Soon after, Winston was bathing Dervla's injuries with the warm water laced with a heavy dose of antiseptic solution. With the dried blood removed, her injuries still looked nasty, but a lot less frightening. While Winston tended to Dervla, Bennett left the room to make a phone call. I heard Jackson speak to Bennett outside on the landing.

"Your officer said you wanted to speak to me… What's the problem?"

"Ah, Jackson … yes … there's been a bit of an accident. We need to fly a doctor over from Saint-Marie. Is it possible for one of your planes to be on standby to bring a medical team across?"

"I'll organise it. Tell them to call the hangar when they are ready to leave and the plane will be ready when they reach the airstrip."

Jackson hurried off and I heard Bennett make one more call. He had wandered further around the gallery so I couldn't hear what was said, but I assumed his call was to organise a doctor. Then he returned to Dervla's room. After telling Winston to stay with the patient, Bennett rounded up his officers and disappeared.

I seemed to have become invisible to Bennett so, after he and the others left, I settled down to help Winston keep watch over Dervla. One thought attacked the forefront of my mind: where was Frankie? Not only was it one of her guests who was attacked, it is her good friend lying here seriously injured. Whoever our hostess is, she might look like Frankie, but she is not Frankie.

Time dragged on with little visible change in Dervla's condition. Winston occupied himself interspersing making regular checks on her vital signs with checking outside the room for anything which might constitute a danger. A check on the time revealed I had been sitting cross-legged on the hard floor next to Dervla for over an hour. My backside became numb some time ago. While I have no intention of leaving this room, I do need to stand and move about a bit to crank my circulation back up to normal.

When Winston returned from his latest prowl outside, I levered myself off the floor. On wobbly legs, I wandered about the room for a few moments until I was sure my legs were not going to give way under me. For want of anything better to do, I strolled across to the window. As I leant on the windowsill taking in the glorious day outside, the two golf carts crossed my field of view and disappeared along the track through the rainforest.

"I think the doctor Bennett ordered is about to arrive. The golf carts are headed for the airstrip." Winston seemed unmoved by my announcement. He appeared preoccupied with his patient. The now familiar lead ball was back in my stomach again. "Winston, is everything okay? You look a little concerned."

"Sorry…? No, nothing is wrong. I think your friend might be starting to regain consciousness." I rushed back to Dervla's side. My heart was beating wildly. A pang of disappointment hit me. I couldn't see any change in her. My disappointment must have showed. Winston sought to ease my concern. "You won't notice much visual change, but her vitals suggest an improvement. Anyway, as you say, the doctor is likely to be here soon. We will learn more then."

Hanging about doing nothing is not my style. Today is giving me a hard lesson in how to do it.

Chapter 10

Two women, each looking a ball of business, alighted from one of the carts and followed Sampson's directions to the front steps. Dwayne, carrying a bag in each hand, trailed along behind them. Bennett met them at the steps and ushered them inside. Feet clattered up the stairs and, within moments of the women's arrival, Bennett was knocking on Dervla's door. Brief introductions identified one of the women as a doctor and the other as a specialist nurse.

They commandeered the patient and the room. While Winston was allowed to stay, it was made clear I was not required. After a brief argument, and plenty of reluctance, I exited the room. My first task was to locate Bennett. There is a whole string of questions to which I want answers ... and I intend to obtain them by one means or another. Bennett appeared to have vanished from the castle, so I marched across to the staff quarters. No one there; this was not shaping up to be one of my better days.

The only other place I thought the police might go today was the derelict cottage where the action took place last night. Did I want to traipse through the rainforest again this morning? In all honesty, I didn't. Besides, the medical team upstairs might finish up soon, and I might be allowed back in with Dervla. As I entered the lobby, the sight of Winston coming down the stairs suggested it was not likely to happen any time soon.

"You've served your purpose and been thrown out now as well, have you?" I asked as Winston reached the bottom of the stairs.

"The medical team have taken over to give me a break for a while. The good news is, they confirm your friend is moving towards regaining consciousness. Don't get too excited. It will be a slow process – and that's a good thing. It allows the brain to heal as it happens."

"Thank you. That is good news. Do you happen to know where I might find Inspector Bennett?"

"I haven't seen or heard from him since he left the room earlier. He might be back at the staff quarters." I shook my head. "Then, I'm sorry, but I can't help you. I'm going back to the quarters to make myself a coffee. Could I interest you in joining me?"

Tempting though a coffee was right now, I had more important matters to deal with first. A sudden rethink of the situation sent me scurrying across the lobby to the kitchen. Delphine had a large mound of pastry on a table in front of her and was covered to her elbows in flour. "I don't want to interrupt you, Delphine, but is it possible for me to make myself a coffee?"

"Certainly not; I will make you coffee. You poor thing; you must be worried sick. How is Miss O'Reilly?"

As no amount of argument would persuade her to let me make my own coffee, I perched on a stool and watched her. Her question about Dervla's condition spawned a fresh idea. "It has been a different sort of vacation so far, Delphine. Finding my friend like that this morning is just about the last straw. I've been worried sick for the last couple of days about Miss Dubois, and now this happens. This was supposed to be a special time; a get-together of three old friends. And now I seem to be the only one left standing. Will something happen to me next?"

Delphine looked uncomfortable. She hesitated a tad too long before attempting a response. I expected an evasive comment – I'm too polite to call it a lie – would be forthcoming. Perhaps my stony look changed her mind. With a sigh of resignation, she poured herself a coffee and came and slid onto a stool opposite me.

"I don't know what is going on in this place, or what to expect next." She looked close to tears. Her usual unruffled façade began to crumble.

"Delphine, I know you are close to Miss Dubois, and I think you are concerned for her too. As she is someone special we both are worried about, what can you tell me about where she is and what's happening with her?"

She buried her face in her hands and I heard her sob. When she looked up, tears streaked her cheeks. "I don't know, Miss Tessa, I don't know. That's why I'm so worried … and I don't know what's happened to Mr Charles either. Not that he would be concerned about what's happened to his wife."

Ah hah, so my earlier assessment of the situation here was right. I need to tread carefully if I want more from Delphine. One weak moment doesn't mean she will open up completely.

"What happened on the night of the birthday party? Frankie … Miss Dubois seemed to evaporate into thin air sometime during the night, and long before the night ended. I don't remember seeing her for a while before the power went off. And the last I saw of Mr Charles was when he went out with Sampson and Dwayne to check on the generator."

"I don't know. That's the truth. I didn't know she left the party early. Most of the night, I was here in the kitchen. I just finished cleaning up when the power went off, so I went to my rooms. As I went past Miss Dubois' suite, through the crack under the door, I saw a pale light moving about in there. Nobody answered when I knocked, so I called out a couple of times. Still nobody answered, but the light went out. I let myself in. When the lights went out, I grabbed a small torch which always hangs on the wall over there and put it in my pocket. I didn't need it to find my way through to my rooms, but I turned it on as I soon as I opened Miss Dubois' door. She was startled by my entry and shouted at me."

"What was she doing when you entered?"

"Just sitting on the edge of her bed and holding a large candle. The candle wasn't lit, but I smelled it had been. It was the light I saw moving about in the room before she blew it out."

"You said she yelled at you. Did she often yell at you?"

"No, never before."

"Okay; what did she say? How did she seem?"

"Something was wrong – very wrong; I could tell as soon as I saw her. She told me to get out … told me she needed her privacy and accused me of daring to come into her room without permission. I don't know how to describe …"

"I take it she had never spoken to you like that before…" Delphine shook her head. "But you didn't leave her room as she told you to, did you?"

"No. I couldn't leave her alone."

"Tell me how she was. Was she crying … distraught … angry? How was she when you found her?"

"…Perhaps distraught … No. Depressed, or despondent maybe … It was as though the life had been sucked out of her. Apart from that brief moment when she yelled at me, she was like an empty shell, a hollow copy of herself."

"What did you do? Did you leave her alone as she asked?"

"No, of course not; I could see she needed help. I sat on the bed next to her and held her tight while I talked to her. After a while, she said she was tired, so I helped her to bed. Then I sat in the big old chair in her room until I was sure she was asleep before I went to my own room."

"Did Mr Charles come back while you were with her; did you see or hear him come back later?"

"I don't know whether he came back or not. I didn't hear or see him, and I don't go into his rooms until after he comes to breakfast in the morning. He didn't come to breakfast next morning or today."

"Doesn't he share the same suite of rooms as Miss Dubois?"

"No … he has his own rooms. Uhmm … he often works late at night and well … you know … it would keep his wife awake if he had the lights on in the room for most of the night."

"What work does he do?"

"He's a writer. I thought you knew that. I think he must be one of those night owl people who prefer to work at night, and often until the early hours of the morning. Most nights, Miss Dubois is in bed by eleven o'clock; more usually soon after ten o'clock."

"How is their relationship?" Delphine gave me a stern look I tried softening the question, but there are only so many ways to ask a simple question. "I mean, do the couple seem happy together?"

"I really couldn't say, Miss. In my position, I have no way of knowing such things."

I knew I was pushing my luck but it was worth a try. "Am I correct in thinking you haven't seen Mr Charles since the night of the party?" She shrugged and then nodded. "Do you think Miss Dubois knows he isn't around? Maybe that's what is upsetting her. She is worried about him. When she rushed into the dining room the morning after the party, she was looking for her husband."

"She was looking for him for comfort and support. She had a terrible shock earlier that morning. That's what triggered her near-hysteria."

This is like paddling a boat with a feather: I'm working hard but going nowhere fast. It might be better to check on Dervla or search for Bennett than to waste more time trying to extract information from Delphine. Give it one more go, I told myself.

"What shock…? That morning they discovered Anton's murder. Did it have something to do with how upset she was?"

"Of course it did! She was fond of Anton; encouraged and supported him all the time. Finding his body like she did would be enough to tip anyone over the edge."

"Frankie… Miss Dubois found Anton's body? I thought one of the men found him early that morning."

"Yes, Sampson found him first thing. He came straight back here to tell Mr Charles about it and to ring for the police. Mr Charles wasn't in his rooms and he couldn't get the police, so Sampson stayed here in the castle trying to contact the police. It was nine o'clock or so by the time he spoke to them. Sometime while all that was happening, Miss Dubois went for a walk and found Anton. There was no one else around at the time, so she rushed back here to tell her husband about it."

"…And, by the time she arrived, she was quite distraught and Charles was nowhere to be found … and still isn't, it seems." Delphine was anxious to return to her baking and I wanted to check on Dervla, so I took my leave.

Dervla's door was closed so I knocked. The young nurse opened the door a fraction and told me in quite definite terms to go away. Having delivered her message, she closed the door in my face. There wasn't much opportunity while the door was open, but it was enough time to note Winston hadn't returned to his patient. Dervla remained on the floor but had moved, or been rearranged, in the interim. I hoped it was the former and it indicated she had regained consciousness.

As prising answers out of Bennett was the only other thing on my agenda for today, I went to my room to prepare to search for him. After changing into the slacks, long sleeves and the now muddy Nikes I wore last night, I headed downstairs. On the way down, I discovered both mine and my captive's torches were in the roomy pockets of my slacks. A detour into the hall for bottled water and I was set to go... but to go where? I decided it was worth checking the staff quarters again before enduring another trek through the rainforest.

The staff quarters remained empty. It was too good an opportunity not to poke about. Careful not to leave evidence of my snooping, I looked through loose papers, files and at charts pinned to the wall. My efforts turned up nothing of interest, or help in finding Bennett. It left only the derelict cottage in the rainforest clearing as his likely location. I started across the lawn in the same direction as I took last night. As I passed the front steps, a thought hit me: why would he be at that cottage?

If he thought the cottage held evidence to assist with his investigation, he would have his officers search the place. He might go with them for an initial look around in daylight, but I doubted he would hang about there for long. Much of the morning had disappeared. I could hear guests in the back garden indulging in morning tea. Bennett had been gone since around breakfast. It was then a terrible thought occurred to me: what if the plane which brought the doctor and nurse to the island transported the prisoner back to Saint-Marie – and Bennett accompanied him? I did not want that to be the case.

I plonked down on the bottom step to consider the situation further before rushing into the rainforest. Without consciously doing so, I was fast convincing myself Bennett would not be at the cottage. If he weren't, I wouldn't need to go there. I did want to look at the cottage, but not necessarily right now. My problem was, there was nowhere else apart from the cottage where Bennett could be... Or was there? It only took a couple of seconds to think of other places: the air strip, Saint-Marie ... or Anton's cottage and studio. Oh, I did like that last possibility.

There was one major problem with the possibility Bennett was at Anton's abode. I didn't know where it was. Think, Tessa, think. You must have some idea where it is. Then I remembered Frankie introducing me to Anton. When explaining who he was and where he lived, she did a vague wrist-flap in the direction now off to my right as I sat there on the steps. For want of a better idea, it's worth taking a look over there to see what I can find.

No tracks led off the lawns in the required direction until I reached the edge of the rainforest. Almost directly opposite the front steps, a narrow track disappeared into the trees. After about a hundred metres, it emerged again into the open to run along an escarpment above a sheer drop to the sea below. The view was spectacular. I promised myself I would spend time admiring it later but, right now, finding Bennett was more pressing.

An abbreviated headland separated the first small bay I encountered from the next slightly larger bay. Bingo! There, central to the bay and commanding the most magnificent view were a small cottage and the burnt out remnants of a second small building. If the burnt out building were Anton's studio, he could find no more inspirational place to work. Lost for a few moments in the beauty of the place, a noise coming from the cottage brought me sharply back to reality. Should I dive for cover in a nearby stand of trees, or should I investigate? For the space of a couple of heartbeats, I did neither; just stood hesitating on the spot.

In the end, no decision was required. I glimpsed Bennett inside the cottage as he passed by the open door. Enough time wasted on indecision, I strode to the door, knocked and called out. "Inspector ... Tom, may I come in?"

A few hurried footsteps and Bennett was at the door. "What the hell are you doing here?"

"I happen to be looking for you; oh, and good morning to you too." His throaty chuckle in response suggested things might be amicable between us – at least for the moment.

"It seems you found me. Has something else happened to have you looking for me? First, how is Miss O'Reilly doing?"

"I wish I knew. The doctor turfed both Winston and I out and took over the room. I tried to see how Dervla was before I came looking for you, but was told nothing by the nurse, other than to bugger off that is."

"Is Winston on duty outside the room?"

"No. He said he was told go for breakfast and then to rest or resume normal duties. The basic message was his services were no longer required by the patient. I think he wasn't too happy about it, and a bit concerned."

"Perhaps I need to have a chat with the good doctor ... and Winston needs reminding who gives his orders. You still haven't said why you were looking for me."

"I wanted to have a chat with you ... about the case, of course ... and I think it's becoming urgent. I know you want to go to sort Winston out, but might you spare me a few minutes before you rush off?" There was a strong note of resignation in his agreement. "Is there somewhere we can sit while we talk?"

"We could sit inside, but it might not be the most pleasant experience for you. We moved Anton's body inside until it is removed to Saint-Marie. It's all right in there, but it depends on how you are about sharing the place with the body."

"In my line of work, bodies are a part of the trade. Let's go inside shall we?"

While Bennett dragged a couple of straight-backed chairs from around a small kitchen table over to the open doorway, I tried hard to ignore the bundle wrapped in blankets at the other end of the room. We sat side-by-side facing out across the bay, and enjoyed a brief silence before getting down to the serious business I wanted to discuss. Bennett initiated the discussion.

"Have you thought of something else you need to tell me in relation to my investigation?"

His question was gentle. I detected no hint of confrontation or reprimand. Encouraged, I dived in without much preamble. "There are a number of things I wanted to discuss but, first and foremost, I need answers to a couple of questions." I watched his eyebrows shoot up his forehead and guessed he was going to stonewall me, so I rushed on before he had a chance. "Frankie, Miss Dubois, is a friend from a long time ago. Dervla and I are here to rekindle a friendship, but Frankie is invisible. I understand she has taken to her rooms. That may be the case, but I'm not sure it's true. If it is, what is her condition? Is she well? Is she eating? Should the doctor see Frankie while she's here? Has something involving Frankie happened? I'm sorry, but I do need to know. And I do need to see and speak to my friend."

"The short answer to that is, I don't know. Look, can I trust you not to go to the media with any of this stuff? I know you're probably chasing a story, but I can't risk this going out yet."

"No, I'm not chasing a story; I'm not working. I'm spending two weeks' vacation with my friend who seems to have evaporated into thin air. Is it unreasonable for me to want to know what's happening, to want to know how she is, and to at least be able to see and talk to her?"

"None of that is unreasonable, but that doesn't change my answer. I don't know if she is involved in something, or how she is at the moment. Nevertheless, you are right. We do need to find out about her current situation. Perhaps we might do that when we return to the castle."

At last I'm getting somewhere; might as well push my luck a bit further while I'm about it. "Have you seen Charles, Mr

Allerton, or do you know where he is? He seems to have vanished as well, and at the most inopportune moment, I would suggest."

"Charles remains a concern. Your assessment is fairly accurate. He does seem to have disappeared. The how, why, and where of that state of affairs is of interest to our investigation. So far, I don't know whether he had direct involvement in what happened here on the night of the storm, or even if he might be 'collateral damage' from what occurred here. It's part of my reason for fossicking around in the cottage this morning. I live in hope of finding something – anything – which might provide answers or at least shed some light on what happened here, and why."

"Am I reading too much into it, or is it a little strange for Anton's studio to be sacrificed but not his cottage? What needing obliterating would be in his studio, while nothing in the cottage required the same attention?"

"They are the same questions I am asking myself. I haven't found any answers yet."

"What do you know of Anton Benoir? I only met him the afternoon before the party. Frankie said he was an artist, but that was all. Somehow, I think the arrangement which provided him with accommodation here was more complex than simply supporting a budding artist. I searched for information on Anton and his work, but drew a blank. While maybe still to make his mark in the art world, I would expect to find some mention of him in some capacity. There was nothing."

"Like you, I know nothing about the man other than he is supposed to be an artist of some sort. There are a few small sculptural pieces in the ruins of the studio, so it's safe to assume he was a sculptor. Other evidence suggests he also was a painter. I first thought this might be nothing more than Charles supporting another emerging creative individual."

"Are you telling me that's not what you think now? In Charles' absence, Frankie might be the only one who could shed light on the matter … if we could speak to her. Have you found anything in the cottage or in the studio to help explain any of this?"

"Not as such; if anything, I've come across a few inconsequential things which tend to raise more questions. Do you have any ideas?"

"Maybe not ideas; more like intuition... I had formed the opinion that Anton's presence here might be a grace and favour type arrangement. In return for this place, he provided special services when required. I think some of those services included attendance at dinner parties and the likes whenever guests were on the island. I don't know the reasoning behind such attendance, but I got the impression at the afternoon tea when I met him, he was no more thrilled to be there that I was."

Bennett appeared to consider my comments for a while before springing up off his chair. "We've managed to identify quite a few mutual questions without finding any answers. Perhaps our next move should be to check on your friend, Miss Dubois. Come on; let's see if we might have a word with her."

Chapter 11

As we climbed the front steps of the castle, Bennett asked, "How do you suppose we might go about getting an audience with Miss Dubois?"

"Delphine, the housekeeper, said Frankie had locked herself in her rooms. Even Delphine can't get in to see her, and I think they have a close relationship. They are not just employer and employee. They are friends. I suppose the best we can do is to ask Delphine how we might gain access."

The housekeeper was not helpful. She confirmed Frankie's door is locked from the inside, and she thinks the key is left in the lock. Delphine leaves trays of food outside Frankie's door. When she checks later, the tray remains outside, but it looks as though Frankie has picked at it. Bennett was not happy with the situation and decided to try his own approach to gaining access to Frankie.

He marched down to the door Delphine indicated and thumped loudly on it. "Miss Dubois, it's the police. This is Inspector Bennett. I need to speak to you as a matter of some urgency. Please unlock the door so I may come in to speak with you."

His approach met with silence. He tried twice more, with the same result. Losing patience, he bellowed, "Miss Dubois, I demand you open this door. Open it at once or I will be forced to take more forceful measures."

This time, he extracted a response. "Go away. I do not wish to speak with you or anyone else. I demand my privacy. My door is locked and will stay that way."

Bennett's face turned a glorious shade of red. That, combined with his clenched fists, suggested his blood pressure was about to skyrocket.

"Let me try. I probably won't do any good either, but it won't hurt to try." I tapped gently on the door and kept my voice soft and non-aggressive. "Frankie, it's me, Tessa. I'm worried about you. We haven't seen you around and are concerned you're okay. Could I talk to you, even just for a few moments, just to be sure you're okay?"

There was no response, so I waited a couple of minutes – while Bennett impatiently marked time beside me – before trying again. "Frankie, Frankie, please say something. It's not right for a hostess to invite friends to stay with her and then refuse to see or talk to them. You know better than to do that. Please, talk to me."

After a brief silence, at last Frankie answered. The catch in her voice was obvious. She was crying. "I'm sorry, Tessa. I know it is rude of me, and I so want to spend time with you and Dervla, but it's just not possible. I should have known better; never invited you to come. This is not a good place, not a good place for my friends to be, but I thought … I thought … What I thought doesn't matter. I made a mistake, that's all, and now I've probably lost the two best friends I ever had. I am so sorry, but you and Dervla should – must – leave this island as soon as possible. Now please leave me be."

Stunned, I was at a loss as to what I should do – could do. In desperation, I looked at Bennett, hoping for some suggestion. None was forthcoming. The inspector, standing hands on hips, was intent on studying his boots. After a few seconds, he looked up and motioned for me to follow him. He led us into the kitchen. Delphine was with us outside Frankie's room while Bennett tried his best to have the door unlocked. When that met with no success, and all appeared lost, Delphine abandoned the cause and returned to her kitchen.

"I'm sorry," she said as we entered the kitchen. "I knew it was useless to try, but I thought you, as a police officer, might persuade her to open up." She returned her attention to vegetables she was preparing, but she wasn't quick enough. I saw the tears well up in her eyes. Soon they would tumble down her cheeks, and she would not want us to witness that. "Tom, perhaps you and I should leave Delphine to get on with her work while we go elsewhere to think about the other questions plaguing us."

We were at the kitchen door when Bennett stopped suddenly, turned on his heel and marched back into the kitchen. "Is there a master key to this place?"

"I'm not sure what you mean by a master key, but keys for every door in the place are kept in the keys locker in the office."

While technically not part of his suite of rooms, Charles appeared to have commandeered the office which was located adjacent to his rooms. "Is this a general office used to manage the running of this place, or is it Charles' private domain?" Bennett asked as he surveyed the office from the doorway.

"It's hard to say," Delphine began hesitantly. "It is the main office for the island. We all have occasion to work in here. Mr Allerton doesn't approve of course. He wants it to be just *his* office. He tried to kick us all out, but Miss Dubois pulled him into line."

"I see," Bennett murmured. "So, who does use the office?"

"Well, I do. This is where I do all my paperwork, and Sampson keeps his records of what's happening on the island in here. Of course, Miss Dubois uses the office quite a bit too. The fax machine is in here and our main computer. So, we all work here from time to time as part of our jobs. Oh, and of course Mr Allerton uses it. He likes to make it difficult for us to come in here to do our work."

Delphine's forthright comments surprised me. In my brief conversations with her, I had found her a model of discretion. But here she was airing her dislike for Charles Allerton for all to hear. Deep down, I think Delphine's feelings for the man run to more than 'dislike'. I made a bid to soften the questioning of the housekeeper who was showing signs of becoming distressed.

"Delphine, I understand Mr Allerton is a writer." She sniffed contemptuously. "I suppose that means his work demands he has office space of some sort. If he didn't work here in this main office, where else would he do his writing?"

"He has his own office in there," she said, jerking her head towards the room next door. "When they moved to live here, Miss Dubois made changes to the building to create Mr Charles' suite. Those changes included an office for him. It's even more spacious and this one, so I don't know why he needs to work in here."

"Is that the keys locker over there?" Bennett asked as he pointed to a shallow cabinet mounted on the wall along from the desk. Delphine nodded. "Is it locked?"

"No, I don't think so. It never is, and it's not supposed to be."

Bennett walked over and tried opening the cupboard. It was locked. Delphine didn't believe it and bustled over to try opening it herself. It was locked. "I... don't... understand. It is never to be locked. If there is an emergency, everyone must be able to access the necessary keys to deal with it. Valuable time could be lost, if it were locked, while people tried to find someone to unlock it."

"As you say, it is strange. As the officer in charge of an investigation on this island, how do I obtain a key to unlock that cabinet?" Oh dear, Bennett seems to have hit a nerve. Delphine was quite agitated by the question. A hard look from Bennett produced a response.

"Well I'm not supposed to ... Only Miss Dubois is supposed to have a key. But, a few months ago, she gave me a copy of it for safekeeping. I don't know why, but I now have a key to the keys locker."

"I think we need to look at the keys in there to make sure they are all present and accounted for. Would you mind fetching your key, so we can check?"

Delphine brought the key, handed it to Bennett and stood to one side while he unlocked and flung open the cabinet. "Why are there empty hooks?" The keys rattled as he ran his hand over the rows of keys, all neatly tagged and numbered.

"The empty hooks at the bottom are spares. They put in more hooks than we needed for the keys we have."

"Yes, I understand about the ones at the bottom, but what about these other empty ones?"

"Eh...? What other ones ... only the hooks at the bottom of the cupboard should be empty." Delphine came around to the front of the cabinet and elbowed Bennett aside for a better look. "No. No, those keys should not be missing. These ones up here; they are for doors here in the castle. I have no idea what this one was for. Uhmm, the others are for various places in and around the grounds." The housekeeper fingered each empty hook as she spoke, all the while shaking her head in disbelief.

"Who would know? How do we find out which ones are missing?" I detected a hint of excitement in Bennett's voice when he asked his questions.

"There is a register." Delphine turned to face the desk. "It's kept here in the drawer." She pulled open a drawer and froze. "Who did this? What a mess..." A rhetorical question not directed at anyone in the room. "It's not here. The register is not in this drawer where it always is."

"Try the other drawers," Bennett suggested.

I heard Delphine open two drawers in quick succession. It was when she opened the second drawer I heard her gasp in alarm. "It's in here; on top of everything else in this drawer. It's not supposed to be here. It lives in the bottom of the top drawer. Nobody has looked at it in months. We didn't have any need to once all the keys were in the cupboard and recorded in the register."

She identified each key as Bennett called out the numbers on the empty hooks. The first two were for bedrooms here in the castle as she indicated earlier. A single one missing from a row further down was for one of the guest cottages in the grounds. After identifying it from the register, she stood looking perplexed for a few moments and didn't hear Bennett call out the next number.

"Delphine, what does this number belong to ... and the one beside it which is missing as well?"

"I'm sorry. I didn't hear you. Please tell me the numbers again."

A look of horror spread across her face when her finger running down the page came to the last two numbers. Without answering, she looked up at Bennett. The colour had drained from her face. "Those keys are for Anton's cottage and studio. Why would anyone take those? He never locked up. Most of the buildings around the grounds are never locked."

"The shed you said one of the keys belonged to, does it happen to be the shed in which the generator is housed?" Her response to Bennett's question was a half-hearted shrug.

"I think so, but I'm not sure. Sampson would know. ...But I know it is another building we never lock. What would be the point of locking it? Apart from when guests are here, only a handful of us are on the island. In Miss Lucille's day things were different. She employed a huge staff and people came and went all the time. If you wish to speak to Sampson, he should come in soon. It is almost lunchtime ... and I am running behind with lunch. So, if you will excuse me, I must get on with it."

Bennett asked her to leave the key register on the desk and to leave the key cupboard unlocked. His requests didn't appear to cause Delphine any discomfort. After she left for the kitchen, I queried Bennett about those requests.

"I think our first priority is to speak to Sampson, not just about that shed, but about a few other aspects of what has happened here. Then, depending on the outcome of that conversation, we might return to this office. I'm inclined to spend some time poking around in Charles' suite of rooms. It's high time we gave his disappearance some thought. And I'm sure we need an update on your friend's condition. I will come with you for that one. No uppity young doctor is going to tell me to bugger off. Any questions...?"

"None I can think of. So, what do we do now?"

"We go and sit quietly in a corner of the kitchen, out of Delphine's way, while we wait for Sampson to come in for lunch. If we play our cards right, the four of us – or five of us if Dwayne is there too – might lunch together."

Our wait was short. About five minutes after we took up our positions in the kitchen, Sampson bounced in, closely followed by Dwayne. Without much obvious difficulty, Bennett engineered for us to eat in the kitchen with the three staff members. Once we took our places at the table, Bennett opened the conversation by asking Sampson about the shed for which the key was missing.

Sampson confirmed it was the generator shed, and claimed he couldn't remember it ever being locked in his time on the island. In a bid to relax the staff and eliminate the appearance of an official interrogation, Bennett asked each of the staff how long they had been on the island and what changes occurred during their time here. Dwayne was the most recent addition to the staff, having worked here for three years. While Sampson looked only a young man, he arrived just over ten years ago. "We had a party to celebrate his tenth anniversary," Delphine told us.

Delphine's story was fascinating. She spent her whole life on the island, both during Miss Lucille's time and now with Frankie. Her mother was the housekeeper before her, and still lived with her daughter here on the island and in the same wing as Frankie's suite of rooms. I commented on how difficult it must be in the kitchen at times like this when there are mobs of guests. "You produce two dishes for every course at dinner every night, and a variety of food to choose from for lunch each day. In addition, there are all the extra morsels which accompany morning and afternoon teas."

"Yes, it gets busy, but we've had plenty of practice over the years. I doubt I could manage entirely on my own when there are big numbers such as there are now. On such occasions, my mother helps with some of the lighter tasks, like peeling the vegetables, cutting up fruit, making iced tea, and preparing salads." I was too polite to ask how old her mother is, but the question intrigued me.

Then Bennett returned to the original intent of this friendly lunch with the staff. "Sampson, please run through events as they occurred, and as you remember them, on the night of Miss Dubois' birthday party."

While Sampson collected his thoughts, Delphine got up from the table. "I'll leave you to discuss this with Sampson. I need to attend to the dining room. Dwayne perhaps you might help me." Dwayne suggested the inspector might want his input to the discussion. Bennett assured him it was okay to leave, but asked him to return to the discussion when he was through helping Delphine. As soon as the pair bustled off to deal with the dining room, Bennett returned his attention to Sampson and the outstanding question.

"There isn't much to tell about the night while the party was in progress." Sampson began slowly, but soon warmed to the task. "Nothing unusual happened until we lost power, and then that storm broke. Dwayne and I brought lanterns and torches from the storeroom. We left some lights with the guests in the hall, before Mr Charles, Dwayne and I went to the generator shed. Mr Charles thought the generator ran out of fuel. I knew that wasn't possible. I filled its fuel tank just before the guests came down for dinner. It is routine for me to do it at about the same time every day."

"Was the shed unlocked when you arrived?"

"Yes, but why wouldn't it be? The shed is never locked. It wasn't that night either."

"So, you all went into the shed and checked the generator's fuel supply?" Sampson nodded. "Had it run out of fuel?"

"No, the tank was almost full. The level hadn't gone down much since I filled it earlier."

"Why did the generator stop working? Did you identify the cause?"

"Mr Charles said it must be a problem with the unit itself; perhaps some part broke. We tried to find the problem, but the lanterns are not bright and it was difficult to see much in the dark shed. When we accepted there was nothing we could do, Mr Charles said we should leave it until the morning and take a look at it then when the light was better."

"Okay, you couldn't get the power back on, so what did you do?"

"We came back here. By then, the storm was full-on. It blew a gale and the rain came down in sheets. We were soaked through by the time we made it back here."

"All three of you came back together?"

"Yes ... ah, no. Dwayne and I came back to deal with the guests. Mr Charles wasn't with us. He was still poking about the generator when we left. He told us to go and he would follow along shortly. Both Dwayne and I were busy with the guests after that. I didn't see Mr Charles come back to the castle." I sat silently making mental notes as the questioning took place until a thought morphed into a verbal question.

"Think back, Sampson, to the last time you saw Mr Charles. Where was he and what was he doing?" Bennett shot me a hard look for interrupting. I ignored it.

"I don't remember. Let me think. He walked to the door of the shed with us as we were leaving. Oh yes; he said he might hang back for a while to see if it stopped raining before he returned to the castle. Then Dwayne and I took off at a trot through the rain. We hadn't gone far when I thought I heard a noise from the shed. At least, it came from behind us somewhere, so I looked back. That's when I saw Mr Charles pick up his lantern, look up at the sky, and then step out of the shed. He had something – a rag or sack bag – draped over his head. I thought he changed his mind about waiting and decided to follow us back."

"After you reached the castle, you didn't wait for Mr Charles to arrive or look for him afterwards?"

"No, Miss Tessa. It was not right for guests to be left unattended in such circumstances, so Dwayne and I went to the hall the moment we came back. We knew what we had to do. We didn't need Mr Charles to tell us. After all the guests were organised and things settled down, we went to our quarters. I assumed Mr Charles went directly to his rooms when he arrived. He would be as drenched coming back as we were and would want to shower and change into dry clothes. That's what we wanted to do, and it's what we did as soon as we took care of the guests." For a moment I wondered why I hadn't seen the two men return, but didn't pursue it. It probably was while I dozed at the top of the stairs.

Bennett seemed excited by Sampson's details of events, and resumed his questioning. "So, you don't know whether Charles came back to the castle that night or not?" Sampson shook his head. "Okay. Tell me what happened next morning. Was the power back on when you got up?"

"No, there was no power. I was out of bed early – before five o'clock – and went straight to the generator shed to see if I could make it go, so Delphine would have power for breakfast and the guests were not inconvenienced."

"Did you get it started?"

"Not at first but, after a few tries, it started. I don't know what was wrong with it. It didn't start because of anything I did to fix it."

"That's strange, but lucky for the guests. What did you do after the generator was working again?"

"I suppose I was shocked when it started. I was about to come back here but, at the door, I turned around and just looked at the machine. I was still confused about why it wouldn't start last night but started without too much trouble this morning. That's when I saw the smoke; while I stood in the doorway."

Chapter 12

"What smoke…?" Bennett and I chorused in unison.

"The smoke coming from the direction of Anton's cottage; I wasn't concerned about it. He built a rock fireplace out front of the cottage and collected fallen timber from the rainforest. He kept strange hours ... seems creative types do. Anyway, Anton often lit a fire at odd times and sat outside beside it; sometimes drinking coffee, sometimes something else."

"Was he a heavy drinker?" Why is that of interest to Bennett's investigation, I wondered.

"No, not at all; he only had the occasional glass of wine, and sometimes a port or rum. The most he drank was an occasional bottle of beer."

"So you wandered down to check on the smoke coming from the direction of Anton's place; then what happened?"

"Before I reached the clearing, I realised there was too much smoke for it to be coming from his fireplace. I ran the last part of the way. The studio was alight and too far gone to be saved. That was obvious from the moment I saw it. Anton didn't seem to be anywhere around. I became worried. What if he was in the studio when it went up in flames? What if he had some sort of accident in there which started the fire? The door to his cottage was open, so I rushed over to see if I could find him. I ran into Charles as he was coming out of the cottage. He looked terrible. Before I could ask him what was going on, he gestured with his head out towards the fireplace. That's when I saw Anton. I started to run towards him. Mr Charles didn't come with me. I wondered why and stopped to look back at him. He just shook his head at me. I knew then Anton was dead, but I had to see for myself. I'm sorry; I can't go on. I need to take a break."

Sampson's voice cracked as he asked to stop. "Anton and I were friends; good friends. I still can't believe he is gone."

Relief for all of came when Dwayne bounded back into the kitchen. "Have I missed much?' he asked as he scanned the solemn faces around the table. "Sampson…" he exclaimed when his eyes fell on his fellow staff member. He turned angrily to Bennett. "What did you say to him? What have you done? It has been hard for him over the last couple of days without your coming in here and making things worse."

The shocked look on Bennett's face was priceless. In spite of the gravity of the situation, it was all I could do not to laugh. One thing was clear. Dwayne was angry and he was not about to back down. I felt obliged to try rescuing the situation. Sampson beat me to it. He managed to convince his colleague Bennett had done no wrong, and we were going to take a break for a while.

Bennett and I took the hint and, after a few reassuring words to both Dwayne and Sampson, we left the kitchen. "Tessa, my thinking was everything happened after the storm that night. Now, I'm wondering if it began before the storm." As we entered the lobby, Bennett suggested, "Time we checked on your friend's progress, I think." I needed no persuading.

I wanted to check on Dervla, but a couple of questions to ask Sampson remained. Perhaps I might catch him later on my own. Any further thoughts of Sampson evaporated. We were outside Dervla's room and Bennett was pounding on the door.

An angry nurse confronted him through a narrow gap in the door. Shooing him off with her hand, she told Bennett to go away. He was having none of it, flashed his warrant card at her and shoved the door wide open. Once inside, he stopped for a brief word with the nurse. "I dictate who does what around my investigation, my girl, not you." With that, he left the stunned nurse in his wake and marched across the room to the obviously irate doctor. I drifted along on his coattails, hoping he would provide a human shield from the explosion I knew the doctor would deliver.

"Don't bother, Doctor. Your officious attitude cuts no ice with me when it comes to victims involved in my investigation. I see the patient has improved sufficiently to be moved onto her bed. Now, can we stop playing silly buggers please, and you tell me about her injuries and her condition?" The doctor turned on him and was about to erupt. The inspector's stony look changed her mind.

"It is highly inappropriate to barge in on a doctor when they are with their patient. I would appreciate…" She didn't have a chance to finish whatever she was about to say.

"That's enough. You have been cloistered in here all morning. It is obvious the patient has improved. I'll have your full status report now, thank you." She pulled herself up to her full height and gave him a haughty glare. As she opened her mouth to retaliate, Bennett continued. "…Or I will have you and your offsider removed from this room, and the island if necessary." There was a notable change in the doctor's demeanour.

While the exchange between the other two took place, I concentrated on Dervla, and edged out from behind Bennett to stand by the foot of her bed. She looked different; more peaceful now as if she was asleep as opposed to unconscious. As I stood watching, her eyelids fluttered and opened a little for a fraction of a second. I heard her murmur something indistinct. The others heard it too. I called Dervla's name softly. There was no response.

"Well, Doctor…" Bennett began as he gestured towards Dervla.

"Yes, all right. Miss O'Reilly shows signs of regaining consciousness. That is the best sign we have so far. Even when she fully regains consciousness, she will be groggy for some time, and there may be residual effects from her injuries." I did not like the sound of that last bit. It caught Bennett's attention as well.

"Like what; what residual effects are we talking about here?"

"It's probable she will not be able to remember anything about the attack; nothing at all quite likely. And, as I said, she will remain groggy and sleep a lot over the next couple of days, but there will be periods of lucid consciousness along the way."

A brief conversation between the inspector and the doctor ensued before Bennett realised Winston should be a part of their discussions. He called Winston, who arrived a few minutes later. The other four went into a huddle on the other side of the room while I sat beside Dervla, stroking her hand and talking to her. As the discussions on the other side of the room seemed to be progressing amicably, I risked making a suggestion. "As the doctor and her nurse haven't had as much as a coffee since they arrived, maybe this is a good time for you all to adjourn and continue your discussion in the kitchen or the dining room."

No one objected and, after I promised to call at the slightest change in Dervla's condition, they left. Glorious silence filled the room. While I continued speaking in hushed tones to Dervla, it did sound loud in the changed environment. The solitude lasted about an hour before all four of them returned.

The nurse bustled about handing over and giving instructions to Winston. Bennett came over to stand beside me at Dervla's bed. "The plane will arrive in about half an hour to take the medical team back to Saint-Marie. Winston will take over caring for Miss O'Reilly and also will guard her during the day. I will arrange for a cot to be brought up so he can sleep in this room. Another officer will be on guard outside the room at night while Winston sleeps. You may spend time with your friend at Winston's discretion."

While Bennet outlined those arrangements to me, I noticed the doctor packing their equipment into various bags. Winston's briefing concluded, the nurse came over to assist the doctor with their gear. Then the room was quiet once more. The inspector helped carry their bags down to the waiting golf carts. Winston trailed along behind to see them off. Minutes later, through the open window, I watched the golf carts travel along the track and disappear into the rainforest. Bennett chose to ride to the airstrip with the medical team. A couple of minutes later, Winston let himself back into Dervla's room.

I remained at the window while Winston checked on Dervla. "I don't think you will see much happen in the next little while. If you have something else to do, I suggest you take care of it and call back later this afternoon to see how she is doing." He was right. There was no point in both of us sitting here with long faces and bored out of our minds. I told Dervla I would be back and left.

Unsure what to do with myself, I went to my room, and scribbled out a few notes from our earlier discussions with Delphine and Sampson before heading downstairs. Guests straggled out to the back garden in anticipation of afternoon tea's arrival. Not sure I wanted to suffer the mob, I wandered over to the front door instead of joining them under the Poinciana tree. The golf carts returned and drove around to the kitchen's rear entrance. One paused long enough at the front steps to allow Bennett to alight.

"I believe it is time for afternoon tea," he chirped as he bounded up the steps. "Are you coming through to the back garden?"

"You go on through. I'll be along in a moment."

I wasn't sure it was the truth, but it worked. Bennett didn't hang around. He continued straight through the hall and out into the garden. Soon after, Sampson and Dwayne wheeled out afternoon tea and set it up on the long trestle tables. After filling glasses and helping everyone start on the food, Sampson left Dwayne in charge and disappeared around the side of the building. Assuming he was going back to the kitchen, I allowed him a minute or so before heading to the kitchen in search of him.

He was helping himself to a long glass of iced tea when I entered the kitchen. "Sampson, I don't want to interrupt your afternoon tea, but I wonder if we might chat while you go about it." He gestured for me to pull up a chair. I did, and he placed a glass of iced tea in front of me as he joined me. How long did I have before Bennett came looking for me and/or Sampson? Speed might be the essence of what I hoped to achieve without Bennett's involvement.

"Sampson, this morning, when we talked about the morning you found Anton's studio burnt down and his body lying outside, we didn't ask you what happened afterwards. Would you mind continuing the story for me, so I have a clear picture in my mind of the morning's events?"

"Okay. I was shocked. Mr Charles and I had a few words about the situation; nothing important, just comments about the terrible event. Then Mr Charles said he had something to do. No ... he said there was something he needed to look at, and he left me there."

"That's odd. Where did he go? What did he want to look at?"

"I don't know, but he took off into the rainforest. The track from here to Anton's place stops at the clearing where Anton lived. From the other side of the clearing, there is no track leading further around the island. I've only been a little way beyond Anton's, so I have no idea where Mr Charles was going, or why."

"So, you were left on your own in the clearing with Anton's body and a burned-out studio. What did you do? Did you wait for Mr Charles to return?"

"I wasn't thinking too clearly, so I hung around. I suppose I was hoping Mr Charles would come back to tell me what to do. After about fifteen minutes, I decided to try calling him, but he didn't answer. I'm not sure the mobile service was working at the time. So I waited another fifteen or twenty minutes but, when he still didn't return, I decided to come back here to ask Miss Dubois what I should do. As I walked across the clearing to the start of the track, Miss Dubois burst in. She looked terrible, as though she had been running. Her hair was everywhere and wet, and I don't think she finished dressing properly."

"Did she say anything; give you any indication why she was there?"

"She was looking for Mr Charles; kept asking me if he was there or if I had seen him. Nothing around her seemed to register with her. She kept asking me the same questions even though I explained to her Mr Charles had been there but went off to look at something. I don't know if she wasn't listening, or if she couldn't take on board what I told her." Sampson studied his almost empty glass and drifted off into his own world for a few moments. I let him be for as long as I dared before continuing my questioning.

"Apart from asking you about Mr Charles, did Miss Dubois do or say anything else? Did she give you instructions about what to do?"

"No, nothing; all she did was ask about Mr Charles. I tried to get her to calm down, but she ran off back towards here. She wasn't right, you know; not right in the head I mean. But she only glanced at Anton's body. She already was distracted when she arrived. What she found at Anton's place when I was there didn't cause it."

"Do you think she already might have known about Anton; maybe been there before you arrived?"

"I don't know but, what you say might explain why she was almost out of her head."

"So, Miss Dubois returned to the castle and you were left there alone again. What did you do?"

"I was concerned about Miss Dubois and ran after her. I don't know where she went. I left straight after her, but I didn't see her anywhere on the track and she wasn't back here in the castle when I arrived. Delphine and I knocked on her door. It wasn't locked and she wasn't there. We tried Mr Charles' suite and the office, but neither Mr Charles nor Miss Dubois was around. We returned to the kitchen, and I told Delphine what happened. She told me to ring the police on Saint-Marie while she got on with making breakfast. I couldn't get through. The phones weren't working."

After Sampson refilled our glasses, I encouraged him to carry on with the story. "After we set breakfast up in the dining room, I returned to the kitchen with Delphine. Every few minutes, I tried calling the police again. I think it was a bit after nine o'clock when I finally got through to the police station at Honoré on Saint-Marie. The rest you know. Inspector Bennett and his men arrived as soon as they organised a plane. While I waited for them to arrive, I rounded up the guests and brought them all over to the hall as he requested. Then Dwayne and I took the carts to the airstrip to collect the police when they arrived."

"What about Miss Dubois, did you see her again?"

"Oh yeah, I forgot about that. Not long after we set up breakfast and I came back to the kitchen, Miss Dubois rushed in through the front door and into the dining room. You were in the room when it happened." I confirmed Dervla and I were there when Frankie came in. "Delphine heard her carrying on about Charles being missing. Delphine murmured something about the woman being hysterical, before she rushed out to see what she could do for Miss Dubois. She took the woman to her rooms and was gone from the kitchen for a while. I don't know much about what happened afterwards as that's when I stayed close to the phone and kept trying to raise the police."

Delphine, who had been absent from the kitchen, returned as Sampson finished his tale. As she removed the empty glasses from the table, she told me, "I took her back to her room, quietened her down a bit, gave her one of her tablets – some sort of sedative I think – and put her to bed. She seemed to go to sleep almost immediately, so I left her room and came back to the kitchen."

"At any time, did she give either of you any indication why she was so concerned about Mr Charles and where he was?" They exchanged a look before both of them shook their heads. Delphine stopped on her way to the sink with the empty glasses and added an afterthought.

"I don't think she was capable of telling us anything. You saw what she was like when she rushed into the dining room. She just continued like that until I quietened her down. There was no chance she was going to make any sense, even if I pressed her about what was wrong."

The only other piece of information I received was about Frankie's behaviour that morning. It was extraordinary. Neither of the staff had seen her like that before, and I think it left them stunned. As I had asked all the questions I intended, I stood to leave, and was thanking them for their time when another question occurred to me. It would have to wait till some other time, because that's when Bennett appeared in the kitchen. As I expected, he demanded to know what was going on. I gave him my sweetest smile and told him I'd come to talk to the staff about my friend, Frankie, and to ask if they had any more news of her. He looked sceptical but accepted my explanation. Moments later, we were on our now all-too-familiar perch on the front steps.

"I do want to go back and spend time with Dervla, but I don't want to make a nuisance of myself and end up having Winston chuck me out of her room. If I can manage to wait a bit longer, I'll go to see her when I go up to change for dinner."

"I can assure you Winston will not chuck you out. If anything, he'd probably welcome the company. I checked on your friend after afternoon tea. She was still asleep."

"There is something I've been meaning to ask you. What are you doing about Anton's body? You can't leave it there in the cottage for much longer. It's already a grisly package to transport to the airstrip. Would they be happy to have it on board one of their planes without its being in a coffin of some sort?"

"I'm aware of the time factor, and, no, the airline is not happy to transport it. It has been a waiting game, but it should end tonight. We were waiting for the rare occasion when a boat could come ashore at the island. Happily, it happens at around dusk tonight. The police vessel is positioning itself in the bay as we speak. Sometime between six and seven o'clock tonight will be a window of opportunity to bring the boat to the beach and load the body on board. I collected a special body bag from the plane which came to collect the medical team. In about an hour's time, my officers and I will return to Anton's cottage to make ready for the boat's arrival. I would appreciate it if you could see your way clear to stay with Miss O'Reilly while we carry out that operation. It would free up Winston to help."

"Of course, I'll stay with Dervla. Do what you need to, and use Winston for as long as you need him. I'm happy Anton's remains are being dealt with at last."

"In the meantime, we could continue to sit here chatting, or we could undertake something more productive in terms of my investigation ... only if you feel inclined to be involved, of course."

"Let's go. What do you have in mind … and is it a covert operation, or do we need others to assist?"

His chuckle and the sheepish look on his face told me what I wanted to know: this was to be covert. "Come on then. This is our chance while everyone remains engaged with afternoon tea." He bounced up onto his feet and extended his hand to help me up.

Trying to look as though we were not up to anything untoward, we sauntered across the lobby and headed down the hallway to the office. After consulting the key register, Bennett spent a few moments in front of the open key cupboard trying to work out which key he wanted. At last, he lifted one off its hook and, with it held in the air in triumph, he crossed to a door in the side wall of the office. The key unlocked the door, and he beckoned me to follow him into the adjoining room.

"If my guess is correct, we are now in Charles' suite of rooms, and this room should be his study. Jesus! What happened here? It's been trashed."

I barrelled into Bennett's back when he stopped abruptly in front of me. After disengaging myself, I stepped around from behind him to see what he was fussing about. The room was a shambles. It looked as though a tornado went through the place. Bennett rushed on through adjoining doors, firstly past a walk-in wardrobe/dressing room, then through a bedroom and into a sitting room. All areas had suffered the same fate. A substantial wooden door in the sitting room suggested this was the suite's main access from the hallway.

We returned to our entry point and began a search of Charles' study. Furniture was knocked over and much was broken. Every desk drawer was removed and emptied. The paper strewn about the floor came from the filing cabinets where every drawer was empty, its contents rifled through before being dumped out. A recliner lounge chair in a corner of the room had its upholstery slit open and its padding pulled out. An expensive looking office chair behind the enormous timber desk suffered the same fate.

A monitor on the desk was knocked over and lay face-down on scattered documents. While the cable and a laptop stand remained, the laptop was missing. I found it under the desk, smashed. On close inspection, I discovered its hard drive was missing.

"Now, what worth stealing would a writer store on his hard drive?" I treated Bennett's question as rhetorical and continued scratching around through the mass of paper everywhere.

The sliding doors of a credenza-type cupboard against the wall behind the desk were removed and thrown on the floor. One of the doors bore evidence of being stood on. At the site of impact, the wood was splintered and long cracks snaked away from it. Empty now, the cupboard's contents appeared to have been scraped out onto the floor. Bookshelves lined the far wall behind the ruined lounge chair. While they were stripped bare, only a couple of books were on the floor ... not many for a writer's office.

Chapter 13

With nothing amongst the debris warranting special attention, we moved to the walk-in wardrobe/dressing room. A hanging rack ran the length of one wall. The top of a built-in set of drawers served as a dressing table. A full-length mirror, a small set of drawers and a hat stand were the only other furniture in the room. It seems Charles was much inclined to sartorial elegance. I counted no less than eight pairs of shoes ranging from boots to casual slip-ons. Some were slashed open. Others had their heels prised off.

Shirts, trousers, suits and jackets were slashed and torn apart. While now all ruined and thrown about the room, they constituted a considerable wardrobe. To me, this seemed incongruous with a Caribbean island lifestyle; on a private island. A tie rack ripped off the wall intrigued me. What could a tie rack hide? Some of the ties were sliced open; such a waste of such beautiful silk.

As expected, his bathroom didn't have much of a story to tell. The vanity unit was ransacked, and the mirrored medicine chest on the wall above the vanity unit treated the same way. Its contents were scraped out into the vanity unit. Pills spilled out of their bottles. Bottles of lotions popped their caps leaving sticky residue over everything. The lid of the toilet cistern was cracked and on the floor beside the pedestal.

While only sparsely furnished, the bedroom screamed 'masculine'. The bed was huge; probably king sized. A pair of unremarkable looking bedside cupboards kept the bed company. Reading lights had silvery anodised aluminium shades. The bedcover was lightweight and featured an abstract pattern in black, grey and white, with the occasional splash of red. The only other furniture in this room was the companion recliner lounge chair to the one in the study.

A lack of furnishing hadn't spared the bedroom from the same treatment as the previous rooms; the mattress, bedcover and chair's upholstery all slashed and torn apart. Whoever did this was thorough, with nothing overlooked as they worked their way through the rooms. A silly thought occurred to me as I wandered around in the bedroom: it's as well the room isn't carpeted, or they would have ripped the carpet up as well.

Moving into the sitting room produced no surprises. It received the same treatment as the other areas. I felt a wave of anger spread over me at the sight of the irreparable damage suffered by some of the expensive looking furniture. Nothing escaped damage.

There was sight of only so much mayhem and destruction I could stand. "Tom, I think I'll check on Dervla. There is nothing I can do here. I'll leave you to it."

"I'll come with you. I just checked the time. I need to round up Winston and my other officers and go to Anton's place to prepare for the boat's arrival to remove his body."

We backtracked through the suite of rooms to the main office. Bennett locked up and replaced the key on its hook. Then we were out in the hallway and on our way to the lobby. It felt like stepping out into fresh air after Charles' rooms.

Dervla was awake when we arrived. Winston's transition from nurse to police officer took only moments. Before departing with Bennett, he drew me aside and gave me instructions on looking after his patient. While Dervla looked groggy, it didn't appear 'looking after her' would result in any surprises. As soon as the two police officers departed, I dragged a chair over to the bed and made myself comfortable.

While the doctor's words about the strong possibility of Dervla remembering nothing of the incident remained with me, I decided it was worth trying my luck. After exchanging only a few words, I tested her memory.

"I'm not even going to ask how you are. It's obvious you're a long way from normal. Finding you as I did gave me quite a shock. I'm not sure I've recovered from it yet … just as you haven't either. What do you remember about what happened?"

"Nothing; there is a vague memory I think of being on the floor at one stage, and then later being lifted and moved. The next memory I have is of being here in bed. What I am aware of is my aching head. There are a few other aches and pains as well, but nothing compared to my head."

"Try to think back before that – before being on the floor. Can you remember getting out of bed this morning?" She screwed up her face as though thinking required some major effort.

"Sort of, I think. Yes … Yes, I remember getting out of bed. I think it was early; earlier than usual."

"You hadn't changed into your day clothes when we found you. You were just as you are now. Is it likely you hadn't been up long when you were attacked?" I saw the blank look and the slight shake of her head which suggested I wasn't going to get an answer I liked. I tried a different approach. "What's your normal routine every morning when you get out of bed?"

"Nothing exciting; I head to the bathroom for my morning ablutions before dressing for whatever is scheduled for the day." I saw something akin to a spark of recollection make a brief appearance on her face.

"Did this morning start the same way? It's obvious it didn't progress to the stage of your dressing to face the day. So, I presume something intervened. Soon after you were out of bed, something threw your routine off track."

"Yeah, this morning was different. I didn't go straight to the bathroom. There was something… Something I had to do … Something I remembered… Oh, I don't know. There is something there in the back of my mind, but I can't access it. It's like I can't see what I did this morning."

It looked as though I might have plumbed all there was of her memories. Winston's instructions included not stressing her, so I avoided asking more questions. For something different, I stood up and moved over to the window. "It's been a glorious day; not too hot with a pleasant light breeze all day. The police are still here. I can't report noticing any progress with their investigation. So, goodness knows how much longer they will be here, or how much longer before the other guests are free to leave."

"What are you looking at out there?" The question was asked in a very quiet voice; a strange tone.

"Eh...? I wasn't looking at anything in particular; just gazing at the scenery. It's still the same. Might be a few more flowers out today, or maybe fewer, but nothing else has changed since you last saw it."

"That's just the point... I think I saw something this morning."

Oh God, is she hallucinating, developing false memories, or something? False memories will not help in finding out what happened and who did it.

"Perhaps you did, but it would be out of keeping with your usual routine. Would you go to the window to admire the view as soon as you got out of bed?" Dervla didn't answer. She seemed to be wrestling with something in her mind. "Don't stress yourself by trying to remember things. Let it be. Things will come to you in their own good time."

I hoped I sounded more confident than I felt. There are any number of recorded cases of people suffering similar trauma never regaining those memories. All of a sudden her face lit up. I knew she dredged up something from her memory bank.

"I did go to the window as soon as I got out of bed. I wanted to check on something. It was early; much earlier than I usually wake up. The sun hadn't come up yet. I don't know what time it was, but it was during the period of semidarkness just before the sun comes up."

"Did you hear a sound outside you wanted to check on, or a strange birdcall perhaps?"

"No-o-o, I don't think so. My mind is telling me it wasn't something from this morning I went to check. It was something I already knew about. How can that be? Why would I want to check something I already knew about?"

"That's a good question, but I'd don't think I have an answer for you. Maybe it was something you saw earlier, like sometime yesterday, and you wanted to check if it was still there today."

"Maybe … Yes, I think you're right. I wanted to check if something was still there this morning. But what was I looking for? Did I expect what I saw from my window to have changed since whenever I last saw it?"

"It could have been anything: a bird, flower, someone wandering in the grounds… To develop some idea of what it was, we probably need at least a rough idea of when you saw it; if it was during yesterday or last night. Something earlier, from sometime since we arrived, will be hard to pin down. I don't think you'll be able to dredge up the memory right now, so it's probably best to leave it for a bit."

My comments had Dervla looking despondent. I searched for something else to move the conversation to a different topic. Having opened the can of worms for her, if I didn't move her on, she would do herself no good trying to remember what she saw. "Okay, so you went to the window first thing to check on something outside. We don't know what it was and we're not going to worry about it for now. So, do you have any memory of what happened after you went to the window?"

A soft knock at the door interrupted proceedings. Dwayne with a tray loaded with food stood outside. "We were instructed to bring food to Miss O'Reilly. Miss Tessa, you are to encourage her to eat some. Leave the tray outside when you're finished and I'll collect it later." Having thrust the tray into my hands and delivered his message, Dwayne disappeared down the stairs. After kicking the door closed, I advanced to the bed with the tray held out in front of me.

"I don't feel hungry. They shouldn't have sent food up. It will be wasted … unless you eat it." Dervla's excited look accompanying her afterthought disappeared when I assured her

I wasn't going to eat it, and insisted she at least try some of the food Delphine made for her.

"Now, my friend, try eating something." As I spoke, I drifted back to the window. "There's not exactly a sunset outside, but there's a strange light casting beautiful shadows from the trees across the lawns. It's a sort of gold light coming through the trees."

When I looked around at her, she was staring intently at the tray of food in front of her. "You must try to eat. The sooner you have your strength back, the sooner you will be out of bed; out of this room and enjoying the world outside." For a few moments there was no response from Dervla. She continued staring at the tray.

Then she started murmuring, constantly repeating the same single word. "Lights … lights … lights." Her eyes snapped wide open. She turned to face me, almost upsetting the tray in the process. "There's something about lights. Argh, it's not coming through. But I know it's important."

Her look implored me to help her remember. Taken by surprise by her outburst, I was at a loss as to what to say or do. She tried to push the tray away from her, sloshing the fruit juice out of the glass. As I dived to rescue the tray, an idea came to me. With the tray safely on the side table, I sat down beside the bed.

"Let's think about those lights, shall we. Don't you do any thinking; you just close your eyes, relax and listen to me babble on for a bit. Are you up for it?" She whimpered her agreement. I began without a clue what I was doing.

"Let's talk about lights. I saw some lights a couple of nights ago. I saw them again last night too. They moved about. I didn't know what they were. The first night was when the power went off. There were lanterns and torches moving around all over the place. I don't think the lights I saw were anything to do with them. These lights were…"

"It was at night and they were outside! That's why I went to the window this morning; to see if I could make sense of what I saw."

"So, you saw lights outside last night?"

"Ye-e-s... I think it was last night. Yes, it must have been last night, because it was this morning I went to the window to see if I could work out what they were."

"Okay; perhaps they were the same lights I saw. Where were the lights you saw?"

"They were... they were moving about, but they were..." She stared at some indeterminate spot on the bedcover and chewed her lip.

"Don't force it; just relax." She heaved a huge sigh and I saw her shoulders slump. When she looked up at me, tears were not too far away. "See, your memory is not too bad at all. I saw lights moving about outside last night, and you remember seeing them too. I wonder if they will be there again tonight. I must remember to watch for them."

I had no intention of looking for lights tonight. There would not be any. All I hoped was my waffling on about lights might loosen further memories for her. Dervla went quiet and seemed to retreat into herself. I returned to the window.

"It's a shame you're laid up and can't come to the window. Those last rays of sunshine coming through the trees are quite beautiful." I pulled out my phone and tested it for a photo. "No, I can't capture the light for you. The trees are too far away."

"That's it! The lights were moving about in the trees over there beyond that big garden bed with the tree fern in the middle of it. There were two lights. I watched them for a little while, and then I went and knocked on your door to tell you about them. You didn't answer. I don't know if you weren't there, or if you were asleep. When you didn't answer, I came back here and watched them for quite a while. That's right! After some time, there were a lot of lights moving about in those trees. At first I thought it must be the guests in the cottages going back after dinner. Then I realised the cottages aren't in that direction."

"Wow, what happened after that?"

"I was tired of watching them and I was becoming sleepy. I thought I would rest for a while and get up later to see if they were still there. I fell asleep … and then … uhmm … and then … Damn! I can't remember what happened after that."

"Don't fret about it. Look at how much you remembered already. Who knows? After a good night's sleep, by tomorrow more memories might return. Nevertheless, you have to be prepared to accept the possibility not everything will come back to you. Sometimes that's the way the psyche protects itself after a serious trauma. It stops the person reliving it."

"I don't want it to be so in my case. I want to know who did this to me; to know why, and for them to pay for what they did. None of that is possible if I can't remember what happened."

"Dervla, while it might not seem like anything is happening in that regard, the police are working on it." I noted the sceptical look she gave me. "I believe what happened to you is not an isolated incident, but part of a bigger story. A story we are still trying to piece together to determine its full extent." My theory received nothing more than a shrug. Since I held the floor, I thought I might as well continue. "I don't know how long it will be before Winston returns to look after you, but I recommend you do eat something before he does. If you think I'm a nag, I'm nothing compared to what Winston will be like."

To reinforce my suggestion, I retrieved the tray and placed it on the bed in front of her. She lifted the cover a little way off one of the dishes, a mouth-watering aroma wafted out. My stomach almost went into convulsions at the first whiff. I realised I was hungry. In case my stomach started grumbling, I moved back to the window so she wouldn't hear. After a sneak peek under all the covers, I heard the clatter of one of them. At least she found something on the tray interesting.

It was a bit after seven o'clock when Winston returned to Dervla's room. He apologised for being so long, but he stopped at the kitchen for a quick meal before coming upstairs. By the time he arrived, his patient had consumed about half of the food on the tray. Dervla received his tick of approval. As Winston would be on duty all night, he suggested I go to dinner with the others before coming back to see Dervla later if I wished. My stomach endorsed the idea. I ducked to my room nextdoor to freshen up before heading for the dining room.

As I crossed the lobby, I decided I wasn't up to making polite conversation just yet, and detoured out to the front steps. I was about to sit down when Bennett strode across the lawn towards me. "Beautiful night isn't it?" he asked as he climbed the steps. "If you are out here, I take it Winston is back at his post." I confirmed his assumption. "How about you join me in a drink to celebrate a tricky but successful operation this evening?"

"I interpret that as Anton's body having departed the island. Yes, I think I would like to raise a glass in his honour." We stood in silence for a few moments drinking in the night air and all it carried on it before going into the dining room.

Some of the guests already were there with pre-dinner drinks in hand. After exchanging a few greetings and grabbing ourselves drinks, we moved to the opposite side of the room. "Anything interesting happen while my men and I were otherwise engaged this evening?" he asked as soon as were alone.

"No, nothing; I sat and chatted with Dervla when she was awake and felt up to talking. They sent a tray up to her room, and I managed to persuade her to eat a bit. Winston is now with her." How glib I am becoming at telling white lies. That one rolled off the tongue as though it was the truth. I don't know why I didn't want to tell Bennett about Dervla's returning memory, but my gut was telling me 'not yet'.

Once dinner was over, I didn't intend hanging about downstairs. While I felt as though I hadn't a moment to myself all day, I wanted to spend more time with Dervla. Winston's presence would be an impediment to working with her to dredge up further memories. Another potential problem was Bennett. He might decide he wants to chat after dinner. I will need to make a slick escape if I don't want to be trapped downstairs.

My escape was uncomplicated when the time came. While one of the women engaged Bennett in conversation, I quietly beat a hasty retreat. Dervla's door was locked, so I knocked gently. Winston opened the door a crack, then opened it for me. He probably saw the horror on my face as I looked over at Dervla.

"Come in, come in. She is okay. I gave her the medication the doctor left for her and she went straight to sleep. That's what the pills are for. While she sleeps, the brain has a chance to heal itself. When she is awake, she will spend her time trying to remember things and generally working her brain overtime. That impedes the healing process. Feel free to stay with her if you like, but she is unlikely to wake before morning."

"Thanks, Winston, but I think I'll take myself off for an early night. Will you be on duty all night?"

I will be sleeping on the cot in the corner, but not until one of the other officers comes on guard duty at midnight. He will be stationed outside, not in the room."

As I left, I saw Bennett crossing the lobby below on his way to the stairs. I quickly dashed into my room, locked the door and made for the shower. Not only was I in need of a shower, but I could use it as an excuse for not answering my door if Bennett came knocking. Afterwards, feeling a bit refreshed, I spent some time writing up my notes from today. When I finished, it was still too early for bed, and I wasn't sleepy. There was something else I wanted to do all day, but an opportunity never presented.

A cautious look outside my door revealed no one on the landing. If Bennett was still upstairs, he wasn't visible. This was my chance and I didn't intend wasting it. Not wanting to draw attention to myself by turning on lights, before I left my room, I slipped my small torch into my pocket. Then I was down the stairs and across the lobby in near record time. Once I entered the hallway and was unlikely to be seen, I quietly made my way to the office.

In the office, I stood still in the darkness for a few seconds to listen for anyone coming to investigate my presence. Not a sound came my way. By torchlight, I searched the key register on the desk. Armed with the number I required, I checked the key cupboard. Yes, both keys I needed were on their hooks. A check on the time told me it was too late to do what I planned. It would have to wait until tomorrow … and might involve trying to give Bennett the slip somehow.

As I stepped out of the office and into the hallway, I froze. A rear view of Delphine greeted me. She walked away from me along the hall and was entering the lobby when I saw her. Her arms didn't swing by her sides as she walked. It looked as though she carried something. My assumption was confirmed by a profile view of her when she turned to make her way to the kitchen. She carried a tray. I assumed it was from Frankie's room. A tray was outside her door when I went past a few minutes ago. Maybe I should have risked paying Frankie a visit in spite of the time. Now, the moment had passed. I crossed the lobby and continued to my room.

I knew there would be no lights moving about in the rainforest tonight. Bennett and his merry men ended that nonsense this morning. Nevertheless, I had to check. "Christ, there's a light out there again. It's too early and it's not supposed to be there. What's going on? Is it Bennett doing a mop up; looking for more evidence perhaps?" My empty room didn't offer any response. Should I try to find Bennett, or is it Bennett out there, I asked myself as I stood riveted to the spot.

A few moments later, the light disappeared, and stayed gone for the next ten minutes. No point in watching nothing happening, so I got ready for bed. I couldn't resist one last look before I fell into bed. There was no light in the rainforest. I resolved to tell Bennett about it in the morning … after what I knew was going to be a restless night.

Chapter 14

Today did not start well … and it is becoming a habit. I awoke early and feeling like death after a lousy night's sleep. It's a situation I've experienced quite a few times in the past when working as an investigative journalist. I can expect it when the questions are piling up, answers are not forthcoming, and I feel I'm not gaining traction with the investigation.

Before heading down for an early breakfast, I perched on my broad windowsill, stared into the distance, and took a couple of minutes to develop a plan for today. Straight after breakfast, I would spend time with Dervla, if she is awake. After that, I need to avoid Bennett so I'm free to go in search of Frankie. Then, the day may evolve according to whatever happens with Frankie. Thinking of Frankie gave me something else to add to my list of things to do today: ask Delphine whether there is any change in Frankie's behaviour or situation. I doubted there was, but it was worth finding out before doing anything else.

With the first part of my day sorted, I went to breakfast. The advantage of being in the dining room so early is eating alone and unbothered by having to make polite conversation. As I dawdled over my coffee, I wondered what the other guests were really like. I hadn't bothered to find out and still knew nothing about most of them. Marian Nettleton was the only one with whom I had any conversation. It provided a little information about her, but the experience didn't have me lusting to know her better. I eased my conscience over avoiding the other guests by telling myself they hadn't gone out of their way to talk to me either.

Breakfast over; it was time to look in on Dervla. I hesitated before knocking. Isn't there supposed to be an officer on guard duty out here? Sounds came from inside her room, so I assumed

Winston was on duty again. When he let me in, his refreshed look surprised me. He looked heaps better than I looked – and felt – and was bright and chirpy. "The cot is quite comfortable," he assured me, "and Miss O'Reilly slept all night. She seems much improved today."

Dervla was awake and appeared anxious to speak to me, but Winston wanted to give me a situation report before I went to her. Good manners dictated I be patient. In my initial short time after entering the room, I learned Dervla's breakfast tray had not yet arrived, and Winston had not had breakfast yet either. I couldn't let the opportunity pass by, so I told Winston I would stay with my friend while he went for breakfast, and did whatever else he needed to, before returning. He jumped at the chance. Moments later he was on his way out the door.

"Thank God," Dervla murmured. "I didn't think we would ever get rid of him." I gave her a questioning look. "Argh, he's doing a great job of looking after me, but I don't need so much looking after now. I would prefer he only came to check on me occasionally, and didn't spend every minute of the day in here."

"Oh yes, you are feeling better; almost back to normal by the sound of that gripe." She giggled and I felt my spirits rise. "So, as we are stuck here together for a while, what would you like to talk about?" Dervla frightened me by hauling herself upright in bed and becoming agitated. Her eyes sparkled as she leaned in close to whisper to me.

"Iwaswrong.Igotitwrongyesterday.Iknowhowithappened."

Jesus, I hope this isn't the start of some psychotic episode. Should I discourage her from talking about it, or is it better for her to let it out? I didn't have a chance to decide. She rushed on while I pondered the best approach.

"Don't look like that. I'm fine, but the sequence of events I gave you yesterday was wrong. The first part of the story was correct. I saw lights out there moving about in the trees. After watching them for a few minutes, I tried your door without success. So, I came back here and watched the lights for quite a while. It looked like they would continue all night. I grew tired of watching, and decided to rest for a while before checking if they were still out there. Now, here's how things really played out after that."

"Before you go any further, I've been told it is not good for your recovery to work your brain too hard, or to become agitated or excited. Promise me you will stop if you start to feel stressed talking about those events." She promised, but I knew there wasn't a hint of truth in it.

"Oh, do shut up and listen. It was while I was half awake this morning, it came back to me. I woke up early this morning. Winston was asleep and I didn't want to wake him. After a while, I dozed off for a few minutes. It was more like being half awake and half asleep. Anyway, during that time, it came back to me."

"Okay, what did you remember differently from yesterday?"

"Yesterday, I told you I had a rest after watching the lights for some time, but fell asleep and slept until early next morning. I was wrong. I did fall asleep, but only for a little while; maybe an hour or so. Then I went to the window again and saw there were lots of lights moving about through the trees. I wanted to ask you what you thought about it, so I started for the door. Half way across the room, I thought maybe I should throw my robe on over what I was wearing. But, I was in a hurry. I wanted you to see the lights before they disappeared. So, I told myself not to worry about the robe as there would be no one about outside. I didn't even have shoes on."

"Fair enough; you were coming to get me and dressed just as you were when you got out of bed."

"You used to be a light sleeper and, although I hadn't been able to wake you when I tried your door earlier, I was determined to pound your door down if I had to. Anyway, having decided I didn't need my robe, I raced the rest of the way to the door. It was locked but the key was in the lock, so I unlocked the door. I was in a hurry. So I flung open the door and rushed out and…"

She let out a stifled scream.

"Dervla, Dervla, relax … you're okay … I'm here … we are safe." She was shaking. I put my arms around her and held her tight for a few moments. "What happened just now? Why did you scream? Did you remember something else?"

Winston's instructions about keeping her calm were forgotten. I bombarded her with questions. It's probably not the right thing to do, I told myself. Calm her down first, and then ask her what caused the scream. As I held her, I felt her shaking subside. She pushed me away from her, wiped her face on her sleeve and stammered out an apology.

"I'm sorry … I didn't mean to scream … I don't want Winston rushing back in."

"He can't. I was told to keep the door locked and to identify who was outside before opening it to anyone. If Winston knocks on the door, I'll tell him to go away and come back later. How will that do?"

"Thank you. When all this came back to me earlier this morning, I only reached the point where I dithered about whether to put on my robe or not. The last bit of what happened just came into my head when I reached that point in my recollection of it. It's when it happened isn't it? That's when I was attacked."

The right words – no words – would come. All I could manage in response was a nod.

"Why did my memory stop there? Why can't I see the person who was outside and attacked me when I rushed out of here?"

"I'm not a psychologist, but I think it has something to do with your mind protecting you; protecting and preventing you from reliving the trauma associated with the next part of the story. This will sound rubbish, but you must not dwell on it. It's easier said than done, I'm sure, but you must not try forcing the memory to return. You will drive it further into a dark recess somewhere deep in your psyche."

"How am I supposed to do that? I want to know – need to know – who did this to me, and why they chose me. I saw the person. I must have seen him!"

"I don't think they chose you. Most likely it was a case of wrong place, wrong time."

After spending some time soothing her fears, she was more or less settled again when Winston returned. "What have you been talking about? Has she been upset? She looks wrung out. I told you to keep her calm."

"I dozed off and had a bad dream, Winston. That's all. I was so glad Tessa was here with me when the dream woke me. She's a special friend."

It took all I had not to let my jaw drop as Dervla fed him her impressive story. Nevertheless, he insisted she take another tablet. She fought not to take it. I was standing behind Winston, so he didn't see me signal her to take it. She relented and, within minutes, she was sound asleep again.

"Miss O'Reilly doesn't want a babysitter, Winston. Your continued presence in this room has begun to upset her. She doesn't feel comfortable and can't relax with you here all the time. I know you have your orders and must do as you're instructed but, when I leave here, I will go in search of Inspector Bennett to relay the same message forcefully to him. I am going now, but I thought it fair to acquaint you with my intended course of action." The poor man didn't deserve such an earful. He did an excellent job of caring for Dervla. Without strong intervention, the present arrangement might remain in place for far too long and result in hindering rather than aiding her recovery.

I marched off, leaving Winston not too happy in my wake. It's not his fault he's spending his time looking after Dervla. I know he is following orders, and I shouldn't have spoken to him as I did, but his nursing technique is smothering his patient. When I reached the lobby, I had to make a decision: whether to go in search of Bennett to tell him to pull Winston off his nursing duties, or to talk to Delphine about Frankie. In the end, the choice wasn't difficult. If I spoke to Bennett first, I could forget about the rest of my plans for this morning. I would be stuck with Bennett for the duration. That settled it; head for the kitchen.

My appearance took Delphine by surprise, and it was no secret she wasn't overjoyed to see me. There was no offer of coffee or tea. It was okay. I wasn't here for refreshments. With the climate in the kitchen not particularly welcoming, I decided the best approach was to ask my questions and depart as soon as possible. So, without any preamble, I launched into my questions.

"Delphine, have you seen or spoken to Miss Dubois since we spoke yesterday?"

"No."

Okay, this shows promise of not going well. "Are you still leaving trays outside her door?"

"Yes."

"You have made it clear I'm not welcome in this kitchen and you don't want to speak to me so, one last question and I will leave you to get on with stewing over whatever it is you are unhappy about. Is Miss Dubois eating any of the food you leave for her?"

She shook her head. "Not much… All she does is pick at some of it. She has tea and coffee making facilities in her rooms, but I don't know if she is even bothering with that."

This time, as she answered my question, there was concern in Delphine's voice and etched on her face. It's not unexpected she is concerned, I suppose, given the close relationship she has with her mistress. As the housekeeper, there are protocols to follow and a standard of behaviour to maintain but, if someone I cared about was causing me so much concern, I would have invaded Frankie's room ages ago … and apologised for it later if needs be.

And that's exactly what this concerned friend of Frankie Dubois is about to do. On leaving the kitchen, I checked Bennett was nowhere around before heading for the hallway running past Frankie's suite of rooms. Trying to make as little sound as possible, I rushed along the hallway and into the office. A quick check no one followed me along the hall, and I strode across to the key cupboard.

From memory, I lifted all the keys I needed from their hooks. Still no sign of anyone coming to catch me in the act. I let myself into Charles' study. Moving quickly through his rooms,

I locked doors behind me and pocketed the keys. A final door confronted me. If I was right, through this door were Frankie's rooms. I hesitated. In her fragile state, someone rushing into her room might push her over the edge. I hesitated long enough to draw a couple of deep breaths to prepare myself.

That little voice in my head was on my case. *Come on, Tessa, come on. Open the door. Go in. It's now or never,* it chanted in my ear. It was right. I had to go in. I had to know if she was all right. And, above all else, I needed to know what was happening here on her island.

The layout of Frankie's suite replicated that of Charles'. I stepped into a miniscule study and made my way between a walk-in wardrobe and bathroom to come to her bedroom. My first view of Frankie's bedroom made me gasp. She heard me and looked up with vacant, unfocused eyes. Almost buried in a large lounge chair off to one side of the king sized bed, Frankie looked emaciated and unkempt.

In my best attempt at a soft and soothing voice, I tried to avoid alarming her. "Frankie, it's me, Tessa. I've been worried about you. You haven't been around for us to catch up and talk about old times."

She didn't seem alarmed by my unexpected presence. There was no reaction and no response. It was as though she was heavily drugged. A bottle of pills was on the bedside table on the other side of the bed. I couldn't read the label from where I stood, but I had a fair idea about its contents. I kept up the mindless chatter in the hope of breaking through to her.

"Dervla has been asking after you too. She wanted the three of us to sit down and swap yarns as we used to do all those years ago. All your guests are still here. Like the rest of us, they probably are missing your company as well."

At last, she looked at me. I knew she was focused now and probably seeing me for the first time since I arrived in her bedroom.

"Where's Charles? Is Charles here? Has he come back yet?"

To risk telling the truth or not…? Instinct told me there was no point in lying. She probably knew he still was 'missing'.

133

The truth might be the kindest approach in the long run. She no longer looked at me. Her eyes were constantly moving, scanning the room as if for the first time.

"No, Frankie. Charles hasn't returned. I don't know that he will. Where was he going, do you know?"

Open so wide they resembled saucers, her eyes bored into me. Tears welled up in them. She tried to say something but nothing came out. I watched her shoulders slump and the tears roll down her cheeks. This was not going as I hoped, but maybe the tears were a sign she was returning to reality.

"Gee, I could do with a coffee about now. Would you like a cup too? How do we go about getting a cup?"

Without a word, she lifted her arm a few centimetres and gestured towards the doorway into the next room.

"You sly thing; you have your own set-up in your room. I suppose it avoids having to annoy Delphine when you feel like a cuppa." I kept the verbal connection going as I walked to the doorway.

Through the doorway was a sitting room. Over to one side against the wall, a small table held a coffee machine and associated paraphernalia. It had a small bar fridge tucked in underneath. Having seen all I needed, I went and stood in front of Frankie.

"How about you have a nice shower and freshen up while I make us a coffee? Then, while we sip our coffee, we can have a long chat about old times."

There was no argument, and I took her attempt to escape the chair as acceptance of my suggestion. After helping her to her feet, I supported her on her wobbly legs to the bathroom. Before venturing into the sitting room, I stood outside the bathroom door until I heard the shower running. Trusting she would be all right in there on her own, I went to make the acquaintance of her coffee machine.

"How hard can it be?" I asked the universe as I eyed it off. It was a capsule-type machine, but an unfamiliar one. The capsules were no problem. An open packet was beside the machine. I selected two mugs from a group upside down on a cloth on one corner of the table, and checked they were clean. In the past, both of us drank our coffee black. I still did. If Frankie had changed her habit, I could add whatever was required later. With everything set up ready, the only thing left to do was to tackle the machine itself.

After running my hands all over the machine, I found a switch, tried my luck, and managed to power it up. Various coloured lights winked and blinked for a while before the illuminated image of a cup became fixed. Okay, I guess it means the machine is ready to go, I told myself. Now to find out how it makes coffee. More fiddling with bits of the equipment and I worked out where, and how to feed the capsules into the relevant aperture so they didn't fall straight through. The only thing left to do was to tell it to 'go', and I knew which button did that.

"Perhaps I should check Frankie is all right before I make the coffee," I murmured.

The shower had run for what seemed a long time. What if she had passed out in there? Neither of us would enjoy the experience of my rushing in on her if she was all right. I stood listening outside the bathroom door while I considered what to do. A discretionary approach occurred to me: knock on the door and ask is she still takes her coffee black. If she doesn't answer, I'll know something is wrong and I will investigate. As I was about to implement my plan, the shower stopped running. Frankie was okay.

I scurried back to the coffee machine, double checked everything was ready, and pressed the button to start the coffee flowing. Almost instantaneously, steaming brown liquid flowed into the mug below the outlet. I felt a certain degree of elation at mastering the beast and having made at least one cup of coffee. As I replaced the spent capsule with a fresh one for the second cup, Frankie wandered into the sitting room.

Her wet hair was raked back off her face, and she was wrapped in a dark green towelling robe designed for someone about four times her size. The sight of her brought home to me the full extent of her deterioration. She held up her hand to stop me as I made a move to rush over to help her. Perhaps it was the start of her road to recovery as she made a show of tottering under her own steam to one of the chairs and collapsing into it.

Keep it light and bright until you find out how things are, I told myself. "Do you still take your coffee black? I can add sugar, and I saw there is milk in the fridge if you want it."

"Just black, thanks; nothing has changed."

With my chair drawn up close, we sat facing one another sipping our coffee in silence. After about a minute, Frankie broke the silence. "You said Charles hadn't returned. Does any-one know where he is or where he went?"

The coffee seemed to have instilled new life into her. Her voice was stronger, and her bearing more confident. She was regaining control of herself and the situation. The last thing I wanted to do was to ruin that progress.

"As far as I know, Frankie, Charles hasn't returned or been seen since the storm. Nobody seems to know where he went or why. Do you have any ideas about why he is missing?"

She didn't answer, looked away and avoided meeting my eyes for a few moments. When she looked at me again, I saw something in her face; in her eyes. It wasn't exactly anger but something had changed. Something had touched a nerve.

"Why didn't you come sooner? I didn't expect you to take so long."

"I'm not sure what you mean, Frankie. Dervla and I came according to the arrangements you put in place. We arrived as planned and you and Charles were there to meet us. I don't know why you expected me to come earlier."

"Oh, I'm not talking about then. I don't mean when you arrived here on the island. I mean now. Why didn't you come to find me sooner?"

I made like a goldfish: my mouth opening and closing with no sound coming out. My vocal chords finally kicked in again. "Are you asking me why I didn't come sooner to find you here in your rooms?"

Almost convinced I misinterpreted her question, I needed clarification before I offered an answer. She gave me a dismissive shrug. Okay; so I didn't misunderstand the question. Now, how to answer it without incurring more damage?

"Until I spoke to Delphine, I didn't know where you were or what was happening. All she could tell me was that you were in your rooms. She went on about respecting your privacy; how she didn't know how you were because she couldn't intrude when you obviously wanted to be alone. It was by chance I found out about the keys, and managed to sneak in here today while no one was around. I'm sorry I disappointed you – let you down – but I was unaware you waited for me to come to you."

Again, another shrug, this time accompanied by a dismissive flap of her hand. It was clear I was not one of her favourite people at the moment. She wasn't going to get away with it. If she was going to be so dismissive of me, she needed to tell me why … and in detail.

"Well, Frankie, I find this most disappointing. In fact, I find this whole visit to your island to be nothing but one complete and utter disappointment so far. You may well want to castigate me and dismiss me for having disappointed you, or whatever, but I am not leaving this room until you tell me what is going on here … and I mean the *whole story,* not just why you are pissed off with me right now."

Oh dear, I breached the dam. Tears gushed down her face and her shrunken frame was wracked with heart wrenching sobs. I raced over and wrapped my arms around her until the sobs subsided. "Let's talk, Frankie, like we used to. Please tell me why I am here on this island and what is happening here. Will you do that for me?"

She dried her eyes and sniffled a few times before giving me the most abject defeated look. "I owe you that much, and I am desperate for your help. Will you help me, please?"

Chapter 15

"I'm not sure where to start," Frankie began after a couple of hesitant starts. "I don't even know when the situation began; long before my time I suspect. What do you think of my husband, Charles?"

Now, I wasn't expecting that, but I suppose it's best to establish how the land lies and get the hard questions out of the way early. "I don't think I have an opinion about Charles. There hasn't been opportunity to talk to him since you collected us at the airstrip."

"You're being evasive. I take it, you don't think much of him. Tell it as it is. I won't be offended."

"Okay; I wasn't impressed by him from the start. There has been little opportunity since to change my mind. That aside, I was surprised you married him. I assume you are married, even though you retain your maiden name."

"Yes, we are married. He can be charming if the situation calls for it. But, I was either drunk, or it was a moment of severe mental aberration when I agreed to marry him. We only knew each other about five seconds beforehand."

"I didn't know you married. Dervla found out about it in the course of some research. At the risk of being out of line, the marriage doesn't seem to be working. It doesn't appear a happy one. While it's none of my business, I would like to know something about Charles: his background, how you met, that sort of thing."

"Charles was and remains an enigma. He purports to be a writer; needed his own study so he could lock himself away to write. His muse comes at night, or so he claims. So, he spends much of the night hours writing. Because of that, he insisted we have separate rooms so as not to keep one another awake by our different sleep patterns. I think it was nothing more than a ruse to avoid sharing a bed with me. And, of course I own this place. Where better for a writer to unleash his creativity than here in the solitude of Île Verte?"

"Are you saying you believe he only married you to be able to live here? Were you living here at the time you were married?"

"No, I wasn't living here then, but my thinking was I might move here at some time in the not-too-distant future. Just before we were married, I brought Charles here to show him the place. I had talked about it, so he knew of it, but had never seen it. It was straight afterwards he started pressing me to move here to live full-time. I was still working part-time. Thanks to my great aunt's bequest, I was well off and didn't need to work anymore. Anyway, almost straight after we were married, he persuaded me to come here to live. At first, I believed about his writing and the environment being good for his creativity. Now I'm not so sure about his motivation."

"When I found out through Dervla who your husband was, I recognised his name and looked him up as an author. I have to admit to being surprised at his receiving a gong when his body of work is so small and virtually insignificant. Has he produced much writing since you've been here?"

"I've not seen any evidence of productivity, creativity, or anything else since he came to the island. Oh, he locked himself away in his rooms for much of the time, and spread out into the main office, but I've not seen any evidence of what he does with his time."

"At the time you met him, and up until you moved here, was he working only as a writer, or did he earn his living in some other way?"

"If I believe everything he told me, he was a writer and made his living that way. I don't think there was much truth in it. Yes, there was a handful of published works citing him as the author. But, when I think back to that time, there was something else going on; something else in his life besides writing. I've no idea what it was, but his behaviour was strange at times, and his explanation for his absences as 'research for his writing' didn't ring true. I was a fool, Tessa. I can read people better than that. Somehow, I fell for his stories and I believed him. At least, I believed him for a short time before I came to my senses again."

I wanted to ask about the arrangement under which Anton lived on the island, but felt it might too sensitive for her to handle yet. So, after I made a mental note to explore their marriage again at some later time, I cast my mind around for something else to explore. Frankie's birthday party came to mind.

"Frankie, I was a little surprised by the guest list for your birthday bash. I'm not being critical, but types of people I expected you to invite weren't there. In fact, I found the guests a strange bunch. Marian Nettleton told me you met about eighteen months ago, but it sounded as though your husbands knew each other from well before that. What about the other guests, how do you come to know them?"

"You're right. Charles and Terrence Nettleton worked for the same mob years ago. I don't know what they did, but there are a few others they both worked with as well. Various numbers of them have dinner together whenever Charles is in Paris. I rarely attend. I'm rarely invited! One of those rare times was when I met Marian Nettleton. It seems Terrence couldn't get away without her that night, so Charles found himself forced to insist I accompany him to dinner. I discovered on the way to the restaurant, my role was to keep Marian entertained while the men discussed 'more important matters'. And, no, I don't know what such matters were."

That's good to know. It sounds like Frankie doesn't think any more of the Nettletons than I do. Now, it's time to see what I can find out about the others.

"What about the other guests, Frankie? The Seymours and the Nettletons seem to be close. Did they know each other before coming here to your party?"

"I don't know for sure, but I think so. I only met the Seymours when they arrived here. They are friends of Charles … as are most of the guests. You know Jackson, the pilot who brought you here. I've known him for years, and he always is so obliging. I like the man and he often comes to dinner here. And, of course, Anton was a guest. He also always came to dinners and anything else happening here. It's so sad; tragic. I shall miss him terribly. Not every day, but most days, I visited his studio to see what he was working on. We sat and talked; sometimes as he worked, and at other times over coffee. He was my friend … in spite of what Charles liked to think."

"What did Charles like to think?"

"Argh, I don't know. It was as though he thought he owned Anton. Don't get me wrong. Charles never questioned my relationship with Anton. He just carried on as though he owned him, as though Anton was some special project of his."

"What about the other guests in the cottages, are they close friends?"

"One couple in the cottages is from Guadeloupe. They have been business associates of mine for some years, and have been here twice before I think. The other couple are English but live in France now. Charles often has dinner with the husband when he is in France."

"It seems Charles had a good deal of say in who was invited to your birthday party. Were you okay with that?"

"Not really, but I'm not telling this story very well. Let me start again."

I gave her a 'go to it' gesture. She looked off into the distance and started a narration that sounded as though she was reading straight from her memory bank, delivered in a flat tone, devoid of inflection or emotion.

"It had been a while since we had visitors stay over. I told Charles I planned to invite a few friends over for my birthday. He wanted to know when that was, and when people were likely to arrive and leave. He …"

"He doesn't know when it's your birthday?"

"Birthdays, wedding anniversaries and the like are of no interest to Charles. I told him the date, and I anticipated people would arrive a day or so before and leave the day after. We had a bit of a row. He said it was too short notice for people to make arrangements to be here, and couldn't I put it off for a couple of weeks. I insisted my birthday was when it would happen, and I would not change the date. He realised I was quite determined, and seemed to accept the situation. His interest switched to my guest list. Whom did I plan to invite? Apart from you, I didn't have a clue at that stage, so I claimed to be working on it but, of course, it would include Jackson and Anton … and maybe the Martins from Guadeloupe."

"Is that when he put forward his invitees list?"

"He said, of course I had to invite the Martins. They would be insulted if I didn't and it might affect our business relationship with them. Then he suggested the Nettletons and the Seymours: *You and Marian got on so well in Paris, it would be good for you to catch up again, and it has been a while since you spent time with Kate Seymour.*"

"I had never met Kate Seymour until the day she arrived here. It was much the same with the Grevilles, the other couple in the cottages. I hadn't even seen either of them before their arrival."

"I'm pleased this was to be YOUR birthday party. So, then the Nettletons and the Seymours arrived earlier than you planned."

"They were supposed to arrive the day before the party. Only you and Dervla were to arrive earlier. Then I discovered Charles had changed their tickets, and they ended up being the first to arrive. He claimed that, because they were coming from such a distance, they needed time to recover from their travel to be in a fit state to enjoy the party. I planned to put them in the cottages, and everyone else, except Anton of course, would be in rooms in the castle. I hadn't given Delphine the arrangements when Charles went to her and insisted those two couples were given the big guest rooms in here. When I gave Delphine the list of allocated accommodation, she told me about Charles' demanding the other arrangement for his friends. To save embarrassment, I went along with it."

"I admit to being a bit confused by all this. You were such a strong person. Why did you go along with it? Why didn't you just scrap the whole idea? After all, it wasn't really your fortieth birthday."

"I wanted a reason to bring you here. To make it look authentic, I needed to invite Dervla as well. It's not that I didn't want Dervla to come. It was you I wanted ... and I was pleased when you both said you would come. Then I had to concoct a story about you both contacting me about my forthcoming BIG birthday, and how I felt obliged to invite you both to stay for a few days."

It gave me pause for thought. If Charles saw Dervla and me as 'obligation invitees', it might explain his lack of interest in getting to know us. While a plausible explanation, my gut told me it wasn't the case. Without being able to give precise examples, something about Charles' interaction with Nettleton and Seymour stood out in some way. And, I still needed more information on how and why Anton came to reside on the island. Lost in my own thoughts for a few moments, it was Frankie's voice which brought me back to reality.

"Tessa ... Tessa, are you all right? Did I say something to upset you? You've gone quiet."

After a brief apology, I returned to interview mode. "What do you know about Charles' friendship with Nettleton and Seymour? You said they had worked together and often met up in France?"

"I don't know. I asked about their history a couple of times, and received the same answer both times: they met through their work many years ago. Don't ask what their work was, or if they were all in the same line of work, because I don't know. Such information appears to be a state secret which Francesca Dubois should not know."

She giggled. My heart soared. This was the real Frankie coming back. "It might have been a Freudian slip; my calling it a state secret. While I don't know what they were involved in, over the years, I developed a suspicion it was something hush-hush. It's probably nonsense, but the fact he is so secretive about his past, makes me wonder."

"Well, wonder some more for a moment, and answer me this: do you think whatever they were involved in back then continues to the present time? Maybe in some lesser fashion, but is it likely they are still involved to some extent?"

"Again, I don't know, but I admit to sometimes wondering about it? Oh dear, with everything I say, I seem to confirm I'm one of those brainless females who drift through life knowing nothing of what's going on around them. I'm not, am I?"

"The Frankie I knew wasn't."

"I know. But that's what I've become. How did it happen?" I shrugged and tried looking unconcerned. "I don't need you to tell me. I know what happened. I married Charles. I always thought I was a relatively intelligent woman. It seems I was kidding myself. Charles is proof of that."

I was tempted to ask whether Charles was a bully – abusive in any way – or just arrogant and pig-ignorant. Courtesy and good manners told me to form my own opinion, and keep it to myself … at least for the moment. Perhaps a change of subject might lighten the mood a little.

"Tell me about the history of this place; this island and how it came to be yours."

"It's a long family history type saga. Are you sure you want to hear it?"

A knock on the door interrupted proceedings before I could answer. Frankie and I exchanged a look. I raised my eyebrows in question as to whether I should answer the door, or if she intended to ignore it. She whispered, "I'll ask who it is first, and then decide whether to open it or not." I nodded and gestured for her to go ahead.

In a loud, strong voice, she called out, "Who is it and what do you want?"

"It's Delphine, Miss. I've brought a tray for you. Please may I bring it in?"

The confident person who was Delphine the housekeeper sounded much less together than her usual self. Again, I raised my eyebrows in question at Frankie. She huffed a sigh of disgust, and flapped a hand at me to deal with the door. When Delphine saw who opened the door, she almost dropped the tray.

"Please put it over there on the table, Delphine."

Frankie resumed command. After depositing the tray as instructed, and when about halfway to the door, Delphine hesitated for a moment. She spun around to face Frankie … and shot me an angry look as she did so. Delphine was not too subtle at letting me know how she felt about my presence in the room. Frankie noticed.

"Was there something else?" Frankie asked … with icicles dripping off every word. Delphine shuffled on the spot. The poor woman looked stunned by being spoken to in such a way.

"No, thank you, Miss Dubois; I've been concerned about you that's all. May I ask if you will be joining the others in the dining room again soon? And, will you want to see the menus beforehand as is your usual practice?"

"I'll let you know when I've decided. In the meantime, my friend, Miss Tessa, and I have many important matters to discuss. I would prefer there are no interruptions."

As an unwilling spectator, I was embarrassed for Delphine. She didn't deserve to be spoken to that way. The woman was genuine in her concern for her mistress. Why would Frankie speak to her in that way? I observed a strong bond of friendship between these two women. Why would Frankie turn on Delphine like this?

Dismissed in no uncertain terms, Delphine let herself out. Still stunned by what happened, I continued to study the floor tiles for a few moments after the housekeeper left. When I looked up at Frankie, I realised she watched me trying to work out what happened.

"Oh, for goodness sake, Tessa, don't look like that. The stunned-mullet look does not suit you. What have you found so objectionable?"

"Well, since you ask, you just gave me another taste of it. The way you addressed Delphine, and me just now, was uncalled for. Perhaps you are best left alone to wallow in whatever it is you are wallowing in. Your last performance indicates whatever is wrong with you continues to render you unfit for human company. I'll take myself off to a more hospitable environment, and leave you to fester in your misery. Oh, and before I leave, I doubt you are interested, but I'll tell you anyway. Dervla is recovering after almost being killed. She is still laid up and suffering severe memory loss, but is improving."

Having said my piece, I stood up, nodded my goodbye, and headed for the door.

"Don't go! Please don't go, Tessa. I didn't mean to attack you … or Delphine. I will apologise to her later. Please, sit down again. There remains so much I need to talk to you about."

"You know which room I'm in. If you wish to speak to me, perhaps you might come to find me when you feel ready to continue our conversation in a civilised manner."

Frankie looked as though I slapped her across the face. I knew her remorse was genuine, but I wasn't about to let her get away with it. The thought uppermost in my mind at the time was about changing the date on our tickets home as soon as Dervla was fit to travel. So far, my time on Île Verte had proved it a long way short of a Caribbean idyll.

"Please Tessa; I'm sorry. Please sit down."

Unsure of what I should do, I stood looking down at her. I watched her reach for the phone and, without taking her eyes off me, made a call.

"Delphine, please forgive my rudeness … Yes, I know, but that's no excuse … Thank you … Could I impose on you to bring another lunch tray for Miss Tessa, please? … Wonderful… thank you." She gave me a pleading look. It was enough to melt my resolve. "Your lunch will be along in a few minutes. Tessa, please at least have lunch with me. Then leave, if you must."

It wouldn't be two minutes later when Delphine arrived with a second tray. We wasted no time moving to the table and settling down to an excellent lunch. At some point during my meal, I remembered Dervla and my mission to have Winston's nursing duties curtailed. I hadn't intended spending so much time with Frankie. Finding Bennett to organise Winston's removal from Dervla's room was a high priority for this morning. Now it was afternoon and I still hadn't done anything about it.

Frankie noticed I was otherwise preoccupied and became concerned. "Are you okay, Tessa? Is the food all right, or would you prefer something else?"

"The food is wonderful as usual, thank you. I'm sorry I was rude. I was thinking about Dervla."

There followed a long conversation about what happened to Dervla and my concern Winston was smothering her with unwanted care and attention. "So, my mission this morning was to tell Inspector Bennett to remove his officer from Dervla's room. But, it is now afternoon and I still haven't done it. I'm feeling guilty about it – and about not having looked in on Dervla since I left her soon after breakfast."

A torrent of questions followed about Dervla's attack, her memory loss, who was nursing her, who were Winston and Inspector Bennett, and probably dozens more. I answered them as best I could, but so many of the details she wanted, I didn't have. If nothing else, her questioning alerted me to how little I had achieved in investigating the attack on our friend.

"Well, we shouldn't be sitting here all afternoon when there are things to be done. Come on. Let's check on Dervla first, and then find this Inspector fellow and sort things out."

Thank you, God, Frankie is back. "I'm not sure you should go charging about the castle in a green towelling bathrobe. Perhaps you should dress first, while I take these trays back to the kitchen."

She giggled. "It's tempting to go out like this. It would shock the toffee-nosed guests ... maybe enough to make them go home."

"Nice thought; but the police are not letting anyone leave the island yet."

As I let myself out, I saw Frankie disappear into her walk-in wardrobe. The two trays and their contents stacked as best I could were a precarious load. I was relieved when Delphine saw me coming and rushed to rescue my load. "I think your mistress is about to leave her den and re-enter the real world. I'll do my best to protect her from anything likely to send her back into hibernation."

"If she is emerging, she is back to Miss Dubois again. She won't need you, or anyone else, to protect her. She is one strong lady." Delphine's wide smile as she spoke said volumes about the two women's relationship. I breathed a silent Amen.

By the time I returned to Frankie's room, she was dressed and ready to face the world again.

Chapter 16

We encountered Inspector Bennett as we crossed the lobby on our way to check on Dervla. I introduced him to Frankie before launching into my spiel about removing Winston. Bennett was not inclined to comply. My long lost friend, Frankie Dubois, displayed her colours in fine form.

"Has Miss O'Reilly broken the law in some way?" Bennett looked confused, but Frankie rushed on. "I mean, has Miss O'Reilly broken the law in some way by allowing herself to be violently attacked and almost killed? ...No? ... Then, as it appears she has not broken any law and is not in custody, please remove your officer from her room at once. I will not have one of my guests treated as though she is under arrest for the crime committed against her. Surely your officer might be better utilised in investigating the crimes carried out on my property, than in smothering a young woman with unwanted and unnecessary care."

Frankie's berating of Bennett left him slack-jawed and momentarily struck dumb. When he finally recovered sufficiently, he took up the challenge. "I assure you, Madam, your guest is receiving the best possible care. I will be the judge..."

"No, Sir, you will not be the judge. I am here to tell you she is subjected to more care than she requires; unnecessary care. And, such care as you see fit to impose on her, is robbing her of her privacy. The whole situation can only be viewed as one of unlawful incarceration. You and your officer have created a situation which is contrary to Miss O'Reilly's will. If you do not remove your officer from her room immediately, I will lodge complaint with my close friend, the Police Commissioner."

"That won't be necessary," Bennett snapped and gave us both a dark look. "I have wasted enough of my officer's time. I need every one of my men out here working on the investigation." Having delivered his broadside, Bennett stormed up the stairs and knocked on Dervla's door.

Discretion appeared a wise move, so Frankie and I made an unscheduled trip through the hall and out onto the rear deck to check out the back garden. On returning to the lobby, we were greeted by the sight of Winston negotiating the stairs while loaded with his folded up cot and a few other bits and pieces. Again, discretion came into play. We lingered in the doorway to the Great Hall until Winston exited the building via the front steps. As soon as he reached the front door, we raced up the stairs.

Our next surprise came at Dervla's door. It was locked. Was this a touch of spite on Bennett's part? Frankie sprang into action. She thrust a key into my hand. "It my master; go in." Then she turned on her heel and was off like a flash down the stairs again.

The sound of her shoes on the tiles told me she was at a flat gallop crossing the lobby. In the hope of catching some of the ensuing action, I leaned as far as I dared over the railing. I could see as far as the bottom of the front steps. It seems Winston lost hold of his load as he went down those steps. Frankie caught up with him as he scurried about picking it up again. Her voice reached my ears, the fire in it intimidating even from my distance.

"The key, please ... The key to Miss O'Reilly's room, give it to me now." Winston's reply did not carry up to me, but it was obvious he refused. "Officer, I am not interested in anything your inspector said. He will be the least of your worries when I call my friend the Police Commissioner to report your illegal imprisonment of one of my guests. Now, I'll have that key thanks ... or I'm off inside to make a phone call."

"Miss Dubois, we are trying to keep her safe. What if they try to finish the job and attack her again?"

"We will worry about who enters her room and who doesn't. No, I don't want any more excuses. The key please... When you find your inspector, please tell him I have an urgent matter to discuss with him."

I have to hand it to Frankie. She played the part of ruler of her dominion to perfection. With the issue of the key apparently sorted with Winston, I unlocked Dervla's door using Frankie's master key and slipped inside. Dervla was sitting propped up in bed with a face as long as a wet weekend. Her face lit up when she saw me.

"Are you alone? Is Winston out there too?"

"No, Winston is not outside, and somehow I doubt he will be coming back. But I'm not alone. Frankie will be along shortly. Now, how have you been since I last saw you?"

"I am fine ... apart from the gaps in my memory. And, I am sick of being treated like an invalid. All I need is to get out of this bed, to take a shower and walk around for a bit."

"Do you think you can get out of bed; you won't topple over if you try to stand?"

"Only one way to know for sure; let's give it a go. Help me out from under all these bedclothes. Anyone would think we are at the North Pole the way he has kept me wrapped up. Someone should tell him we are in the tropics, and even we Poms can handle the climate without so much mollycoddling."

Her spirit is alive and well, even if her memory still isn't. "Okay, you've convinced me you might be ready to try out those legs of yours. Hang on to me as you push yourself upright."

Frankie joined us at that point in the exercise. With one of us on either side of her, Dervla tested her legs. While a bit wobbly at first, within moments she was striding around the room unaided. "Ladies, if you will excuse me, I am off to take a shower."

We made ourselves comfortable and waited. It turned out to be a long shower. Dervla eventually emerged in a bath robe and with a towel wrapped turban style around wet hair. "That was wonderful. I almost feel human again. The whole time I've been locked up in here, I've been dreaming of going to sit in the garden to soak up some sunshine. Do you think we might give that a go?"

"If you feel inclined to try, we could go out to the back garden. It's almost afternoon teatime, but it means the others will probably start streaming out there as well. If you'd rather avoid the other guests, we could sit in my courtyard and have Delphine bring us afternoon tea on a tray." Frankie's offer of afternoon tea in her private courtyard met with unanimous support.

While Dervla dressed and tried to tame her unruly still damp hair, Frankie and I waited outside. Frankie called to organise afternoon tea while we waited. Then, with more than a little trepidation, and with one of us on either side of Dervla, ready to catch her if she looked like falling, we set off on our trek to Frankie's courtyard.

Our journey was incident free. We did pause for a few moments at the bottom of the stairs. The descent left Dervla a little breathless, but the rest of the way didn't present any difficulties for her. An abundant and somewhat indulgent afternoon tea arrived almost the moment we were seated around the small table in the courtyard outside Frankie's suite.

The overheard conversation between Frankie and Winston came to mind. "Frankie, you told Winston to find Inspector Bennett and to send him to you as you had something urgent to discuss with the inspector. Depending on the good inspector's mood at the moment, he might be out there looking for you by now."

"Don't worry about it. It won't hurt him to have to wait to find me. I'd enjoy making him stew for a while."

"I was thinking more along the lines of, if he can't find you, he will ask Delphine where you are. He could arrive here at any moment."

"Ah no, that won't happen. He might ask Delphine for our whereabouts, but he will get nothing useful from her. Rest assured; our afternoon tea will not be disturbed by the arrival of Inspector Bennett."

After we made some small inroad into the delights on the table, Frankie asked for details of what happened to Dervla, and admitted to feeling completely out of touch with happenings over the last couple of days. I was concerned rehashing it all might trigger some adverse reaction in Dervla. She held no such concerns and insisted we discuss it at length.

Frankie proved an excellent listener. Between Dervla and I, we gave her chapter and verse on the night and right up until the time Dervla's attack took place. Then it was Frankie's turn to hold the floor. Her questions came thick and fast, and I found myself amazed by her ability to retain so much information given to her in such a short time span.

"I don't doubt you know what you're talking about, but could those lights you saw moving around in the trees be the other guests going back to the cottages?"

"No, the lights were in a different part of the rainforest, nowhere near where those cottages are. And, they were erratic; not made by people following a direct path to their cottage." So far, Dervla sounded strong and unperturbed by discussing the night's events.

"Dervla is right … to a certain extent. The lights were not your guests returning home, but they were located at a cottage. There is an almost derelict cottage in a clearing some distance away from everything else. It's where the activity was based that night."

Both women looked hard at me for a while when I finished speaking. Frankie found her voice first. "There is one old cottage which has been out of use for some time. Well, for as long as I've owned the island anyway. There is a story attached to it from my great aunt's time. We are not going to go there now though."

Dervla appeared to have been deep in thought until Frankie finished speaking. "Tessa, you knew about those lights. You went to investigate them? I suppose you must have if you know about the cottage. What else can you tell us about that night? Oh, don't worry. I'm not going to collapse in a quivering heap because we talk about it."

"She is right. And talking about it might help her in some way." Frankie wasn't telling me something I hadn't already thought about. Nevertheless, I wasn't convinced it was the right thing to do. Peer pressure is an interesting thing. I succumbed to it.

My recount of the events in and around the derelict shack occupied the next few minutes. As I talked through the events, some vague thought tried to develop. I couldn't bring it to the fore, or develop it fully. But, something told me it was important. It was an important fact I'd overlooked. While the other two discussed what I told them, I worked on my ghost of an idea in a bid to make it materialise. It didn't happen, and I knew it would bother me for the rest of the day ... and probably tonight!

Instinct told me it was important. Was I losing my touch as an investigative journalist? Determined not to let it beat me, and have it keep nagging me, I rewound my memory of the night and replayed it. There were no gaps. The story was complete. Through the frustrating murkiness of my thinking, I heard my name mentioned. "Sorry; I wasn't listening. What did you ask me?"

The two women giggled. "I wasn't talking to you, I was talking about you." Dervla managed to say between giggles.

It appears Dervla had reached the part of her story where she was on her way to tell me about the lights. As it was when her memory of the event ended, I guessed Frankie and the rest of the story were left hanging. Dervla's mood changed in an instant. When I looked up at her, she was shaking her head. I suspected revisiting the next missing piece of her story hit her hard.

"Don't try to force it, Dervla. Remember, the missing bit might never return. Would that be such a bad thing?"

"I wasn't thinking about that, Tessa. But, since you mention it, for me, it will be a bad thing. If I can't remember ... if I don't know who attacked me, it will bother me for the rest of my life. I'm quite convinced of it. Nevertheless, it wasn't what I was thinking about. When I opened the door that night, I was on my way to your room. I intended making enough noise to wake you so I could tell you about the lights. But, you weren't there anyway.

You already were out in the rainforest chasing those lights. It didn't matter how hard I banged on your door, there wouldn't be any response."

Her comments weren't intended to make me feel guilty, but they did. I doubt things would have turned out differently even if I were in my room at the time. I decided not to mention it, or my guilty feelings, but added a little more clarity to the story instead.

"You saw many more lights when you checked after you woke from dozing off, and you intended telling me about them. It was then, when you opened your door, you were attacked. But, when I first spoke to you, you told me you knocked on my door earlier; when you first noticed the lights. It would have been before you fell asleep. I think you saw only two lights in the first instance. It was the first time you knocked on my door to tell me about them and received no response. It's likely I already was on my way to investigate the lights, or maybe I was in the rainforest by then."

Frankie sat in silence during the exchanges between Dervla and me. While she sat there, only half listening to our discussion, Frankie found a myriad of new questions to ask. She took the opportunity to air some of them.

"Tessa, as you seem to know about the derelict cottage, I assume you were there when the action took place. What can you tell us about when the action focused on and around the cottage?"

"Not a great deal I can think of, but I'm not sure what you want to know. There were two lights because two people were involved. The clearing provided some sort of meeting place for them. My initial view of proceedings was, a meeting was in progress. I watched them for a while until it appeared the meeting ended. One person started back through the trees towards the castle. The second person remained at the site and went into the cottage. I have no evidence to back it up, but I formed the opinion the second person might be camping in the cottage."

"Where were the police? Did they get involved in any of this?" Frankie sounded quite indignant strange things could happen here while there was a police presence on her island.

"They did come, and tried to surround the cottage. The person in the cottage was alerted by sounds from outside and fled. He too tried to make his escape through the trees in the general direction of the castle. The police, who were on the other side of the cottage at the time of his escape, didn't see the exact direction of his escape route. They spent some time thrashing about in the trees as they worked their way back towards the castle."

"So, you were watching the place when the person escaped? Did the police know you were there … know you'd seen it all?" The excitement in Dervla's voice was mirrored in the way she moved forward to perch on the edge of her chair.

"No. At the time, I don't think the police knew I was there."

"But you did see it all?" Frankie asked. "So, what happened, did the police catch the escapee?"

"Yeah, they … Christ, that's it!"

"What…?" both women exclaimed in unison. "Did you remember something else?" Frankie asked.

"Oh yes. Something bothered me all afternoon; something I missed about the night's events. I just realised what is odd about it." Both women were now sitting on the front of their chairs and leaning forward over the table towards me. "Let's go back to when the person made a break from the cottage and headed into the trees. The police realised he'd gone and circled back to re-enter the trees at almost the same point from which they emerged earlier. They took after him, but followed much the same route as they used to find the cottage. The escapee's route split the gap between mine and the police's routes out of the trees, but the escapee's route was closer to me."

"God, you could have been attacked too." Dervla said.

"Possibly, if he knew I was there."

"What did you do?"

"He knew the police were after him, but he wasn't aware of my presence. Anyway, the opportunity arose to do something about it, so I used a fallen branch to trip him. It became a bit hectic after that. He fell flat on his face and dropped his torch. I jumped onto his back, and managed to signal to the police with his torch. The police found us, cuffed him, and dragged him out of the rainforest towards the castle. By the time I picked myself up and found my way back out onto the lawn, everyone had disappeared. There was no sign of the police or the escapee. I still don't know how they managed to disappear so quickly and completely."

"So, what was the elusive thing you remembered a few minutes ago when you were talking to us?" Frankie's voice was not much above a whisper, and something told me perhaps she too had come up with the same question as bothered me.

"It's not one thing it's a whole lot of questions: who was the escapee, what did they do with him, where is he now, and how did they pull off such an amazing vanishing act after emerging from the rainforest?"

"Well, how did it all happen and who was it? Is it what you remembered?" Dervla's excitement was almost palpable.

"Don't get excited, Dervla. I don't have the answer to any of those questions. The questions only occurred to me now. My gut tells me something is not right about all of this."

Frankie drummed her fingers on the table as she stared into her empty coffee mug. When she spoke, it was low, slow and deliberate. "I assume the police were called after Anton was discovered and they arrived sometime after. If my assumption is correct, they have been here for several days, during which Dervla was attacked. Do we know anything more about what happened at Anton's place? I suppose the question is, what has their investigation turned up so far? Dervla's been incommunicado but, Tessa, have you heard any more about what happened?"

"Not a thing; all I've been given to believe is that Anton's body was taken of the island last night. The guests are still here, and are becoming agitated about not being able to leave. At the risk of sounding sceptical, I was told the escapee from the derelict cottage was flown off the island the morning after he was captured. I can't confirm it. I have not heard a name mentioned, and I still don't know what happened during the intervening period from when they handcuffed him until supposedly they flew him off the island."

"You are an investigative journo, Tessa. I think it's time we looked for some answers. I'm not sure we should involve you at this stage though, Dervla." As she finished speaking, Frankie and I looked at Dervla. We expected her to make some comment. I saw nothing but shock etched on her face.

"Dervla, are you okay? What happened?" My guilt feelings were back big time. What had we done to upset Dervla so badly?

"Anton is dead? How? ... When? ... Are you sure? Why wasn't I told?"

I shot Frankie a look and hoped she understood the message was for her to play along. "At the time, you were a bit preoccupied with being unconscious. By the time you were back with us, Anton was old news and we were more concerned about you."

"There was nothing we could do for Anton, but we were keen not to see you end up the same way."

Thank you, Frankie. You understood my message.

Tears trickled down Dervla's cheeks. "It's such a tragedy. I liked Anton. He was nice. I was hoping to spend some time with him before we left. Tessa, you seemed to get on well with him too."

"I had little enough to do with him but, you are right, I did like him. Somehow, I thought we might be kindred spirits. I suppose, now we will never know."

"Has his brother been notified?"

Frankie's question caused Dervla and me to exchange looks. Having just stated how much we liked Anton, could we be so insensitive as not to think about his family. They might remain ignorant of what happened. Dervla didn't know anything about the event, so it fell to me to answer. "I'm unaware if his family has been notified. Neither Dervla nor I was in a position to contact them. It is something we should follow up with Bennett."

"…If he will talk to us after my performance earlier. I imagine he will come in for dinner tonight. It might be the time to ask him. In front of a dining room full of people, he might feel inclined to play nice." Frankie's suggestion made sense and received our support.

Dervla caught my attention. She had her hand pressed hard against the side of her head. "Do you have a headache? Are you okay?" It was obvious she wasn't, but the question slipped out anyway.

"Yeah, it's a headache of sorts, but I'm also feeling light-headed with it; giddy. Maybe I should go back to bed for a while."

"You are not going back there. Tessa, give me a hand with this couch. It converts to a double bed. Dervla, you are staying here in my suite of rooms until we know it's safe for you to go back to your own room."

Within minutes, the couch had morphed into a bed and Dervla was tucked up in it. After checking all the doors were locked we left her to sleep. As we headed along the hallway, Frankie made an interesting suggestion. "There is still some time before dinner, and still plenty of light outside. How about we wander across to Anton's place for a bit of a poke about?"

Chapter 17

While I had no knowledge of what motivated Frankie to suggest going to Anton's place, it was worth doing. My only concern was we had little time for a decent 'poke about', as she called it, before the light failed. I quietened my misgivings with the notion it was a preliminary visit. One we might follow up tomorrow if we thought it warranted.

Frankie set a cracking pace, making it hard to talk as we strode along. "What is this all about, Frankie? What do you hope to find or do there?"

"We will know when it happens. I just have this almost overwhelming feeling something is not right. Something about the investigation into what happened at Anton's place and his death is not right. Added to that, there is the matter of my missing husband."

"Charles…? What has Charles got to do with anything? Aren't his disappearance and Anton's death likely to be two separate incidents?"

"I don't know, but I am beginning to wonder. There are so many things going round in my head at the moment, I can't think straight. Sometimes, when this happens, I just let instinct take over, and go with whatever it tells me to do. Right now, it's telling me I need to look around Anton's place. If you have qualms about doing that, please go back. You don't need to put yourself through something you find uncomfortable, and I'm perfectly all right on my own."

"That's not going to happen. I don't have any qualms associated with Anton's place. All I'm trying to ascertain is why we are going there, and what we need to do there. And, if I'm honest, I do hold some concerns about how revisiting the site might affect you."

"Needless concerns, Tessa; I'm back to normal … or, I will be when I know what happened here."

As Frankie tried to reassure me she was okay, we broke out of the rainforest and into the clearing at Anton's place. Nothing appeared to have changed since my previous visit. I knew the only change likely was Anton's body gone from inside his cottage. Frankie stopped in the middle of the clearing and stood, hands on hips and swivelling from the waist, as she inspected the site.

Her visual inspection complete, she walked slowly across to a couple of large rocks some distance out front from the cottage. A large, slab-like rock was partially buried parallel to the ground and protruded about forty centimetres above it. After studying it for a few moments, Frankie bent down and ran her hand, almost in a caress, across the rock. Then, she straightened and stood still and erect in front of the rock as if offering up a silent a prayer or paying homage in some way. It was a bit too spooky for my liking. I didn't want to intrude on her private moment, but the event was becoming a bit eerie.

At last, she moved a few paces away from the rocks and stood examining the cottage and the remains of the burned out studio. "Should we start with the studio or the cottage, Tessa? What's your preference?"

Did I have a preference? Not any I was aware of, but the studio somehow seemed the safer bet. Frankie agreed. As I followed her over to the studio, I searched the ground around us for any hint or clue as to what happened here.

Frankie was almost on the studio's doorstep when a patch of grass caught my eye. It was a little way off to one side, and a couple of metres out from the building. I left Frankie to her own devices and detoured to the patch of grass. The only out-standing thing about it was its slightly different colour from the surrounding grass. It could be due to anything, I told myself. This was Anton's art studio. It might be where he threw out the water he washed his brushes in, or anything else needing disposal. I realised I didn't know what sort of artist Anton was. Was he a painter, a sculptor, a potter, or what?

"Something I haven't asked before, Frankie: what type or artworks did Anton produce here? What he did will tell us the types of materials he had in his studio and how they impacted on the fire."

"He was multi-talented and worked across a wide spectrum; a painter ... landscapes and still life stuff and the odd portrait ... a sculptor in both wood and clay ... and he occasionally dabbled in silversmithing. I believe he worked as a printmaker in the past as well, but without the necessary presses, or whatever is required, he didn't continue with that."

"If he was a painter, it is likely he had highly flammable materials stored in his studio. Did he have a kiln of any sort to fire his clay sculptures?"

"Ye-e-s, I think so. Yes. Soon after he arrived, he built a small gas kiln. Then he discovered how difficult getting cylinders of gas to the island can be. Sometime later, I think he bought – or built – an electric kiln. I remember him talking to Charles about needing an uninterrupted power supply when he was firing."

Frankie's information gave me plenty to think about. First, I decided to concentrate on the patch of grass which caught my attention. I bent down and ran a finger over a section of it. It left a slight oily residue. One sniff and I knew it was some sort of accelerant. ...Might mean nothing, I told myself. It could be turps he used in the studio. My gut believed otherwise.

Taking a fresh tissue from the small pack in my pocket, I rubbed it firmly over the patch of grass. A colourless oily mark resulted. The fact it was colourless told me this was not from Anton cleaning his brushes. If it were, I would have picked up traces of colour from the paints he used. There was none. Whatever spilled here was fresh and uncontaminated by anything in the studio. To ensure a good sample, I gave the grass another good rub with the tissue.

My problem was what to do with the sample. I didn't know how long before all trace of it disappeared from the tissue. It needed to be sealed up in something. Devoid of any obvious suitable container, I left Frankie wandering around the shell of the studio and went across to the cottage. A small lidded plastic container in a kitchen cupboard was ideal. In spite of vigorous sniffing, I couldn't detect any existing smell in the container. So, I decided it was okay to use, folded my sample tissue into a tight parcel and sealed it in the container. Small enough not to be obvious, the container slid easily into one of the roomy pockets of my cargo shorts.

As I exited the cottage, Frankie called me. Her voice had an edge to it. I wasn't sure whether it was excitement or alarm. Nevertheless, I was a ball of apprehension as I raced to the rear of the studio to where Frankie waited.

"What does this look like to you? I was just about to pick my way through the ruins when it caught my eye. What do you think?"

"Hmm ... may I reserve my judgement until after we inspect the place a bit? But, I agree it's worth thinking about in the meantime."

Frankie drew my attention to an area in the rear section of the studio where a good deal of flammable material had been stored. "Do you know what was here before the fire?" Frankie shrugged. "It's difficult to tell, but it looks as though canvases were stacked along the wall. Do you know what media he worked in?"

"Mostly oils, but also acrylics sometimes, and even watercolour occasionally; I think his preference was oils."

"So, if canvases were stacked there, a high proportion of them might have been oil paintings?" My thoughts were not going anywhere I liked, but I knew there was some justification for it. "Let's see if we can pick our way into other areas of the studio. What we find in there might tell us more."

As we worked our way through towards the front of the building, I noticed the fire damage was less severe. The only other area to suffer as much damage as the rear section was what appeared to be a storeroom. Frankie confirmed, soon after Anton converted the place to a studio, this small area was partitioned off and had shelving added to serve as his materials storeroom. Turpentine and acetone supplies likely were stored in here and, as far as I could tell, it looked like canvases were stored here too.

While I stood trying to record to memory every detail of the effect of the fire on the contents of storeroom, something else invaded my senses. "Frankie, do you smell anything?"

"I assume you mean besides the smell of smoke and burnt plastic. No. Should I? What else is there?"

If only I was sure… I left her question unanswered for a few moments while I wandered away from the gutted storeroom and into a less damaged section of the building. Frankie asked her question again, and this time I felt obliged to answer … and was almost sure of what I was about to share with her.

"I'm almost convinced I smell accelerant in this building. It is strongest in that back section where the canvases were stored against wall. There are other smells mixed with it in the storeroom area. You get a better sense of it when you move out here into the front section of the building. The smell isn't so noticeable here, but you get a whiff of it wafting through from other parts of the studio."

Frankie came and stood beside me. "This was Anton's main work area. He said the light coming through the front windows was perfect. I often sat here and chatted to him while he worked. We had many mugs of coffee in here, or sitting out there on the big flat rock. I can see the damage and I know what happened, but somehow I can't believe I won't be having coffee here again. I can't believe he is gone, and he won't come bouncing back at any moment with his camera slung around neck after having been out to take photographs for his work." She is not the first person I've encountered in my work who expressed those same emotions.

I climbed over a pile of burnt rubble to exit the studio via the front door. It was good to take in a couple of deep breaths of clean air. Lost in my thoughts about what occurred in the building, it took me a while to notice shadows were now quite long. Daylight was fading fast, and it already would be quite dark along the rainforest part of the track.

"Come out of there Frankie. It's late. We should have started back to the castle before this. Hurry up; let's go. Besides, we need to check on Dervla before dinner."

"It's not so late. Stop worrying. There's still plenty of light for us to go back to the castle."

"After everything that's happened here, I do not want us to be in the rainforest in the dark. How fit do you feel? Do feel up to jogging at least part of the track?"

She objected on the grounds there was no need for such concern, but I started jogging and she was faced with deciding whether to come with me or make her way back alone. As I hoped, common sense kicked in and she jogged with me. When we reached the lawns in front of the castle, she dropped back and stopped. I looked around to find her doubled over and gasping. Jogging obviously was not a regular part of Frankie's daily routine.

By the time she staggered to the front steps, her breathing was all but returned to normal. "I might be a bit late into the dining room tonight. I definitely need another shower after all we've done this afternoon." She wasn't the only one, but I didn't share the thought with her.

About half an hour later, a pale but alert Dervla accompanied Frankie into the dining room. My entrance a few minutes earlier placed me amongst the first guests to arrive. As has become my fashion, I selected a long glass of a fruit juice concoction before moving to the opposite side of the room from the drinks cabinet. A few more guests joined the congregation before Frankie and Dervla appeared. The two women, drinks in hand, joined me in being unsociable. Frankie scanned the assembled guests.

"I don't see Inspector Bennett. Has he been in yet?" I shook my head. "Does he generally eat in here with the guests?"

"Yes. Bennett eats in here with us while his officers eat with your staff. He sometimes arrives late if they have been out poking around somewhere in the grounds."

Dinner was a subdued affair, with we three women being treated as highly contagious. We sat on one side of the table, while everyone else chose seats on the opposite side. The most noticeable thing about dinner was the complete avoidance of Frankie by her so-called guests. As well as the missing police inspector, I noticed the pilot, Jackson, also was absent. We wasted no time over our meals, and left before desserts arrived.

On our way to Frankie's rooms, Dervla remembered her medication was still in her room upstairs. I volunteered to fetch it for her. Frankie objected to my going alone. She wanted to come with me, but I did not want Dervla left alone. In the end I won the argument. The guests were still at dinner when I crossed the lobby and climbed the stairs to our rooms.

There was no evidence of anyone having been in Dervla's room in her absence. Everything seemed as it was earlier this afternoon. As I reached for the bottle of pills on the bedside table something made me stop. I froze and let my eyes wander slowly over all I could see from there. Nothing jumped out at me, but my gut kept telling me something was not right. I did another slow scan of everything in front of me, from peripheral vision to peripheral vision. Still nothing seemed amiss. Perhaps I was just being paranoid, and my instinct had gone haywire. "I don't believe that for a moment," I told the empty room as I bent to pick up Dervla's book from the floor where it had landed face down, open, and in danger of cracking its spine.

My hand reached out for it ... and recoiled instantly. The book wasn't on the floor when we left this room earlier today. When we helped Dervla out of bed, the book was amongst the bedclothes. It became tangled in them after Dervla laid it aside on the bed after reading for a while. I had untangled the book and placed it on the bedside table, in front of the bottle of pills. At the time, the bottle of pills was in the centre towards the back of the bedside table, and the book was near the front edge. Now, the book was on the floor, and the bottle of pills had moved forward and to the side of the table nearest the bed.

With the tissue over my hand so as not to mark the book, I picked it up and put it on the bed. Dervla's tote bag was on the lounge chair. I fetched the bag and, employing my tissue again, carefully placed the book and the bottle of pills in an empty plastic bag I found in the tote. I tried to focus my mind on Dervla and not on what might have happened in this room during the last few hours. No woman likes to be without their personal grooming materials, so Dervla would probably appreciate her wet pack from the bathroom. It struck me as soon as I entered the ensuite. This is not how Dervla left it. The top of the vanity unit was tidy ... too tidy. The hairs on the back of my neck stood up.

Dervla was a creature of habit almost to the point of being obsessive. She had lined up in a neat row on the vanity unit various face creams and other toiletries, along with a hairbrush and comb. Her open wet pack sat on the narrow glass shelf between the vanity unit and the big wall mirror. Now, the wet pack was closed and on the vanity unit. All the bits and bobs Dervla neatly arranged on the vanity unit had disappeared. Using my trusty tissue again I opened the wet pack. It was no surprise to find those items dumped in the wet pack. I added the wet pack to my plastic bag and thanked the gods for such a large bag.

As I was about to leave the room, I realised carrying a plastic bag containing the selected items looked as though I was carrying an evidence bag. I was, but I didn't want it to be obvious. My eyes strayed to Dervla's large tote bag. "I'm sure she wants that too," I told the universe as I dumped my plastic bag into the tote and slung it over my shoulder. Then I was down the stairs and across the lobby in a flash, and rushing down the hallway to Frankie's rooms.

I breathed an almighty sigh of relief when Frankie opened the door and I saw both women were okay. Frankie caught her breath. "What happened, Tessa? Are you all right?"

"Me...? Of course I'm all right. Why wouldn't I be?"

"You don't look all right. How you look is tense and uptight." Frankie barely finished speaking when Dervla chimed in.

"You were gone a long time. It shouldn't take you so long to retrieve a bottle of pills. What else happened while you were away?"

"Would you two mind if I sit down before this Inquisition continues? I am quite all right. There, now that's out of the way." The two women exchanged a look. I chose to ignore it. "Dervla, this medication of yours, how important is it for you to continue with it? Do you feel as though you need to keep taking it? From memory, the stuff they gave you to take is a heavy duty sedative. While it's understandable if you feel you need the medication, I wondered if it is necessary for you to continue with it."

"I didn't know what they were, and thought they were some sort of antibiotic to help heal my scalp wound. If, as you say, those pills are sedatives, I'd prefer not to be doping myself up all the time. But, I'm not sure how I…"

"Good," I rushed in before she could say any more. "Let's see how you go without them. If you start having nightmares or anything, we will rethink the situation."

Frankie studied me as I spoke and seemed to pick up on what I was trying to do. "I think you're right, Tessa. If Dervla keeps taking them for a bit longer, there comes a time when she does have to come off them – even if it means a few rough times afterwards. Dervla, the longer you stay on them, the harder and more rugged it will be when you stop taking them. Don't stress about it, just see how you go without them. We'll both be here with you if you start to struggle."

While I don't think she was too confident about it, Dervla agreed she didn't need sedating and was happy to try going without the pills. Relief flooded through me. I knew someone had been in Dervla's room and the bottle of pills was moved during her absence. The only reason I could think of for it is somebody tampered with them. While I wasn't sure how Dervla would cope without the medication, there is no way I will let her take any of those pills again.

Frankie was deep in thought for a few moments before deciding to share those thoughts with us. "I'm not at all comfortable with you continuing to occupy your room upstairs, Tessa. With Dervla down here now, your room becomes isolated from everyone else. If anyone is concerned about what Dervla might remember, they wouldn't have to be too bright to work out she probably shared her memories with you. It might put you at risk of becoming the next incident on this island."

Dervla picked up on Frankie's line of thinking and added to it. "I have to admit to feeling safer with the three of us together. I know you two are not likely to admit to feeling the same way but, if we let common sense prevail, it would tell us it's the wisest approach."

"I hear what you're both saying, but I don't feel inclined to sleep on the floor. And, while Frankie's suite of rooms is well appointed, they are a bit short on beds if the three of us are to stay together. So, under the circumstances, it seems..."

"Nonsense, that's not the situation at all." Frankie's indignation was obvious. There is another couch next door like the one Dervla is sleeping on, and there is a king-size bed there too. Your only decision to make, Tessa, is whether you want to sleep in the room next door, or if we are to move the other couch in here for you. But, it is the only decision to make. You will not be going back to your room upstairs."

I started protest about all my belongings being upstairs. It didn't get me anywhere. Frankie cut me off again. "There are two options: Delphine could collect your belongings and bring them here or, as an alternative, Sampson could accompany you to collect your belongings. Which would you prefer?"

I took Frankie aside. "The room next door is part of Charles' suite. I hardly think it appropriate for me to sleep in there."

"You are perfectly safe. He will not come back in the middle of the night and ravish you."

"That's not what I was thinking. I can't just move into someone else's space without their permission, or them knowing about it. When they came back, they would be offended to find someone had invaded their private space."

"He won't be coming back. No, Tessa, don't argue. He won't be coming back, not tonight or ever."

"You don't know that."

"Yes I do. Oh, I don't mean I know what happened, but I do know he won't be back. Charles can't come back ... because he is dead."

Chapter 18

The matter of fact manner in which Frankie shared with me her belief her husband was dead left me stunned. It was a while before I could follow up on her statement. Delphine's arrival with the rest of Dervla's belongings created an interruption which gave me time to think about Frankie's conviction regarding Charles' demise. I was unaware Frankie organised earlier for Delphine, as soon as she finished in the kitchen after dinner, to clear out Dervla's room. Now she had all her possessions, Dervla's only interest was in taking a shower. Dervla out of earshot gave me an opportunity to press Frankie about Charles.

"Frankie, please tell me why you think Charles is dead. You seem quite calm about it, if you really believe it is the case."

"I'm not sure how to explain it. I *know* Charles is dead. But, without evidence to confirm it, I just won't let myself *believe* he is dead. I've known he was dead since the moment I saw Anton's body and Charles was missing. Don't misunderstand me, Tessa. I didn't love the man. If there ever were any such feelings, they died a long time ago. I discovered early in our marriage, he was not a nice person. Oh, he could be charming but, underneath, he was rotten to the core. There was nothing decent, honest or truthful about him."

"But you were distraught when you couldn't find him that morning, so you must still have some feelings for the man."

"Finding Anton's body almost pushed me over the edge. It was that and the fact I knew, for Anton to be killed, terrible forces were afoot on this island. More terrible things would follow. I had no doubts about it … and I still don't. "

"Call it my journo's nose for a story if you will, but I have a sense of the history of this island being tied up somehow in what has happened and in your reason for inviting me here after all these years."

There was an abrupt end to our conversation when Dervla walked in and sat down with us. Our attempt to change the subject and create the impression we were discussing something else failed dismally. "Come on, ladies. What happened to me didn't render me deaf. Why are you so interested in the history of this place, Tessa, and why shouldn't I hear about it too?"

Dervla was right. Trying to protect her from everything might not be the best strategy. "Okay. It will probably sound a bit naff but I sense there is something in the history of the place which might shed light on those incidents happening here over the last few days. We were trying to exclude you from our discussions for no reason other than maybe to protect you from being upset by anything we discovered. Perhaps the best way forward now, Frankie, is to continue our discussion, and for Dervla to tell us if it becomes uncomfortable for her."

With no argument raised by the others, I continued from where I left off. "Okay. For your information, Dervla, the point we were at when you joined us was my asking Frankie for the history of this place. She was about to launch into the story. You have the floor, Frankie."

"I suppose the story begins somewhere further back than this island. I'm not sure whether you know it or not, but I inherited everything here from my great aunt, Lucille Dubois. Lucy was my grandfather's only sister – only sibling actually – and she turned out to be something of a rebel. I don't mean that in a bad way. She was ahead of her time in her thinking and her approach to life. It was her approach to life which led to her being ostracised by the family."

"I like the sound of this woman," Dervla murmured. "She sounds like my kind of woman. The sort I'd like to be if I wasn't constrained by such things as having to earn a living and my employer's idea of appropriate decorum."

Frankie gave a wry grin. "She wasn't one to be constrained by any such nonsense. I don't know all the details, but it seems she was something of a party girl before such a term was in common usage, and maybe she was a bit too liberal with her affections. Anyway, when grandfather became head of the family, Lucille, who was much younger than her brother, was enjoying life to the fullest and causing the family a great deal of embarrassment. The cringe factor became too much for grandfather and he ostracised her and cut off family support."

"This is beginning to sound like a tragic romantic novel from the early 1900s. Her situation would be desperate once the family cut off all support." Already I was beginning to develop an emotional connection with Lucille.

"It could have been a disaster for her, but grandfather overlooked an important factor. Lucille had inherited from her grandmother. She received the bequest by way of an annuity; a fairly substantial annuity for the times. Nevertheless, life became difficult for her. She became *persona non grata* in upper-class circles as a result of grandfather's bringing his influence to bear. Invitations to parties, balls and the likes dried up, and the only would-be suitors showing any interest in her were from well down in the order of things. She took herself off to Spain; somewhere in the Catalonia area. We don't have a lot of information about her life there. From what we know, it seems she continued with the lifestyle she enjoyed, but tempered it to a more respectable level. About two years after she moved to Spain, the family discovered she had married a well-heeled upper crust Spaniard."

"Ah-hah, maybe it's not a tragedy after all. It certainly explains the Spanish influence in this place." I couldn't help hoping this feisty lady made a good life with her Spanish husband and did well for herself.

"In the tradition of all good stories: *but wait, there's more.* Lucille was a good catch. She was a beautiful woman with independent income. One who liked to entertain, and enjoyed the social roundabout of parties and other events. It made her quite appealing to her husband who had enormous landholdings and was involved in various enterprises. She always was an independent spirit, and it appears she remained so during her marriage. It suited her husband. Lucille made her own life in many ways, and wasn't demanding of his time and attention. It left him free to immerse himself in his commercial enterprises and, not so long after they were married, provided him with free time to return to his womanising ways."

Dervla giggled. "See, Tessa, you shouldn't make rush judgements. It looks like it is going to be a tragic tale after all."

"I suppose whether it's a tragedy or not depends on how you see it. I'm sure it was difficult for Lucille when she discovered the truth about the man she married. But, in historical true tradition, you can't keep a good woman down. At the time, divorce wasn't common. And, it just wasn't the done thing in a primarily Catholic environment. Nevertheless, it was never going to get in the way of a strong-willed woman like Lucille. There was a divorce – messy and acrimonious. It ended with Lucille gaining her freedom … And a significant slice of her husband's assets."

"Hooray for Lucille…!" Dervla and I chorus in unison. We were enthralled, and waited for the next exciting instalment in the story when Frankie broke the spell.

"I could go a mug of hot chocolate right now. Anyone else feel so inclined?"

Dervla and I exchanged exasperated looks before confirming we were interested. Frankie had the phone in hand and called our order through to Delphine. "It should be here in about ten minutes," Frankie announced as she ended the call.

"While we are waiting for our chocolate, and to avoid another interruption to the main story, may we change tack for a moment?" The other two nodded. I continued. "What can you tell us about the derelict cottage in the rainforest, the one where all the action was the other night?"

"Off the top of my head, nothing much other than I believe there is a story attached to it. There have been a couple of occasions when I thought to look it up in Lucille's records, but I haven't. I don't know the story, but I think it must be significant. The cottage hasn't been in use in my time, and I don't think it was used for a long time before then. Do you think it's important in some way?"

"I've no idea. It intrigues me and I would like to know more about it. Was it in such poor state when you inherited the island?"

"It wasn't great, but structurally it was okay. I haven't been near it since soon after I took over the place, so I imagine there's been significant deterioration over the years since then."

I was about to ask another question which nagged me all evening when Delphine arrived with our hot chocolates.

"IneverthoughtI'dbedrinkinghotchocolateonatropicalisland intheCaribbean,"DervlaquippedasDelphinedistributedthemugs.

By then, two questions were nagging at me … and Delphine was just the person to provide answers. "Delphine, do you know if Inspector Bennett had dinner tonight?" Her look told me my question surprised her. "He didn't come to dinner in the dining room while we were there and I thought he might have eaten with his officers instead."

"No. His officers ate with us and he didn't join us tonight. Now you mention it, I don't think he dined in the dining room. As usual, I was in and out of there a few times during the evening. I don't recall seeing him there. I hope he is not ill."

"Perhaps send Sampson to check," Frankie suggested. "Tell Sampson to take the key. If the inspector doesn't answer the door, he should take a quick look inside to make sure the inspector hasn't had an accident or something and is in need of attention."

Frankie gave me a hard look as Delphine scurried off to find Sampson. No words were needed. I knew we shared the same thought. Was Bennett another 'incident' to happen on the island? Conversation did not return to historical topics while we dispatched our hot chocolates and their melting marshmallows. I found myself hoping Delphine would return soon to report on Sampson's expedition to Bennett's room. I had an unpleasant feeling about Bennett, and there was still the other question nagging me. The question I wanted to put to Delphine, but didn't have the opportunity when she brought the chocolates.

With our mugs rinsed and back on the tray awaiting collection, I began the process of bringing our focus back to the story of Lucille Dubois and this island. "Now, when we left her, Lucille had divorced her husband and done very nicely out of it. I imagine her life changed substantially again then. What did she do next?" I had barely posed the question when a knock at the door interrupted proceedings again.

A tentative looking Delphine entered the room. "Excuse me, Miss Dubois, but I thought you might want to know how Sampson got on."

"Thank you, Delphine. I was hoping someone would report back to me. What did he find?"

"Sampson banged on the door for quite a while but nobody answered. He did as you said, and used the key to check. The room was empty. There was no sign of the inspector. I asked Sampson and Dwayne if they saw the inspector during the afternoon or this evening. It seems no one has seen him since afternoon tea. Is there something we should do? I sent Sampson over to the old staff quarters to ask the other police officers if they know where the inspector is. I'm still waiting for him to come back."

"There is little else we can do except wait to see if he's around in the morning. Please let me know what Sampson finds out from the other officers when he returns."

Delphine picked up the tray and was on her way to the door when Sampson appeared in the doorway. One look at Sampson's face, and I felt my stomach tighten. Whatever he found out, wasn't good news. Frankie took charge of the situation.

"Sampson, we just mentioned you. Come in. How did it go with the police officers? Do they know what's happening with Inspector Bennett?"

"I'm sorry to interrupt, Miss, but I was concerned after talking to the officers. They said they thought he was in his room. Because they don't normally see him again after he goes to his room to freshen up for dinner, they were not aware of anything to be concerned about. They also said they were unaware of anything to do with the investigation which might've kept him from dinner. A couple of them seemed a bit concerned. Officer Williams attempted to dismiss their concerns by telling them an idea probably occurred to the inspector and he didn't want to wait until morning to follow up on it."

Williams's comment didn't sit well with me or, at least, it didn't sit well with my instinct which now screamed *RUBBISH* loud and clear in my ear. "Did those who showed some concern about the inspector accept Williams's explanation?"

"I'm not sure, Miss Tessa. I don't think they did really, but Williams is the senior officer and I don't think they were game to argue."

"Thank you for doing that tonight, Sampson. We might talk again in the morning. It is too dark outside to do anything now. All we can do is wait to see what the morning brings."

Sampson and Delphine sported sombre looks as they departed. I saw Frankie rub her hand across her face. It didn't wipe away her concerned look. I felt obliged to intervene somehow in the heavy silence which descended over the room.

"That was not the news we wanted. Perhaps we should abandon our journey through Lucille's life until we're all in a better frame of mind."

"No!" Frankie almost shouted. "I've been infected by your notion of somehow the history of this place having something to do with what's happening here. I think we should continue with the story. I don't know of anything which will help but, as we go through it, one of us might pick up something relevant. I know we're all feeling a bit tense about Bennett at the moment, but none of us would sleep if we went to bed now. Besides, it is still early. I move we continue with our history lesson; all those in favour…"

"Yeah, I suppose so. Now, where were we?"

"Now, what's wrong with you, Tessa? Five minutes ago you were keen to hear more of the story."

"I still am. I was trying to run back over the story so far to find out where we were up to with it. So, carry on… Damn…!"

"What now?" I couldn't blame Frankie for being a bit exasperated with me.

"I'm sorry. A question is nagging at me. I was going to ask Delphine about it when she brought the chocolates, but there wasn't opportunity. So, I made a mental note to ask if she came back. And then I forgot to ask her every time she was here. It's not important. The world won't end because of it, but it probably will annoy me for a long time tonight."

"Right," sighed Frankie, "that's taken care of the question. Now may we…"

"It might have taken care of Tessa's question, but I have one too." We both raised our eyebrows at Dervla. "I'm allowed to have a question, and here it is: what do we think has happened to Bennett? We seem to have a great deal of interest in the fact he didn't come down for dinner tonight. What am I missing about all that?"

"I don't know anything has happened to him, and it's quite possible nothing has. It's the age old complaint: there's never a policeman around when you want one. I wanted to talk to him about something and thought dinner would be a good opportunity; plenty of people around for a defined time meant it couldn't become too involved. His absence was just another frustration to add to today's list."

Dervla nodded to indicate she accepted my answer, but her face said she was sceptical. Best I move things along before the night degenerates too far. "Frankie, I sure we have dealt with everything and are ready for you to move on with the story. What was Lucille's life like after her divorce?"

"She stayed in Spain for about a year afterwards, in a different part of the country from where she lived before the divorce. How much she loved Spain is the stuff of family legend. After about a year, she took a trip to the US; to California and Florida, and then on to the Caribbean. She sailed the area for a while before spending time on Guadeloupe. Anyway, the Caribbean worked its magic on her, and she decided this was where she wanted to put down roots. This island was exactly what she wanted; a place to escape everyone and everything. It took a while to secure ownership but, even before she held title, she engaged a talented Spanish architect to draw up plans *for* this castle. She brought him to the island several times so they could plan the layout and where to build everything."

"It would be a monumental undertaking even in a more civilised and populated location." In my mind, something of this scale was not a project I could manage, even with the most accomplished architect around to assist me.

"How long did all of this take to complete?" Dervla was as overwhelmed by the magnitude of the undertaking as I was.

"Oh, it took quite a while just to clear areas and build temporary accommodation for Lucille and her architect when he visited. The castle was being constructed as other works were going on around it, resulting in the gardens and the outbuildings being more or less completed long before the castle. If I remember family stories correctly, it took something like five years to complete construction of the castle. Of course, some parts of it were habitable before the whole place was completed. Lucille took up residence in the first completed 'wing' as soon as it was possible. As you might appreciate, difficulty accessing the island always was a problem, but more so during the construction phase. Works would be held up for weeks, even months some-times, because conditions were not suitable for boats to land here. The airstrip didn't happen until many years later."

"Did she spend the rest of her life here on the island, or was this a sort of holiday home for Lucille?"

Dervla's question paved the way for what might be a slightly indelicate one I wanted to ask but I let Frankie deal with Dervla's question before asking mine.

"No, it wasn't a holiday home. It was never intended to be. This was where Lucille had decided to make her home. She spent the rest of her life here on the island."

"Did she die here, or did she return to Europe towards the end of her days?" I hoped my question wasn't too offensive for Frankie.

"Oh yes, she died here. Nothing was ever going to make her leave her island." Great, now I want to know where she is buried, but I think I leave that for another time.

"Did you come here as a child?" Dervla asked.

"Yes, we came here at least once a year when I was little. After my grandparents died there wasn't the obligatory attendance at the traditional Christmas get-togethers. They usually lasted the whole week, and involved lots of eating, lots of church, and lots of being bored out of my mind. Both grandparents – my father's parents – were gone by the time I was about thirteen. After that, we spent every Christmas here with Lucille. We continued to come for our annual vacation visit as well, which meant we were here twice a year. Sometimes we stayed in the castle. But, if Lucille had other guests at the same time, we stayed in the cottage Anton was living in. The staff Lucile allocated us for the duration of our stay occupied the cottage Anton used as his studio. They were a husband and wife team. The wife was our housekeeper and the husband helped out around the place when required, and went back to work at the castle when he wasn't needed by us."

It was interesting Frankie never mentioned this place or her visits here during our university days. Maybe the visits ceased by then, for Frankie if not for the family. I decided to ask the question. "Once you left home to go to university, did you continue to visit here?"

"I always came here at least once a year right up until Lucille's death. My mother passed away before I went to university, but my father continued to come here twice a year for a number of years. I think he and Lucille gradually drifted apart due to differing opinions and outlooks on life. His visits dropped to once a year – usually for Christmas – and then ceased all together a few years after I graduated."

Lucille had won me over. She was my kind of woman. I'm not surprised the young Frankie I knew was close to her great aunt. In many ways, I think they were kindred spirits, but perhaps Frankie was not quite as 'liberated' as Lucille was in

179

her youth. From what I remember of Frankie's father, she would not have been allowed to deviate far from what he considered 'proper behaviour'. "Was your father still alive when Lucille died? I'm intrigued by her leaving the island to you and not to a male descendant."

"My father was alive for a couple of years after Lucille died. He was killed in a plane crash, so died relatively young. Bitterness runs in my family and grudges can last forever. Lucille remained bitter about her treatment by her brother. Then, whenever we visited, my father, a pompous, arrogant man in the family tradition, couldn't help himself. He always tried to interfere in Lucille's life; to dictate what she should or shouldn't do. As I said, bitterness and grudges last a long time in this family. The will Lucille made soon after she acquired this place stated quite clearly that none of her estate should pass to any male member of the family line. It also bequeathed this island to me. A codicil added soon after I graduated university provided for her whole estate to pass to me."

What a fascinating story! It managed to plunge me and Dervla into stunned silence for a minute or so after it ended. And, it had filled in quite a slice of the night. I knew it was late, but didn't realise how late until I looked across at Dervla. She looked wrung out and was having to prop her head up.

"It's late; time for bed, I think." No one argued.

Chapter 19

Frankie rattling around in her bedroom woke me. My watch told me it was early. "Why are you up so early this morning? After our late night, I didn't expect anyone to surface early today." Mindful of not waking Dervla, I spoke in a stage whisper.

"No need to whisper; I'm awake." To confirm her statement, Dervla threw back the covers, swung her legs over the side of the couch and sat up.

"I didn't mean to wake anyone, but..." Frankie was all set to launch into an expanded apology until Dervla cut her off.

"You didn't wake me. I woke up about an hour ago and have been dozing on and off since."

I checked my watch again to be sure I hadn't misread the time. "It's too early for breakfast. What shall we do to fill in time until then?"

"You didn't go to collect your belongings last night, so I suggest we go *en masse* to retrieve them before breakfast ... or, if you would prefer, I could ask Sampson to accompany you. They are your only options."

A shower and fresh clothes would be wonderful. "Okay, you win. Everyone get respectable; we're going on a pilgrimage to my room."

Too early for the rest of the guests to be interested in breakfast yet, we encountered no one on our way to my room. The other two insisted they would wait while I took a shower, and promptly made themselves comfortable. Then, it took only a few minutes to pack up my belongings before heading back to Frankie's rooms. An idle thought occurred to me as we crossed the lobby: how long were the three of us to be cooped up together in Frankie's suite of rooms before life returned to normal?

There was still some time to wait for breakfast. Instead of sitting around looking at one another, I decided to use the time usefully. "Let's take a few minutes to plan our day shall we? What are today's priorities, and in what order should we tackle them." Taken by surprise, the other two exchanged blank looks. "Okay, I'll start the list. High on my agenda is finding Bennett. I don't mind if you two have other things to do, but I want to talk to him. Anyone else have any suggestions?"

"I want to go back to Anton's cottage. Yesterday, we nosed about in his studio. Today, I want to subject the cottage to the same treatment." Frankie seemed deep in thought as she spoke. What occupied her thinking became clear when she continued. "Why are the police still on my island? Where were they yesterday when we were out and about? Apart from during my 'discussion' with Bennett about removing Winston from Dervla's room, they were invisible. Well, not quite all of them. We know where Winston was and, while I had Bennett's ear, Williams appeared. What were the other two officers doing? I half expected Anton's place to be swarming with police, but they never came near it while we were there."

"Okay, Anton's cottage is on the list of things to do today; anything else to add?"

No further ideas were forthcoming. Mention of going through Anton's cottage gave birth to the germ of a thought. It refused to mature sufficiently for me to make sense of it until well after breakfast, when it hit me. Was Anton's camera burnt in the studio fire? Perhaps it was something he photographed, inadvertently maybe, which led to his death. While we hadn't agreed what we should do first, I had no doubt we would be going to Anton's place.

I thought Bennett would front up for breakfast, and I would be able to put a couple of questions to him before Frankie dragged us off to Anton's place. He didn't show while we were in the dining room … but we were early starters, and finished before some of the other guests wandered in. Regardless of what else Frankie might have in mind for today, I will devote some time to locating the elusive inspector.

"Fran -kie," Dervla started tentatively as we hiked through the rainforest section of the track. "What do we do if the police are going over the place when we arrive? They are bound to want to know why we are there and what we are up to."

"We are not up to anything. This is my property and I have a valid reason for going there."

"Yes, I know it's your property, but it is also a crime scene – and is off limits to everyone except the police."

"Leave it to me, Dervla. I am prepared for such an eventuality." Dervla shot me a questioning look. I shrugged. I had no more idea what Frankie had in mind than Dervla did.

We shouldn't have worried. There was no sign of the police, and nothing to suggest they were there after we left the studio yesterday. Frankie led the way into the cottage without hesitation and we traipsed in after her. "What are we supposed to be looking for?" Dervla looked uncomfortable about being in the cottage.

A frustrated look flashed across Frankie's features, so I stepped in to avoid what might have been a harsh answer. "We are not looking for anything in particular, Dervla. It's more a case of scanning the place for anything odd or which might in some way suggest what went on here." Anton's camera came to mind again as I spoke. "Frankie, did you see Anton's camera anywhere in the studio yesterday? Do you know where he kept it?"

"Nowhere in particular, I don't think. It generally was lying around wherever he dropped it when he came in. I saw it here in the cottage a couple of times, but most of the time, I saw it in the studio. What's your interest in the camera?"

"Just curious about what he photographed recently. I assume it was a digital camera...?"

"Yeah, an expensive-looking top of the range model..."

"Did he have a laptop or computer of some sort? If it was a digital camera, it's likely he downloaded his images onto a computer."

"Uhmm ... I think ... yeah, he did. It used to sit on the small table over there near the window."

The table was bare now. The power outlet in the skirting board behind it tended to support Frankie's memory of a laptop being here. But, it wasn't there now and nor was its power supply cable. Three possibilities came to mind: Anton took it to the studio and it was incinerated in the fire, he put it away somewhere for safekeeping, or it was stolen. I did not want it to be that last option. I rushed to a nearby sideboard-type cupboard and, in a frantic waste of energy, threw open door and drawers.

Very little of anything lived in the cupboard. Its most abundant content was empty space, closely followed by dust. My next target was a large cupboard against the wall on the other side of the room.

"What are you looking for?" Frankie demanded. "Tell us what you are looking for and we will help you."

Up to then, the other two had wandered around the kitchen dining room area, admiring everything but touching nothing. Before I could answer, a comment by Dervla brought things to a standstill.

"This place is a surprise. It is well appointed for a bachelor pad ... and for an artist at that. Most of the artists I know live in grotty, almost unsanitary chaos. Did your staff look after him, Frankie?"

"Eh ... look after him...? Oh, I see what you mean. No, he had to do his own thing. I provided some basic furniture and fittings, but the rest of it was his doing."

"Remarkably tidy soul then... Would have made someone a good husband. Did he sell much work?" Dervla's line of conversation was interesting, and not what I expected.

While Frankie looked to be pondering whether he sold his work, I jumped in to move my objective along. "Instead of wandering around sightseeing, could you please help look for the missing laptop? Go through every cupboard and drawer – every possible space – where a laptop might be hidden."

"Hidden...?" Frankie echoed. "You think he hid his computer somewhere in here?" I just nodded and shooed them off on their mission.

A few minutes later, Dervla yelled at me as I walked into the next room. "I've already checked everything in there. There is nothing much of anything, let alone a computer."

The same story applied to every room in the cottage; no laptop. While the other two rechecked some places within the cottage, I wandered across to the studio ruins. With no idea of where to start looking for either the camera or a laptop, I simply climbed over the rubble in the front door opening and started from there. The front area of the studio suffered the least damage. While poking about in this part of the building was filthy work, it was relatively easy going.

Such easy-going meant I could be sure of accomplishing a thorough search. Then, as I picked my way through to the rear of the building, I encountered increasing degrees of fire damage. I had pinned my hopes on finding at least one of the sought objects in the destroyed storage area. The degree of damage in there made it difficult to feel confident about the outcome of my search. Nevertheless, the result was disappointing.

I was in the rear section of the building where yesterday we discovered the burnt out stock of paintings when I heard my name being called. Frankie and Dervla were out front of the cottage looking for me. I joined them in perching on some of the big rocks in the clearing while we reviewed our search results. It didn't take long. There wasn't much to review. In spite of our best efforts, no camera or laptop was discovered.

"If we believe those items were here before, and they are nowhere to be found now, do we assume they have been removed? And, if we assume that, whom do we think removed them?" Dervla's questions came as no surprise. The same ones bothered me, and I felt inclined to canvass ideas on the matter.

"It's possible we might be jumping to conclusions if we assume they've been stolen at this early stage of our search. While I don't support the assumption, I also have no clues as to where else they might be. This area seems to be the centre of Anton's life. Frankie, were there any other places on the island Anton was attached to, or frequented regularly?"

"He roamed the island freely, even around to the other side where there is little to see except rainforest and beaches. I don't think he was particularly attached to any of those places. They were just places he went to in his search for inspiration for his artworks. Nowhere comes to mind as a place he might stash his camera or laptop."

"Tessa, it is sounding like maybe it's not too soon to assume they were stolen. How long are we going to avoid accepting the reality of it?"

Dervla was right, but I wasn't ready to concede defeat. I told myself I'd make one last try. "Frankie, you are my last hope. Is there anywhere you can think of Anton might stash his equipment for safekeeping?"

"Maybe we're overlooking one important factor, Tessa. Maybe the police removed those items as part of their investigation. If you think they might contain something of interest, it's likely the police thought so too."

"The possibility did occur to me, Frankie. I can't help thinking, if we knew what was going on here – why Anton was killed and his studio torched – we might be in a better position to work out what, if anything, happened to those items, other than Anton stashed them somewhere safe."

"For Anton to take deliberate measures to keep his camera and laptop safe, suggests he knew what might happen. Perhaps it also says something about the bigger picture; about the game at play here. Because of all the incidents which occurred, I'm inclined to think there is a much bigger game happening on this island."

"Thank you, Dervla, for voicing my exact take on the situation here. I did not mention my thoughts, for fear of giving them credence by their very utterance. Frankie, do you have any thoughts on the subject?" I noticed Frankie had withdrawn from the conversation and was staring off into the distance. Mention of her name brought her back to us.

"I ... am ... not sure. I wasn't ignoring the conversation; just revisiting some childhood memories. As I told you, when we visited here when I was a child, we often stayed in this cottage.

It looked a lot different back then; inside I mean. There was more furniture, better furniture, and…" Without completing the sentence, Frankie sprang up off the rock and started towards the cottage. "Come on, there's something I want to check."

Dervla and I bounced up off our seats and rushed after Frankie. She stopped just inside the front door, causing the two of us to slam up against her. We were standing just inside what had been Anton's kitchen/dining room/sitting room. The minimal furniture in this large space hadn't presented too many likely places for anything to be hidden, and I felt confident my search was thorough. We both stood watching Frankie, and waited for the next instalment of this latest drama.

"Don't look at me like that. I haven't lost the plot. I'm trying to remember. This used to be our sitting room." She gestured towards the end Anton used as a dining room/sitting room. She then turned to face the other end of the space. "This end of the space, where Anton had his kitchen, was my father's area. He had a writing desk, bookshelves and a big overstuffed lounge chair there. And, I think there was a cabinet against that wall, maybe a drinks cabinet."

"It's all very interesting and nice to know, Frankie, but how is it useful in our current quest?" Dervla swivelled her head from side to side as Frankie spoke, looking from one end of the area to the other.

"I don't know if it helps us at all. But, I think I remember something else about this room; something intriguing to me as a child."

While Dervla and I stayed where we were, Frankie slowly picked her way along to the kitchen end and then stopped. Standing still, she visually inspected every inch of the floor. Then I saw her straighten up as if electrified by something. I rushed to join her.

"What did you see? What have you remembered?"

At first, Frankie didn't answer, choosing instead to stare across the floor towards a small cupboard against the back wall. "Give me a hand to shift this cupboard, please."

This was Anton's pantry cupboard, and was packed with cans and packets of foodstuff and was heavy. It took a fair amount of grunting to persuade it to move. While it looked as though it had been moved in years, once we moved, it was obvious that was not the case. Between us, we dragged it out from the wall about a metre. I thought that might be far enough for whatever Frankie wanted to see.

"I need it out further. I'm not sure exactly where this thing was." After more heaving and shoving, Frankie halted the exercise. "That's it; that's enough. Now, it should be about here somewhere. Give me a hand to look please, Tessa."

I followed her lead and studied the floor, but I had no idea what I was looking for, and couldn't see anything out of the ordinary anyway. But Frankie could. Dervla wandered down to where we were messing about with the cupboard, but stood a little way off to keep out of our way.

"Dervla, have a look in the drawers. See if you can find a big knife or something I can use as a lever. It needs to be substantia; strong."

After rattling through drawers of cutlery and kitchen tools, Dervla held up a large chef's knife and asked if it was suitable for whatever Frankie had in mind. Frankie looked sceptical, but motioned for Dervla to bring it over to her. She inserted the tip of the blade between the tiles. It disappeared down a gap to a depth of about fifty millimetres.

"I hope this thing is strong enough and doesn't break."

I watched Frankie trying to lever up the tiles. I examined this floor the same as she had done. I didn't see any gap in the tiles or anything at all different about the area in question.

"Dervla, see if you can find another tool of some sort for Tessa to use. I think it needs the two of us on either end of this slab to lift it. It needs to be strong though or it will snap off and might jam the slab."

"Hang on a minute; I think I saw something outside which might do." She returned moments later brandishing what looked like a fireplace poker. "It was out by that rough barbeque area."

It required more muscle and grunting, but victory was ours. "That's disappointing," Frankie said, and the look on her face reflected her comment. "There used to be a floor safe, or something similar, here in the old days. Looks like it was removed. I wonder why they bothered. I doubt it would have been easy."

Instead of the safe Frankie remembered, we were looking down into what appeared to be an empty hole. Well, maybe it wasn't quite empty. All we could see was a folded up old sack bag. It was about 100 millimetres below the floor level. I wondered about the floor safe which once occupied the space. Surely it would require more depth than we could see at the moment.

"Don't give up yet, Frankie. Let's see what's under the sack bag." I reached in and hauled out the bag. It didn't come out cleanly, but simply unfolded leaving most of it still in the hole "That's interesting. I expected a cloud of dust to come up to meet us. The fact there was none suggests this bag hasn't been in there long."

Excitement had us both scrabbling at the bag. Both trying to haul it out at the same time, we obstructed one another. I sat back on my haunches and gave Frankie free rein to get it out. We both gasped in unison. Frankie found her voice first. "Now, what does that tell us?"

Dervla rushed over to peer over our shoulders. I managed to find my voice.

"I don't know what it tells anyone else but, to me, it says Anton knew something and had something sensitive he wanted to protect. He would not have gone to the trouble of removing that slab and hiding the laptop and camera under the floor for no good reason."

"What do we do with them now?" Dervla asked. "Should we leave them where they are and tell the police about them so they can come for them, or should we remove them now and give them to the police when we get back to the castle?"

"What do you mean? ... Give them to the police! ... Not bloody likely, and not until we've had a damn good look at what's on them."

"Thank you, Frankie, my thoughts exactly. After we know what's on them, then we will decide if we're going to give them to the police. Ladies, here are my thoughts on our situation. So far, we've uncovered very little in relation to the incidents which happened here. What we have learned suggests to me there might be more than one game afoot here. It might not be the case, and it might prove to be all part of one grand overarching masterplan. If only we could get a handle on what the masterplan might be, or who might be driving it, things could start making sense. In the meantime, our immediate problem is how to get this stuff back to the castle and safely into Frankie's rooms without anyone else being aware of what we've found and what we are doing."

"I think I might have a solution for how to transport them without having them obvious to any interested onlookers. Anton had a canvas bag he used to sling across his body when he worked outdoors. He carried pencils, brushes, paints and that sort of stuff in it, and sometimes his camera. I saw it hanging in the cupboard in his bedroom. We could put the camera in it and one of us could wear the bag back to the castle."

"Good thinking, Frankie. That would work for the camera. Now we have to think about how to disguise the laptop." I hadn't seen anything in the parts of the cottage I searched, and I didn't expect we would find something suitable.

"Wait a moment. I just remembered something. Dervla, that cupboard beside you – the one under the sink – open it please. Yes, it's still there. A couple of weeks ago I brought Anton some pineapples and mangoes in it and I kept forgetting to take it home again."

Dervla removed a large opaque plastic bag from the cupboard. It was white with large bright orange and purple daisies all over it; the sort of bag women take to the market when they go to buy fresh fruit and vegetables. The most important thing about it was, it wouldn't look incongruous in any way if one of us had it slung over our shoulder when we returned to the castle … and it would hold the laptop.

With the items bagged and ready to go and the slab replaced in the floor, I was anxious to leave the cottage. Excitement ran through me like an electric current, but so did something else. I wanted to be away from there and safely back in Frankie's rooms as soon as possible to avoid encountering anyone while we were carrying those precious items.

Frankie grabbed the tote bag and slung it over her shoulder. I picked up Anton's artist's bag and hung it across my body. No matter how I arranged it, the bag was far too obviously what it was. Dervla came to the rescue.

"How about we shorten the strap so you can wear it over your shoulder? Leave it long so it hangs about hip level. Yeah, that looks good. Now, stand still while I drape this shirt over the bag. There … what do you think, Frankie? Doesn't she look like a woman who went for a walk with her bag and took her long sleeved shirt off when the day warmed up a bit?"

As Dervla hadn't been to the cottage before, she didn't realise she wouldn't have a problem with being in the sun. So, to protect her alabaster white skin, she took the precaution of throwing a long sleeved shirt over her top. The shirt draped over the bag completely changed its appearance. We tried looking nonchalant as we strolled across the lawn and up the front steps.

At the top of the steps, Frankie halted. "Change of plans; it's morning teatime and the guests are already gathering in the great hall. I think we'd rather not be seen crossing the lobby. Let's go back and come in through the kitchen entrance. That way we won't be seen crossing from the kitchen to the hallway to my rooms."

Delphine and the two staff members looked a bit startled as we traipsed in. Frankie laid a finger across her lips to request their silence, and we carried on unhindered through the kitchen, down the hallway and into Frankie's sitting rooms.

Chapter 20

A collective sigh of relief went up as Frankie locked the door behind us. Frankie's phone rang a couple of moments later. It was Delphine asking if we would like morning tea brought to the room. About ten minutes later, Delphine and Sampson arrived carrying trays laden with enough to feed twice our number.

In between bites of some cream-filled treat, Dervla asked, "What happens now? Which piece of equipment do we look at first?"

"There is something I'd like to do first, before we look at either of those pieces of equipment. It shouldn't take me more than a couple of minutes to check something. While I'm away, could you to please sort out the cables and plug them in to make sure they're fully charged when we start to explore the contents?"

"Yes, Dervla and I could do that, but I want to know where you think you're going. Wherever it is, you're not going alone."

"Frankie, don't make a fuss. I just want to go into the hall to see if Bennett is there for morning tea. I'll just go out through the kitchen, go around and come up the front steps and into the hall. If Bennett is not there, I'll grab a cracker or something and leave again, retracing my steps to here. Nothing will go wrong with that."

"Actually, it's all wrong to start with. As the three of us went for breakfast together, it would be expected the three of us would appear together for morning tea. Your turning up alone would generate unwelcome interest … and that's apart from the fact I wouldn't let you go on your own anyway. Come on, Dervla. Wipe the cream off your face. Let's get these things plugged in and charging, and then we're off to the great hall to be seen together."

I knew it was pointless to argue, so I didn't bother. A few minutes later, we startled the staff again as we made our way out through the kitchen. Morning tea was in full swing when we arrived. Frankie and Dervla smiled and spoke to a few people on our way to the table with the food. My focus was on checking the crowd for Bennett, not on being sociable. He wasn't there. I signalled the other two it was time to leave. We each picked up a morsel from the range on offer and edged our way out into the lobby. As we crossed the lobby, I murmured to the other two.

"Bennett wasn't there. Are his officers likely to be having morning tea in the kitchen? I don't think I want to encounter them on our way back to Frankie's rooms. It would be better if no one other than the staff knew where we are camped at the moment."

"I see your point. You two stay out of sight outside the kitchen while I check out who is inside. It won't look strange if I suddenly appear in the kitchen of my home."

In the event, Frankie didn't have to venture further than the kitchen doorway. Only Delphine remained there, the two male staff members having gone to resume their duties. It took us no time to be back securely locked in Frankie's sitting room. We allowed ourselves a few minutes to dispatch more of the overly abundant morning tea before loading up the trays and placing them outside the door. Then, it was down to the serious business we somehow managed to delay for so long.

By some mysterious means, I became appointed team leader for the exercise. It suited me, and I was more than happy to get on with discovering whatever Anton's two pieces of equipment might have to offer. I elected to start with the laptop. He probably downloaded his photos onto it, except for any last-minute ones with which he didn't have time to download. I held my breath as I waited for the computer to boot up and silently prayed access wasn't password protected.

"Shit! I knew it would be. You wouldn't go to all the trouble of hiding something without putting in place every possible means to protect its contents in the event it was discovered."

"What are you mumbling about? What have you found?" Frankie demanded.

"What I've found is the need for a password to access anything on this machine. I suppose it's too much to ask if you might know what it is."

"Hmm … We-ell, I'd don't *know* what it is, but I could suggest a couple of things for you to try. I've always wanted to go onto Charles' computer to see if he really was writing when he locked himself away for hours in his study. Of course, it was protected like this one. Anyway, one day a while back, I was bitching to Anton about it, and somehow it led onto a discussion about passwords. He claimed the average person picked something useless like their birth date, pet name, or home town. Too many people know such information about you, or could easily find it. I admitted I would be guilty of choosing something similar. So, I asked him how to choose a worthwhile password."

"I hope he didn't suggest some random number, or cypher type approach." I had visions of our efforts and excitement being all for nothing.

"No, of course not. He suggested picking something about yourself. Something which you probably never had occasion to share with anyone else: the name of a favourite artist, favourite tune or composer, where you lost your virginity … that last one took me by surprise. Anyway, from all that, I can suggest a couple of ideas to try. Anton never shared his favourites with me but, from our many conversations across a range of topics, a couple of possibilities come to mind."

I was up for trying anything that might get us in. My only concern was that there might be a 'three strikes and you're out' type of additional safeguard. If there was, it would limit any guessing game about a password. With no other option available, I was prepared to listen to whatever Frankie suggested.

"Okay, don't try anything just yet. Let's brainstorm a few ideas first, and then see where we go from there."

Having no argument with such approach, I gave her free rein to suggest possibilities. Dervla didn't have much to contribute, and admitted she was one of those who uses something half the world probably knew. On the other hand, Frankie worked hard dredging her memory banks and, after a couple of minutes, brought forth her first idea.

"He never said who his favourite musician was, or if he had a favourite tune, but I know he liked jazz and we often discussed it. There were a couple of musicians whom we often mentioned. If I had to pick one he mentioned most often, it would be Charlie Parker."

'Charlie Parker' seemed an unlikely password to me, but it might develop appeal if I think on it for a bit. I opened my pocket notebook to a new page and wrote the name as the first item on what I hope would become a short list. While I did so, Frankie sat deep in thought and staring off into the distance. I waited for the next clue.

"Y-e-ah ... either one of those, but which one?" Frankie's thinking aloud was frustrating, but I bit my tongue rather than interrupt her thought processes. Finally, she was ready to share. "I was thinking about his favourite authors and artists. I didn't get too far with the authors. But, his favourite artists, the ones he talked about most often, were Dégas and Botticelli. I know he admired the changes Botticelli brought about in the way artists worked but, I think his favourite artist might have been Dégas."

To be on the safe side, I added both artists' names to my so far short list. In a bid to try to speed things up, I jokingly asked if Anton ever felt inclined to share with her where he lost his virginity. Frankie turned bright red.

"Good God, no. Our conversations were never so personal. But I was trying to think of places he often mentioned or referred to in some way which suggested they might hold special meaning for him. Give me a moment longer to think on that one."

I obliged. What else could I do? Frankie held all the aces in this password game.

"Yes, I think there is a place name worth a try. I don't know what Anton's connection was to it. He only mentioned it twice that I remember, but I could tell it was special to him. Definitely worth a try: Ordino."

"Ordino…? That's a little village in Spain isn't it?" I had nothing more than a vague recollection of the name in relation to a story I once covered. I didn't go there, but another journo I worked with at the time went there on holidays. As I recall, she called it a quaint little village and raved about its beauty.

"Not quite in Spain; it's in Andorra, the tiny country sandwiched between France and Spain – or Catalonia if you're being precise. On one occasion, he waxed lyrical about the old stone houses in the village."

Being precise about Ordino's location wasn't a high priority for me right now. I added the village's name to my list of potential password clues, but this process was getting us nowhere fast. My gut told me 'Ordino' was obscure enough to make it a good password. Without waiting for any further suggestions from Frankie, I typed it in.

"Bingo! We're in. Now, let's see what his hard drive has to tell us."

All the usual stuff was there: programs, emails, documents … and an extensive gallery folder divided into two sub-folders. One held what I assumed to be photos of Anton's paintings. Frankie confirmed it. The other sub-folder held images he had taken of places and scenery on the island. Quite a few were of luxe-looking cruisers anchored in a bay somewhere. A few older ones were from other places, some of snowy winter scenes. Maybe some of those were from Ordino.

"Any idea where those boats were photographed," I asked.

Frankie took a closer look. "I think they were anchored in the bay between here and the Saint-Marie. He would have photographed them from the other side of this island. I wonder why he was interested in them. It seems quite a few visited the bay over time."

It was a good question. The bay was not on the usual routes used by boaties in these parts, and Saint-Marie had not much to offer the well-heeled sailor. The owner of any one of those luxury yachts would have to be well-heeled.

We spent the next hour dividing our time between examining the laptop and the camera. I confirmed the last shots he took were still on the camera. Anton had not downloaded them to the laptop before stashing everything under the floor. While finally being able to access it all had created a frisson of excitement, realisation of the magnitude of the task ahead somewhat took the edge off it.

Frankie's phone disturbed the silence of her sitting room. "No, thank you, Delphine; we will eat in the dining room. ... God, look at the time. Have the others arrived for lunch yet. ... Okay, that's good. We will escape via the kitchen again. Call me if the police officers arrive before we reach the kitchen." As soon as the call ended, she was on her feet. "Come on you two. It's lunchtime. We need to be through the kitchen to be outside ready to come up the front steps before certain other people take over the kitchen."

By eavesdropping on her phone call, I was way ahead of her and had closed down the computer. Using her master key, I let myself into Charles' rooms and stashed both the laptop and the camera in an empty suitcase on the top shelf in his walk-in wardrobe. I reasoned that, as these rooms were already searched and trashed – and Charles hadn't returned since it happened – they were unlikely to attract attention again. Paranoid maybe but, having found the laptop and camera, I was not about to lose them again ... and I certainly didn't want them falling into the wrong hands until I knew all their secrets.

Just to vary the routine, this time we didn't come into lunch by the front door. Instead, we wandered around the back garden and spent some time looking at the various plants before climbing the back stairs and ambling through the great hall on our way to the dining room. Something caught my eye on our way through the hall and made me stop for a moment. Frankie noticed I had dropped behind.

"What's wrong, Tessa? What happened?" I shook my head and rushed to catch up to the others. "It's important we stick together; safety in numbers and all that stuff."

She expected me to explain why I had stopped. It wasn't the right time or place. Besides, I wanted to think about what I'd seen before I said anything to her. "Sorry; I was busy sightseeing. Come on; let's join the others in the lunchtime feeding frenzy."

Lunch held no interest for me. Bennett's absence from the table again disturbed me and occupied my mind. After pushing food around my plate for what seemed like a polite period of time, I checked the other two's progress with their meals. Their plates were almost empty, so I felt safe in suggesting we didn't linger longer than necessary. It had the desired effect. Moments later, Frankie pushed her chair away from the table and stood up.

"If you've finished lunch, Dervla, we might continue our sightseeing. There are a few other special plants I'd like to show you. Are we right to go now?"

This time, we exited through the front door and wandered out onto the front lawns. I shepherded them off in the direction of that derelict cottage in the rainforest. At the large garden bed about halfway between the castle and the rainforest, I stopped and feigned great interest in some of the plants in the garden bed. I intended using this pause in proceedings to explain why I brought them this way, Frankie jumped in ahead of me.

"There is nothing special in this garden bed, so why did you carefully orchestrate our arrival here? What are you up to, Tessa?"

"Bennett wasn't at lunch again today. I don't believe in coincidences, and I have an unpleasant feeling about his absence. We talked about going to have a look at that derelict cottage. My instinct insists I go there now. I'm not asking you to come with me, but I am going to look at the cottage now."

"No problem; but we are not going to go charging off into the rainforest from here. We are going to take a leisurely wander a short distance along the track towards the airstrip. Not far along, is an ill-defined track which should take us to where we want to go. Perhaps a more covert approach might prove worthwhile. You never know who might be watching."

Damn! Why does Frankie always have to be right, I wondered as we started off along the main track. Frankie led the way and made a show of pointing out various orchids in the trees as we went. Earlier, on my way through the great hall, I grabbed a small bottle of water and shoved it in one of the pockets of my cargo pants. It was an impulse based on habit. Now I regretted it. The weight of the bottle dragged my trousers down on one side and, every couple of minutes, I found myself having to hitch them up again. Ditching the bottle would appear crass and could offend Frankie. There was nothing for it but to persevere.

"Okay, this is where we turn off onto the track to the clearing with the derelict cottage. Watch your step. These days, it's *almost* a track, if you know where it is."

The overgrown route we followed confirmed Frankie's description of it as 'almost a track'. Nevertheless, the going was a little easier than thrashing and bashing our way through the rainforest as I did the other night. This track was an obstacle course of fallen branches, overhanging trees and deep leaf litter … and home to hordes of mosquitoes.

While I wasn't enjoying the experience, my concern was for Dervla. Was she up to this so soon after her attack? We hadn't considered her recuperation at all today. A wave of guilt flooded over me. I took to stealing sideway glances at her as we trudged through the rainforest. She seemed to be managing as well as any of us. After about ten minutes or so of hard slogging, a clearing opened up ahead of us. At the rear of the clearing stood the derelict cottage.

Having reached our destination, we regrouped just inside the clearing and took a few moments to survey the area. Between us and the cottage was the fireplace of roughly placed rocks where the two men sat the other night. The depth of ash in it suggested plenty of use in recent times. While the cottage presented as no lesser sad sight by daylight, somehow it looked less frightening than it did at night.

"A priority will be to research the story associated with this cottage. I don't remember ever being told the story but, somewhere along the line, I worked out it related to some tragedy. Why are you so keen to check it out, Tessa?"

"I'm not sure why. I suppose one reason is, after the episode here the other night, I wanted to see what the place was like. It was hard to gain a proper feel for the place in the dark. But, if I'm honest, my gut is telling me I might find answers here to some of my questions about what is happening on this island. Don't ask me what I'm looking for…" I knew that was the question Dervla was about to ask. "I'm working on the assumption I'll know it when I see it."

"Right; that makes it easy – not at all." Frankie said, and added a disbelieving shake of her head for emphasis. "So, what do you want us to do?"

"Uhmm … I want to look around out here first, without trampling on any existing evidence. No, I don't know what I'm looking for. I'm just looking. Maybe you two might make yourselves comfortable on those big rocks beside the fireplace while I look around out here. Then, we could have a poke about inside."

No argument, so I left them to sort out their seating arrangements and began a slow and methodical prowl, gradually working my way in towards the cottage. The footprints from the escapee's dash for freedom remained visible across the clearing. A whole mess of prints entering the clearing from the right hand side of the cottage were by Bennett's men when they stormed the place. But, there were other footprints, several tracks of them, all leading to or from the cottage.

Those tracks gave me pause for thought as I tried to rationalise their existence. Of course there would be tracks if the escapee was using the cottage as his hideout. He wouldn't spend his whole time indoors. I had almost convinced myself of the veracity of such thinking when I noticed another important factor. Those tracks all came and went from the rainforest. I could accept the escapee might wander around in the clearing, but I struggled with the concept of his making frequent trips into the rainforest. After photographing the tracks with my phone, I continued working my way towards the cottage.

Frankie called out, "Have you discovered anything yet?"

"Yes. I've discovered the mosquitoes here are vicious. I think we should…"

A sound from inside the cottage made me freeze midsentence. The other two stiffened but remained seated. I put a finger to my lips and beckoned them over to me. With our heads together, I whispered, "I was about to say we should check inside. I still think it's what we should do, but are you up to it? I've no idea what we might find in there, but I have a suspicion it might be a person."

"I'm up for it, and none of us is going in alone." Frankie looked at Dervla and continued. "I'm not sure you should come with us. One hit on the head is more than enough, and I don't want anything else happening to you while you are here."

"You can think what you like, but I need answers … and I have a score to settle. I don't know if the answers are in there, but I'm as sure as hell going to find out. So, how do we do this?"

Armed with no great strategy or even a hint of a plan, we tiptoed to the door which now hanging at a drunken angle after coming off its top hinge when the escapee made his break for freedom. "I'll lift and drag the door open while you and Dervla rush in. Don't go in too far. Just go as far as the opening. Then the three of us will go in together."

… And that's what we did. At least, that was the intention, but we stopped short after only a couple of paces into the interior of the cottage. A collective gasp went up from the three of us. While the other two stood rooted to the spot, I did a 360 degree pivot to be sure there no one else was around. No one other than the person tied up in the corner. Having found no other persons in the building, I rushed to the one tied up.

Chapter 21

"Christ! It's Bennett. Frankie, give me a hand. Let's see if we can sit him up and remove that gag."

Bennett's condition was worse than poor; barely conscious, and drifting in and out. We hauled him into the sitting position against the wall and tried removing the gag. The gag, a length of filthy cotton material, had a huge knotted arrangement shoved hard into Bennett's mouth, and its tails tied in a tight knot behind his head. Neither Frankie nor I had any success untying the tails. Frankie did a version of that self-frisk thing in which you check all your pockets.

"Now, if we were half decent Boy Scouts, or whatever, we would be carrying a trusty pocketknife. We have to remove the gag, but how the hell are we going to do it if we can't untie it?"

I knew it was a fruitless exercise, but we appeared to be in what was once the cottage's kitchen. I wrenched open the drawers of what remained of the cupboards. No surprise I suppose, no knife left conveniently about. At the other end of the room, a window was broken sometime in the past. Broken in from the outside, it left shards of glass littering the floor.

They are the closest thing to a knife around here, I told myself as I raced to the other end of the room.

After selecting a couple of the most suitable looking pieces, I was back kneeling beside Bennett. I tried to allay his fears and keep him calm. "I don't know if this is going to work, but it's the best option we have. I'll try not to damage you in the process, but I can't guarantee it. So, please stay as still as you can and bear with me while I try this." His eyes flashed open. He looked up at me and blinked to signify his understanding.

At best, the process of cutting through the gag was brutal. I eventually worked out the best way to approach the situation was to insert a glass shard beneath the gag and then saw through towards the surface. The only problem was the gag was tied too tightly for the glass to slide between the gag and Bennett's cheek. The only way to achieve it was for me to push his cheek inwards as hard as I could and then quickly slide the makeshift knife into position.

To cut with it, the glass had to be used on its edge. While I'd chosen the piece with the narrowest pointy end, the width of the shard made the mission almost impossible. Nevertheless, I got on with it … and Bennett received the inevitable cuts and scrapes in the process. He stiffened, and winced, and screwed up his eyes on numerous occasions as I sawed away at the fabric, but he never fought me or pulled away. After what seemed like forever, final threads parted, and the cut ends hung loose. I eased knotted arrangement out of his mouth. For a few moments it seemed his mouth would never work properly again after being stretched open for so long.

As I worked on removing the gag, Frankie, using a second piece of glass, sawed at the ropes binding his wrists. They were tied behind his back and around the leg of a big old cast-iron wood-fired stove. The stove was never going to move. Bolts in the concrete anchored its feet to the floor.

"I could do with some help around here. I don't seem to be making much impression on this rope." Frankie sounded desperate.

My intention was to help her with the ropes after dealing with the gag, and was about to when she asked for help. As I went to scramble to my feet, Bennett croaked something. I didn't understand. I put my ear close to his mouth and asked him to repeat what he said. It was a rasping croak, but this time I understood him: *water*…

Perhaps the habits of a lifetime should be maintained, even if they pull your trousers down on one side. I whipped out the bottle of water and, cradling his head in the crook of my arm,

I held the bottle to his lips. He tried gulping it down. More ran down his chest than down his gullet. "Just small sips … I know you're thirsty, but just take small sips." He nodded and did as I instructed.

After only a few sips, he was exhausted. I knew he was still thirsty, but he began choking, even on the smallest sip of water. "Rest for a minute, Tom, and then we will try again. While you do, I'll give Frankie a hand with those ropes. Just lean back against the wall and relax."

Scrambling back onto my feet was a challenge. After kneeling for so long, my legs weren't inclined to take my weight. I managed to struggle halfway up before taking a breather. Bent over and supported by my hands on my thighs, I noticed Dervla was not with us. "Where is Dervla? She hasn't wandered off on her own has she?"

"No. I haven't gone anywhere. I'm here in the doorway keeping an eye out for uninvited visitors." The relief at hearing Dervla's voice gave me the impetus required to become erect.

"Here, wrap this tissue around the end of the glass you're using. It might stop the glass cutting into your hand for a while." As I eased myself down to my knees beside Frankie, I noticed her hand was bleeding from a couple of cuts inflicted by the glass she was using. The tissue won't last long before the glass shreds it. I reached around to retrieve the recently removed gag and tore it into two pieces. Each of us, then with a piece of the gag wrapped around our tool, attacked the ropes with renewed vigour.

Frankie yelped in surprise as the rope she worked on parted. Bennett was becoming agitated. He needed more water. Leaving Frankie to continue sawing through my rope, I moved around to the other side of Bennett and helped him drink a little more. He calmed down again, and the water seemed to lubricate his vocal chords. This time, his words were clearer and louder.

"You must leave. Don't let them catch you here. They are ruthless and would not hesitate to kill you. They have taken my weapon."

"I didn't think your lot carried weapons."

"We don't but, after the call from MI6, I thought it wise to carry my side arm. I need you alive to warn the authorities. Otherwise, there is no future for anyone on this island. They have backed themselves into a corner. There is no way they can just up and leave the island now. Please go. Leave me here. I'm resigned my fate, but I don't want lives lost my account."

"*Mon Dieu!* We will not leave you here. Such merde on my island...! What is behind all this?" This is the Frankie I remembered; the one who reverts to the odd word in her native tongue when stressed or angry. "Ah, the second rope is broken. Tessa, please finish untying the inspector. I have a call to make."

As she made her way to the door, I heard the beginning of her call. "Delphine, there are a couple of important things I need you to do. They are urgent, and I want you to be very careful and to make sure no one is aware of what you are doing. Go to the bedside table on the left-hand side of my bed. Under some personal hygiene products and some other stuff, you will find a handgun. It is loaded. The safety catch is on, but you should handle it with care. Take it and then go to Mr Charles' bedroom. In his bedside table you will find another handgun. Take this one with you as well."

Concerned about what Frankie was organising, I abandoned Bennett's ropes and followed her to the door. From there, I heard more of the conversation with Delphine.

"...Stress to them the urgency of what they must do. After the men hitch the spray rig trailer to one of the carts, they must remove the tank from the trailer, and then cover that part of the trailer with a tarpaulin so no one can see the tank is missing. Then, without hurrying, they must look as though they are going out to spray weeds along the track to the airstrip. They need to leave the cart and the trailer beside the main track and use the old track to the derelict cottage to bring the handguns to me. I will..."

I heard enough. Whatever Frankie was planning might happen quite soon. Bennett needed to be free and able to be moved. I needed to finish dealing with those ropes. After a few moments, his were arms. In spite of his shoulders being stiff and sore from his arms being tied back behind him, he eased his hands around to the front and began working on reinstating circulation. My next task was to sever the rope around his ankles.

That rope didn't present the same degree of challenge as the ones around his wrists. Within a few minutes, his ankles were free. I worked on them to restore circulation. Frankie returned after her phone call and helped work on Bennett's ankles. We were about to try hauling him to his feet when Dervla put us on high alert.

"I hear sounds. I think someone is coming. What do we do?"

"Move back inside and stand behind the door." I called my instruction as loud as I dared under the circumstances.

Frankie scrambled to her feet. "Incoming friendly or unfriendly do you think? I'm hoping it's friendly. There's been just enough time for Sampson and Dwayne to arrive. I'm hoping it's them."

She went to the other side of the doorway and peered out. After a few moments I saw her relax and step out into the open doorway. "In here please, Men. We need a hand." As the two men passed her to enter the cottage, Frankie asked, "Did you bring the two items I asked for?" She received confirmation. Both men dived into their pockets and each produced a handgun.

Then Frankie took charge of the situation again. "We have an urgent but extremely delicate operation to carry out. I need you to take Inspector Bennett out to the golf cart and hide him in the spray rig trailer in the space usually occupied by the tank. Make sure he is well covered with the tarpaulin so no one can see what is in the trailer. This could be dangerous. If you feel concerned about it in any way, you must say so now. I won't be angry or upset." The men just grinned at her. "If you are sure you want to do this, keep one of the handguns. You must protect yourselves at all costs."

Both men laughed. Sampson explained. "When we were given the two handguns to bring to you, we knew something serious was happening. We came prepared. These protective jackets we wear when spraying proved useful." In unison, both men reefed open their long, loose protective jackets to reveal the rifles they carried tucked in against their sides. "We can take care of ourselves – and the Inspector – if required. You keep the handguns. I hope you don't need to use them."

While Frankie talked with her two staff members, Dervla and I helped Bennett to his feet. His struggle to stand on his weakened legs lessened as we helped him take small steps to encourage them back to life. Bennett overheard Frankie's instructions to her staff and was not happy.

"No, Men, I can't go with you. I am barely able to stand, and I cannot go tramping through the trees. I would slow you down ... not to mention putting your lives in danger. It would be better if you helped these ladies get away from here."

"Inspector Bennett, these are my staff members. They take their instructions from me. And, my instructions are for them to take you safely back to the castle and keep you concealed until I return. There will be no argument. That is what will happen." This is the second time Bennet has unleashed the dragon in Frankie. He should realise by now he won't win against her.

Bennett was about to continue the argument, but Sampson advancing towards him made him stop. Sampson's face was almost split in two by his wide grin displaying a lot of straight white teeth. Bennett's attempt to back away was useless. In one swift flowing movement, Sampson hoisted Bennett in a fireman's lift over his shoulder and headed for the door.

"Come on, Dwayne, let's take this bloke home." He had a question for Frankie on his way past. "Will you be okay to get away from here, Miss Dubois? The inspector might be right. Maybe we should be taking you back to the castle."

"We will be fine, Sampson. You have your instructions. Please be on your way."

Bennett called over his shoulder as they carried him out. "Mind how you go... please."

The three of us stood in the doorway and watched the two men – and Inspector Bennett – cross the clearing and disappear into the rainforest. Then Frankie took command again.

"Tessa, choose your weapon." She held out both handguns for me to choose from. "I know it was a long time ago we were members of the university's pistol club, but I assume you remember how to use one of these." Too stunned to pay much attention to either weapon, I simply reached out and took the nearest one. "Good choice; in case you're wondering, that is Charles' gun."

When she spoke, all colour seemed to have drained from Dervla's face. "I hope you are being overcautious; over dramatic. Why the guns…? You don't really expect to have to use them, do you?"

"Not unless we have to, Dervla. Now, that's enough of this standing around chatting nonsense. We need to get out of here. Follow me. I think it wise to avoid the track we used to come here." With that, she pivoted and strode out into the clearing.

Frankie crossed the clearing at a sharp angle to the left to enter the rainforest after only a short distance across open space. Dervla and I rushed to catch up with her. After that, the route was reminiscent of my night in the trees. It was rough going as there wasn't even an ill-defined track to follow. Our pace was slow, partly due to the conditions, but also out of concern for Dervla. About fifteen minutes after we entered the rainforest, Frankie halted.

"We've been heading roughly towards the airstrip. Just up ahead, we should emerge from the trees and onto the main track. 'Caution' is the keyword for this last stage … in case anyone happens to be patrolling the track."

Her words made my stomach tighten. I instinctively slid my hand into my pocket and wrapped it around the handle of the weapon nestled there. For a moment, I was amused by the memory of how annoyed I was by the bottle of water pulling my trousers down on one side. Now, the gun in my pocket was doing the same thing, but it didn't bother me at all.

No welcoming committee waited for us when we emerged from the trees. Somehow managing to maintain a leisurely attitude and pace, we set off for the castle. As we approached its front lawns, Frankie resumed tour guide mode. We didn't head directly for home, but continued along the edge of the front lawn … with Frankie stopping every few metres to point out some plant or another.

At the far corner of the lawn, we turned to circle back to the main building, passed the entrance of the track to Anton's place, and ended up in the back garden. Afternoon tea was all but over when we arrived. Only Jackson and one other guest remained yarning near the food table, which was now bare. Frankie commented on the fact loud enough for the two men to hear.

"Oh dear, it looks like our horticultural jaunt has deprived us of afternoon tea. Make yourselves comfortable while I see if I can organise a little extra for us."

As she approached the steps, Sampson and Dwayne came down them to clear away the remnants of afternoon tea. I saw Sampson give Frankie a slight nod, before announcing they would return to the kitchen to ask Delphine for something for the three of us. Frankie was beaming as she returned to us. "All is well. Let's rest our legs after our long walk."

The knowing look she gave us suggested her 'all's well' comment had nothing to do with afternoon tea, but told us Bennett was safe. Safe … but where and how, I wondered. We all relaxed a little when Jackson and his companion wandered back into the building. In spite of being alone in the back garden after their departure, no one uttered a word other than about plants. It wasn't until Sampson and Dwayne returned with our afternoon tea we learned of their trip back with Bennett. Sampson gave us the details.

"No problems, Miss Dubois; when we were close enough to be seen from here, Dwayne walked beside the cart and pretended to be checking for weeds. After a short distance, he climbed on board and we drove around to the shed. We didn't want to leave the inspector in the trailer or in the shed in case people investigated our disappearance. So, we continued searching for weeds all the way around to Delphine's place. Bennett was smuggled in through the side entrance, and Delphine's mother is looking after him. We put the trailer back in the shed and replaced the tank. After all that, we still managed to be on time to set up for afternoon tea."

After the two men went back inside, there was little conversation as we indulged in the goodies Delphine provided. Then it was our time to go inside and to work out what to do next. On our way through the great hall, Frankie announced in a voice loud enough for the world to hear, "Come with me. We can exit through the kitchen. I want to thank Delphine for afternoon tea."

It was obvious Frankie was creating the impression we were on our way outdoors again. I didn't really feel like peering at more plants, but I would go along with whatever she planned. Our time in the kitchen was brief and consisted of nothing more than a brief conversation between Frankie and Delphine. Then, Dwayne walked through the lobby and entered the kitchen. He reported no one in sight on the upstairs gallery or the ground floor. It was our cue to escape the kitchen and head for Frankie's rooms.

In spite of being pleased we weren't going to look at anymore plants, I wanted to talk to Bennett and not spend time sitting around in Frankie's rooms. Once we were back in her sitting room, I voiced my thoughts in the most diplomatic way I could.

"Of course we need to talk to Bennett. I wanted to come back here while we worked out how best to achieve it. Tessa, you seem to have a reasonable rapport with the man, so you might be best to talk to him. My relationship with him so far is unlikely to be conducive to extracting information from him. My thinking is this: Dervla and I will remain here while you talk to Bennett. As a journo, you are much better at asking the right questions to extract any information he has. How does that sit with you?"

"I'm happy to question the man. Whether I would be successful is another matter. My real concern at the moment is for Delphine and her mother. It's unacceptable for their lives to be put in danger because we didn't better manage the situation. I don't know what else we can do with Bennett, but there has to be some way we can keep him safe while removing the other women from potential danger. I'm open to ideas."

After a short discussion, it was agreed our best move would be to bring Bennett back to Charles' rooms where, between us, we should be able to keep him safe while extracting whatever information he has. As usual for me, the big question was how to move bodies about in this vast building without the rest of the world knowing about it. I voiced my concerns

"Oh, don't worry about that. This wing of the building is very good at isolating its residents from the rest of the place. Anywhere in this wing can be accessed without going near the lobby, except for the kitchen. That includes Delphine and her mother's quarters at the far end. The bit you know of this wing might seem straight forward, but it's like a rabbit warren with passageways running all through it. I agree we can't leave him with the women. Maryann might argue she is the best person to care for him, but their quarters are not really designed to take in an extra person."

We both looked at Dervla in surprise when she asked, "Who is Maryann?" It wasn't too hard to work out the woman referred to was Delphine's mother. After enlightening Dervla, there was unanimous agreement we should spirit Bennett out of the women's quarters and into Charles' rooms.

To my surprise, the exercise involved little time and almost no fuss. As soon as Bennett was settled in his new accommodation, Frankie made us all coffee and we got down to the serious business of information extraction. In line with our previous agreement, I led the questioning. You didn't need to be a Mensa member to work out what the first question should be.

Chapter 22

"Let's start with the most recent stuff. Who was responsible for your enforced stay in the derelict cottage, and why?"

"I think you found him officious."

"Williams…? One of your officers was responsible?" The man struck me as a ball of ambition. Surely this would do his future prospects no good at all.

"Yes, Williams was one man involved in what happened to me. I brought four officers to the island with me. Williams and one other apparently were playing for another team, while Winston and the fourth officer, Patrick, were squarely on my team. I knew something was amiss soon after we arrived here. It's why I tended to send the officers off to investigate various issues while I poked about on my own. I became suspicious of Williams' behaviour, and he sensed it. Make no mistake, my days were numbered. I overheard Williams telling his offsider I would be found somewhere out in the rainforest some distance away from any of the buildings. The plan, as far as I could determine, was for me to die from lack of food and water, and then for my body to be taken out into the rainforest in the hope it looked like I had become lost and died out there."

A sharp intake of breath by Dervla made me wonder about her presence, but I didn't have time to dwell on it. Bennett cut across my thoughts.

"I couldn't believe my luck when I discovered Tessa McNally was one of the guests here. I knew… No, I hoped your nose for a story might be my salvation. After everything happening here, I hoped you would want answers and would do your damnedest to find them."

"If we can leave the more recent stuff for a moment, I think I'd like to go back to the beginning … to when this series of events began. For us here on the island, it all began the night of Frankie's birthday party and, more specifically I think, when the storm occurred. Perhaps it might be more accurate to say everything which happened here began *after* the storm. Regardless, the storm heralded an interruption of idyllic life in paradise. Coincidence lacks credence in my world. There was too much coincidence involved over the course of that night. Not the least of it was you and your officers already being at the airport when Sampson finally managed to contact you. I don't buy luck being involved."

"No, luck didn't play a big part in it. The storm the previous night was particularly severe on Saint-Marie. But, severe tropical storms aren't uncommon in this part of the world. Our phone lines went down and the radio tower sustained damage. The usual pockets of habitation on the island likely suffered damage. After such an event, it is not unusual for me to fly over the island to assess the damage. On this occasion, I made the magnanimous gesture of inviting all of my officers to come along. That's how come we were at the airport when Sampson got through to me on my mobile. I already planned to fly over of Île Verte to check for any damage here as well."

"Okay, I'll buy that up to a point. Your 'magnanimous gesture' smells like another of those coincidences I have difficulty swallowing."

"You're right. It was an almost spur of the moment decision, but it wasn't a coincidence. Miss Dubois, how much do you know about your husband's life; what he did, what he was?"

"What is there to know? He was a writer. It's common knowledge, and it was for his writing he was awarded his gong. I suppose, in his earlier years, he found employment in other capacities until his career as a writer took off."

"Frankie, didn't you ever discuss his earlier life; what he did before you knew him, and before the world knew him as a writer? Do you even know where he lived or worked during those early years?" I struggled to believe two people could form a relationship and marry without ever having explored such background details. I saw the redness creep up her throat and expand across her face. Christ, I hadn't meant to embarrass woman, but my questions must have been too close to the bone.

"It will be difficult for you to believe … it's difficult for me! … but I don't know any of what you're asking. Oh, don't get me wrong. Over the years I did ask about where he had lived, the places he visited, his work, how his writing career began… Every time, to every question, his answers amounted to nothing more than a fob-off. I gave up trying to get to know the man and I suppose, after a while, I didn't want to know him. What I did know was enough to convince me I didn't like what he was, and certainly didn't love him."

The pained look on Dervla's face was almost heartbreaking. After Frankie finished speaking, it took Dervla a while to find her voice. It had a catch in it. "Why did you stay with the man? Why continue to live in such an unhappy situation where you were virtually bullied by the man you married? I suppose the big question is, why did you marry him in the first place?" Then Dervla bit her lip and shook her head a couple of times before continuing. "I'm sorry, Frankie. It's none of my business, and I didn't mean to be so rude or to upset you."

"You see, Inspector Bennett, I have two very loyal friends. Our friendship goes back a long way, and you have no idea how much I regret having lost contact with them for so long. All three of us always spoke our minds without fear of repercussion. So many times I thought how my life would have been different if we remained in contact. I often imagined Tessa telling me to wake up to myself and ditch Charles Allerton."

After a few moments of uncomfortable silence, Bennett cleared his throat and tentatively entered into what could be sensitive territory. "I see … Miss Dubois, perhaps I am in a position to fill in some of those blanks for you, but I'm not sure …"

"For God's sake, Bennett, call me Frankie. If you know anything to fill in any of those gaps – anything at all – then tell me. I'm not some delicate petal who can't handle whatever it might be. So, roll it out … and let's all get to know my husband a little better."

Not wanting to nod and have everyone see me, I gave Bennett a long, hard blink which I hoped he would interpret as confirmation he should proceed with sharing whatever he knew of Charles Allerton. The good Inspector read me correctly.

"It's difficult to know how, and where, to begin. Perhaps, in this case, it isn't at the beginning, but much closer to the end." Bennett paused for a moment to unscramble his thoughts. I used the time to try dealing with the frisson of excitement coursing through me, and trying to ignore my tightening stomach. Having sorted out his thoughts, and whether I was ready or not, Bennett launched into his story.

"The real reason I was at the airport the morning after the storm, was due to a call I received on my mobile about half an hour before I spoke to Sampson; a call from MI6 in London. They started trying to reach me during the height of the storm the previous night, and were becoming frantic when they couldn't contact me. The contents of the call are classified, and I don't intend sharing them. Nevertheless, I can tell you it centred on concerns about Île Verte, and was the catalyst to send me and my officers to the airport."

"MI6 …? Why would they …"

"Perhaps, if we let Tom continue, it might become clear." I didn't want Frankie holding up the rest of the story by asking questions which Tom's information might answer. He took the hint and rushed to continue his story.

"MI6 called me because what was happening here – or what they believed might be happening here – was of concern to them. I knew of their interest in this area before I left London to take up my post here. At the time, I didn't take much notice of it because, if something of interest to the British spooks was happening in this part of the world, it would be MI5 who were interested. Over the three years I've been here, I've managed to learn a little bit about their concerns. This is where the story jumps into a different timeframe. Not long after he graduated University, Charles Allerton became a spook. He worked with MI5 for a number of years before switching to MI6. His work during those years had him moving about a fair bit, particularly in troubled hotspots. Eventually, research for his writing became the smokescreen to cover his many visits to various places in Europe and the Middle East. While, ostensibly, his gong was for his work as a writer, he earned it as a spook. Anyone with any interest in the matter would realise his paltry body of writing would never earn him such recognition."

"I'm sorry, Frankie, but I arrived at that conclusion before we left London. I suspected there was something else but, without more time to research, I just had to accept that there was something strange about it." She shrugged in reply and Tom continued.

"Somewhere along the line, probably not too long before you were married, some sort of bad smell attached to Charles and a few others in his group. A couple were tried quietly under the Secrets Act, found guilty of treason or something of that nature, and disappeared off the face of the earth into some prison arrangement somewhere. The rest of them escaped trial and, in essence, were exonerated of any wrongdoing. In spite of that, the smell continued to linger on two or three of them."

"You're telling me Charles was one of those under scrutiny for breaching the Official Secrets Act? I can't believe it. Apart from anything else, he didn't have the balls for it." Somehow, I managed to stifle a giggle. I had not expected to hear that from Frankie.

"Let's say any smell attaching to him was by way of association. Regardless, they could hardly retain him in full active capacity when his other smelly associates were dismissed. The long and short of this story is, Charles continued to work in a limited covert way for the spymasters. His many visits to various places overseas to research for the writing he supposedly was doing here on the island tended to be command performances. And, his continued association with some of his doubtful former colleagues would be difficult for him. They worked together; were close friends and allies. But now, whenever they met up, he was torn between yarning over old times with them, and sussing out for his masters what they might be up to."

"Without telling me anything you shouldn't, am I right in assuming some of those 'smelly associates' might be here on this island at the present time?" Bennett chose not to answer, but dropped me a hint of the nod. "Here is a left-field question for you, was Anton somehow involved in all this cloak and dagger nonsense?"

"Miss Dubois ... Frankie, what do you know about Anton Benoir's background?"

"Other than he is French and an artist, not much else. I don't think he spent his whole life in France, but spent short periods of time in out of the way places. I imagine it was in the pursuit of his art. I don't know if he was a *friend* of Charles, but Charles knew him or knew of him. It was Charles who arranged for him to come to the island, and then suggested he take over the cottages to stay and work here."

Bennett was hesitant in asking his next question. "Did you have much to do with Anton while he was here? Did he ever share anything about his life with you?"

"We were quite close. Don't read anything into the comment. I think we both had no one else to talk to. Apart from that, I think he genuinely enjoyed my company as much as I enjoyed his. So, yes, I spent quite a lot of time talking to Anton. Now you're asking, I find it strange to admit I still don't know any more about him than I did when he first arrived."

"What about you, Tessa, did you learn anything about his background? You seem to get on well with him." I didn't feel comfortable under the hard look Bennett gave me.

"I liked what little I knew of Anton. We exchanged a few sentences the afternoon before the birthday party, and about the same amount of conversation at the dinner later. None of it provided any insight into the man's background. I did form the opinion we might have been kindred spirits as a result of our

217

shared view of the mob we were with. But I know nothing of Anton. Oh, I believe he has a brother. I remember you, Frankie, asking if anyone had advised his brother of Anton's death."

Frankie nodded and confirmed my statement. "Yes, I believe he had a brother. He mentioned him a couple of times, not in any particular context. The brother, I think, was his only family. I have no idea what happened to his parents or any other members of the family as it was never discussed. I assume it was more a case of what I assumed from unrelated conversations. But, while on the subject, I'm surprised his brother hasn't arrived on the island ... Or, is he being prevented from coming here?"

"Umm ... Perhaps there are a few things to sort out before we proceed to answering your question. First of those: Anton Benoir was not his real name. His real name doesn't matter at this stage. There is no brother wanting to come to the island. There is no brother, not as such."

"Of course he had a brother. They corresponded regularly, and I know he often called his brother. They had long chats two or three times a month. I'm sorry, Inspector, but in this matter you are wrong. Anton did have a brother."

"Yes, I don't doubt there was much contact between the two men, but the other man was not Anton's brother. I suppose, for the purposes of this conversation, we should think of him as Anton's handler. He has lived in France for a number of years, but he's not French. And, nor was Anton. If we had to allocate Anton a nationality, we might be tempted to say he was Spanish. Even that would be wide of the truth."

"Tom, you described the man Frankie thought was Anton's brother as Anton's handler. In my world, that translates as Anton was also in the spook business. Which side was he on? Whom did he work for?"

"Again, that's not something for this conversation. Suffice to say at this stage, he was not a British spook, but worked closely with and for them. He worked closely with Charles for a while. Then, as I understand it, a messy situation developed. Somehow, Anton's life expectancy became considerably shortened. I suspect that's why Charles brought him here and persuaded him to stay. Now, in answer to your question Frankie, Anton's handler does know of his demise but, for obvious reasons, won't be coming to Île Verte."

"This is all very interesting, Tom, but I'm not sure it's answering any questions. If anything, for me, it's creating a whole lot more. Nevertheless, we should proceed, and I do have a difficult question to ask." Bennett gave me an exaggerated cringe which I ignored. "On the night of the storm, or early next morning, Charles Allerton seems to have disappeared. Having listened to what you've said so far, I now believe there might be one of two possible scenarios involved: either he has been spirited off the island for his own safety or something to do with his spooks work, or he won't be coming back because he can't. He won't be coming back because he is no longer alive. I'm sorry, Frankie. They are the only possible explanations I can think of."

"In a sense, you are right on both counts. Just before my 'disappearance', the commissioner called me. Two fishermen out in the bay pulled Charles' body from the water. He still had his phone on him. When the tech boys checked his calls log, they discovered Charles had tried ringing the police station, my mobile and the commissioner. He rang each of the numbers several times starting from soon after midnight and continued over the next few hours. It appears the last call he made was to the commissioner. The message he left contained a special code word. Charles stated he was on foot running on the causeway which was covered at the time by water no more than ankle deep. He intended swimming from the end of the causeway to shore on Saint-Marie."

"Did he drown? I don't believe it. He was an excellent swimmer and had swum across to Saint-Marie a few times." Frankie was becoming agitated – not unreasonably I suppose under the circumstances – but it did have the potential to hinder finding out anymore. I cut in with a question to keep the information flowing.

"Was he asking the commissioner to meet him at the beach where he came ashore?" I told myself it was an unnecessary question. Why else would he give the commissioner such details if he didn't want the man to meet him there?

"His message did not say so, but I suppose it was because his message was cut short. The tech boys isolated the sound of a shot at the point where the message stops. The body they retrieved from the bay had a fatal gunshot wound."

"Why did no one help him, answer his calls? He might still be alive if…"

"Frankie, stop it. Think about why he kept trying to call those phone numbers. It was the night of the storm and all communication networks were down." With Frankie stunned into silence, I put another question to Bennett.

"Is it possible, before he attempted to leave the island, Charles already knew Anton had been murdered?"

"It's possible Anton's death, and Charles' concerns about what else might follow were the motivation behind his attempt to swim ashore. This might sound insensitive, but I want to leave discussing Charles to one side for now. Frankie, in your statement when we first arrived, you said you were up early the morning after the storm, earlier than usual, and went for a walk along the track towards Anton's cottage."

"Yes, in spite of a restless night, I woke early. The generator wasn't working yet, so we still had no power. I tried to call Delphine to ask if she was okay to make breakfast, but the phones were still out too. Then I remembered the second stove was gas not electric, so she would be okay. I wanted to see if we suffered any damage from the storm. There was nothing obvious here around the house so, as I was up and outside, I decided to go for a walk. Something suggested Charles was out walking too and he might be on the track to Anton's. I did want to make sure Anton's place was okay anyway, so I went that way."

"You didn't see Charles along the track or at Anton's place?"

"No, I didn't see him, but initially it didn't mean much. Charles had devised his own walking track which took him past Anton's and on further through the rainforest. I think it comes out at the only beach on the island accessible by boat. Once I reached the clearing, saw the studio was on fire, and then found Anton's body, I didn't know what to think. I ran back here, but

Charles wasn't in his rooms. I ran a short way along the main track to the airstrip calling out for him. Somehow, I knew he was missing, but I ran back here in the hope he had gone into breakfast and was in the dining room the whole time."

"You found Anton's body. What can you tell me about that; about how Anton was when you found him?"

I stiffened and shot forward in my chair ready to protest the insensitivity of the question.

"No, Tessa. Don't interrupt. It's an important question for me and the investigation and – as difficult as it might be – it's something Frankie needs to confront again before she can start putting it to rest. So, Frankie, anything at all you remember from that terrible moment when you found Anton's body, please."

"As I told you, Tessa, he was lying on his back over on that big flat rock. Well, he wasn't so much on the rock as the top half of him was sprawled across it. And ... And ..."

"Take your time, Frankie. Don't rush it; just let it come back to you."

Tom was doing his best, but I felt my anger rising. I knew what he was trying to do, but I wasn't sure Frankie's psyche was up to it. He made sure I didn't have a chance to intervene.

"Frankie, think about Anton lying on that rock. Was he wet? Maybe it happened during the storm the previous night."

"Yes ... er, no. He was wet, but only a bit. He would be soaked if he was out there during the storm. Maybe it sprinkled a bit after the main storm moved on, and that's when he got wet."

"Anything else you saw about the body? Any marks or ..."

"Something was sticking out of his chest. It looked like a bit of stick of some sort. I didn't go close enough for a good look."

"A crossbow bolt...!" I yelped, just about startling the socks off everyone. "And one is missing from one of the artefacts in the great hall."

Chapter 23

"Tessa, what's all this about crossbow bolts? If you know how Anton was killed, why didn't you say something before this?" Bennett's look was savage. It made me uncomfortable, even though I had nothing to feel guilty about.

"No, Tom, I didn't know how he was killed, but Frankie's comment about something sticking out of his chest suggested a possible answer. Early today, on my way through the great hall, I noticed something was wrong with one of the displays. A shield hanging on one of the walls ... it's not a real shield, just a slab of timber in the shape of a shield. The particular exhibit consists of a crossbow and five bolts for it mounted on the shield-shaped slab. As I started to say, on my way through the hall, I noticed something was wrong with the display. One of the bolts was missing. I actually leaned over the table to see if it had fallen off and was on the floor below. It wasn't. And, I noticed the crossbow was slightly skewed to one side. On my way through the hall again later today, the crossbow had been straightened and all five bolts were back."

"Full marks for being observant, Tessa, but I think it likely a bolt did fall off the display and a staff member replaced it and straightened the bow."

There was nothing wrong with Tom's speculation about what happened, but instinct told me that wasn't the case. "Frankie, is it possible to call Delphine to ask her to find out if one of the staff mended the piece?"

Frankie was way ahead of me. She had her phone out and was dialling Delphine as I spoke. Her call was short. All three staff members were in the kitchen at the time. A troubled look clouded her face as she ended the call and turned to face us. "None of the staff knows anything about it and, therefore, none of them did anything to the display."

"Whoever availed himself of the handy weapon would need a ladder to reach it." I tried visualising the exhibit hanging on the wall. It was high; too high for me to reach without a ladder of some sort. But, a tall person might not need a ladder as such. "On second thought, a tall person might be able to reach it if they stood on a table. They would need something higher than a chair, but a table might just about do the trick. The missing bolt must have been retrieved and replaced on the wall sometime after Frankie found Anton and before Sampson did."

Bennett went to say something but stopped before anything came out. After what appeared to be a moment's thought, he tried again. "Yes, that fits. Frankie, perhaps you should tell me about the guests who were invited to your birthday party."

"You already know about them. You interviewed each of them as soon as you arrived on the island. What more can I tell you?"

"Well, you could start by telling me how well you know each of them and how they came to be invited to spend time here to help celebrate your birthday. I'm sure you must know lots more people, but only these few were invited. Were they special in some way?"

"Oh, I see. I think you are aware of my association with Tessa and Dervla and how they came to be invited. Now, let's see what more I can tell you about the others."

Details of all the other guests and Frankie's relationship with each of them took little time to recount. It didn't include anything I didn't know before, but something did catch my attention. Frankie made it clear the Nettletons and the Seymours were Charles' invitees. I already knew that, but the bitterness in Frankie's voice as she explained their presence almost took my breath away. There was more to their presence than she admitted to, and I suspected their forced inclusion on the guest list had not happened without a fight on Frankie's part."

"So, are you telling me you are not close friends with those couples, don't particular like them, and the fact that they are here is down to Charles? Is that an accurate summation of the situation?"

"Yes ... as much as I hate to admit it."

"Why do you say that, Frankie? It is perfectly all right and only natural to like some people more than others." Frankie's revelations about the two couples seemed to bother Dervla more than I could understand, but I let it go by without comment.

In spite of Dervla's soothing words, it did bother me Frankie was forced to suffer people she didn't much care for at her birthday bash. More important to me was the fact she let Charles bully her into inviting those people. It was not like the Frankie I knew all those years ago. But, perhaps *she* didn't invite them. Maybe it was *Charles* who invited them. In view of the story Bennett shared with us about Charles' past employment, why would he invite them? For the moment, the question shall remain another one of life's mysteries.

A sudden change in our situation occurred when someone checked the time. It was almost time for dinner, and none of us had done anything about getting ready for it.

"You all must go to dinner as usual. I can't join you, of course, and will remain here in these rooms. It is important everything appears normal. It might be expecting a bit much, if what I think is true. Nevertheless, everyone must try to look quite relaxed – perfectly normal – when you go in to dinner. It goes without saying, you will come under close scrutiny from certain quarters. Try not to let it rattle you should it become obvious. And Frankie, you must start devoting more attention to your other guests. To ignore them in this way will be quite a deviation from what is expected from such an experienced hostess."

The next few moments were spent discussing how we should arrive at dinner so as to dispel any suspicion Dervla and I spent the entire day with Frankie. In my opinion, it wouldn't matter how we arrived, if anyone were interested in the three of us, they already knew what we did today … hopefully, except for our rescuing Bennett. Our agreed plan was for Dervla and I to leave via the kitchen and re-enter the building from the back garden. Frankie's arrival in the dining room would follow her usual pattern.

There were the usual few moments of checking everything was in place before I left for the backyard with Dervla. Not the least of those was who would have which weapon. The final arrangement was Frankie would carry her gun, while I carried Charles' weapon. An extra handgun Frankie produced from somewhere became Bennett's weapon. With the weapons sorted out, I was ready to leave Frankie's rooms. I looked for Dervla to check she was ready to go. Dervla wasn't in the sitting room ... and she wasn't anywhere else in Frankie's suite of rooms.

"Christ, did she leave without me? Did anyone see her go?" My whole nervous system had moved to panic mode. The other two looked stunned. Frankie managed to find her voice.

"She has been bleating about becoming independent again; about not continuing to be a burden for us to look after. She might have decided to test herself out there on her own." I was almost at the door by the time Frankie stopped speaking.

A blood-curling scream rent the air. I was racing along the hallway towards the lobby, with Frankie and Bennett close on my heels. Dervla was up ahead, just a couple of metres in from the entrance to the hallway. She was hysterical and cringing up against the wall. Wrapping my arms around her, I held her as tightly as I could. Her legs seemed to turn to jelly. She slid down to the floor, dragging me with her. She tried to speak, but body-wracking sobs prevented it. She managed only a couple of gulps of air before regaining sufficient control to croak a few words.

"It was him. I saw him…"

"Him…? Who? Who was the man you saw? Talk to me, Dervla. Tell me what you saw; what terrified you."

"It was him, I tell you. I remembered everything. Seeing him again brought it all back to me. He was going to kill me

– again. I know who attacked me, and he was going to do it again; to finish the job this time. He had a knife, a large knife."

"Take a couple of deep breaths … that's it. Now, who was it you saw? Tell me his name."

"Nettleton…! Terrence Nettleton…"

"He came at you here in the hallway? Was he lurking along here somewhere?"

"No. He was crossing the lobby when I stepped out of the hallway and into the lobby. As soon as he saw me, he came at me. I raced back into the hallway and he followed me. I screamed when he pulled out the knife. My scream scared him off. He turned and raced out of the hallway."

As I untangled myself from Dervla and scrambled to my feet, I glanced back at my two companions. With weapons drawn, both Bennett and Frankie stood on guard behind us. "Help me take her back to your rooms please, Frankie. Then, we need to review our situation, and quickly."

With Dervla settled in one of Frankie's armchairs, I led off the review of our situation. "It's probably safe to assume keeping out of sight and trying to hide has become a waste of time. It appears Nettleton now knows at least Dervla is holed up somewhere along this hallway. It wouldn't take much to work out where we all are. To date, our approach has been a defensive one. I think it's time we went on the offensive. We must neutralise Nettleton, and as soon as possible, if we are to prevent any further incidents. I suppose the question then is: what do we do and how do we go about it?"

"Well, sitting here talking about it won't neutralise anything. We need to take down Nettleton and render him incapable of creating any further mischief. Frankie, I recall you mentioned Nettleton and Seymour were here at Charles' invitation. I'm wondering if we shouldn't consider Seymour to be in cahoots with Nettleton, and would prove just as dangerous if Nettleton is taken out of the equation." Bennett paced around the room as he spoke. It was likely he was applying some thought to a strategy we might implement.

While Frankie admitted her opinion of Seymour might be a little jaundiced because of how he came to be on the island, she supported the idea he might be as dangerous as Nettleton. Her support for Bennett's thinking seemed to galvanise him into action. He asked whether she thought Sampson and Dwayne would be willing to participate in our endeavours to take down Nettleton and Seymour.

"Of course they would. They wouldn't go against me if I asked them to, and they already helped Winston and Patrick capture your two rogue officers. They might only be my staff, but they are astute, and they are well aware of what's happening here. I'll call them to join our council of war if you wish. What about your officers? We have to rule two of those out of course."

Frankie's mention of police officers Williams and his colleague gave me a moment of panic. "What have we done with those two officers? Is there any chance Nettleton might mount a rescue bid?"

"That's unlikely," Frankie said with some conviction. "Even if Nettleton knew where they were being held, he would not be able to free them. I am fairly confident and that." She might be, but I needed further reassurance. "Don't worry, Tessa. It's quite likely Nettleton has no idea where they are. They're being held in a deep concrete cellar under the old dairy. You don't know about the old dairy, and neither does anyone else I suspect. It's long been out of use and, while it's still a sturdy structure, over the years it has become hidden in the rainforest. Even if Nettleton managed to find it, I'm confident he wouldn't be able to break into the cellar."

"That's a good point you raised though. It would be worthwhile stationing a couple of men near the dairy in the off chance Nettleton does go there. If Sampson and Dwayne will assist Tessa and me, I will utilise my two remaining officers, Winston and Patrick, in guarding the place."

A few moments later, a knock at the door heralded the arrival of Sampson and Dwayne. Each carried a rifle slung over his shoulder. Bennett took charge of the gathering. "In a moment, I will call Winston and send him and Patrick to guard the dairy.

Then the four of us will go in search of Nettleton. Frankie you will remain here to stand guard over Dervla. Does anyone have any problems with those arrangements?"

When no arguments were forthcoming, I posed my next question. "Okay, we all seem to be in agreement, so where do we go to look for Nettleton?"

Ideas were not plentiful, but it didn't matter. Bennett tentatively suggested the derelict cottage in the clearing in the rainforest. I wasn't at all convinced Nettleton would head for there. No one else questioned his suggestion, so I went along with it. We encountered yet another delay. Bennett moved out of the sitting room and into Frankie's bedroom to make a call. At the end of the call, he returned to the sitting room looking reasonably pleased with himself.

"Right; I suggest we move out into the hallway and wait there until the next stage of the operation is complete before heading out to search for Nettleton. Frankie, what about the wives? Are the Nettleton and Seymour wives likely to be involved in their husbands' operations, or are they merely window dressing?"

"I don't think I would consider either of them window dressing. I will keep an eye out for them. I hope I'm misjudging them."

After Bennett sent Sampson and Dwayne on their way, he and I hung about in the hallway until we saw Winston and Patrick drag an uncooperative Seymour down the stairs and out front door. I raised my eyebrows at Bennett.

He chuckled. "I do hope he will find the cellar to his liking and my other two officers to be convivial company."

Then, at last we were on our way and the search for Nettleton was in full swing. I was curious about where Bennett sent the two staff members, but didn't have the breath to ask the question as we galloped flat out across the lawn. We maintained our pace as we turned off and headed along the main track towards the airstrip. Suddenly, Bennett slowed his pace, almost causing me to crash into him. He seemed to be closely examining the side of the track as he trotted along. All became clear when Sampson and Dwayne stepped out onto the track ahead of us.

"No sign of him, Inspector. We hid in close to the shack and waited. When there weren't any sounds coming from around us, we went in and checked the cottage. Then, when we didn't find him, we hid in the trees again for a while to see if he arrived. After a couple of minutes, we gave up and came back out here to meet you."

"Okay, it seems my supposition was way off the mark. I'm not sure where to search next, but I suppose we should concentrate on the castle and its immediate surrounds." We started back along the track when an idea occurred to me.

"Does anyone know when the next low tide is?"

After a quick glance at his watch, Sampson replied, "It should be dead low tide in about an hour." A spark of excitement lit up his eyes as he realised where my question was heading. "... and tonight's low tide is the lowest for this quarter."

"Does it mean it will be low enough to leave the causeway completely clear of water at least for some brief time at dead low tide?"

"Yes; for about twenty minutes or so while the tide turns and it's at its lowest point, there will be no water over the causeway, even none over the lower section beyond the point."

"Does anyone remember how long ago Nettleton did his runner from inside the castle?" My question raised nothing more than negative head shakes. "I put it at about half an hour, or maybe closer to an hour. Even though it won't be dead low tide for maybe another hour, sometime during that hour, the tide should be low enough to safely use the causeway."

"Yes, Miss Tessa, you are right. The tide is probably low enough already for water to be no more than ankle deep across it."

As Sampson and I discussed the implications of the low tide in relation to accessing the causeway, Bennett pulled out his phone and moved a short distance away to make a call. His call ended as we finished discussing the causeway. On returning to our huddle, he asked for suggestions on what we should do next. I was happy to volunteer a suggestion.

"You remember the beach where you brought in a boat to remove Anton's body…?" Bennett nodded. "That's where I think we should head for. If I'm honest, I think we might be too late. I hope I'm wrong but, if I'm right, our quarry might already have escaped. I wonder how good a swimmer is Mr Nettleton. At such a low tide, the distance to the beach on Saint-Marie would be somewhat reduced."

"Aah yes; that possibility is covered." Bennett winked at me and tapped the side of his nose. I suspected the Commissioner had been pressed into service again and would be spending some time patrolling a certain beach on the other island.

No further command was needed. Together, we raced across the lawn and headed along the track towards Anton's place. While the track was good underfoot in daylight hours, it was difficult to maintain speed over it in the dark. Nevertheless, risking our ankles, we raced on with as much speed as possible until we reached the clearing. Here, our course deviated briefly. While the two staff searched the ruins at the studio, Bennett and I searched Anton's cottage. Having found no sign of Nettleton, we entered the rough track which carried on through the rainforest to its terminus at the beach and the causeway.

Scrambling down the low bank onto the narrow strip of beach in the dark was treacherous. With no clearly defined track and plenty of rocks jutting up to meet us, some skin was sacrificed before we were standing on the beach. Sampson produced a small torch and shone it along the sand. Apart from the disturbance created by our arrival, the torch picked up a recent line of footprints heading across an otherwise pristine area of sand and towards the causeway.

"Nettleton…" Bennett grunted. "We are too late, but at least we know where he is going." His phone came out again for another rapid but brief call.

While Bennett made his call, Sampson played his torch along the length of the causeway. It was dead low tide. The water level was about 300 to 400 millimetres below the surface of the rocky causeway. The torch's beam highlighted the slippery nature of the rocks.

"What is the slippery-looking stuff on the causeway?" It seemed to me, anyone trying to run along the there was inviting significant injuries. Some of the rocks looked quite sharp and, with the slimy looking stuff on them, they were accidents waiting for any foolhardy trespasser.

"Some of it is moss, and some is a form of kelp," was Sampson's economical response before he let out a quiet yelp. "There he is. See, along there on the lower end section of the causeway."

I was amazed by how far out the causeway stretched. Nevertheless, in the distance and barely picked up by the torchlight, a figure hurried away from us along the rocky surface. Finding himself spotlighted by Sampson's torch probably spooked Nettleton. As Sampson kept his torch trained on the retreating distant dim figure, we watched in frustration. Then, the figure appeared to slip and disappeared. Did he slip, or was it a poorly executed dive? Whatever happened, the result was the same: the figure went off the side of the causeway and into the sea. Sampson continued playing his torch over the area where Nettleton went into the water, but it was too far away for it to do much good.

"Dwayne and I will go along to the end of the causeway to see if we can pick him up swimming to Saint-Marie."

"Thanks, Sampson, but that's not necessary. We have to accept he has left the island. Our only hope now is the commissioner and his men will arrest him when he reaches the beach on the other island." After a couple of heartbeats, Bennett added, "If he makes it to the beach over there... The tide already has turned. I imagine the current will be quite strong between the two islands on the incoming tide."

"What if he is just hanging off the rocks out there, waiting for us to go away before scrambling back out of the water? Shouldn't we make sure he is not still out there?" This was the first contribution Dwayne made during the exercise, and his questions made sense.

Without waiting for Bennett to answer, the two staff men were off and running towards the causeway. I watched in awe when, like a pair of mountain goats, they picked their way fast along the rocky causeway. Whether Bennett's shouted instructions reached their ears is unclear.

"The moment water nears the top of the causeway, get back here… and make it FAST."

I couldn't help but think the two men out there wouldn't pay Bennett's instruction much heed, even if they did hear it. The prospect of the spectacle we might witness if they didn't comply kept my pulse racing until they were both safely back on the beach.

"No sign of him out there," Sampson reported. "The tide is coming in fast now. We should leave the beach quickly before it goes under water too." No further prompting required. We scrambled back up onto higher ground.

While I stood staring at the causeway, Bennett moved some distance off to make another phone call. As we turned and jogged our way back towards Anton's place, Bennett confirmed the commissioner and his men were in place.

Chapter 24

While I could see no conceivable reason for us to hurry back to the castle, we kept up a good pace all the way; trotting where necessary and galloping where possible. I really must do something about my fitness. Much of my time spent on this island so far has seen me gasping for breath and stiff and sore from so much exercise. It was as we raced across the front lawn towards the front steps I considered the matter of unfitness to keep my mind off my aching legs. That's when we heard it and I was propelled back into the real world of Île Verte.

"Shit…! That was a shot. Come on … the women …," Bennett yelled at us in between gasping for breath.

At the sound of the shot, Sampson and Dwayne took off like a pair of startled rabbits. They stepped up into top gear, leaving Bennett and me in their wake. I heard Sampson bellow, "Check on Delphine," just before the two men separated. Dwayne peeled off and headed for the entrance to the kitchen. Sampson, with us doing our best not to lag too far behind, bounded up the front steps.

"Careful. Check it out first. Don't go rushing in. Easy does it." It was good advice on Bennett's part, but it was obvious Sampson knew what he was doing. By the time we entered the lobby, Sampson had unslung the rifle from his shoulder and was inching his way along the hallway towards Frankie's rooms. Dwayne joined him and followed Sampson's example.

"Wait here in the lobby, Tessa, until I give you the all-clear to come to Frankie's rooms."

Bennett is kidding himself if he thinks I'm going to do that. I liberated the gun from my pocket, and tacked myself onto the tail end of the phalanx of drawn weapons moving along the hallway.

The shot had the two women on high alert for even the slightest sound. In spite of our best efforts at stealth, Frankie's door flew open. Framed in the doorway, Frankie stood there with her weapon trained on the group of us in the hallway.

"Don't shoot, Miss Dubois. There is only us out here." Sampson's voice wasn't loud, but his words were clear ... and they did the trick. Frankie lowered her weapon. At the same time, she seemed to deflate a little.

"Thank God. Quick; come inside. Were you followed?"

A quick glance around the room told me all I needed to know about the shot we heard. "Frankie, where is Dervla? Is Dervla okay?" Frankie looked about ready to go into hysterics, and didn't seem to hear my questions. I grabbed her by the biceps and shook her. "Frankie, answer me. Where is Dervla?" My voice had risen to several decibels above necessary. A nervous little voice answered my questions.

"I'm here, Tessa. Frankie made me hide in her walk-in wardrobe. I'm all right, but I heard a shot. Is Frankie all right? Is it okay for me to come out now?"

"Yes, Dervla; come out and join us. Frankie is a little shaken but okay. All of us are okay. All of us except Mrs Seymour, that is. She had a close encounter with Frankie's handgun."

"Nothing serious though…" Bennett added from down on his haunches beside the wounded woman on the floor. "Her right arm might be out of action for a while. I imagine it will mend okay."

Bennett's phone rang while he was crouched down beside the woman. He stood and motioned for Sampson to keep her covered. In spite of moving away a few steps, I overheard his conversation ... that is, I heard his side of the phone call: *Commissioner, what news do you have? ... Good... Okay, well, please keep us informed ... London? ... Oh, I see ... Yes, very good of them ... Ah, we already worked that out... They were a bit late, but thank them for me anyway.*

There was an extended pause in the inspector's side of the conversation. I presumed the commissioner was passing on information. Then, it was Bennett's turn to speak again: *There is one other matter. We have a number of packages to remove from the island... No, these are not normal removals... That's correct ... So far, the count is four, but who knows... Yes, I agree that would be best... Okay, I'll leave it in your capable hands to organise something.*

Bennett returned and stood looking down at the wounded Mrs Seymour who remained curled up on the floor. Sampson gestured at her with his rifle. "Do we put her with the others? And, what do we do about the wound?"

As he removed the phone from his pocket, Bennett replied, "No, I think we need somewhere else for this one. We'll talk about that while Winston patches her up. Keep an eye on her for a bit longer while I organise Winston."

This time Bennett left the room to make his call. Dwayne volunteered to fetch the castle's comprehensive first-aid kit. My concern for the wounded woman slowly increased. She had lost quite a lot of blood. I have no idea how much, or at what point such loss becomes critical. Her face was now quite drained of colour, but I don't know whether that was due to blood loss, or the fear which accompanied her realisation of the difficult situation ahead of her.

Winston and Dwayne accompanied Bennett when he returned to the room. Dwayne opened the first-aid kit on the floor beside the woman and Winston set about attending to her wounds. The shrieking and moaning she produced as Winston got on with it were too much for Dervla. I noticed she became quite agitated before escaping into the bedroom to distance herself from the drama taking place in the sitting room.

Overlooked while everything else was happening, Frankie had quietly slumped into one of the lounge chairs. She looked quite shaken, and I knew shock was setting in. I had a quiet word in Bennett's ear. "The two women are suffering the effects of what happened here. I'm going to take them to the kitchen and make them a coffee or something. It will be better if I remove them from here for a while."

After reassuring himself I was all right and not about to collapse in a great heap, Bennett agreed to my removing the women, but insisted Dwayne accompany us as our 'protection detail'. As Bennett held the door open for us to leave, I asked quietly about his plan.

"It remains a work in progress. I will continue working on it when you stop talking to me and allow me to think about it in peace." A bit miffed by his response, I put an arm around each woman's waist and shepherded them towards the kitchen.

Dwayne rushed up and did a fancy two-step around us so, with weapon at the ready, he could lead the way. Delphine looked somewhat less than her usual regal and inscrutable self when we arrived in the kitchen. While my two companions and I sat around with mugs of hot chocolate, Delphine took Dwayne off to one side.

"Who would have thought it; hot chocolate on a tropical island," Dervla murmured again more to herself than to anyone else on this occasion.

"It's comfort food – nectar for the soul – regardless of where you have it." The sharpness of Frankie's response suggested she was a long way from being okay after her harrowing event.

Maybe if I get her to talk, about anything, it might help her cope with the shock she seems to be trying to hold at bay. I embarked on a program of mental gymnastics as I searched for 'safe' topics to engage Frankie and help take her mind off recent events. That exercise hadn't progressed too far when Bennett joined us in the kitchen.

"...Any chance of another mug of whatever they're having?" He directed his inquiry to Delphine, bringing her discussion with Dwayne to an end. Moments later, she plonked a mug of hot chocolate down on the table in front of him. "Oh God, hot chocolate... Never mind, it will do. I would have preferred something a little stronger."

"I could put a dash of rum in it for you," Dwayne volunteered. Bennett's eyes lit up, and a splash of rum was duly added.

"Dwayne, I have given the other men instructions about Mrs Seymour and the plan for the rest of the night. Please go and join them in Miss Dubois' rooms. The others will fill you in on what is to happen." As soon as Dwayne was on his way, Bennett turned his attention to Delphine. "Thank you for remaining at your post tonight, but I think it's time for you to stand down. I'm sure your mother heard the shot and is probably quite concerned about what's happening out here. As your services won't be required again tonight, it is best if you retire to your quarters to set your mother's mind at ease."

Not inclined to leave the kitchen, Delphine began to protest, and indicated soon there would be four mugs needing to be washed. I stepped into quash that one. "Don't worry about these mugs, Delphine. We will rinse them out when we're finished. You need to be with your mother, and you both need to try for a good night sleep."

While reluctant to leave, she accepted the situation and left us sitting at the table with our half-drunk mugs of chocolate. My offer to rinse our mugs when we were finished was not some magnanimous gesture. There were a million and one questions I wanted to put to Bennett, and I wasn't sure of getting any answers in front of the staff. As it turns out, I wasn't going to get any answers in front of the other two women. My first question, innocuous though it was, was fobbed off, providing clear indication of how things were going to be.

A few moments later, Dwayne popped back into the kitchen and spoke quietly to Bennett. "We're on our way now, Sir. Miss Dubois' rooms are now empty again." His message delivered, Dwayne hurried out to the lobby.

"Right, it's time for you two ladies to catch up on some sleep. Come on, let's get you back to your rooms and make sure you're tucked in safely." As he finished speaking, Bennett gave me a hard look. I wasn't sure how to interpret it but decided discretion was probably the best approach. I tried looking blank and didn't respond.

In what I assumed was a bid to create an air of relaxed confidence, in a leisurely stroll, Bennett led us back to Frankie's rooms. Bennett and I checked out Charles' rooms while the two women, readied for bed. Then, once they were both settled in their beds for the night, Bennett bade them both good night and tried reassuring them they would be safe from now on.

"What about Tessa?" Dervla's strident demand pulled us up at the door. "Why isn't she going to bed like the two of us? What's going on, and why aren't we informed?"

"I never had a chance to finish my interview of Tessa. In view of most recent incidents, it is now critical I do so. It's imperative I have every grain of information about what's happened on this island if I am ever to piece this investigation together." Then, Bennett pushed me out of the door and pulled it closed behind us.

"Okay, Inspector, now perhaps you would like to tell me why I'm not back there catching up on my beauty sleep as well."

"For Christ' sake, Tessa, there is so much we don't understand about what's going on here. I need someone I can discuss it with; someone who thinks logically and has an analytical mind. If, for some reason you're averse to helping, just say so and piss off to bed."

"Not averse at all, just wanting to know what's going on. This isn't going to be a one-way street. I have a whole bucket of questions requiring answers, and you are the only person around here likely to have answers to them."

We settled back at the same table where we recently drank hot chocolate. As soon as we were perched again, Bennett launched into our discussion. "I think we should trade questions. You lead off, and I'll ask the next one."

"Where do I start? Oh, I know: what happened to the man you arrested after he escaped from the derelict cottage? I believe he was flown off the island, but who was he and where is he?" Bennett's brow furrowed bringing his eyebrows almost together. When he looked up at me, there was a strange slightly stunned look on his face.

"Uhmm ... Why is it important to you?"

"Why don't you answer the question? If this conversation is to continue, it will be on the basis of trading information. Unless you are prepared to do so, perhaps I will go to bed after all. Is the answer to my question such a top-level secret, you can't share it with me?"

"No. There's nothing secret about it. When you asked the question, I just realised I didn't know the answer to any of it. You are correct about the prisoner being flown off the island. Officers Williams and Taylor escorted him back to Saint-Marie in one of Jackson's small planes, and then escorted him to Guadeloupe on a commercial flight. I haven't had time to follow up with Guadeloupe to find out what they managed to extract from the bloke."

"Wouldn't Guadeloupe contact you as a matter of course to pass on anything they discovered?"

He agreed it was the usual procedure, and admitted he had heard nothing so far. While he tried to create an impression of no concern about it, he was a poor actor. "Don't ever take up poker, Inspector. You don't have the face for it. Would it be too late tonight to call Guadeloupe to ask for a report?" He confirmed it was too late, and he would leave it until first thing next morning. "If I may say so, Tom, you appear frustrated by this investigation. Is there something in particular bothering you?"

"Argh, all we've done so far is neutralise dangerous elements. While I suppose that is a positive, the investigation itself is not gaining any traction. I'm not getting anywhere with it."

"It seems to me we are amassing a cast of thousands, without having settled on a script. What I…"

"Tessa, it has been a big day, and it is now a late night. Forgive me, but I have no idea what you are trying to say."

"In simple terms then, there are five people in custody here on the island and presumably one more now being held on Guadeloupe. Should any other guests be added to that list?"

"We don't know; not yet anyway."

"Exactly … and the main reason we don't know is because we don't know what is behind everything happening here. Therefore, we can't anticipate what else might happen … and who might be involved. What I am saying is: we don't know what the script is and, therefore, we don't what and who is involved in the next act of this show. …Or to use your jargon, we don't know the motivation behind all this. On the other hand, perhaps you do know and it is only the rest of us who don't know."

"All I have discovered thus far is an association at some time between Allerton and three of the prisoners. None of that speaks to motivation."

"Three of the prisoners…? You told me about Allerton's association with Nettleton and Seymour. Who is the third member of the band?"

"Mrs Seymour…" My jaw almost hit the floor. I gave him a 'gimme' gesture.

"Mrs Kate Seymour, or the former Catherine Randell, worked for the same company of spooks way back when. In spite of there being no hard evidence against the blokes who found themselves out in the cold, they were cast adrift anyway. Without hard evidence there couldn't be a trial, and they couldn't be locked up. Randell also was a covert operative. She worked alone on select missions and wasn't part of the men's gang. They had no hard evidence against her either and, while they suspected her collusion with the men, they couldn't prove it. After the men were dismissed, the section announced a reshuffle with the possibility of redundancies. It's no surprise Randell was found to be surplus to requirements and made redundant."

"It would have been handy to know that before Frankie had to shoot her. Who else among the guests do we not know about?"

"We only received the information after Seymour was shot. It appears she was in cahoots with the men via her relationship with Seymour. About twelve months after the dust settled following the London shake up, then living in France after a period spent living in Switzerland, the couple quietly married. By then, they had slipped below the section's radar and nobody was aware of the marriage."

"Oh, handy to know… Should we be looking at Marian Nettleton in the same light? Is she a danger still on the loose?"

When MI6 rang the commissioner to share the news about Mrs Seymour, the commissioner asked them to look into Mrs Nettleton. Who knows how long it will be before we hear anything back? In the meantime, she won't be able to as much as sneeze without our being aware of it."

"Everything we know so far only links them together. We don't know what they did to get them tossed out on their ears, or what they might have been up to since then. While we might assume Charles and Anton were killed to stop them interfering in some bigger initiative, it's the nature of that initiative which holds the key to everything."

"I see your point and I agree, but uncovering it is beyond our resources. It's up to London now to identify their end game."

"In the meantime, you are going to keep Marian Nettleton under close surveillance. What about the other guests – the business couple from Guadeloupe and Jackson – are they also mixed up in all this."

"I think it safe to discount them and assume them to be genuine guests. Anyway, apart from you and Dervla, they are Frankie's only other real invitees. Everyone else was here at Charles' invitation. And, before you ask, no, I don't know if it means anything."

"So, what are you going to do with Mrs Seymour? I understand you don't want her in the cellar with her husband and the others, but I imagine your options are limited."

"There is a solid lockable room upstairs in the main part of that old dairy. Sampson said it was where they sterilised all the cheese making equipment, and where they stored it after it was sterilised. According to Sampson, locking it was the only way they could be sure the equipment remained at food grade standard and one of the workers hadn't used bits of it for other purposes. By keeping her at the old dairy along with the others, I only need one officer on guard duty, and the two I have at my disposal can rotate shifts."

"As it seems the danger has been neutralised, I will return to sleeping in my own room. After we leave this kitchen, I will collect my things from Frankie's rooms and move back upstairs.

I'll take my little friend here with me." I patted the gun in my pocket as I added my final comment.

Bennett wasn't at all happy with my moving back upstairs but, after a short debate, he backed down. He intended keeping guard over Frankie and Dervla – just in case – and, with me out of the way, he could sleep on the sofa I had been using. There didn't appear much else to discuss, mainly due to the lack of information relating to any of my questions. And, it was late. The effects of the day were catching up with both of us. Bed became more appealing by the minute.

I wondered how to end our interlude in the kitchen without appearing uninterested in the investigation and Bennett's thoughts on it. For a moment, I thought my dilemma solved when Bennett's phone rang. He started walking away from me as he answered the call, then stopped and returned to his seat at the table. It was a short call. The one side of it I heard was not particularly enlightening. All I learned was the identity of the caller: the commissioner.

After the call ended, Bennett sat staring at his phone for a few moments before turning his attention to me. "That was the commissioner. They have him... wasn't much fight left in Nettleton by the time he reached the beach on Saint-Marie. They will hold him there until his 'friends' from this island join him over there. Then they all will be flown to Guadeloupe to stand trial."

It was all the information I was likely to get tonight, and I felt weary. "I think I'll head back to Frankie's rooms to collect my stuff. Are you coming, or do you have things to attend to elsewhere?"

We left the kitchen together. After collecting my belongings and saying goodnight to the others, I raced upstairs to my room. It had been searched, but I knew my computer was safe. Quite by accident, while searching Charles' rooms earlier, I discovered a well-hidden floor safe in his walk-in wardrobe. A set of drawers were parked over it. Before I left Frankie's rooms tonight, I checked on my computer. It remained where I hid it.

Unsure what sort of night lay ahead for me, I eased myself into bed, and offered up a silent prayer to whichever god might be listening for sleep not to be elusive or a stranger tonight. A question nagging me since we left the kitchen continued to bother me as I waited for sleep to arrive: what was the motivation behind every incident here on this island since the stormy night of Frankie's birthday bash?

Chapter 25

Sluggish after a restless night and oversleeping this morning, I dragged myself into the almost deserted dining room for breakfast. The absence of Frankie, Dervla and Bennett sent a spike of fear through me. Now, as I raced along the hallway to Frankie's rooms, I was wide awake and on the verge of hyperventilating.

Bennett almost received a fist in the face when he swung open the door as I went to pound on it. "Is everyone all right? Where are the other two?"

"Why wouldn't we be all right?" He waited for my answer before dealing with my second question.

"You three were not at breakfast. I was concerned something happened. So, where are the women?"

"They didn't wake early. It took them ages to decide whether they were going to the dining room or if they would ask Delphine for breakfast on a tray. I ended up deciding for them. We are about to go to the dining room. That is, we will go when they finish titivating themselves up for the day ahead."

"Titivating themselves up...? We are talking about Frankie and Dervla, aren't we? Neither is into 'titivating' ... well, Frankie has been known to, a bit. Let me in so I can find out what's going on."

"I'm not preventing you from entering. In fact, please do. See if you can hurry them along. I'm in danger of dying of starvation before we ever make it to the dining room this morning."

"Oh, hark at you. You've just spent the night with two beautiful women, a blonde and a redhead, and you're carrying on like this. One can only assume things did not go your way last night."

"You are right. Things did not go my way last night. The pair of them yapped until some ungodly hour of the morning, when all I wanted to do was sleep."

Still chuckling at Bennett's sour disposition, I strode into Frankie's bedroom. Both women were dressed and ready to go, but Frankie had taken to showing Dervla the various outfits in her wardrobe. "Come on, you two. Breakfast won't wait all day for us … and Bennett is about to collapse from hunger."

After they recovered from the shock of my rude intrusion, there were a few moments delay while they exercised their presumed right to bloody mindedness. I was with Bennett on this one, and I wasn't big on patience either this morning.

"Right, suit yourselves. The inspector and I will be in the dining room should you choose to join us for breakfast." I pivoted and marched out to Bennett still standing in the open doorway. "Come on. We are going to breakfast. What they choose to do is up to them."

I strode out into the hallway. Bennett dithered in the doorway, torn between what he knew to be the logical thing to do and what he considered his duty. I took his arm and towed him out into the hallway. "I've made the decision for you. You are taking me to breakfast. Close the door and let's go." By the time I finished speaking, the two apologetic women had joined us in the hallway and Frankie was locking the door behind them.

My bravado was all show. It helped mask my concern for Frankie. Her appearance this morning shocked me. Frankie is one of those almost surreal drop-dead gorgeous women. She is tall and thin – 'willowy' is an apt description – with flawless skin, and eyes which sometimes look green, and blue at other times. This woman, who seems to glide, rather move and walk like other mere mortals, is topped by a mane of palest blonde hair never out of place. Today, her face is drawn tight over her high cheekbones, and her eyes sport deep purple smudges below them. Perhaps her hair was the biggest shock. Always shiny and perfect, without a bucket of product to keep it that way, today it lacked lustre and looked as though a bird had nested in it.

While reluctant to check my theory in front of a mirror, I suspect, in spite of her recent ordeals, Dervla looks the best of the three of us. Shortish, rounded and with an unruly mop of red hair and grey eyes, she turns heads when she enters a room. She would still do that today. On the other hand, I know what I look like when suffering lack of sleep. I would look more like Frankie than Dervla today ... hence, I'm avoiding mirrors.

As soon as breakfast was over, the four of us returned to Frankie's rooms. While the other two discussed possible plans for their day with Bennett, I slipped into Charles' wardrobe and retrieved my gear I stashed in his floor safe. The hair I stuck across the laptop remained in place. The machine had not been opened. Loaded up with my gear, I returned to Frankie's sitting room. The two women were in Frankie's bedroom completing their preparations to face the day.

"I'm going up to my room. I might be there for a while. You know where to find me if you need me. Good luck coping with those pair in the bedroom." Bennett rolled his eyes and started to protest. Already on my way out the door, I kept walking.

An hour or so after I returned to my room, Bennett knocked on my door. After checking who it was, I let him in. He collapsed in overdramatic fashion into my armchair. "Please, may I hide out with you for a while? Those women have, overnight, turned into a pair of Giggling-Gerties." I pointed out I was working, but agreed to stretch a point and let him stay.

"What are you working on? I hope you're not preparing something to send off to some media mob. The embargo on any information going out remains in place."

"You have trust issues, my friend. I have been researching while you were idling away your time with two beautiful women." My comment caused a spate of good natured to-and-fro between us for a minute or so, before Bennett asked me about the results of my research.

"There is nothing definitive yet. I started by looking into the incident which resulted in our now good friends being chucked out of Her Majesty's Service. Not a lot of success with that, probably as a consequence of some hefty suppression orders put in place at the time. I'm not surprised, but I thought it worth a try."

He agreed. Under the circumstances surrounding the matter, there would be strenuous measures put in place to prevent dirty linen becoming public. There was a hint of disappointment behind his comment. I felt chuffed he thought my research ability such I might have cracked it. The other issue I was researching when he arrived was proving just as disappointing, but I decided to share with him the little I had. I barely made a tentative start when he checked his watch, and then bounded out of the chair.

The last I saw was Bennett scrolling through his phone as he disappeared out the door. It was obvious something important occurred to him, and I was more than a little miffed he didn't share it with me. I tried to push it from my mind and returned to my computer. In hot pursuit of an idea, I didn't hear the tap on my door. It wasn't until Bennett called to me, I realised he was outside.

"Sorry, I didn't hear you knock. Come in; it's not locked."

"Well, it bloody well should be," he growled as he came in. "We still can't be sure we've rounded everyone up. It might not be safe to be sitting here alone with your door unlocked."

"I'm perfectly safe … and it's as well you called out before barging in." I gestured to the gun lying on the table in front of the laptop. Anyone coming through the door would see the computer but would not see the weapon. "Nice of you to return, by the way; I thought it must be something I said sent you scurrying out of here."

"It was something you said. Last night, you asked about the prisoner sent to Guadeloupe. I said I would call them this morning, so I did." I knew his pause was for me to ask what he learned from his phone call. Feeling Bolshy this morning, I decided to ignore my cue.

"Uhmm … all right then … it's as well I called. They know nothing about a prisoner transferred from Saint-Marie."

"Do you mean the prisoner taken into custody here and flown under guard to Saint-Marie didn't make it to Guadeloupe? Is that what you are saying?" Bennett gave an emphatic nod. "Well, if he didn't end up on Guadeloupe, where did he go?"

"Perhaps it's a question for Officer Williams and his colleague who escorted the prisoner off this island."

In the belief we were about to dash off to ask people hard questions, I closed my laptop and stood up … just as Bennett subsided into my armchair.

"I thought we were going to question your rogue officers."

"There's no rush; we've plenty of time. I've left organising the prisoners' evacuation from the island in the commissioner's hands. It could take a while, even days, to organise something. When he has something in place, I'll question them before they leave the island."

"I don't suppose the commissioner has heard anymore from London; hasn't heard anything about Marion Nettleton for instance?"

"Not a peep from the commissioner this morning so far. Now, I noticed you were working on your computer while I was away. Find anything interesting?"

"Not really sure; I found something to get my juices flowing, but I'm not sure it's relevant."

He insisted I run it past him. "You never know, just talking it through might help the pieces fall into place. I'm a good listener … but I reserve the right to ask questions."

"At the risk of sounding completely rubbish, as a result of the few things I read, there is now a kernel of an idea trying to develop. The articles had nothing to do with this part of the world, but I could see how a similar situation could exist here. I don't know enough about this part of the world – the Caribbean, I mean – and what's been happening here in recent times, to know if I'm even looking in the right direction."

"What sort of evidence are you looking for? What sort of indicators would help you work through it?"

"In general terms, I would be looking for an influx of interest from outside the Caribbean; perhaps foreigners investing in new enterprises or infrastructure in the area. From what I've seen in other places, it's how it starts, and is soon followed by the arrival of foreign nationals taking up residence in the area. Some of those might be investors in the new developments, or the foreign-owned developers might bring in their fellow nationals to establish and run the new enterprises or projects. The upshot of this is the development of a foreign enclave in a particular area, or one strongly disbursed throughout a geographical area. As I said, I'm not familiar enough with this part of the world to know if there is any such activity here."

I looked up at Bennett to find him sitting forward on the edge of his chair and leaning on his forearms firmly planted on his thighs. He didn't look up at me or attempt to respond. But the look on his face told me I struck a nerve. With all the self-restraint I could muster, I was determined to remain silent until he was ready to share his thoughts with me. I don't know how long it took, but it felt like forever. At last he looked up at me and ran his tongue across his lips. I saw a gleam of excitement in his eyes.

"If that is what you're looking for – foreign investment – then you might take a closer look at this particular area. There has been quite a bit of foreign investment already on Saint-Marie and Guadeloupe. As far as I know, it's been minor stuff so far. But, I recently heard of a couple of applications to establish new enterprises. I've heard – nothing more than gossip mind you – of a lot of interest by foreign nationals in a number of other places throughout the Caribbean. Even on Saint-Marie in the last few months, I've noticed a few strangers roaming around. They don't look like tourists, and there seems to be more of them than I would expect if nothing was going on. Still, those matters in themselves don't give cause for concern. There has to be more key definitive indicators involved for there to be concern."

"There does appear to be a pattern of operation: key public servants are recruited or bribed; politicians are compromised or bought. It means applications for anything from building permits, to land acquisition, to the issue of visas or the granting of citizenship or permanent residency are unhindered by bureaucracy. I think it begins in an innocuous way, attracting no attention, and then rapidly grows and spreads like some insidious disease."

"Hmm ... Yes, but hasn't it been the way of the world for centuries? Isn't it how many countries were discovered and/or developed? If, as you think, this is a contemporary version of what's gone before, what is the ultimate goal of the current version?"

"That's the part I'm not clear about. Where I can identify it has happened in the recent past, it hasn't been so much a foreign take-over of another country, as a strategic manoeuvre. Everything happens in a slow and covert way. Some time later, it becomes apparent the foreigners have a strangle hold on a country and are now strategically positioned to influence global trade ... or worse."

"By 'worse', you mean the interloper is then strategically positioned to take over – to invade, to attack – another country?"

"There are instances which provide hard evidence to support such thinking."

"Jesus! The scenario you describe already exists on Saint-Marie, and we are nothing more than a tiny dot in the Caribbean. I have only one problem with your reasoning: How could any foreign nation consider Saint-Marie 'strategic' ... and for what?"

"I don't know. It's one of those elusive and indeterminate variables you encounter in such research. Only people closer to the action might have information which helps determine, one way or another, whether something is going on or not."

Bennett might not want to know, but I could see the Caribbean providing a desirable strategic stronghold for any power interested in North America. On further thought, several unsettled countries in South America – and the lucrative drug trade emanating from some of those countries – might hold a certain appeal.

After being lost in thought for a few moments, Bennett asked, "What attracted your interest in such a situation developing in the Caribbean?"

"Frankie talked about Anton being a keen photographer. What he might be photographing intrigued me. We searched everywhere, and eventually found his camera and laptop hidden where they were unlikely to be found … and wouldn't have been except for Frankie's childhood memories of the cottage. The majority of his shots were of the bay between here and Saint-Marie, and the many luxury yachts anchoring there over a period of time. It's not on the regular tourist route, so why were so many wealthy visitors coming into the area?" I handed over Anton's laptop and camera – and the password, and suffered his wrath for having withheld them. I didn't mention the copies I made of anything I thought might be useful in the future.

Further discussion was avoided when Bennett received a phone call. It was brief but had Bennett up out of his chair again and heading for the door. "It was the commissioner. He has arranged for the removal of the prisoners from the island. I've got about an hour in which to interrogate my rogue officers."

"I'm coming with you," I yelled after him as he bounded down the stairs. I don't know if he heard or not. Regardless, he didn't argue, so I locked my door and raced after him.

Williams was his first target. The sullen young officer, looking considerably less than his usual immaculate self, was uncooperative and strenuously resisted being dragged up out of the cellar to be interviewed. I observed his subsequent interview, which went nowhere and told us nothing. Rather than waste too much time on Williams when it was obvious he wasn't going to tell us anything, Bennett ended the interview and locked the man in the dairy's former cold room. The move alarmed me.

"He won't get any air in there. That's how cold rooms are." I couldn't understand why Bennett just didn't return him to the cellar. He was handcuffed again, so probably wouldn't cause much of a problem.

"There's enough air in there to last him until we move them out. A few minutes of panic on his part might be useful in the long run … might soften him up a bit."

Taylor, the second rogue officer, was openly terrified when Bennett dragged him up from the cellar. He offered no resistance, and was ready to *spill his guts* as they say in the classic movies. As the interview progressed, I found myself almost feeling sorry for the bloke. Bennett started his questioning by focusing on the now missing prisoner they were to deliver to Guadeloupe. Taylor wasn't troubled by loyalty to his fellow officer.

"Williams knew the man, Sir. Williams had his orders, but I didn't know about them until later. I thought he took the prisoner to Guadeloupe like we were supposed to, but his orders were to let the man get away."

"Taylor, you say you thought Williams took the man to Guadeloupe, why didn't you know it didn't happen? You were supposed to accompany Williams and the prisoner until he was handed over to the police on Guadeloupe." Bennett's voice had descended to a deep growl.

"I know, Sir, but I got a call just before we took off for Saint-Marie. My wife had gone into labour. It's our first child and I was upset about missing the birth. I knew she would be upset and angry about it too. I told Williams about it. When we arrived on Saint-Marie, we had about an hour's wait before our flight to Guadeloupe. The prisoner wasn't giving us any trouble so, about half an hour into our waiting time, Williams told me to go to the hospital to be with my wife. He would take the prisoner to Guadeloupe, and would catch up with me again when he returned to Saint-Marie."

"So, in the belief Williams would complete your mission, you went off to the hospital. What happened after that? When did you find out about the prisoner's 'escape'?"

"My son was born around mid-afternoon and I left the hospital soon after. I expected Williams to return on the flight which arrives at about six o'clock. He hadn't told me how or when we were to come back to Île Verte, but I knew it would be too late for the small plane to bring us back then. Williams called me at around five o'clock. Due to inclement weather, his flight was cancelled and he wouldn't return to Saint-Marie until the next morning. He said he was unsure of the timing, but arranged to meet me at the Honoré police station on his return."

"He didn't mention the prisoner at all during that call?"

"No, Sir, he never mentioned anything about Guadeloupe. Later, I knew something was wrong. I had an early dinner and was on my way back to the hospital when I thought I saw Williams go into a house at the far end of town. I told myself I was being stupid and went on to the hospital, but I couldn't put it out of my mind. I knew one of the nurses on duty, and knew she lived almost directly across the road from the house I thought I saw Williams go into. I asked the nurse who lived in the house over the road. When she mentioned the name, I knew it was Williams I saw. His latest girlfriend lives in that house."

"Did you do anything about it?"

"When I left the hospital, I parked along the street a bit from the house and waited. The lights were on inside when I arrived but, by about ten o'clock the place was in darkness. I waited until nearly midnight, but it looked like he was spending the night, so I went home. He arrived by taxi at the police station at nine o'clock next morning. He kept the taxi waiting while he came inside to tell me our flight to Île Verte was leaving at ten o'clock. I went with him in the taxi to the airstrip. He still didn't say anything about the previous night or Guadeloupe. I wanted to know what was going on, so I asked how things went on Guadeloupe. He just said everything was normal; as expected."

"So, when did you find out what happened?"

"It wasn't until the next day. I confronted him about what I saw and demanded to know why he lied. He told me about letting the prisoner escape and how he was following orders. He wouldn't say whose orders they were, but I knew they weren't official. He kept telling me I was implicated because I hadn't followed orders, and it would not go well for me if I spoke to anyone about what happened. I didn't know what I had become involved in, but I was scared. I guessed the deaths here somehow were a part of it. I had to go along with Williams … even when he abducted you and tied you up in that cottage."

At that point, Bennett's phone rang. He told the caller he would call back in a couple of minutes. With Taylor back in the cellar, Bennett returned the commissioner's call. Bennett's contribution to the conversation amounted to nothing more than murmuring *I see* a couple of times. As soon as the call ended, Bennett called Winston. This time, I knew exactly what was happening: A helicopter will land on the front lawn in about ten minutes. Once it has landed, bring Mrs Nettleton out in handcuffs to put her on board with the others.

Then it was my turn to receive my orders. "You must go back into the castle now to join Frankie and Dervla. I don't expect anything untoward to happen, but I want to know they are covered in case anything does happen. I can't spare me or one of my officers to take care of them."

Chapter 26

While I could see the possible need for me to look after the other two women, I can't say I was happy to remove myself from the action. I need not have worried. After my brief explanation of the situation, neither woman wanted to be hidden away inside when everything was happening out on the front lawn. We barely had established that when the thump of the chopper's rotors as it came into land echoed through the building.

We tiptoed along the hallway to keep watch for Winston and Marian Nettleton coming down the stairs. I heard a phone ring somewhere upstairs and presumed it was Bennett calling Winston. A few moments later, Winston escorted Marian down the stairs and to the front door. They stood just inside the door for about a minute as if waiting for some signal to proceed. Then they were out and on their way down the front steps. It was also our cue to move into the lobby to find a vantage point allowing a good view of activities taking place out front.

The commissioner and a number of men in camouflage uniforms stood beside the helicopter. Winston delivered Mrs Nettleton into the safe hands of one of those men. He loaded her onto the chopper. Then Winston accompanied the commissioner and the other uniformed men to the old dairy. Shortly after, they returned with the prisoners under close guard. Bennett and his other officer, Patrick, also returned with the party.

It seemed the well-choreographed event was over in a matter of minutes. Everyone clambered back on board and the chopper lifted off, leaving only the inspector standing on the lawn. He stood watching the machine rise above the tree tops and disappear. By then, we had moved out onto the top step. "I knew it was too much to expect you three to stay safely out of the way," he yelled as he strode across the grass towards us. Delphine intervened before he could say much else.

"I assume you will be interested in morning tea about now."

"Oh, yes please, Delphine. Might we have it in the great hall this morning, please?" Frankie's request proved unnecessary.

"Morning tea is laid out in the hall. I'll just make the coffee if you are ready." Delphine was on her way to the kitchen when Dwayne arrived, accompanied by the Martins, Grevilles and Jackson from the cottages.

As everyone made their way into the great hall, I caught Bennett's arm and held him back a little. "It would be a good thing if the five guests who accompanied Dwayne had the reason for their enforced extended stay on Île Verte explained to them. I imagine it is now safe for them to leave and they are free to go." Bennett acknowledged my comments with a shrug and a nod.

His explanation of everything happening on the island over the previous few days was brief but succinct. It did not include even a hint of what was behind it all. The other five guests stood shaking their heads in dismay. Bennett allowed them a moment to digest all he told them before addressing Jackson. "Perhaps, if everyone could be packed and ready to go by lunchtime, you might arrange for your plane to collect everyone after lunch, say, sometime between one and two o'clock."

Jackson took himself off a short distance to make a phone call. While he was about it, the other couple assured Bennett they could be ready within half an hour if needed. Such hurried preparations were unnecessary. Jackson returned to the group and announced the plane would leave Saint-Marie at one o'clock. The timing suited Bennett.

"Good; Dwayne please organise the golf carts to collect the passengers at about one o'clock for the trip to the airstrip. There will be six of us."

Six passengers… It could only mean Bennett planned to fly out this afternoon as well. No, no; this won't do. He can't leave, not with so many questions remaining unanswered. Loathe to make a scene in front of the others, I leaned in close and whispered, "Could I have a word, please – outside." We left the buzz of excited chatter behind us and strolled out onto the rear deck.

"Before you start, Tessa, let me tell you I will return first thing tomorrow morning ... hopefully with more information than I have now. There are things I must do which I cannot do here. The commissioner and my two officers will return to Saint-Marie from Guadeloupe on this evening's commercial flight. I will have a working dinner with the commissioner and will continue to work with him into the night. You and your friends should use the time until I return to relax and recover as much as possible."

The three of us spent until lunchtime in Frankie's private courtyard. We sipped iced tea, indulged in only sparse conversation devoid of any mention of the events and tragedies of recent days. In spite of everyone trying to be upbeat, lunch was a controlled and sombre affair. And then the guests boarded one of the golf carts, and we joined Bennett and Sampson on the other cart for the run to the airstrip.

As the plane lifted off Île Verte, Sampson murmured, "It will be good to have life here back to normal again."

If only it were possible, I thought. For Frankie, I'm not sure life will ever return to what it was before her birthday bash. It was a thought I revisited later as we sat in the back garden in the cool of the late afternoon.

"Frankie, I know Dervla will need to return home as originally planned, but I am free to stay for as long as I choose. We still have a few days left of our scheduled stay here on the island, but I think I would like to stay on longer with you. Once things settle back to normal around here, the reality of your situation will hit you. I would like to be here to help you through it."

"I think I would like that, but let's talk about it again closer to your scheduled departure date. As you say, I know the reality of it all will hit me some time, but I don't think it will be as devastating as you might imagine. Charles will be missed – a loss – but only for a brief time. In reality, losing him will be more like having a weight lifted off me. Now is not the time for such discussion, but I will explain as soon as I feel able."

We helped Dervla move back into her room before preparing to go down for dinner. Conversation flowed a little more freely over dinner, mainly about what each of us had done over recent months. In spite of the chatter, aided by a very nice red wine, the dining room seemed cavernous and empty. The day had not been a strenuous one for any of us, so no one felt weary. In spite of it, after a quick nightcap on the rear deck, each of us retired to our room for an early night.

My concern for how Dervla would settle back alone in the room next to mine, dictated I should sit up for a while in case she needed support. Doing nothing is not one of my strong points, so I grabbed my laptop and made myself comfortable in my armchair. The journo in me had picked up the scent of a story, not one which would contravene the embargo on what happened here, but something possibly relevant to it. It was after midnight when I stopped to review the mountain of research I ferreted out.

"Safe to say Dervla is coping okay," I told the universe. "Time for me to call it a night." I was tired by the time I sunk into bed, but sleep, deep, restful sleep, was a long time coming. The outcome of my research kept my mind churning until well into the morning.

*****

The thick head caused by last night's research and poor sleep accompanied me to breakfast. On the other hand, my two companions looked disgustingly bright and refreshed this morning. As we neared the end of breakfast, Sampson dropped into the dining room to tell Frankie Jackson had called. He would return Inspector Bennett to the island at about nine o'clock. The sour look on Frankie's face after Sampson departed concerned me. As soon as Sampson was out of earshot, her comment matched her face.

"So, the inspector will be back in a bit over an hour. Are we supposed to be excited, or should we spend the time bracing ourselves for his return?"

"Frankie, what's wrong? Why make such a comment?"

"How long has he been on this island, and what has he discovered? We still don't know what was behind Anton's death. Why was Charles shot? Bennett has told us nothing. I suspect it is because he hasn't been able to find out anything. He's out of his depth with his investigation. A total waste of time."

"I think you are being a tad unfair, Frankie. Bennett's return to Saint-Marie yesterday was to seek some of those answers. I suggest you wait to see what he has learned before dismissing his efforts as a waste of time. There was so much more I wanted to throw at her, but I realised some of the information Bennett shared with me, he hadn't shared with Frankie. I don't think he intended I should pass it on to her, so I bit my tongue.

"You appear to be getting on quite well with the good inspector, so I wouldn't expect much else from you."

Breakfast was over, and there was nothing more to be said. On our way out of the dining room, Dervla claimed she had things to do in her room. As I climbed the stairs with her, I wondered whether the exchange of words between Frankie and me might have caused her retreat. She didn't volunteer any information and I didn't pursue the matter. I was pleased Dervla went to her room. My time in my room would be brief. I needed to collect my notebook … and then I had issues to pursue.

On my way along the hallway, I tried mentally rehearsing what I would say. It was to no avail when Frankie opened her door. Her tear-streaked face just about broke my heart. "I'm so sorry, Tessa. I don't know what came over me. I didn't mean those things I said."

It took a few minutes for us both the regain our equilibrium. But, once things settled, I felt it safe to pursue the reason for my visit. "If you feel up to it, there are a few questions I'd like to ask you. If it becomes too stressful, we will stop." She nodded and admitted she thought it might help.

"Okay; at the risk being personal, I want to ask you about Charles. I don't think yours was a marriage made in heaven. I suspect it was a whole different place, and not one in which you were happy."

"I wasn't happy, but I felt trapped. He wasn't a physical bully … well, only a couple of times, and then it wasn't serious … but, the way he treated me was bullying, only in a different way. He put me down, derided me and insulted me at every opportunity, even in front of the staff on occasions. I lost all self-esteem and retreated into my shell."

"But, you found the courage to arrange a birthday party. Why did you invite me to you birthday bash – when we both know you weren't actually turning forty? What prompted all this?"

"Not what, but who; It's all down to Delphine and her mother, Maryanne. They said they had suffered the way he treated me long enough. If I did not stand up to him – do something about it – they were both leaving. Maryanne came here as a young girl. Delphine was born here. They know more about this island than I ever will, and their loyalty and support has sustained me all these years. I couldn't survive without them. It took me a while to pluck up the courage to do anything, and it was with their help I came up with the idea of the birthday party. I needed you here, Tessa. I have followed your career, and I knew I needed you here to save me."

"Save you from what? From Charles, from yourself, from wasting your life … what was I going to save you from, and how?"

"All of the above and more. There was something else involved too. I knew it … sensed it I suppose … but I couldn't work out what it was. I knew it involved Charles, and me and my island somehow facilitated whatever he was up to. What he wasn't doing was writing. I'm sure he hasn't written a word since we were married."

"Whatever possessed you to marry him? I'm sure he wasn't the only person ever to show an interest in you."

"Oh, you have no idea how charming and attentive he was – before we were married. You're right, there were plenty of others hanging around, but they were more interested in my family connection than in me. And, great aunt Lucille's bequest brought a whole swarm of them out of the woodwork. I suppose I had hit a brick wall in my life; found myself questioning everything. My career was going well, but it had lost its excitement. My life didn't seem to have much purpose or direction. Charles paid me a lot of attention before I decided to move here to the island to live. I continued working for my old firm from here on a contract basis for quite a while. It meant many regular trips to France. My life was going nowhere, I had no family, and no real ties apart from to this island. Somehow, I came to the idea sharing my life with someone would give it more purpose, more meaning. So, the charming Charles became part of it. And then he took over my life and forgot how to be charming."

"Initially, there must've been some real feelings on Charles' part for him to commit to spending the rest of his life on an island in the middle of nowhere. Perhaps the magic – the novelty of it all – wore off. I would be the least knowledgeable person to offer advice on such situations, not having notched up any long-term relationships in my past."

"No I don't think there was ever any magic involved. Almost from the time we were married, his focus was on establishing his own suite of rooms – to better facilitate his writing of course. As soon as his rooms were ready, he moved in … or more precisely, he moved out of my rooms, out of my bedroom. I provided him with a home, a lifestyle and enough income to be comfortable. So, I suppose it made me important in his life, but not as a wife. I was an opportunity; a convenience. I know you're probably wondering why I didn't tell him to go. I did, several times, but when he refused to leave, what could I do? Having Anton here was the only thing keeping me sane."

"I know you were fond of Anton. I think you still have to deal with his death. The challenge of dealing with it is likely to come once everything here settles down."

"I'm not sure 'fond' describes what I felt for Anton. Truth is, I don't know what I felt but, whatever it was, it was strong. There was a strong bond between us. It was as though we were… Argh, I don't know how to describe what it was. I was a lot older than him, so I won't allow myself to think it was some sort of romantic attachment."

"Maybe not, but it seems you were kindred spirits. Two people who shared the same interests; who saw the world in the same colours. You've talked a lot about your life with Charles, but there hasn't been any mention of what he was doing when you met him."

"You mean, apart from his supposed writing career? I suppose, the short answer is I don't know anything apart from his supposedly being a full-time writer when I met him in Paris. I'm sure I don't need to tell you there was little evidence of his having written anything for a long time before we were married."

I decided to push on with my questioning in the vain hope it might shake loose some flashes of forgotten memory. "Were there never any clues, any references, to suggest what else he might be doing with his life before you married?"

"No. It was as though he dropped onto earth the day before I met him. Oh, I asked questions – tried to work conversations around to elicit information – but nothing was forthcoming and, more importantly, he did it in a way that didn't make me feel I was fobbed off. What about you, Tessa, was there no one you ever wanted to settle down with?"

"No. A few nice, but short-lived, relationships along the way, but nothing more. My career and its associated lifestyle haven't been conducive to any permanent arrangements … and still isn't. It's not something I hanker for. Maybe it's because I haven't met the right person yet."

Our conversation came to a sudden end when Jackson's light plane was heard coming in to land. We went in search of Sampson or Dwayne with the idea of going to the airstrip to welcome Bennett back. Sampson was already at the airstrip, and Dwayne was nowhere around. Frankie and I sat side-by-side on the top of the front steps and waited the twenty minutes before Sampson delivered Bennett to the front door.

At the same time as the golf cart arrived, Dervla joined us. Frankie and I stood to welcome Bennett. "What, no red carpet...?" He chirped as he came up the steps. "Still, I suppose it's good to know I'm welcome."

"How welcome rather depends on the information you brought with you. Sampson, take his bag to his room. It's a little early, but I think we might start with morning tea." Frankie, becoming more her usual self, let us know she was in charge.

With only the four of us for morning tea, the vastness of the great hall felt almost overwhelming. Little time was wasted on small talk before Bennett, recognising our desperation for information, took the conversation in the direction we wanted. "So, where shall we start? Let me have your first question."

"We could start at the beginning, in which case our first questions relate to Anton." I jumped in ahead of Frankie in the hope of preventing her earlier waspish attitude making a reappearance and maybe derailing the whole process before we're off the mark.

"Yes, please. Can we talk about Anton?" A so subdued Frankie had me nervous. I was waiting for the wasp to resurface. I let her continue. "Why was he killed?"

"Ah, yes; let's tackle the hard ones first. To answer those questions, and probably anything else you want to know about Anton, I need to tell you a story." I saw Frankie move forward into the attack position on her chair. "Relax and listen, Frankie. It is my way, or not at all." With the game plan explained, Frankie slumped back in her chair, but the dark look remained on her face. Satisfied, Bennett continued.

"First, let's call young Anton by his proper name." I heard a simultaneous gasp from Frankie and Dervla, but Bennett seemed not to notice and continued without missing a beat. "In real life, he was Mathieu Bergeron. Mathieu had no brother; no living family. The man he corresponded with, and you believed to be his brother, is Lucien Charvet. He was not related to Mathieu in any way. Lucien was Mathieu's handler; his contact."

"False names ... handler ... this is starting to sound like an extract from a spy novel." Dervla looked at Frankie as she spoke, but Frankie didn't notice. She was too stunned to notice.

"Are we back in spooks territory again?" The question probably was unnecessary, but I felt I should ask it so none of us was under any misapprehension about what we were discussing.

"Yep, we're talking spooks again. London recruited Mathieu some time ago to work undercover. He infiltrated a small circle of men who met semi-regularly in Paris, and whose interest London felt might not be in the best interest of others ... if you get my meaning. For quite a long period, Mathieu fed valuable intel back to London before something went awry. It wasn't confirmed at the time, but there were strong indications his cover was blown. Nobody knew how, but it was obvious Mathieu had become an endangered species. London arranged for him to disappear, but left him with one contact ... a sort of 'in case of emergency' thing. That contact, another of London's undercover operatives, was Lucien Charvet."

"So, somehow, London 'disappeared' Mathieu – complete with new identity – here to Île Verte. Was Charles involved in this sleight of hand?" Frankie's voice was sharpish, but the wasp hadn't yet returned.

Bennett studied Frankie for a moment while considering his words before answering. "Back when Charles was thought to be involved in the misbehaviour which saw Nettleton, Seymour and a couple of others dismissed from the Service, he too was dismissed. None of them was prosecuted due to a lack of hard evidence, although circumstantial evidence was overwhelming. Later, Charles was cleared of any wrong doing. While records will show Charles never rejoined the Service, he continued to have contact, and proved useful on a couple of occasions in carrying out successful operations for London."

"What did you call them, Tessa...spooks? Inspector, are you telling me Charles continued as a spook?" Frankie's stunned look turned to one of disbelief.

"I'm afraid so, Frankie. Because he had been tarred with the same brush as Nettleton, Seymour and the others, Charles' continued involvement with London was kept quiet. It allowed

Charles to meet with his former colleagues in Paris on a regular basis for some time afterwards. Then something happened. It spooked Charles. He wanted out of Paris; out of France. I'm sorry, Frankie, but it seems that's where you came in handy."

"So, I was his ticket to escape to a remote island. It helps explain a few things – like a marriage that was nothing more than a sham. But, after our marriage, he continued to meet with those men in Paris. It wasn't a regular thing, but it was often. If something frightened him enough to want to escape Paris, why did he keep going back?"

"He promoted his life as a full-time writer and, as such needed to meet with his agent and editor in Paris every so often. By not severing ties completely with the others, it gave his escape increased credibility and, in a strange way, helped keep him safe."

"…Until they killed him." Frankie's voice was flat and she appeared deep in thought. "I'm sorry, Inspector, but I think I need some time to absorb this information. Perhaps we might take a short break before meeting again in the dining room for lunch at twelve o'clock?" She received unanimous approval. "Good; I will inform Delphine."

Frankie was out of her chair and supposedly heading for the kitchen to speak to Delphine. The three of us left behind exchanged looks. "Best we give her a bit of space to digest everything. I might go to my room until lunch." I hoped mentioning going to my room would encourage Dervla to do the same. It was Bennett who picked up on the hint.

"Yeah, me to; I need to unpack, and I have calls and paperwork begging for attention. This might be a good time to knock over some of it."

It worked. The three of us climbed the stairs together. After I let myself into my room, Dervla and Bennett continued together to their respective rooms. I judged fifteen minutes to be ample time before slipping out and hurrying along to Frankie's rooms.

Chapter 27

"A bit too hard to hear, wasn't it?" I said as Frankie let me in. "I know you suggested time alone, but I was concerned for you, and wanted to check you were okay. How are you holding up?" She shrugged. "If you would rather I left you alone, just say … or, if you want to talk, I'm here for you."

"Please stay. Talking might help me understand it better. I just don't know what to say. I had no idea about any of it … and Anton *was* an artist."

"Yes, he was, and it worked well as his cover while he was here."

"Did I miss something, Tessa? If all Bennett said is true, I don't understand why Charles would invite the Nettletons and the Seymours here; why he would risk exposing Anton … or Mathieu, if you prefer. From the line of work you are in, you know more about this spooks business than I do."

"I don't know why they were invited. Maybe a situation developed, and exposing Anton was a way of flushing it out into the open. It's a question for Bennett when we meet again."

This morning's revelations resulted in lunch being a low key event. Rather than hold up the staff who wanted to clear the table, when we finished eating, we moved to Frankie's sitting room. As soon as we sat down, Frankie asked why Charles invited the Nettletons and Seymours. Bennett picked his words slowly and carefully.

"We are led to believe a situation of some sort was suspected or had developed. London knew about it and agreed an offensive move was essential to prevent something far bigger developing. Charles' invitation might have been designed to call out whoever was behind it."

"So one of them killed Anton, thanks to Charles' strategic manoeuvre backfiring. How stupid could he be?"

"No Frankie, I don't think that's how it happened. I'm sure, if surveillance equipment were available at the time, the equipment would show the Nettletons and the Seymours were inside the castle throughout the duration of the storm. But, it would also show the crossbow and its bolt being removed from its display during the blackout. Early the next morning, Jackson came across Nettleton standing on a table pushed against the wall under the crossbow exhibit. When he questioned Nettleton about what he was doing, Nettleton said he was checking the display to see if it were a real crossbow and bolts, or a decorative reproduction."

"He wasn't checking anything! He was returning the bow after it had been used. He shot Anton!"

"No. As I said before, those four people made sure they were accounted for at the time of the murder. I believe Nettleton removed the bow and the bolt from the display – and was returning the bow later when Jackson saw him – but he didn't kill Anton. Someone else did." Bennett was displaying exceptional patience with Frankie.

"The bloke in the derelict cottage…!" I blurted it out before engaging my brain. I gave Bennett an apologetic look. "Sorry; maybe you had better explain."

He threw his hands up in resignation, and then delivered an abbreviated version of the events surrounding the arrest of the bloke hiding out in the derelict cottage. I noticed this version did not mention the man's meeting with Nettleton prior to the man's arrest. In my opinion, that wasn't fair, so I stepped in to correct the 'oversight'.

"Earlier, I saw lights moving about in the trees – the same ones you saw Dervla – and I went to investigate. I found the derelict cottage and hid in the trees at the edge of the clearing to observe a meeting taking place around an outdoor fireplace out front. The meeting was between Nettleton and the bloke hiding in the cottage. As we now know, it was Nettleton who attacked

Dervla later. He was on his way back to his room after the meeting when Dervla surprised him."

The furrows in Frankie's brow told me she was deep in thought, troubling thought. What troubled her became clear when she asked her next question. "I still can't understand why Charles would invite those people here, and risk Anton, when he knew what they were like."

"We believe something forced Charles to risk it. We don't know what and, if they know, London isn't saying. All I can think of is how Charles' must have felt when he found Anton's body the night of the storm. His feeling of guilt might be what drove him to try to swim to Saint-Marie for help. I wish we knew what initiated such a risky move in the first place. It might answer a few other questions as well." Bennett sounded apologetic as he tried explaining to Frankie. He would be overwhelmed by feelings of frustration and inadequacy ... and I felt for the man.

"So, who did shoot Charles? In his case, it was a bullet and not a crossbow bolt. Why would the murderer use two different methods?"

"We don't know it was the same person in both cases. And, we don't know the time frame in which the two incidents occurred."

"Yes we do! It was during the storm." Frankie's frustration had her barking. While I could sympathise with her, I felt for Bennett. He was doing the best he could to answer her questions.

Bennett was shaking his head as he responded. "We don't know that. Anton left the party early. He might have been killed earlier before the storm hit. We are reasonably convinced Charles found Anton's body after he and the two staff checked on the generator. There might have been a couple of hours between those two incidents. London assures us they don't know what precipitated this whole situation. They claim they heard nothing from Charles or any of their other operatives for some time prior to Frankie's birthday party."

"It sounds like the suggestion is whatever situation triggered the invitations arose suddenly, and Frankie's birthday party provided an unforeseen opportunity for Charles to respond to whatever it was." After I said it, a worrying thought occurred to me. I found myself hoping Frankie wouldn't start blaming herself in part for what happened, and was relieved when she didn't appear to react.

In his most soothing voice, Bennett continued trying to help Frankie understand they too were frustrated by the lack of details. "I hoped Charles might have kept a diary, journal or some other paperwork which would shed light on events leading up to the party. We didn't find anything, but his rooms already had been turned over when I looked through them. I think it goes without saying, Nettleton and friends probably looked for the same things as I hoped to find. The big question is: did they find anything? Somehow, I don't think they did."

Frankie was up off her chair and pacing around the room. "Whatever else Charles might have been, he was meticulous. If he knew the danger – and it appears he was well aware – he would have an insurance policy in case things went bad. I mean, he would have some form of documentary evidence explaining everything and implicating those involved. It was the nature of the man. If you didn't find anything, whoever searched his rooms first must have it." A long, heavy silence filled the room after Frankie finished speaking.

She knew Charles better than of any of us, and what she said made sense. I felt a heaviness descend over me. The thought we might never know why two people lost their lives that night was hard for me to handle. What must it be like for Frankie? I suppose I half expected her to fall to pieces. She didn't. With a determined look on her face, she kept pacing the room, but her pacing stepped up a notch to become more heavy-footed. Her sudden halt took us all by surprise.

"Tessa, come with me. There's something I want you to look at."

Caught off guard, I scrambled out of my chair and strode after Frankie who already was out of the sitting room. There was a moment's delay while she unlocked the connecting door to Charles' suite.

"In here," she yelled over her shoulder as I followed her through the sitting room towards Charles' bedroom. "Now, tell me, what's your opinion of that thing?" she demanded as we stood facing the wall opposite the foot of his bed. "You've seen Charles' rooms, his furniture and everything. Does it fit with everything else? Does it look like it belonged to the man who occupied these rooms?"

The 'thing' in question was screwed high up on the wall in front of me. A glass-fronted display case had its wooden frame screwed to the wall. About a metre by 600 millimetres, it looked quite shallow, maybe 50 millimetres deep. Tacked to a mount board inside the case was a piece of textile of vaguely Middle-Eastern design and of average quality at best. Unless it held some sentimental attachment, I could not understand why anyone would want to hang it on their wall. I tried choosing my words carefully.

"While I don't know its story, I don't see it as something a bloke would hang on his bedroom wall. What do you know about it? Did Charles ever tell you its history?"

"No, and I certainly had plenty to say about it going up on the wall. He told me this was his room and he would decorate it however he liked. It has to come down. I want it removed now."

"Yeah, Frankie, I probably would take it down too, but is this the appropriate time to be fussing about it?"

"Tessa, at the risk of making a right fool of myself, I want it taken down now. Don't ask why or give me a hard time about it. I'll call the men to come and take it down."

Bennett wandered along to see what we were up to and now stood leaning against the door jamb. "I'll take it down for you. I should be able to reach if I stand on a chair. All I need is a screwdriver." There was something about Bennett's voice. It was low and soothing, but I thought I detected a hint of excitement in it.

While the hunt for a screwdriver happened, I used my phone to photograph the room from various angles, all of which included the display case. For the final shot, I stood on the bed to be almost at the same height as the case, and zoomed in for a close-up of the case and its contents. As I climbed off the bed, Frankie and Bennett returned with the requisite screwdriver and a four-rung ladder. Not wasting any time, Bennett positioned the ladder and began unscrewing the case from the wall. The hunt for a screwdriver had involved Sampson, and he arrived to see why the tool was required.

His arrival was timed to perfection. He was able to support the case while Bennett removed the last two screws. I helped Sampson lower the case onto the bed. We all gathered around for a closer look at the textile it contained … all except Bennett, that is. He remained up the ladder. His exclamation shifted our interest from the textile to the wall.

"Well now, what have we here?" Bennett wiped his hand across the bricks several times, with each pass pausing almost imperceptibly over a couple of bricks. "Sampson, hand me the screwdriver again please."

As he used the screwdriver to lever out the first brick, he grunted and muttered to himself. "Bastard is loose, but doesn't want to come out. Ah, here it comes."

The first brick came out and was soon followed by the second brick. As he removed them, Bennett handed them down to me. "They look as though they were thinned down a bit. Are the other bricks up there the same thickness?" The face of the bricks was the same size as all the other bricks in the wall. It was only the depth of the brick which seemed wrong.

Bennett didn't answer my question. He was preoccupied with scrabbling around in the cavity created by the extracted bricks. Such scrabbling included much grunting and many surprised exclamations, but nothing to explain what he was doing. Then, it was all over.

"Here, hold this." A bundle of stuff was handed down to me. Comprised of a number of loose items, I struggled not to drop any.

Then Bennett was down from the ladder and taking the bundle from me … before I had a chance to examine any of it.

All I managed to identify in the brief time I held it were two hard-covered small notebooks, more than one data memory stick, and possibly a disc or two. As Bennet slid everything into a large plastic bag, I tried improving my knowledge of the items which came out of the now gaping cavity in the wall. Everything slid into the bag so quickly and smoothly, I didn't learn any more. Where did the bag come from anyway? Do coppers go around with large plastic bags in their pockets as a matter of course?

Frankie did not see the material retrieved from the wall cavity. Sometime after the display case came down from the wall, Dervla wandered in to see what was keeping us. She caught our attention when she murmured, "Vaguely Moroccan perhaps…"

The textile grabbed her interest, and she and Frankie became engrossed in analysing the pattern woven into it. With all the material from the secret cavity secured in the plastic bag, Bennett gave me a meaningful look as he shoved the bag down the front of his shirt and squashed it as flat as possible to prevent a tell-tale bulge. Then he engineered his escape from the room. "Jesus! I just remembered something I meant to look at in my room; back in a few minutes. Don't do anything exciting without me."

The two women looked up from the textile, but Bennett was on his way out. Frankie raised her eyebrows at me. I shrugged and shook my head to signify I didn't know what his hasty departure was about … and hoped I looked convincing. Bennett and I would be having a quiet conversation later about why he did not want Frankie to know about the material he found.

During the subsequent twenty minutes, at Frankie's insistence, we turned the display case over onto its front. Convinced the case held some hidden secret, Frankie wanted to open the case and remove the textile. The trusty screwdriver was pressed into service again to remove the screws holding the back of the case in place. With the back removed, the mounting board with the textile tacked to it was lifted out. Frankie fetched a pair of nail scissors and snipped the threads holding the textile in place. We then had three pieces – case, mount board and textile piece

– none of which held any secrets. Leaving everything spread across Charles' bed, two dejected women and I traipsed back to Frankie's sitting room.

Delphine arrived a few moments later to inquire about afternoon tea, and met Bennett at the door on her way out. "I've asked Delphine for afternoon tea in the back garden. They will bring it out in a few minutes. Perhaps we might move out there now to take in some fresh air while we wait." We all rose together and followed her out through the great hall and into the garden.

Dervla announced we had only a couple more days left to spent on Île Verte. It cast a dampener over the group. I saw Bennett's face fall, and I received a quizzical look from Frankie. "Oh, I'm sorry Dervla, I meant to tell you earlier. I realise, because of your work commitments, you need to return home as planned. Freelancing allows me more flexibility. I offered to stay on a little longer with Frankie once every-thing settled down here to make sure she was okay before I left her alone. Will you be all right flying back on your own?"

"Of course I will be all right. I usually travel by myself. It is good someone is able to stay with Frankie for a while. I was concerned we would all leave the place at once, and things might catch up with her once she was alone."

"Miss Dubois will not be alone." Delphine's haughty comment and stern look assured me Frankie would be in good hands after I left. Whether it was due to clearing the air between us, or the afternoon tea waiting for us, the group seemed to relax. After afternoon tea, Frankie thought she would like a rest before dinner. Dervla supported the idea. I was happy to spend time in my room or somewhere else on my own, but I really wanted time alone with Bennett to interrogate him about a number of things. In the hope he wouldn't disappear in a hurry when the others left, I made a point of settling back with yet another long glass of iced tea.

"Not in a rush to go back to your room?" he asked quietly as the others made their way across the lawn.

"Not particularly interested in going to my room at all."

"Good; that gives us time to sit and chat. Shall we walk, or are you happy to remain out here?"

I was happy to remain where I was, and I didn't want to waste a moment of the time I had with him. "Why didn't you want Frankie to know about the stuff you found in the wall cavity? Surely she has a right to know."

"Thanks for playing along. At the time, I didn't know what any of it contained. On the one hand, I didn't want to get her hopes up only to find they were love letters from some unknown female. On the other hand, if she knew about the stuff, she would want to see it – read it or whatever. As it is subject to the Official Secrets Act, she can't. It's best she remains ignorant of its existence. Who knows, maybe at some time in the future, she might find out about it."

"For you to say it comes under the Official Secrets Act, I assume you looked at some of it."

"I glanced through one notebook. Some of it is in long hand. The rest of it is in some form of cypher or code. As I plan to spend a couple more days here 'wrapping things up', I hope to spend some time on it before I have to hand it over to the relevant authorities. Enough about that stuff … I am pleased to hear you are staying on for a while. Perhaps you – and Frankie if she feels inclined – might visit Saint-Marie occasionally while you are here. If Frankie comes, there is nice accommodation available over there. If you come on your own, my beach shack has a reasonably comfortable spare room in its annex."

"I should like to see your annex. And, if you find yourself needing some help with any of the material you found, I'd be happy to help."

"And I would see details of it all in an article sometime soon…?"

"Of course not; at the moment I'm pursuing a different line altogether for an opinion piece. Maybe we should freshen up before dinner. Then, after dinner, we might engineer an early night, and somehow make a start on that material."

We climbed the stairs to our respective rooms together.

Chapter 28

This afternoon's rest period seemed to work wonders at lifting spirits, resulting in dinner being considerably brighter and chattier than lunch. Dervla dominated conversation. She spoke to her office and received news of two new – and apparently exciting – projects she would be managing on her return. Her enthusiasm eased my mind and erased any concerns about her being offended by my not returning home with her. In spite of the changed mood, dinner didn't drag on.

Dervla went off with Frankie to look at something Frankie wanted to show her, while Bennet and I went upstairs. With the two women otherwise engaged, we didn't need to resort to a clandestine meeting. We went straight to Bennett's room and got down to business. He spread out the stash from the wall cavity on a small table he dragged out into the middle of the room.

"Have you looked at any of the stuff on the memory sticks?"

He hadn't, and I marvelled at his self-restraint. I wouldn't be able to stop myself. They would be in my computer as soon as I was back in my room. Bennett handed me a stick. "See what is on this one while I create an inventory of all this material. Chain of evidence and all that, you know how it goes."

It didn't occur to me when we came upstairs, but I should have collected my laptop on my way past my room. A quick trip, to collect it … and I collected something else while I was there. A couple of minutes later, I added a small plastic container to the stash of material on the table. "You might find its contents interesting and useful to your investigation." I explained the sample of accelerant I collected from that patch of grass outside Anton's studio. The expected lecture about withholding evidence followed, but was neither severe nor long.

Moments later, everything had settled down, and I had the memory stick's folders up on my screen. The folder names told me nothing, and the last dates the folders were accessed meant even less. Okay, that's enough fiddling about, I told myself. Open the folder at the top of the list.

"Christ! How many files are there in this folder? ...And they are all large." Counting the files as I went, I scrolled to the end of the list of files in the first folder. "Tom, after opening the first folder, I am now looking at a list of fifteen files; every one of them large."

"Well, don't just sit there. Find out what they contain. I'm almost finished the inventory. After that, I'll start on another of the memory sticks."

Bennett brought a small printer with him to the island. The amount of stuff I wanted to print out far exceeded the capacity of the slow, pint-sized machine. I resorted to copying everything onto my hard drive instead. There was a limit to how much of that I could do before I ran into trouble with my hard drive. My problem was solved when Bennett decided to visit the dining room's liquor cabinet to fetch us something to sustain through the long night ahead. While he was gone, I slipped back to my room to collect a large capacity solid state external drive I carry with me.

My external drive sped up the copying operation. By the time Bennett returned, the contents of the first memory stick were replicated on my drive. When Bennett knocked on the door to be let back in, I had just slipped a DVD into my computer. I let it do its thing while I went to open the door. It wasn't locked, but Bennett had his hands full with a bottle of scotch, a bowl of ice, and tumblers. For a moment, I wondered how much work we might manage tonight and how reliable any of it might be, if we applied ourselves to lowering the level of the contents of the scotch bottle.

While Bennett faffed about adding ice and scotch to tumblers, I quickly copied the DVD to my external drive. Then we were both seated at our computers and sipping our drinks as we worked. I gave one more memory stick a cursory investigation – and copied it – before turning my attention to the notebooks.

That's when I decided to put an end to sipping scotch for the rest of the night.

Nothing distinguished one notebook from the other, but somehow one seemed to call me to it. I was to discover the one I chose was the first of Charles' notebooks . Making sense of what he wrote ... or, should that be deciphering his notes? ... would not be easy. "Tom, to me, this stuff looks like a combination of cyphers and codes."

"What's the difference ... and does it matter?"

"Cyphers are where something else is substituted for individual numbers or letters. Codes are where whole words are replaced, including sometimes by symbols. I might play around with this for a while to see if I can identify any patterns."

"You know about all this how?"

"Some time ago, on a long running investigation I worked closely with – became close to, might be more accurate – a cryptographer assigned to the case. He taught me a lot and we ended up working together on parts of the investigation."

I started yawning and the yawns became more frequent. I checked the time. It was after midnight. My eyes were hanging out and a throbbing head heralded the onset of the mother of all headaches. After a hurried goodnight to Bennett, I picked up my gear and headed for my room. I decided a warm shower might help me get to sleep. About ten minutes after returning to my room I was in bed and inviting sleep to visit me.

*****

Awake earlier than usual this morning, I spent the time before breakfast reviewing last night's work. Whatever Frankie and Dervla planned for today held little interest for me. I wanted to return to Charles' material. In particular, the notebook I looked at last night. After spending sometime pondering the situation, by the time I went down for breakfast, two things occupied my mind: how to avoid the others' plans for today without upsetting anyone, and how to ask Frankie a couple of questions without arousing her suspicions. Before breakfast was over, I worked out how to approach both those issues.

"Frankie, I know Charles posed as a writer but, he didn't maintain the image well. A writer reads a lot, and usually has books everywhere. Charles' rooms are all but devoid of books, and the rest of the place seems to be too. Did he have a favourite book, or poetry he returned to often over the time you knew him?"

"Well … was he a writer? You're wrong about the books. The castle has a library containing loads of books, mostly from Lucille's time. It was where Bennett conducted his interviews."

"Of course; I had forgotten about that room." I groaned inwardly. The prospect of searching through a library of books to find one particular book didn't excite me.

"There was a book. I don't know if Charles ever read it, but I often saw him with it … something to do with philosophy, or behavioural studies, or something heavy like that. I think it might be a bit like Freud or one of those blokes. I don't remember him ever being interested in poetry."

"I didn't find such a book in his rooms when I searched them. Might it be in the library? I hoped not.

She thought for a moment. "I don't remember ever seeing Charles in the library. Did you check the office? Despite having his own study, he spent most of his time in the main office. It's possible he had it in there." I told her she had me intrigued about what it might be, and thought I might have a look for it later.

Conversation then turned to what the two women planned for today. Frankie was taking Dervla all over the island to photograph the rainforest, beaches and anything else part of the island's tropical environment. I begged off going, citing a poor night's sleep which left me with a headache now promising to develop into a migraine. To add credibility to my story, I made an immediate escape to my room. Bennett knocked on my door about half an hour later.

"I saw them head off on one of the golf carts. What are your plans for today?"

"First up, I'll search for Charles' book Frankie mentioned. I wondered if it might be one of Nietzsche's works."

"Why do you want it? We have plenty of other stuff to sift through."

"It might be the key to the code used in the notebooks. We have to start somewhere, and it seems as good a place as anywhere."

"If you find it! It's possible whoever turned over his rooms before you searched might have had the same idea."

"The thought did occur to me, but I'm not prepared to give it credence yet."

"If your assumption is correct, we might have a problem. How's your German?"

"Eh...? What's that got to do with anything?"

"Charles Allerton was something of a linguist; fluent in German among other languages. He seems such an obnoxious sod, if he had a volume of Nietzsche's work, it's probably in its original German and not an English translation."

"Shit; that won't make life easy. No ... I'm not going to think about such a possibility until and unless we find the book."

Hidden amongst ancient historical files in the bottom drawer of an unlocked rusty filing cabinet, a file labelled 'Dismissed and Deceased Employees' contained a copy of Nietzsche's 1883 work *Thus Spoke Zarathustra.* "Yes...! Thank you, God. It's an English translation," I yelped, and almost startled the life out of Bennett.

We retreated to our respective rooms to work on various aspects of the recovered material. In my case, it was the notebook. After about half an hour with Nietzsche's book, I felt almost certain a substitution code was used ... but I needed a key to start with. I chose this notebook because the date on the first page (in plain English) was the same as the first file on the first memory stick I looked at. If I'm honest, even then, I was hoping for some correlation between the two. The worrying aspect was the two strange symbols used in the first set of handwritten notes. This was inconsistent with a straight substitution code.

With the material saved on my hard drive last night opened on my computer, I tried comparing the contents of the first file with the first set of notes in the book. About ten minutes later, I had a tentative translation for one of the symbols: the name of a town. Another half hour elapsed before I felt I might have pinned down the second symbol: a person's name. "Okay, let's assume I'm correct," I told the universe. "Where do we go from here?" Without any noticeable help from the universe, it was slow going, but I had made some progress by the time a knock on my door interrupted me.

Dwayne announced Delphine was preparing lunch for us and it would be ready in about ten minutes. Message delivered, he turned to leave, and bumped into Bennett who came to collect me for lunch. "You look a bit 'fog-bound'," he commented after Dwayne left. "How is the work coming along? We need to remember we don't need to kill ourselves over it."

"If you asked me an hour or so ago, I had a different answer. Now, I feel safe in saying I have cracked the code for the first set of notes in this book. If he remained consistent as he went along, the rest of the book should be a doddle to decipher."

Only Tom and I lunched in the dining room. The two women, having taken a picnic hamper with them, didn't return to the castle until around four o'clock. It's as well they were so excited about their day and waxed lyrical about it all through dinner, as Tom and I were brain dead and incapable of nothing more than a few smiles and the odd word or two.

*****

Tom stood with Frankie and me on the edge of the airstrip to wave Dervla off on the first leg of her trip home. He too departed for Saint-Marie the next day. The following week was a time of consolidation. A time in which Frankie endeavoured to come to terms with her changed situation, and I tried to keep her busy, both mentally and physically. By accident, I discovered she had started writing in secret about twelve months earlier. Fearing an unpleasant reaction from Charles to her new-found interest, she kept it hidden from everyone. After some persuasion, she allowed me to read some of it. It was good. She had talent. I encouraged her to keep going.

"Let's talk to Dervla about this. She is a PR professional and could prove valuable in promoting your work ... or at least suggest how to go about it. I can edit for you. I've done a bit of that in my time, not only of my own work ... and I know a publisher or two."

As expected, she put forward every excuse for not going public with her work ... but it really was good and I wasn't about to back down. She finally agreed, but was adamant she wanted something 'meaty'—a really powerful story—for her first release. I had an idea.

"Why don't we research the story associated with that derelict cottage in the rainforest. Even if you don't want the world to know the true story, why the cottage was abandoned might provide the basis for a thrilling fiction yarn." I managed to convince her, and we planned our research, starting with interviewing Delphine's mother, Maryann.

Reluctant at first, Maryann needed encouraging before she began telling the story of the cottage.

"Lucille had it built for her Spanish architect to live in whenever he was here on the island. It took a long time to establish this place and build the castle. Along the way, Lucille and the architect became close ... real close. I suppose, to maintain an acceptable image, they tried to keep their relationship secret. The architect continued to stay in the cottage, and Lucille would join him most nights when no one was around."

"She was quite a girl, judging by what little I know of her." The more I learned about Lucille, the more I liked her.

Frankie was shaking her head. "What did it matter if people knew about it? Who were they to judge? Anyway, what happened? They never married. She was still single when she died."

"It seems the architect didn't feel as strongly about Lucille as she felt about him." Maryanne looked uncomfortable, and needed further encouragement before continuing with the story. "A young couple worked for Lucille. Not long married, the husband was employed on building the castle, while his young wife was a housemaid. It seems the young wife caught the architect's eye."

"Oh dear; it does not sound like this story has a happy ending, but I suspect it will answer my question about what went wrong." Frankie took a deep breath when she finished speaking. It was as though she was preparing herself for bad news ... and bad news was what was forthcoming.

"Late one evening, when everyone was at dinner, the young wife remembered she hadn't yet collected the lunchtime tray from the architect's cottage. She took a lantern and went to collect it. What she didn't realise was, the architect was running late for dinner and hadn't yet joined the others. It seems the architect made advances to the young wife on several occasions and she always rebuffed him. She only went to the cottage that night because she thought it would be safe while he was at dinner with the others. He was still at the cottage and raped her; knocked her about badly according to reports and left her on the floor of the cottage while he calmly took himself off to dinner with the others."

"Oh dear, this is not heading in a good direction," I murmured. No one commented and Maryanne continued.

"Next morning, her husband raised the alarm. The story circulated was, his wife hadn't returned to their cottage the previous night. He retraced her movements to when she went to collect the architect's tray. As the architect hadn't come to breakfast, a group went to his cottage to investigate."

"I don't believe they eloped. How could they get off the island?" I blurted it out before thinking, and immediately regretted it as a dark look crossed Frankie's face.

"No, there was no question of elopement. It was some time before the real story circulated among the workers, and even longer before Lucille learned the truth."

"That is so tragic. How did Lucille react to all this when she found out about it and, more importantly, what happened to the architect?" Frankie sat shaking her head in disbelief as she spoke. I wasn't sure she was up to anymore tragedy yet, but she encouraged Maryann to continue. I didn't object – probably because I was dying to know the real story too.

"Straight after dinner, the husband went in search of his wife. A few of the other workers on their way home joined in the search. They found the young wife in the cottage and took her home. It didn't take too much to work out what happened, and the woman confirmed it. The men waited in the trees until the architect came back to the cottage. Then they rushed the cottage. The architect was never seen again. After they dealt with him, they took his body and belongings and buried them in the rainforest a long way from the cottage."

"You can't leave the story there!" I yelped. "There has to be more to the story than that. What about Lucille; didn't she miss the architect?"

"She didn't see him every day. Some days he worked all day in the cottage. Other days, he was away on one of the sites. The young wife miscarried but was reported as ill. On the second day after her attack, her husband gave notice and the young couple slipped on board a supply ship as it was about to depart after being unloaded. That night, Lucille went to the cottage in search of the architect. With him and his belongings gone, she assumed he left on the supply ship without telling her he was going. Lucille didn't go to the cottage again, but she tried several times to contact the architect and his office in Spain. It was about three months later before she learned something of the truth about what happened. She learned of his attack on the young woman, but I'm not sure she ever knew the whole truth. I think she continued to believe the architect absconded on that supply boat. Anyway, Lucille issued instructions that no one was ever to go into the cottage again. It slowly fell apart over the years."

Apart from Maryann's story, the wealth of information held by the staff was amazing, and their comments led us to other documentary evidence which kept us spellbound for a couple of days. By the end of that first week with just the two of us alone, Frankie had mapped out her story arc and was halfway through the first draft of the tragic romance associated with the derelict cottage.

Chapter 29

Early the next week, Frankie announced she needed to go to Guadeloupe. There were a couple of business matters to deal with: changing her will and to visit the bank. She said she didn't need me to accompany her. I didn't want to anyway … but, I was interested in going as far as Saint-Marie with her. Bookings were made and Jackson flew us to Saint-Marie the next morning. After seeing Frankie off on her flight to Guadeloupe, I took a taxi to the Honoré police station, and found Inspector Bennett sitting behind his desk.

After dumping my bag in the annex of his beach shack, he showed me around town. Things were quiet in his part of the world and, when Frankie called to say she was extending her stay at Guadeloupe for an extra day, I felt a strange light-heartedness surge through me. We spent three glorious days sightseeing, eating, drinking, swimming, and generally mingling with his circle of friends.

My last night before returning to Île Verte had me feeling down, and almost hoping Frankie would call to say she was further delaying her return. Tom picked up on my mood as we walked along the beach after dinner.

"You're quiet tonight. Is everything all right?"

"Yes, of course. I'm sorry; I was thinking about going back to Île Verte; nothing to be concerned about."

"I shall … no, I missed having you around. These few days have been great. I feel a definite chemistry between us, and I think you might feel it too. You don't have to leave tomorrow and, if you do, you don't have to stay away." He was right. There was something; a strong something.

Over the next month, I spent every weekend on Saint-Marie … in the shack, not the annex. But the time for me to leave the Caribbean was overdue. I broke the news to Tom on the last night of my last weekend with him.

"Ah, well now, that's fate for you. My contract here was up for renewal at the end of next month. I've had a word with the Commissioner and he has agreed. He is organising a temporary replacement for me to spend the next twelve months as a sabbatical in London. It's important for us coppers to keep up to date with all the latest developments in policing and technology. I've been on Saint-Marie for three years, and I'm feeling a bit out of touch with the rest of the world."

"You're returning to London for twelve months… and soon? Will they arrange accommodation for you?"

"They will put me up in a hotel for up to ten days while I find a place. If it takes longer than that, I have to pay for the extra time myself."

"Give the hotel a miss. Let me repay your hospitality – and save the police some money. You can stay with me for as long as you like."

"Only if you are sure I won't interfere with your work."

"Nothing interferes with my work. My life is uncomplicated. I'm an early riser – as you already know. I go to the gym almost every day, I write whenever inspiration grabs me, and it often impacts on when meals and sleep happen. That's about it."

"I think I could manage that okay. So, if I don't see you before then, I'll see you again when I arrive in London. But, I will be talking to you – a lot – between now and then."

A few days later, as we sat with our drinks on the rear deck in the cool of the evening, there was no conversation between us until Frankie cleared her throat.

"You haven't stopped smiling since your last trip to Saint-Marie. To state the 'bleeding obvious', as you English would say, you seem to be getting on quite well with Inspector Tom Bennett. And, my nose tells me, he probably is responsible for all the smiling."

"I don't know about any such nonsense, but I am thinking I should return to London soon, but I don't want to abandon you until I'm quite sure you will be okay here on your own."

"How can I be on my own when I have four other people here with me; people who fuss over me far too much? I've finished the first draft of my first book and parked it out of sight for a couple of weeks. I've started on the derelict cottage story. I will do a first edit of the first manuscript while you are still here, and then you can take a copy of it away with you to do your editor stuff. Depending on how much longer you intend staying on the island, I might have the derelict cottage story ready for you to edit as well. When you think either of them is ready – if ever – I will come to London so we can talk to publishers … and to Dervla about publicity. Any problems with any of that?"

I had no problems with it and, two weeks later, I overnighted with Tom on Saint-Marie on my way back to London.

The flight home didn't seem nearly as long and tiring as the trip to the Caribbean. I had two manuscripts to read and edit. Both were damned good page-turner stories. Working on them helped me survive the waiting until the arrival in London of a certain police inspector.

The End

Also by the Author

Revenge is not Enough

Harbour Plaza: built on dreams

On the Way to Istanbul

An Unsuitable House

A Land Too Far

About the Author

KAYLA DANOLI spent her early years traipsing around Australia and then Europe with her parents, and then completed her tertiary education in England before returning to Australia. There were a variety of jobs in various parts of Queensland before eventually making her way towards the coast. She now lives in a small coastal town on the Queensland coast where she works part-time on a charter vessel.

In the early days after settling in that small town, to fill in her spare time, both when at home and while on cruises, she started scribbling down her ideas for stories. These days, she writes whenever time permits. Her *Harbour Plaza* series, previously released in 2015 as monthly eBook episodes, was updated, extended and released in 2016 as the *Harbour Plaza: built on dreams* compilation. *Revenge is not Enough,* also released in 2016, was her first full-length novel.

Paradise Interrupted is Kayla's sixth full-length novel.

Discover more about Kayla and her work by visiting

www.kayladanoli.com

or contact her at

contact@kayladanoli.com

www.ingramcontent.com/pod-product-compliance
Lightning Source LLC
Chambersburg PA
CBHW030630110726
47901CB00002B/387